MW00577797

THE GETTYSBURG CONSPIRACY

A Novel by Will Hutchison

ISBN 978-0-7414-5650-2 Paperback
ISBN 978-0-7414-8298-3 eBook

Printed in the United States of America

Published May 2013

INFINITY PUBLISHING
1094 New DeHaven Street, Suite 100
West Conshohocken, PA 19428-2713
Toll-free (877) BUY BOOK
Local Phone (610) 941-9999
Fax (610) 941-9959
Info@buybooksontheweb.com
www.buybooksontheweb.com

Books by Will Hutchison

Follow Me to Glory
The Ian Carlyle Series: The Beginning

Crimean Memories:
Artefacts of the Crimean War

Will Hutchison is the author
of the award-winning first novel
in the Ian Carlyle Series, *Follow Me to Glory*.

WHAT READERS ARE SAYING
ABOUT THE AUTHOR AND HIS NOVELS...

I congratulate you on a fine yarn; well-written and packed with action. Your clear passion for military history and meticulous research make the tale rich with historical detail and a very good read...

> – Editor Emeritus, *The War Correspondent*,
> journal of the Crimean War Research Society

Follow Me to Glory is to the Crimean Period, what Michael Shaara's *The Killer Angels* is to the American Civil War. Hutchison has put in our hands a tale deftly crafted and full of visual images, which will keep you up reading into the wee hours. I finished it too soon...

> – Keith Rocco, historical artist

Ian Carlyle is back (in *The Gettysburg Conspiracy*) with his most explosive adventure yet. The fate of the Union lies in the hands of this Scottish nobleman. They intend to kill President Lincoln, and Carlyle is caught in a crux of deceit at the wane of the American Civil War in this story of love, loyalty, and betrayal. Were it not for the intuition and heroics of Ian Carlyle, this could have indeed been Lincoln's last address.

> – *The Gettysburg Times*

WILL HUTCHISON IS ALSO
THE PRIMARY AUTHOR AND PHOTOGRAPHER
OF THE CRITICALLY ACCLAIMED
*CRIMEAN MEMORIES: ARTEFACTS OF THE
CRIMEAN WAR.*

Surviving Crimean artifacts are expertly captured on film in superb colour in this beautifully produced book. The authors are to be congratulated on their amazing journey of discoveries, and we are lucky to be able to share the results of their hard work, here served up in such an attractive and convenient form for us to enjoy.

– Editor Emeritus, *The War Correspondent*,
journal of the Crimean War Research Society

No military reference work like this has been undertaken before. Not only is it a goldmine of information, but it is also a photographic masterpiece.

– Regimental Historian and Archivist,
Scots Guards, London

To Rosemary, Robbie, my dear friends,
and the Town of Gettysburg.
They never cease to inspire me.

Introduction and Acknowledgments

The Gettysburg Conspiracy is the second in the Ian Carlyle Series, and the sequel to *Follow Me to Glory*. These are the stories of a young Scottish nobleman, Ian David Carlyle, the second son of the Earl of Dunkairn. The first book's tale follows Ian as he grows to manhood in Victorian Britain, and comes of age as a warrior in the Scots Fusilier Guards during the Crimean War. As an officer in the Crimea, he must face many challenges and his own doubts and fears, to become a true leader of men who go in harm's way.

The Gettysburg Conspiracy brings Ian Carlyle, now a seasoned veteran, into the American Civil War six years after the Crimean War, as an observer for Her Majesty, Queen Victoria. He is forced by circumstances and against his will to become embroiled in a plot to assassinate Abraham Lincoln. He must protect his family, the honor of Britain, and indeed, the President of the United States.

As a historical note, the character of Ian Carlyle is loosely based on the experiences of Charles Henry Fletcher, a real officer of the Scots Fusilier Guards. The storyline regarding Ian Carlyle's mission to observe repeating breech-loading rifles in action is not fictional. After serving as an observer in the American Civil War, Charles Fletcher returned to England and was appointed president of an Ordnance Board committee. Its mandate was to examine numerous repeating breech-loading rifles, including American candidates like the Spencer and Henry rifles, to determine their suitability as a new service rifle for the British Army.

The Americans lost this competition, including Benjamin Henry's rifle. The result of the efforts of Fletcher's committee was the birth of the 1874 Martini-Henry Rifle, a combination of the Martini, or more accurately Peabody-action and Alexander Henry's rifled barrel design. He was a Scotsman, and no relation to Benjamin Henry. This was Britain's first general service rifle designed specifically as a breech-loading, repeating firearm, using a metallic cartridge.

To write historical fiction it is my firm belief that the author must maintain a rigid dedication to historical accuracy, within his fictional storyline. The tale should be one that could have happened, one where its fictional characters, surrounded by real historical figures, could have existed—lending passion and flow to history without distorting it, while bringing drama to the reader.

I have endeavored to do so in this book, but not without the essential assistance and encouragement of friends, colleagues, and historians. I want to take this opportunity to thank them for their time, their wisdom, and their willingness to share both.

Rosemary Hutchison, my wife, my love, and my eternal inspiration, led the first team. I was brilliantly supported by Steve Hanson, Civil War historian and professional editor, who was the primary content/historical editor; Curt Musselman, graphics artist and historian, as my remarkable mapmaker; Keith Rocco, historical artist, who was gracious enough to allow me to use a portion of his magnificent work, "The Last Stand," as cover art; and Peter Culos, historical artist, who rendered the extraordinary sketch of Ian Carlyle surrounded by scenes from the story.

There were many experts in various fields who contributed their time and knowledge to this enterprise. I have listed them in the order in which I asked their help: Timothy J. Reese, graphic artist and historian—the regular army in the Civil War; Tom Clemens, professor and historian—the Battle of Antietam; Beth Miller-Hall—nineteenth century clothing and customs; William A.Frassanito, author and historian—Gettysburg and

Lincoln's visit; Tim Smith, Adams County Historical Society—Adams County history; Al Ferranto, Adams County Historical Society—Adams County history; Thomas Williams, historical consultant—Civil War cavalry; James Getty, speaker and historian—Abraham Lincoln; Del Hilbert, Victorian Photography Studio—Victorian photography; Chris Argonaut, Victorian Photography Studio—wet plate photography; John Wega, Executive Director, USCC Civil War Museum—US Christian Commission; Joanne Lewis, Town and Battlefield Guide—Gettysburg battle and town; Jennifer Roth, Manager of the David Wills House—the Wills House; Bob O'Connor, author and historian—the life of Ward Hill Lamon; Lieutenant Colonel Wade Russell (Ret.), Royal Tank Regiment—British military customs; Lance Sergeant Kevin Gorman, Historian and Archivist, Scots Guards—the history of the Guards Brigade; George Wunderlich, Director, Museum of Civil War Medicine—medicine, medical treatment, and embalming; Dave Kohls—yachting history and seamanship on sailing ships.

Lastly, several historians and friends reviewed the entire manuscript and provided excellent counsel and support. To name a few: B.J. Small, editor, *The Gettysburg Times*; Kathy Nelson-Small; Katherine Brittin; George Vigil; James "Kit" Carson Cooper; and Frank Hall. Of course, my overall editing thanks go out to LinDee Rochelle, whose professional editing of the final manuscript added so very much to the end result.

To each of you my thanks and my friendship.

EVERGREEN CEMETERY GATEHOUSE.

WILLS HOUSE.

WHITWORTH RIFLE.

IAN IN THE FIELD.

ANTHONY CAMERA.

CUSTER'S CHARGE.

GETTYSBURG ADDRESS.

Chapter 1

---

19 November 1863, Gettysburg, Pennsylvania

Cadmus loved this new rifle musket with its finely checkered stock and telescopic sight along the left side. His hands were sweating as he embraced the grip of this elegant killing machine. It was sighted directly at the speaker's platform.

They gave him an Enfield when he was with the army. They had no Whitworths, no telescopic sights, in his ragtag regiment. Cadmus had found the Enfield was good only to about 900 yards. But this little beauty could kill at 1500 yards, and play hell on an enemy at a mile. Today, his target was only 212 paces away—a clean shot, impossible to miss.

He leaned into the eyepiece, saw the white-haired animated speaker magnified three times, filling the scope. It was as though he was right in front of him. If he reached out, he could touch him—if he spoke, the man would answer. It always gave Cadmus a thrill to see the target loom so close through the sight; but this was not his target, not yet. Nerves exposed, mouth dry, he waited, his nostrils wide to breathe deep. He knew this was his one chance to make everything right, only one shot.

At twenty-three, Cadmus Buell, formerly of the South Carolina Palmetto Sharpshooters, was not tall, but thin and muscular, with shocks of auburn hair bristling like a porcupine from his head. He habitually used a lot of grease in a futile attempt to slick it down. Cadmus' rather fat nose flattened into his pointy face, framed by large, bulbous ears. He tried to grow a full beard, perhaps to cover what only a mother could call handsome, but the final effect was an abysmal failure.

On this clear, crisp afternoon in November 1863, Cadmus wore his faded Confederate uniform with the sharpshooter's badge on the left sleeve—a red diagonal stripe with a red star above it. According to plan, his uniform was covered under a long white smock. He did not want to frighten the folks in this small northern town before his big moment. Then it would be different. Then they would all know.

He had moved a chair and a large chest over to the window. It was still uncomfortable, with all the photographic paraphernalia jammed in around him. It was the perfect disguise to conceal the rifle among equipment, camera, and tripod legs. That did not make it any less unpleasant.

Crouched in the upper room of the Evergreen Cemetery gatehouse for several hours, Cadmus was cramped all over—especially his right leg. He leaned out the window and tried to see "Dodger" Kally, who was guarding the photography wagon and the door to the tower. Normally, he could not have missed the huge man scowling up with those knife-like dark eyes, his hairless head shining in the bright sun; but there was no way Cadmus could bend out far enough to spot him. Cadmus genuinely feared this surly Englishman.

Although a crowd milled about the base of the tower, and indeed, the entire gatehouse, no one looked up or bothered with the photographer in the window. He was anonymous, just as they hoped. All eyes were on the platform where the short man with conspicuous white hair was closing his long, tedious speech.

Cadmus perked up. A big, stocky man stood and shouted a few words, but that was not the evil one, either. A murmur rippled through the crowd as they stirred, shifting feet, pressing forward. The soldiers surrounding the platform held their ground, preventing the shoving masses from moving any closer.

A tall, extremely thin man, whose long arms hung loosely by his sides, stood quietly for a moment, then moved to the platform center. Wearing white gloves, he took spectacles from a pocket of his black frock coat and placed them on his nose; he adjusted them as he glanced briefly at the paper in his hands, and in a steady voice, he began speaking. The crowd grew silent.

At the tower door Dodger Kally pulled three times on a rope attached to Cadmus' chair, signaling that this was indeed, the target. It wasn't necessary. Cadmus recognized the evil one as soon as he stood. He could almost feel Satan's presence as the tall man spoke. He had caused it all.

This man caused the war—wanted to free the slaves—invaded his sacred home. This man was the root of the constant sharp pain in Cadmus' leg, like being stabbed with a knife twenty-four hours a day.

Most of all, this man was the reason Cadmus was discharged by his own army, ignored as an unwanted piece of trash. Wounded in the knee more than a year ago, the Confederate army dubbed him unfit for service. They pronounced the war over—for him—said he would limp for the rest of his life.

Cadmus was not ready for that. No, indeed, he relished military life. He came from nothing, an unknown, a nobody. Then almost overnight, in what he considered a stroke from the mighty hand of God, he became a hero! He, Cadmus, was admired by everyone as a sharpshooter ... a killer of Yankee scum.

Cadmus took profound pleasure in the killing and savored the power it gave him. He wanted, craved, that feeling of supremacy and control. He would show them. He thought, *How could they not take me back after this daring act. I'm changin' the world?*

The cramping was gone now, as was the sweat. Even the pain in his leg disappeared, replaced by the satisfying coldness that always overwhelmed him before a kill. He made certain the rifle was securely resting on the trunk, and the percussion cap was solidly seated on the nipple. He rubbed his hand affectionately over the wooden stock, smiling to himself, touching the checkered grip gently, as he would a woman.

Cadmus cleared his mind, centered his entire being on the kill, all sounds and distractions gone. Just as his father taught him, he relaxed, letting out some breath, focused on the chest of the tall evil presence on the platform, and squeezed the trigger ...

Chapter 2

Thirteen months earlier—17 September 1862, near Porterstown, Maryland

It had been an icy winter morning in 1855; the haze hung in deadly silence over the lower reaches of the frozen trenches in the Crimea, thick and occasionally swirling, as though disturbed by graveyard ghosts come alive. The Russian crouched like a beaten dog, waiting for his master, whom he now knew would never come—dead, at the hand of the British officer moving past his cleft in the trench wall.

The officer was shocked by the Russian's scream. He turned in disbelief to face his charging enemy. The long triangular bayonet at the end of the musket was all he could register. It moved straight at him—inevitable.

The lethal point ran him through, piercing his chest with an odd sucking sound, slamming him to the trench floor. The officer looked up in amazement, helpless, saw the dark figure blocking out the blue sky. He clearly made out the coal black eyes and grizzled stubble of beard—grimaced at the full lips pulled back over stained teeth in an insane smirk—he smelled the Russian's foul breath as he bent down.

The Russian slowly pulled the bayonet out. The officer tasted the decay and mud stirred from the trench floor, as blackness engulfed him. Shots fired through a hazy tunnel of sound ricocheted through his mind ... voices ... dull pain—a remoteness and isolation he never knew before. His trusty leopard, the image he concocted as a young lad to fortify his courage in times of fear, was no longer running beside him, no longer invoking that courageous spirit that sustained him through many trying times. He felt his leopard had deserted him. He felt fear. He was alone, abandoned—his life slipping away.

Ian's eyes snapped open. A thin film of sweat swathed his face, accompanied by a rumbling sound that roared in his ears like the hammer-on-iron rhythm of a train passing over tracks. The morning blue sky turned a dingy color, and it was cold. With a start, he realized he was not in the Crimea, but a field in Maryland, in America. The roar was the unremitting patter of rain on wet canvas. The shabby insipid sky was merely the roof of the tent above his camp bed, only glimpsed through sporadic lightning flashes.

"Jesus—not again," he cried out.

A quiet American voice came from the dark, "Ian, you all right?"

"I'm fine, damn me."

"Crimea?" The voice asked.

Ian looked sadly at his friend, barely making him out in the darkness across the tent. "I truly hate this, Hiram."

"Can I help?"

Ian yawned. "Always the Crimea. Silly, ain't it? Always the same damned thing." Although he was not overly tall, his cot was too short. It was made for a smaller man, and prevented him stretching full length.

"It's been raining on and off," Hiram said from the dark. "... and getting worse."

"Raining, yes. One night I simply won't wake. You'll find me at first light, lying here with a ghostly bayonet poking out of my bloody chest, and not a soul about."

"The only cure is time," his friend said, as he rolled over and pulled a worn blanket tight around his shoulders. There was just a chance he could get a little more sleep.

"It's been six bloody years ... You'd think——"

"Doesn't work that way," the American interrupted, his voice somewhat muffled inside the blanket. "Been a lot of years since I fought Indians, but I still wake up a time or two with cold sweats, and I'm not the only poor bastard."

Ian, with more than a trace of sarcasm, said, "Thanks for those kind words, Hiram, yer very reassuring to the mentally deranged."

His friend pressed on. "There were a few occasions in Mexico with the Mounted Rifles that purely keep me awake nights."

Ian swung his legs off the cot, placed them on the rug-covered floor of the tent, felt its rough texture—a small luxury.

Hiram, now wide-awake, was relentless. He twisted back around on his cot to look at Ian, amused by the game. "They'll never go away, Ian, and I suspect you'll just have to live with such horror-filled nights for the rest of your life."

Ian's Scottish accent was light, with the mere hint of the highlands, except perhaps when he was nervous, wanted to use sarcasm or humor, or when he was addressing a young damsel. Then he would slide into a more pronounced delivery without even realizing it. He now slipped easily into a mocking Scottish brogue, "Och, Captain Dryer, yer words give me such grand relief, I canna tell ya. Now I may just quietly take me own life."

Captain Hiram Dryer, commander of the 4th United States Infantry, doffed an imaginary hat as he lay on his bed, sweeping his arm around in an imitation salute. He smiled back. "Why Carlyle, it is my pleasure to serve. After all, we must take good care of our visiting English royalty."

In truth, Dryer's playful banter was welcome. It made Ian focus. Indeed, he was not the only soldier with bad dreams. At least he no longer experienced such moments of madness during the daylight hours. It took him years to break away from the sudden, disturbingly vivid Crimean memories. He had been in a few scrapes over the past few months, and so far no bad or embarrassing daytime incidents—only the damned nightmares lingered.

Ian struck a match and lit a small candle on a camp chair pulled next to his cot, then ran both hands several times through his thick hair. He picked up a wooden-framed mirror from the chair.

The face that greeted him was, in his opinion, neither handsome nor ugly, but merely there, covered in part by a profuse mustache and long sideboards. He was proud of the fact that he was terribly Scottish in demeanor and appearance—a ramrod posture, high cheekbones, a straight nose, and strong chin. He stared at the spread of newly sprouting stubble. *Not quite a full beard yet*, he thought. It gave him a somewhat seedy look.

Ian David Carlyle was a captain and lieutenant colonel[1] in Her Majesty Queen Victoria's elite Scots Fusilier Guards. He came to America with other Guards officers on the Queen's business to observe the Federal army in action against the Confederacy. His army rank when away from his regiment was lieutenant colonel, and he was acknowledged as such by the Americans.

Now he was tenting among the "regulars" of that army at his own request. He was more at home with the regular army regiments, made up of professional soldiers, than with the far more numerous and less disciplined "volunteer" regiments.

---

[1] Before 1871 officers in the Brigade of Guards below the rank of Colonel held a rank in their Guards Regiment and a higher rank in the British Army, itself:

Ensign and Lieutenant
Lieutenant and Captain
Captain and Lieutenant Colonel

They used and were referred to by their higher "army" rank. The regimental rank determined their seniority and their basic function within the regiment, while the army rank determined their army seniority and their function when posted to an assignment outside their regiment, such as staff duty.

Ian found it easier and of more benefit in his observations to keep his rank low key. It helped maintain a rapport with less senior American officers. He habitually wore either his dark blue braided frock coat, which was considerably more subdued than his scarlet dress tunic, or a plain blue unadorned sack coat he acquired from an American officer. Ian's status was visible only in the wide scarlet stripe down his trouser seams, and the Scottish dicing headband and regimental badge on his old battered forage cap.

"I need a shave," Ian said.

He looked at his timepiece, which had been lying in his upturned cap for protection. It was a beautiful silver Repousse Verge open face, made in London by Samuel Smith and Company, and hung from a sturdy silver chain. His father, the Earl of Dunkairn, gave it to him six months before his sudden death from what started as a bad cough. Ian treasured the watch, as he cherished his father's memory.

Thirty minutes until dawn, he thought, *too late to sleep again ... and too many ghosts.* The rain let up considerably, and only a slight drizzle remained to plague the gray dawn.

Ian stiffly pulled on his knee-high boots, and grabbed his rain cape. As he left the tent, plodding through the mud, he replied to Dryer's remark, "Scottish royalty, if you must, Dryer. Scottish, you ignorant Yankee backwoodsman, not English."

Ian heard Dryer's faint laughter amid the snores from the row of officers' tents as he trudged toward the wood line and the sinks behind the camp. The viscous morning fog swirled around his boots as he walked, reminding him of his dream.

Chapter 3

---

17 September 1862, near Porterstown, Maryland

It was morning. Although it had stopped raining, the ground was saturated.

It'll be muddy for the fight, Ian thought, *unless we get a blazing hot sun.*

The fog continued to spread eerily. In the early morning after rain, there was an ever-present smell in the woods, a bold freshness combined with the odor of decaying leaves on a forest floor. The trees showed slightly more orange-brown, slightly less green. A perceptible autumn chill gave a robust hint of the changing season.

Full daylight came and Ian could feel a tightening, a distinct strain in the camp of the United States Regular Infantry Division near Porterstown. The regulars were being held in reserve, much to their regret. They were the best of Major General George B. McClellan's Army of the Potomac, and it seemed he would have them on a tight leash, not wanting to squander his seasoned veterans.

Ian actually thought this very Napoleonic of him, and recalled with dismay the Crimea, when Lord Raglan acted similarly by hording his precious cavalry. That miscalculation cost the British army dearly.

The idea of being the reserve did not sit well with the regulars. *This coming fight might be different. If the enemy numbers are what the general thinks, he surely won't keep the regulars out. That's why I'm here and not at headquarters, or at least one reason.*

Another reason was his distaste for being with a headquarters staff. He recalled Lord Raglan's huge entourage in the Crimea. There were so many mounted staff officers that when they took to the field at the Alma River, the Russians thought it was a sizable cavalry detachment, and promptly began shelling them as a prime target.

Ian chuckled to himself remembering those stalwart staff officers who claimed bravery and courage, yet scattered to the four winds after the first shot, caps flying off, coat tails trailing behind, as they sped away. They were not seen again for the balance of that hot, dangerous day.

He also recalled something a friend said of such officers. "Carlyle, old man, none of us can do anything as incredibly stupid as all of us, when we put our minds to it." That is what he truly thought of the sea of ineffectual staff officers who accompanied General McClellan and his grand army—*mostly volunteers, damned few real soldiers.*

It was shortly after six, and a group of officers gathered for morning coffee. No one talked much; they never did that early. The gathering included Ian's witty tent mate, Captain Dryer, a likable chap for certain, with long side-whiskers and thinning hair. He was not a West Point graduate, but still a damned fine officer.

First Lieutenant John Poland joined them. A visitor from another brigade who commanded the 2nd US Infantry, he sported a short tidy beard, and cut a fine figure in uniform, as bespoke a recent West Point graduate. Dryer's and Poland's regiments were in Sykes' Regular Division in Fitz-John Porter's V Corps.

Ian was munching on a piece of rather decent soft bread covered heavily with jam, and sipping on a tin cup of strong, scalding hot coffee. No milk or sugar—the way some Americans, and he, enjoyed it. The fire, the chill in the air, the steaming brew, and the occasional idle friendly chatter among the officers brought more memories of the Crimea, some of the few pleasant ones from that time.

"Hiram, what orders?" Ian asked.

"Leaving shortly. You'll hear assembly blown. We'll go right in, I believe—"

"Where then?"

"Right up the pike into the next town," Dryer predicted. "Should see plenty of Rebs before we get there, although not many around yesterday."

A Topography Corps engineer officer gave Ian a good map. The next town was a place called Sharpsburg. He had scouted almost into it on his own the day before, riding near Dryer's regiment. Just another of those many activities he was told were too dangerous, and that an "observer" should not be doing.

Poland chimed in, speaking to Dryer, "Pulled you back too soon, you ask me, sir."

"Yesterday?"

"Yesterday. Should have kept pressing," Poland continued. "Longer we wait, the tougher it'll be. Here we sit, guarding a damned bridge."

Ian addressed the outspoken Poland directly, "John, you sound quite keen to be at them. I take it such impatience is the prevailing emotion around here. The air seems pasty thick with it."

With no attempt to disguise his irritation, Dryer inserted, "You can't train such men as these to a fine edge, only to keep them out of the fight. They don't want the glory, that's for the volunteers to dream about—write home to their sweeties about—these men do have their pride."

"We all know that feeling," Ian responded. He learned far too much in the Crimea about the waste in human lives attendant to the word "glory". He felt the scar on his chest, had one of those momentary flashes of the bayonet's sucking sound —even felt the sharp pain. In wet weather he felt the

13

ache, too, from his old leg wound, and the long slash across his back.

Ian recovered instantly, cocked his head to the side, and touched the visor of his forage cap. "I'm pleased to be accompanying you, gentlemen."

Poland said, "I hope, sir, you're still pleased to be among us after this day has passed." His double meaning was not lost on either Ian or Dryer.

Dryer, with a wry grin, looked at Poland. "Now John, you never wanted to live forever ... said so yourself ... too boring you said ... and I wouldn't be too concerned about sitting this one out. It's shaping up."

"Think so, Hiram?"

"Both our brigades will be dancing sure enough—just stay light on your feet."

Dryer changed the subject, "Say, Ian, whatever happened to that huge train of British officers who were with you on the Peninsula? Fletcher, Neville, there must have been a dozen."

"Military observers, guests of General McClellan, as I am. None still about. Felt they'd observed enough and returned to Canada. Och, I dare say, they'd be back enjoying the quiet countryside of jolly old England."

Poland asked, "And you, sir, to what do we owe this honor?"

"More coffee, gentlemen?" Wrapping a cooking rag around the hot handles Dryer took the pot from the fire gingerly.

"I requested to stay on a bit," he smiled, broadly, "wanted to see more of the famed regular army in action."

Dryer and Poland looked pleased, glossing over the irony in Ian's voice. Dryer poured more hot coffee in Ian's cup.

"Truth be known, gentlemen, I'm under orders."

"Orders?" Poland asked.

"Orders ... Yes, from the Queen, so to speak. My government wants to hear more about those breech-loading rifles you're using, like the Sharps, the—"

14

"Ah, so it isn't our charming ways after all?" Dryer cut in, his grin broadening.

Ian continued, "Frankly, I think they're the future. Not merely for special troops such as sharpshooters, but as the general service weapon, for all—and sooner, rather than later."

"Is that why you're toting that impressive Henry repeater around?" Dryer asked.

Ian chuckled. "No, it's a private purchase, and not mine. Borrowed it from one of our commanding general's young, willing lieutenants."

"Why don't they play the damned assembly?" Poland was getting most impatient, fidgeting with his coffee cup.

"Won't he need it—the Henry?" asked Dryer.

This time Ian laughed. "Doubt that. He cut a fine figure as he reported sick yesterday morning, about the time he heard a fight might be brewing." The others nodded, knowingly.

Poland began, "If you ask me—" He was interrupted by a cacophony of buglers, each sounding assembly for their individual regiments—competing like cats over a saucer of milk. Poland, ever eager, jumped up at the first bugle's sound.

His coffee sizzled in the coals of the cook fire as he tossed the dregs from his cup. Poland listened to the hissing sounds, and watched the smoke rise for just an instant, then rushed off to join his regiment. Dryer walked to his tent to get ready.

Ian continued sipping his coffee, staring at the fire—no hurry for him. He was merely a foreign staff officer, granted permission by General McClellan to camp with and accompany the regulars as they advanced. Their discipline and stoic resolve under pressure reminded Ian of his own beloved Scots Fusilier Guards, and the professional military ways he cherished.

There was a time after the Crimea when Ian thought seriously of resigning his commission. He felt he had been properly seduced by that word "glory," and now looked upon such nonsense as the folly of children. He was distressed by the politics surrounding the Crimean War, and disappointed in the politicians he knew were responsible for its being so dreadfully mismanaged.

It took almost three years for Ian to recover fully from his Crimean wounds. The chest wound, which pierced his lung, still occasionally made him short of breath. For most of that time Ian wrestled with the decision of whether or not to resign.

But as Ian's health slowly returned, so did his craving for excitement. *Glory and politics be damned,* he thought. It was always his dream to be a soldier, and he was quite good at it.

In the end it was an easy decision. It was as simple as a fierce devotion to Her Majesty, Queen Victoria, and his country. Ian saw Scotland as a part of the British Empire, although he may have seen it as the very best part. Thus, flawed as Britain was from time to time—mistakes or not— he was bound to the Queen by oath, obedience, and patriotism.

Ian decided to remain in the Scots Fusilier Guards. If this meant overcoming an inordinate fear of long-range cannon fire, and controlling the occasional outburst of rage, then so be it. He would keep his constant and reliable leopard image close, to fortify his courage, but not so close that it took control—no, not that close.

Ian stared into the leftover flames of the cook fire. As it slowly turned to burning embers, the regulars kitted up for their march to the butchery of war. Ian was tired. There had been no real sleep during the restless night. He ran his hand again over the chin whiskers he recently started growing. They were not yet long enough to trim.

Chapter 4

---

17 September 1862, London, England

While Ian reflected on the Crimea on a damp morning near Porterstown, his brother, Lord Peter Carlyle, the Fifth Earl of Dunkairn, sat his tall, slight frame loosely in a comfortable leather chair at White's, his club on St. James Street, London. Peter embraced the lush leather as he took a deep breath, smelled its rich fragrance, and smiled to himself in satisfied comfort.

This was his much-beloved mid-afternoon ritual. It was private time, with none of the constant distractions of family business, or his duties as a member of the House of Lords. In this club, the oldest and perhaps most exclusive in Britain, he could wrap himself in the *London Times*, enjoy a drink or two among the strictly male membership, and no one would dare disturb his peace.

The ritual also included an excellent dinner, followed by cards with select friends, where he lost entirely too much money, entirely too often. On this evening he planned to enjoy gambling and whiskey well into the night.

Peter maintained a comfortable set of rooms very near Belgrave Square for his frequent visits to London from

Scotland, but late at night it was too much trouble to find a hansom cab to bring him home. Thus, as he often did, he had taken a room at White's.

The massive reading room he now sat in was handsomely covered in deep mahogany paneling, its windows surrounded by substantial ornate draperies, and its wall space almost consumed by huge, elaborately framed portraits of past members of the club. The portraits included a sprinkling of members of the Royal Family, going back over a hundred years.

"Ah, Reginald, I'll take a large Taliskers, with a mere splash of water to open it up. That should put some fire in the belly." The neatly dressed waiter nodded and disappeared. He was thinking—*young Lord Dunkairn does not look at all well. Too many late nights and too much gambling, you were to ask me—which none of these high-born types ever does, mind.*

Peter meticulously opened his copy of the *Times*, planted it in front of his face, and began earnestly and pleasantly reading an article by a Frenchman, explaining the American General Pope's recent military engagement around a place with the preposterous name of "Manassas."

It described the Federals as having made a "retrograde movement back toward Washington, with heavy losses." Of course, the French, citing Pope's dispatches, viewed it as a Federal victory, to which Peter merely gave an audible "Hrumph!"—*The damned French. Victory—I mean to say!*

The man who sat himself in an identical leather chair across from Peter was well-set up, with the size and bearing of a military man, but the trim hair, beard, spectacles, and expensive clothing of a wealthy businessman. He studied Peter, who behind his newspaper was oblivious of his presence.

As the man had been warned, Peter Carlyle resembled one of Charles Dickens' quaint characters. He was exceedingly tall, bony, and looked like he had not had a nourishing meal in some time. His clothes hung limply from his body, and were a bit disheveled. The sleeves and trouser legs looked to have been cut a tad on the short side.

Peter's whole disposition gave off a gentle frailness, which made one suspect he had not a clue of the ways of the world he lived in. To the man in the chair, this was a weakness to be exploited.

The man examined his own copy of the Times, then said, casually, "I say, the Prince of Wales seems to be jumping about across the water like a damned rabbit." The Prince happened to be on a spotty tour of various European countries, and was being followed closely by journalists.

Peter read voraciously, especially the news. He had the mind of a scholar, even though he sometimes forgot to lace his boots. He knew exactly what the man referred to, but had no desire to engage him. He merely grunted in reply, hoping the intruder would take the cue. He had no wish to be disturbed.

The man was not to be ignored. He asked, "Do you think the cotton operators in Liverpool are correct?"

A direct question. Now Peter would be rude to ignore the man, and that he could not be. "My dear fellow, I'm afraid I don't take your meaning?"

"It says that they think the American government will be forced to accept peace. Not merely the cotton issue, but so many defeats by the Confederate States army."

Peter had strong opinions against the Federal government in America, and particularly against their President Lincoln. He wanted Lincoln out of the way, and wanted the Confederacy to win their little war, but he also wanted the war to continue for as long as possible. His investments of the family's fortune in the arms manufacturing industry depended upon it.

Now, however, he was becoming truly annoyed by this bumptious stranger, who had interrupted his quiet time. He tried to look haughtily at the man. "I do beg your pardon, sir, but I don't think we've met." Peter was the treasurer of White's Gentlemen's Club, and thought he knew every member.

"We haven't. I'm a guest today."

Ah, Peter thought, *I have you now.* "I see. May I inquire whose guest?"

"None of your damned business, Carlyle," the man hissed in a low, menacing voice. His eyes burned hotly into Peter, who was shocked.

He was, after all, the Earl of Dunkairn. Such crudeness, and in his own club, was not something he was accustomed to. On the other hand, Peter was now becoming decidedly fearful, and it apparently showed. *The man knows my name, yet he's a stranger.*

"Who the devil are you, sir?" asked Peter, with a bravado he did not feel.

"Call me anything you like. You don't need to know who I am, only the parties I represent—and you already know that, don't you."

Reginald came with the glass of malt whiskey, setting it on the small elegant table next to Peter.

"Can I bring you something, sir?" Reginald asked, turning his head toward the man across from Peter.

"No, not at the moment. We wish to be left alone. We'll call you if we need anything else." Reginald looked into the man's eyes, saw the fire, turned quickly and walked away.

Peter was staring at the whiskey. He picked it up and swallowed half the glass. "Yes, I know the gentlemen you represent. What do you want? Haven't I done enough?"

"We need to be informed, Carlyle, merely to be informed. Bring me up to snuff."

Peter sighed. "Of course—up to snuff. Well, my brother has remained with the Federal army to make inquiries regarding repeating rifles, as you wanted. He'll be sending reports to Horse Guards, with a copy to me. I've completed arrangements for his assignment to our legation in Washington, where he is to continue his inquiries and observations. Mind you, he knows nothing of these arrangements yet. That's the best I can do."

"No, it is not ... not by half. Not if you want to remain in our good graces, and I suspect you do. Yes, I suspect you surely do."

Peter lowered his head, but said nothing. He was trapped and he knew it. He also felt shame and no little self-pity. Why had life dealt him such a dreadfully bad hand, why him?

The man persisted, "Well?"

Peter sighed again. "I'll do whatever you want."

"Good of you, Carlyle, but we already know that. There'll be further instructions after your brother's had time to settle."

"Will you be delivering them?"

"No. You won't see me again, and for your own good and your continued health, this meeting never occurred." The man stood up and walked directly out of the club.

Peter looked slowly about the room at the many members sitting in chairs reading, or talking in low voices not to disturb the others. He knew the group this man represented, but not their names or faces. Any one of these fine, elegant gentlemen could be keeping him under surveillance, or even be the chairman of this group.

Peter was always contacted by someone like this fellow, but in the past they were not quite as intimidating. These people surprisingly had the same objectives in this American civil war as he did. A good thing, because the position they had put Peter in did not allow him to do anything but their bidding.

Peter was miserable. He thought about his duty at Lords, he thought about Ian, he thought about their ailing mother, but most of all, he thought about himself. He finished his whiskey and ordered another. He needed to relax, and was glad he had taken a room upstairs for the night.

For the next eight or ten hours he drank himself into a fair facsimile of an incoherent rag doll, had no dinner, and lost over £10,000 at cards.

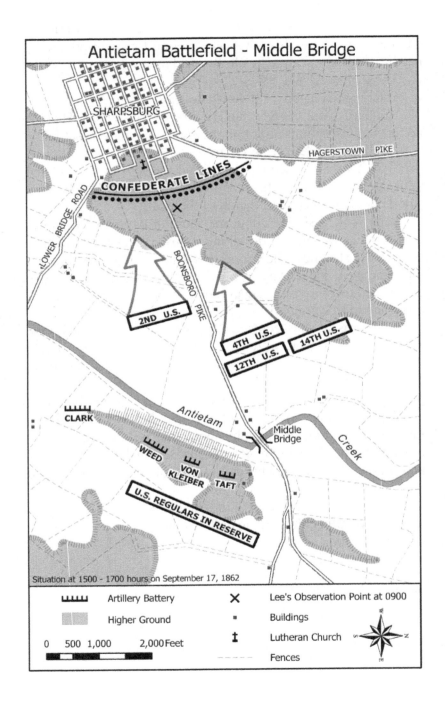

Antietam Battlefield - Middle Bridge

SHARPSBURG

HAGERSTOWN PIKE

CONFEDERATE LINES

LOWER BRIDGE ROAD

BOONSBORO PIKE

2ND U.S.

4TH U.S.

12TH U.S.

14TH U.S.

CLARK

Antietam

Middle Bridge

Creek

WEED

VON KLEIBER

TAFT

U.S. REGULARS IN RESERVE

Situation at 1500 - 1700 hours on September 17, 1862

⊔⊔⊔⊔ Artillery Battery	✕	Lee's Observation Point at 0900
Higher Ground	▪	Buildings
	⌑	Lutheran Church
0 500 1,000 2,000 Feet	-----	Fences

Chapter 5

---

17 September 1862, Sharpsburg, Maryland, near Antietam Creek

The regulars were formed on the Boonsboro Pike and it was time to march. Ian mounted his mare, Jass. He wanted to find a position to see how the battle was being waged, and how the regulars would be employed. Cannon fire opened—the crash of Federal guns could be heard close by, Confederate in the distance.

Ian knew that whatever the Rebels lacked in artillery equipment, they more than made up for in skill. The Rebel guns were about a mile away, along the ridges in front of Sharpsburg. The Federal artillery positions sat on the bluffs east of Antietam Creek. *As good a place to start from as any. May as well face my demons right off.*

When Ian rode up the ridge to the artillery batteries, he saw a magnificent view of the pike leading to Sharpsburg, and a good portion of the battlefield as it developed to the north and south. The artillery pieces were somewhat exposed, but their open field of fire was brilliant, making it worth the risk.

Perhaps because of range, few enemy shots landed to any significant effect around the Federal artillery, but those that did were enough for Ian—enough to rekindle the terror. Ian thought for the thousandth time, *it's so bloody impersonal. You simply have no control. One second you're fine, and the next, you're in pieces.*

As though to place a point on his observations, a solid shot skipped into one of the caissons to the rear of the guns, where Ian sat his horse. It killed an artillery horse nearby, and ripped off the leg of the mounted driver. The hapless artilleryman did not make a sound, gawking in shocked silence as his horse went down hard. Ian thought he heard the snap of the soldier's neck. He lay motionless, not far from the detached lower half of his left leg.

Fear immediately overwhelmed Ian like a giant hammer, slamming into him. The deafening noise consumed him. The acrid smoke made it difficult to breathe. He fought the rising bile, the compelling urge to bury himself in the earth, or gallop back down the ridge to safety. Artillery fire was his old nemesis. He summoned his imaginary leopard from the cave where it rested, felt its calming effect. First time he had a need to disturb the beast in a long while.

A few solid shots bounded down the backside behind the bluffs, narrowly missing the line of regular infantry held there in reserve. *It isn't much safer down there.*

Ian was still shaking and barely in control. He forced himself to ride forward past the caissons to the line of limbers only yards behind the guns themselves. He felt a presence next to him. "What do you think, Carlyle?" a thin, breathless voice asked.

Ian was startled out of his concentration. His mare jigged left at the unexpected sound. "Easy girl." He bent around to find a rider pulling up next to him.

Ian knew the man, vaguely—a journalist, and a photographer. He was popular among the American officers, and traveled with his own photographic wagon for developing images in the field. Ian had bumped into him around the headquarters.

Recalling his name just in time, Ian said, "Beg pardon, old man. Oldham ain't it? You've caught me out. I was most assuredly lost in thought."

"Simon Oldham. Please call me Simon. Entirely my fault for startling you. So, what do you think?" There was the hint of an English accent, but Ian could not quite place it.

A full battery fired not far away, scaring his mare. He was startled himself, but would not allow it to show. He remained in control of his horse and himself.

Ian remembered Oldham as always being wound up and nervous—a bowstring pulled a bit too tight. He also remembered Oldham's shifty eyes, constantly on the move, darting about like a man trying to see in all directions at once. As affable as he seemed, Ian was reluctant to trust anyone who did not look him directly in the eye. Besides, this was a journalist. Wise men and particularly wise soldiers never trusted them too far.

Ian began teasing in a mocking tone. "Aye, Oldham, there's the rub. I was thinking nothin' more deeply than how much my arse was goin' ta ache from this saddle by day's end."

Oldham grinned. "Come now, Carlyle, an Englishman such as yerself must have a printable opinion of today's doings. What about a comment on how badly these 'colonials' fight?"

Ian was not about to be dragged into that not-so-sly challenge. "I think they fight splendidly."

Then to remain in keeping with Her Majesty's edict to her soldiers about maintaining complete neutrality, he added, "As a matter of fact, Oldham, I think both sides fight splendidly."

A well-placed Rebel solid shot hit the wheel of a caisson far down the artillery line, overturning it. Horses were trapped in harnesses, struggling and screaming for freedom, artillerymen scrambled to sort out the tangled mess.

The truth of what Ian believed about the combatants was far different than his words portrayed. When he first arrived in America he was appalled to learn that in the early stages of the war both sides actually elected their officers, based apparently on how well liked candidates were. *How could such an Army survive?*

"And what of this President Lincoln?" Oldham probed, seemingly unperturbed by the occasional incoming artillery. "You can't tell me you think this back country cretin is a stately leader of men?"

Ian was getting a bit put off, but his rising irritation stopped him from thinking about the enemy artillery rounds coming in a heavier now. He had to shout above the din of artillery blasting away and loud commands by the gunners. "Oldham, I don't much like this Mr. Lincoln, but then I'm not too keen on Mr. Davis either. Both made some bad choices as I see it."

There was an uneasy pause; then Ian asked, "Oldham, with all the senior American officers wandering about here, why did you decide to interview me, a British officer, on this particular day?"

"You're right. Damned silly of me. I do humbly beg your pardon. You see the truth is I've upset our 'Little Mac'. I felt it a good time to make myself lost, and spotted you riding alone. Sorry if I intrude."

Ian immediately regretted his outburst. This might well be a fellow countryman, who was only doing his job and being friendly. He said, "I see. It's I who should apologize. Sorry if I was a mite abrupt." Ian paused. "So tell me, how did you manage ta get on the General's bad side?"

"Took an image of some of his staff, without him in it. Very vain, our general."

"I'd have ta say more your general than mine, my dear fellow. By the way, just to keep the air clear, I'm a Scot, not an Englishman."

"Of course, of course you are. Should have chosen my words more carefully."

Oldham was dark and clean-shaven, with bright even teeth. His shoulder-length black hair, thin face, and low thick eyebrows presented a swarthy, but mysteriously handsome man—perhaps a touch of gypsy blood. The only distraction was his darting, restless eyes.

He sat a chestnut mare, too short for his tall, well-proportioned stature. His legs hung down too far. Sitting rakishly on his head was a supple, soft brown brimmed hat. One side was up, and the other hung down over his right ear. Oldham's faded clothing, dirty unbuttoned white shirt, and ragged neck cloth, created the impression of a slightly disreputable artist, or "bohemian"—as the band of journalists with the army called themselves. Ian was reasonably certain this impression was contrived to be just that. *A careful man*, he thought, *vain as well.*

Ian said, "Having a hard time with yer accent—English? Irish?"

Oldham said, "I'm actually Canadian, originally." He moved his horse father away from the guns, down the reverse slope, and Ian followed. At least they could hear themselves think.

"You ride in a military fashion, sir, might that mean you've seen active service?"

"Indeed it might," Oldham replied, "and you're still with 'Little Mac's' army to study the effects of those fast-loading rifles I've been hearing so much about."

My, he is well informed. "Was that a question?" Ian asked. There was an uncomfortable silence between them, interrupted only by the incessant pounding of the guns. Then Ian laughed ... that broke the tense mood.

Oldham returned the laughter, but realized he was not going to catch this officer off-guard. He offered, "The Henry slung over your shoulder was a clue I might be right. May I see?"

Ian unslung the Henry, nudged his mare closer, and tossed it across to Oldham. Oldham's horse shied on the sloping ground. He almost lost it in the transfer, but tugged the reins adroitly with one hand, calming the animal.

He examined the rifle with interest and an easy familiarity. He pulled down the lever to see it was loaded, checked the balance, then snapped it to his shoulder a time or two. His horse jigged a bit, but he remained in total control.

Ian said, "You seem ta know your way about weapons, as well as bein' a dab hand with a horse."

"Was a serving officer in the Rifle Brigade in the Crimea."

"Hmmm. I knew Rifle officers there. Don't recall meeting you."

Oldham explained, "I arrived with a replacement draft in November of '55."

"That would explain it. I was wounded in early '55—sent home. Canadian, is it? I might have had you down for an American. You've no real accent at all."

"I'm not certain that's complimentary. Many Americans take me for one of theirs, but I assure you, my loyalties lie with Her Majesty." Ian nodded his head.

Oldham was still looking at the rifle, paying no attention to the rising cacophony of battle that surrounded them. "Nice piece. Fifteen cartridges?"

"Sixteen, I suppose, with one up the spout."

"Range?"

"No real idea, although some say five hundred yards or more. Who knows, perhaps I'll find out today."

Oldham handed the rifle back. "I thought you 'observers' were strictly neutral?"

"I am, old boy, I am—strictly neutral, but that doesn't preclude a mite of sport, now, does it?"

Ian squeezed his mare and rode forward again, to the guns. He left Oldham to wonder just what he meant by that last comment. *Bloody Canadian, chew on that—ah, perhaps I am, after all, being too hard on him. He seems a likable sort. Besides, an officer having served in the Rifles can't be all that bad.*

Actually, Ian had no planned intention of using the Henry, unless provoked. He merely felt more comfortable with it than without it.

Dismounting, he asked an artillery corporal, "What battery is this?" He measured a calmness in his voice that belied the terror he felt underneath. The leopard purred quietly. *God, I just want to run. Get on Jass and ride forever until I reach England.*

"Company I, sir, 5th US Artillery—best there is," the corporal replied. The corporal was not serving a gun. He had a bandage on his head and blood was soaking through. He added, "Captain Weed's the finest artilleryman in this whole damned army. That's him over there." The corporal pointed to an energetic officer bouncing expertly between his guns, making certain all was in order, and keeping them firing.

"I take it yer in Company I, soldier?"

"Proud of it, sir."

"I dare say." Ian's calmness was a surprise. *Is it getting easier?*

Ian deliberately dug out his telescope, another present from his father many years ago. He went down on one knee about ten yards from the leftmost of Weed's guns, and deliberately jabbed his sword upright into the ground.

He pulled out a large neck scarf, tying it in a simple circle, dropping it over the hilt of his sword. Placing the telescope into the circle of cloth, he began twisting it around until it was tightly secured to the sword, as you apply a tourniquet. That steadied the powerful brass scope, allowing Ian to examine enemy positions without shaking and blurring his view.

"Clever, sir, that telescope thing you're doing," said the I Company corporal, looking on rather shyly.

Ian saw the boy was nervous, standing so exposed on the ridge. He smiled and said, "Learned this trick in a far away land, laddy, where I was so bloody scared my glass kept shakin' and I couldn't see a damned thing." Reassuring the soldier somehow enabled Ian to calm his own rickety nerves.

First, he watched what little he could see of the northern fighting to his right, then tried unsuccessfully to see the lower bridge to his left. There were ridges in his way. His ears told him the firing was dying down from that quarter.

A Rebel solid shot struck the ground thirty yards in front of him with a loud "thwack!" It startled Ian as it skipped over his head and casually took a corner off a supply wagon behind him. He calmed himself, thinking, *It is getting easier.*

Ian turned the telescope back to his immediate front. He gradually followed the Boonsboro Pike from the middle bridge to the town, saw Rebel skirmishers, guns, and—*what in God's name is that?* He could hardly believe what his eyes were seeing.

On the near crest of the ridge just before the town were three Confederate officers; senior officers by the uniforms and mounts, one a big gray.

As he watched in quiet disbelief at their audacity, two of the officers, already dismounted, looked through field glasses in his direction. He jumped back by reflex, before realizing they were nearly a mile away. He was embarrassed at his skittishness. He looked about. No one noticed. *Good, can't have these Americans thinking Her Majesty's officers are jumpy.*

Ian had another start when he realized Oldham was standing just behind him, but he recovered quickly. "Oldham, have a look at this."

Oldham knelt down and looked through the scope. "Bloody hell! What game you think they're playing?"

"No idea, but I suspect it won't last long." Ian was right.

Captain Weed also spotted this strange little group, and was not about to let an opportunity pass. He ran to one of his guns not far from Ian. "Load this damned thing. Solid shot." Under his breath he hissed, "I've got one chance, one chance."

"Already loaded, sir."

"Good." Weed took the handspike himself. He aimed, tapped the spike, aimed, moved the spike again, checked the elevation, then took the lanyard from the "number four" man.

An awed silence hung over his battery's guns. Word had spread among them like a blazing fire. They stopped serving their own pieces to watch their commander's skill. Men now looked toward Sharpsburg, waiting for a glimpse of the trajectory, most not quite knowing the target, others watching intently through field glasses.

Ian was back at his telescope, eyes glued on the three Rebel officers. One, an older man with gray hair and beard, was standing, talking to a big officer with a long dark beard. The third officer, who remained mounted, leaned down from the saddle, as though listening or talking to the others.

Ian heard Weed's voice murmur, "Make this one count, Lord, make this one count." Ian's ears rang when the cannon fired so close at hand. The earth shook under him, and he felt more than saw the gun jump back several feet. He steadied the scope in time to see the impact. It sheared off the forelegs of the mounted officer's horse. The officer fell forward, awkwardly, as the horse buckled. The horse's head dug into the ground.

The officer was struggling to remove himself from the saddle. The big man with the long beard went to assist the tangled rider, pulling him free as the horse completely collapsed. Ian thought he could hear the screaming animal, nearly a mile off.

Oldham, who had his own telescope out, shouted, "Splendid shooting!"

All three Rebel officers, obviously shaken, moved quickly, dragging the two remaining mounts over the crest and out of sight. It was, as Weed predicted, too late for a second shot.

The battery cheered their captain, then returned, at Weeds orders, to serving their guns and sending shot and shell at the enemy.

Ian and Oldham watched the action for a time until Weed seemed to step away from his guns for a moment. Oldham approached him. "Excellent shooting, that."

"Thanks, but I'd rather it had been more effective. They lived. Sorry, must return to my guns."

Oldham was persistent. "A question, Captain. Any idea who they were?"

"My men are already wagering on that."

31

"What's the wager?" Ian asked, having walked over to the pair as they talked.

Weed was amused. "The betting money seems to say it was 'Massa' Robert Lee, himself, and possibly Longstreet. No idea the third officer. Ask me, it being Lee is just wishful thinking. On the other hand, the gray hair and beard, the gray horse—all things are possible."

Ian said, "Whoever it was, you gave 'em a strong lesson in marksmanship. They won't take that chance again.

Chapter 6

---

17 September 1862, Sharpsburg, Maryland, near the middle bridge across Antietam Creek

Ian left Oldham interviewing Captain Weed, who was trying desperately to ignore him. Riding down the slope to where the regular division was formed in reserve, Ian brought his mare up beside Major Charles Lovell, who commanded the 2nd Brigade. Lovell cheerily greeted him, "Good day, Colonel Carlyle, a fine morning to see the elephant."

"That it is, Charles, but this won't be my first time tanglin' with that great beastie."

"I should think not. Crimea, as I recall."

"Your men are in good form. I pity the Rebels this day."

They were riding along in front of the regular division, which had placed their arms in a neat row of pointed stacks and were spread out relaxing on the ground behind them. A supply wagon partially blocked Ian's path, with soldiers working on a broken wheel. He lightly tapped his horse's right flank and worked the reins delicately. She executed an immediate and perfect leg yield, proceeding equally forward and diagonally.

Lovell nodded approval. "That's an exceptional mount, Colonel."

"Bought her in Canada. She's a jewel, as responsive and quick as any rider could ask."

Ian brought two horses with him from Canada when his regiment was sent their by the Queen. One, a sturdy quarter horse gelding named Blackie, currently grazed at headquarters at a house owned by the Pry family. The other, the one he now rode, was a beautiful chestnut bay mare, with black mane and tail, and a magnificent gait. He called her Jass, pronounced as though the "ss" were a "z." She was named in honor of a lovely, passionate lady named Jasmine. He thought a great deal of Jasmine, his first real woman. Perhaps he even loved her, in his own way.

Knowing her independent and strong spirit, he felt she would understand the compliment of naming this splendid and quite beautiful mare after her. The horse, like the lady, is exquisite, alive, assertive, confident, demanding, and even commanding. She will give you her all, but gives up nothing for free—her respect, trust, and devotion must be earned.

A commotion caught their attention. They heard a ragged cheer, saw soldiers jumping to their feet. Lovell looked perplexed. "It's the general, by God. Volunteers get the vapors when he passes. Even my grizzled regulars like him." He shook his head slowly.

"You don't sound like yer a devotee."

Lovell watched as the general rode by his men down the length of the column. He saluted as McClellan passed, then said, "Good organizer, superb, in fact. As you can see, a magnificent presence. After Pope's debacle, he patched up this ragtag army like a great architect rebuilding a grand old house; and did it in days, by Christ ... but in battle—too cautious for my taste—no daring, no boldness."

A voice interrupted, "Can I use those words, Colonel?" It was Oldham, having ridden up beside the two riders as they sauntered down the division line. His horse was puffing. *He must have ridden hard down the slope.*

Lovell thought a moment, measuring his next words carefully. "Ah, but it's not for me to criticize. Good way to kill a career, right Colonel?" Lovell ignored the journalist.

"Aye, that it is," Ian replied.

Ian somewhat agreed with Lovell's assessment, but over the past several months he had gained respect for General McClellan.

Oldham prodded Lovell further. "Some think he'll be your president one day soon."

Oldham allowed that to sink in, then nudged again. "Would that be so bad? He couldn't be much worse than the bumpkin you presently have in office."

Ian listened daily to McClellan's staff chatter away about President Lincoln. They spoke none too highly of him, even referring to him mockingly as a gorilla. Most believed McClellan should be president. The general never took part in these discussions—stood outside the circle, listening, and occasionally showing a half-smile. It was apparent he agreed with them.

Lovell was nervous with the conversation, particularly with Oldham apparently taking notes in a pad resting on the pommel of his saddle. "Let's just say I likely won't be voting for our general in that regard ... Ah, sounds like the ball is perking up." Lovell, by way of changing the topic, referred to an increase in cannon fire, accompanied by the scattered popping of small arms.

By this time they had ridden out onto the pike, and were facing west. Ian could see the bridge leading to the town of Sharpsburg farther down the road. Up on the bluffs to their left the Federal artillery were still practicing a vigorous fire on the Rebels across the creek.

Oldham observed, "Appears McClellan is going up on the bluff with the artillery."

Lovell asked Ian, "Aren't you supposed to be on McClellan's staff?"

"Theoretically," Ian replied, "but thus far I've managed to stay clear of that rather overdone crowd he surrounds himself with."

Lovell uncharacteristically chortled. "Good for you," he exclaimed. "They do make an amazing and amusing sight to us mere mortals."

* * *

It was late afternoon and Ian was now among the regulars, lounging with John Poland in front of the combined 2nd and 10th regiments, lazily watching the men with detached affection.

They drank from canteens, nibbled on meager bits of salt beef and hard tack, and talked in small groups, of whiskey or women or family or sweethearts. Some played cards—keeping their minds busy.

A few soldiers seemed to be in contemplation or prayer, but they were the exceptions. These men were regular army. This was their work, what they were trained to do. The excitement, the sharp focus, would come later, when the action began in earnest. Now was a time to take advantage of the lull in movement and relax—like all warriors have since the Spartans.

Ian could picture these same men in their dirty blue sack coats and forage caps wearing the red tunics and bearskin caps of the Guards—the same faces, the same stoic professionals, even the same friendly, yet merciless banter.

"Hey, Hanson, you got anything but water to drink?"

"Yup!"

"Share with your ol' pard?"

"Nope!"

"Stingy bastard."

"Yup!"

With the exception of skirmishers moving across the creek, the regulars had been idle all day. John Poland was beside himself. He dismounted, hands behind his back, stalking first one way, then another.

"Orders, sir," a frazzled horseman shouted as he swerved to a stop beside them.

Poland grabbed at the paper, read it, and nodded to the courier, saying, "No reply. Carry on."

He took a deep breath—let it out slowly, calming and collecting himself. As he mounted his jittery horse, he shouted to Ian, "We're going in—*first!*" the last word spat out with a huge grin.

Soon Poland's regiment crossed the bridge, marching by the flank. On breaking into open country, Poland deployed the regiment in line by the left flank. His right flank was anchored on Boonsboro Pike. The regiment was moving forward with unbounded precision. Behind Poland came regular field artillery batteries, to replace the lighter cavalry guns already on a ridge to their front. For the regulars, the ball had indeed begun, but for Ian, it was pure frustration.

He could see the enemy muzzle flashes in the distance; hear the shouted battalion commands, echoed by company officers. This was not artillery fire. There was nothing impersonal about musket fire heading right at you. He could almost feel the chomping rhythm of boots slamming into hard earth as the regulars advanced on the enemy skirmish line forcing it back.

Ian found himself involuntarily grinding his teeth. This was a stand up fight, and he was keen to get stuck in, the risk a heady thing.

With difficulty he held back, waited by the middle bridge. Occasional enemy shot or shell reached this area, and the same old fear returned. Ian wanted desperately to go up with the infantry, to fight an enemy he could see and get out from under the random artillery fire. Ian's leopard was waiting quietly to be called upon if necessary, but the need was not so great … yet. In truth, Ian was concerned about his leopard gaining too much hold. He wanted to control his own demons without its help.

He remembered a time in the trenches before Sevastopol when the animal took his soul. He became its slave rather than its master. He killed in a wild, angry rage, without reason, will, or necessity. His own men restrained him, with some difficulty. Ian vowed never again to allow himself to lose that much control. So far he had succeeded, but the day was not over.

Chapter 7

Afternoon, 17 September 1862, the Lutheran Church,
Sharpsburg – within Confederate lines

"Was told to report to Cap'n Donaldson, Gen'ral Garnett's staff. Where might I find him, suh?"

"Who in hell are you, boy?"

"Cadmus Buell, suh, Palmetto Sharpshooters—you Cap'n Donaldson, suh?"

"I'm Donaldson. We have some work for you. I'm told you're the best damned shot in these parts. Is that true?"

"No suh, that'd be a lie. I'm the best damned shot in this here army."

Cadmus was told to report for special duty at a church at the eastern edge of the Maryland, town of Sharpsburg. One of Colonel Joe Walker's lieutenants found him taking a quiet snooze under a tree, and delivered the orders. He was being detached from his battalion in Jenkins's Brigade to go on a special assignment to support Garnett's Brigade in Sharpsburg.

Cadmus was pleased. He loved his work, killing Yankees. It was his passion. He liked all of it—finding a position to shoot from, waiting patiently for a target, sighting in, and firing his Enfield. He liked watching the ball strike the target, exploding a man's chest in brilliant red, and knocking him backward off his feet.

Cadmus Buell had been an ordinary farm boy in Hickory Grove, South Carolina, when war erupted. His four brothers left for the war at the first call. He waited at home for a time, but could no longer hold it in. As 1861 ended, he walked through a freezing rainstorm the ten miles to the county seat, and proudly enlisted in the 2nd South Carolina Volunteer Infantry. His association with them lasted less than two weeks.

Cadmus was by far not the brightest of the five Buell brothers. Most folks merely wrote him off with, "That Cadmus, he's dumb as a stone." Nevertheless, at an early age he showed one unique talent that set him apart. He was a natural marksman.

His reputation for winning shooting prizes at county fairs was well known throughout South Carolina. Thus he found himself almost immediately transferred to special duty with Company G of the newly formed Palmetto Sharpshooters. Not all in this battalion were serious marksmen, and certainly not in Cadmus' class; but some measured up, and were used accordingly. The battalion, itself, routinely performed as ordinary infantry, despite its name.

The expert shooters within the unit were treated differently, with exceptional privileges. Cadmus was given a fine Enfield rifle musket. Over the next months he took a toll in Yankee soldiers. His specialty was killing officers at extreme ranges with one shot. He grew to truly love it. It was the finest thing he had ever done. It made him famous—somebody —and he craved each new kill.

He was a sought-after marksman, praised by his fellow soldiers and his superiors. What they did not know, and he was not about to tell them, was how much he enjoyed the pure ecstasy of killing. Highly acclaimed and even paid bonuses for killing, he gladly would have paid them to allow him the pleasure, without fear of punishment.

"Come with me," the captain ordered.

The battle had raged most of the day to the north and south of the town. Shot and shell rained heavily at times, and the captain was a bit twitchy every time he heard the whine of a cannon ball passing over, the impact of a solid shot smacking into the ground, or the explosion of a shell. He kept ducking as they walked. Cadmus found this amusing, because he was somehow impervious to that kind of fear.

His admirers said his iron nerves made him such an excellent shot. The truth is he was convinced he would not die in this war. He was charmed by some unseen force, which made him indestructible.

He walked behind the captain, smiling as he saw him bob around, seemingly to avoid incoming shot. They walked into what, according to the battered sign out front, was a Lutheran church. The captain led him to a small room with a ladder, which appeared to go up through the roof of the church.

They climbed to the high steeple, where a bell was fastened to heavy iron supports. The tower was not very roomy, but the view was spectacular. He could see the ridge beyond the town, and the rolling land beyond the ridge, all the way to a bridge about a mile east of the church.

There were two officers at hand when they arrived. Both were looking through field glasses, intensely preoccupied.

Cadmus studied the situation, making an immediate assessment, as he had trained himself to do since becoming a stalking killer of men. A few hundred yards east were their own troops, Confederate infantry. A few artillery pieces were scattered thinly on both sides of the road leading to the bridge.

They were battling Yankee infantry, which was slowly, but steadily, advancing from the direction of the bridge on both sides of the road. Some, at least a loose skirmish line, were already reaching the ridge. There was no telling what numbers were in the blind area immediately below the ridge line, where Cadmus could not see, even from the tower.

Infantry reserves and artillery pieces were in the distance all the way back to the bridge and across, beyond it. The artillery was laying a heavy fire on the town, including the church, with telling effect. It looked to Cadmus' trained eye as though his own troops were heavily outnumbered by the approaching enemy.

Cadmus realized that his perch in the high steeple was one of the enemy's primary aiming points. At the same time, he knew that this position was ideal for a fine marksman like himself to bring unrelenting terror down on the closing Yankees.

One of the officers put down his field glasses. "This him?" The tall officer wore an immaculate gray uniform with gilt braid on the sleeves and three stars on each side of the collar. He looked unusually clean, as did the lieutenant with him. Senior officers in Lee's army had developed a decidedly seedy appearance while on campaign, but these two looked fresh from a cotillion in Richmond.

"Private Buell reporting, Colonel, suh."

"About God damned time. Donaldson, you tell him what we want. I'll be down below. Too damn hot up here." The lieutenant with the colonel looked greatly relieved. They climbed perhaps too hastily down the ladder.

"Well, Buell," the captain said, "this is where we find out if you really are as good with that Enfield as you claim." The captain was very jittery, continuing to flinch at the sounds of battle that surrounded him. To his credit, he tried to talk calmly and look nonchalant.

"Darkness is approachin', and those bastards will likely pause for the night, but the colonel thinks they'll attack the town some time after dark. As you can see, we're a little light in strength. The colonel wants confusion to the enemy, and that's what you can give him. From now until you're relieved, you are to pick your targets and kill as many of their officers as you can—up and down their line."

"Yes, suh. What about afta?"

"After—after what?"

"Afta it gets dark, suh. Can't no more see to shoot."

"I'm told there'll be a moon tonight. You just keep shootin' as long as you can see somethin', anythin'. Do you have rations? You won't likely be relieved until tomorrow."

"Don't need none, suh. I got water, and I'll do just fine."

"You understand you're to stay here no matter how hot it gets?"

Cadmus felt in his whole being that this was an important assignment, sent him by God the Almighty to make him even more famous. He was proud to have been chosen. He knew the risks, but just did not care. "I understan'. Stay here no matter how hot it gets."

The captain looked at him in wonder. "Aren't you scared, Buell?"

"No, suh. It ain't my time. Not yet. I got a few more Yankees ta kill fust." Cadmus was all smiles as he watched the captain jerk back from the sound of a shell bursting a fair distance away.

The captain moved nervously to the ladder and started to climb down. "Carry on, Buell, and good luck."

"No luck to it, suh. Not with me behind this here rifle."

Chapter 8

Late afternoon, 17 September 1862 – with the Federal regiments advancing on Sharpsburg

Many of the regular regiments were already across the creek, advancing on both sides of the Boonsboro Pike. *I have no business being here,* Ian thought, *"Little Mac" would definitely not approve.* He had no longer been able to wait by the bridge.

Ian was moving up behind his friend Hiram Dryer's 4th US. Hiram took forward command of all the regulars on the field and orchestrated their advance, first on one side of the road, then the other. Ian placed the Henry loosely across the front of his saddle.

Two Confederate formations came over the ridge from the town to attack Poland's 2nd US, which was still on the left, south of the pike. The Rebels were quickly thrown back by the regulars' concentrated fire.

Poland then led a valiant assault up onto the same ridge within clear view of the town ahead. They suffered losses as soldiers crested the ridge, but their action caused the Rebels and their artillery to withdraw toward Sharpsburg.

It was rapidly growing dark. Poland pulled back some off the crest, and consolidated at a fence along a dirt road. Volunteer regiments moved in on his left. Across the pike on the right, Dryer brought up three more regiments of regulars. The Federals were now in a strong line not far from the edge of town, with a healthy reserve. Skirmishers were forward, occupying the crest.

Ian rode close to Dryer. His friend was impatient, only lightly disguising his annoyance. He had been ordered to hold in place, with no reason why given. They had met very little resistance. He clearly saw an opportunity quietly creeping away.

Highly agitated, Dryer shouted, "Ian, what in hell is the general waiting for? We're here. We could push through this bunch with a company, much less two brigades of regulars."

"I can't disagree, Hiram, but General McClellan must be certain of what's what before committing his reserves."

"Hell's gate. If he needs information, I'll get it for him." With that, Dryer spurred his mount, heading west down the pike toward the enemy-held Sharpsburg.

"Hiram," Ian hissed. "You can't go out alone. Get back here—damn the man!"

No time for thinking. Ian raced after his friend, squeezing Jass into a brisk canter, body bent forward, his head down along her mane. He caught Dryer as he passed his own skirmishers on the last rise before the town. These men looked at the two officers in amazement. Ian was certain he heard a voice close by the pike shout, "Crazy bastards!" He agreed.

"Hiram," he whispered as he caught up and moved Jass on Dryer's left, "Och, man, at least get off the bloody road."

They were in the shadows with the last ridgeline behind them. That and the slowly approaching darkness were all that protected them from a certain and ignominious death. Scattered random shots came their way, mostly from the right. There was an unmistakable deadly buzzing sound as bullets passed. *They're shootin' in our direction,* Ian thought, *but haven't yet seen us as a clear target.*

"Look!" Dryer was pointing ahead, apparently oblivious to the enemy fire.

Dryer was right. Ian could feel it as well as see what was before them. *Hell, I can almost smell it.* The Confederates were strung out badly on a wide front in not much more than a ragged skirmish line, with a scattering of cannon placed among them.

There is no power here, Ian thought. He and Dryer both understood that this was an opportunity for a swift, deadly blow.

A church with a tall steeple stood silhouetted against the sky to their left front. As Ian looked at the steeple, Jass jigged to the right for some unknown reason, bumping Dryer's mount.

That small movement saved Ian's life. He saw a muzzle flash from the dark interior of the steeple, heard with shocked clarity the sound of a shot, then felt a sharp tug at his left sleeve.

"Right, Hiram, get out of here!"

Dryer said nothing, but realized the danger. He swung his horse around and off the pike, heading back toward his skirmishers at a gallop. His abrupt reversal caught Ian off guard.

"Halt, who goes thar?" The voice was very close. Ian froze, but there was nothing for it. He bluffed, saying in a loud hopefully, unshaken voice and his best British accent, "Leftenant Colonel Carlyle, Her Majesty's Scots Fusilier Guards, come to call on General Lee."

There was laughter ahead. A voice came back, "You don't say. Well I'll be damned. Y'all come on over."

Ian prayed they did not see anything but a murky shadow. He was backing Jass away from a dark tree line to his right as he talked, gripping the Henry rifle with sweaty hands.

"Hey—you! I say'd advance and be recognized 'fore I shoot yer dumb ass."

It all happened at once. Jass backed into a hole and reared. A shot rang out. Ian was tossed off the back of the saddle and hit the ground hard square on his butt. As he fell, he felt a bullet whiz by his head like an annoying bee.

Well, that puts paid to it. Jass moved off, and he could hear them coming, feet pounding. He saw a shadow moving in, felt hands grabbing him as he tried to scuttle away. He saw a whitish face with snarling teeth above him—his nightmare ... again.

The leopard took control. He felt the Henry in his hands. His movements were limited, but enough. He smashed the rifle butt into the face above him again and again. He heard the odd crunching of the skull splitting, could feel the wet blood spattering on his clothing, in his face. White-hot rage consumed him—*not this time, damn you!*

The body of the dead Rebel fell on top of him, heavy on his chest. Another shadow moved closer. A voice screamed, "The sum'bitch got Ely!"

There was a flash-bang from where the shadow was, then a sickening "thwack" as the musket ball struck poor Ely's body. The voice yelled, "Got ya – ya bastard!"

Ian struggled, finally getting his arm and the Henry free. Swinging the heavy weapon around with one hand, he fired at the new shadow, heard a yelp as the bullet hit its mark.

Something moved past him, a man running, then another. He could just make out their blue coats. Federal soldiers, two of them, rushing straight at the Rebels.

Must have come from the skirmish line. Thank the Lord. It gave Ian time, time to push Ely's body off, get to his feet, and look for Jass.

Two deliberately spaced shots. Ian turned about in mid-stride to see both Federal soldiers fall, almost at the same time. Quick as that, his rescuers died, and he was alone again.

By sheer reflex, Ian levered a cartridge in the Henry, snapped it to his shoulder, and began firing in rapid succession—eight, nine shots, he lost count. He pumped the lever up and down, and the Henry worked smoothly. The rapid staccato fire it poured out must have appeared to the Rebels like a whole cluster of Federals.

Ian saw three left in the hazy grayness. Two carried poor Ely back into the dark recesses of the trees, while the other covered their withdrawal.

There was a long deafening quiet. Then Ian heard plainly the jingle and movement of horses. Rebel horsemen left the tree line, galloping toward Ian, no more than fifty yards away.

Pistol shots rang out. Between their muzzle flashes Ian saw the silhouette of Jass standing a short distance behind him, turned toward the Federal positions. *Thank God!* Ian ran, stumbling, to the horse. He knew this would be his last chance to avoid capture, prison, or worse.

Ian grabbed the right stirrup tightly, tripping over his own feet and losing the Henry. *No time to mount, lady, only time to pray.*

With his free hand, he smacked Jass's rump into motion. She bolted. He grabbed the stirrup with both hands, and half ran, was half dragged back toward the Federal lines. Ian found himself mumbling out loud, "Please—God—don't let the saddle slip."

Jass took the distance to their skirmish line in stride, with her lopsided load hanging off. Thankfully, Dryer had warned the Federal skirmishers. No one fired at Ian coming through.

Several soldiers halted Jass just inside their position. Ian was shaken and dusty, but he was safe and in one piece.

Chapter 9

Dusk, 17 September 1862, church steeple, Sharpsburg

Cadmus was on his fifth kill, smiling like a dog with an unlimited supply of bones. Some of them may have been sergeants, but he was sure of at least three officers. Two were artillery officers at their guns, and one was a dismounted infantry officer. It was difficult to tell exactly, because he did not possess a pair of field glasses.

All he knew was that each shot resulted in his target flopping back onto the ground, and he swore he saw a blossoming red stain on the chest of at least two. At times like these Cadmus saw himself as a God, with the power of life or death over anyone he chose.

He kept his head well down, hat off, and the bell behind him to cut down his silhouette. This was an excellent position—except for the occasional close musket ball, cannon shot, or shell.

Just as he relaxed with the sight picture on his next target and began squeezing the trigger, a solid shot struck the steeple. The sound of the crash was deafening, and splinters of wood flew about. Miraculously, none struck him. As the debris stopped falling about him, he casually aimed in, fired, and watched as his target was picked up off his feet by the blow of the .577 caliber minié bullet.

It was rapidly growing dark. Cadmus heard a noise and saw Captain Donaldson raise his head and shoulders above the hole where the ladder came through. "Brought you some salt beef and crackers." He handed a sack to Cadmus, who accepted it gratefully.

"I also thought you might need these." He placed his own field glasses on the wood planking next to Cadmus.

"Much obliged, suh."

"Give the glasses back in the morning. You keep your head down, hear?" With that Captain Donaldson disappeared back down the ladder.

Cadmus nibbled on the beef and a piece of hardtack, while he surveyed the land. The glasses brought everything into view more clearly, and helped with the dwindling light.

He counted the bodies he had targeted, but could only find five still lying on the ground, unmoving. *Damn*, he thought, *musta ony wounded one a them bastards.*

Darkness crept in like a shroud, and the intense firing ceased. The Yankees were not yet in the town, but they were close. The Confederate infantry and cannon fell back and consolidated their line more or less even with the church. In numbers they appeared to be little more than a severely stretched battalion.

The Yankees set a line a few hundred yards east of the Confederate line. The ridge was somewhat in Cadmus' way, and he could just make them out.

Cadmus watched as Yankee skirmishers took up concealed positions as best they could behind fences, trees, and bushes. He searched for officers, men with swords dangling, or visible shoulder straps, showing rank.

He wondered why, with their numbers, the Yankees did not attack and overwhelm his comrades below the church tower. Then he saw a strange sight. Two Yankee riders were moving west on the road toward the town and his perch.

To his amazement, they passed through their own skirmishers, and slowed. Through the field glasses he could see they were officers. One wore a French-style kepi, a sword dangling by his side. The other wore an odd cap, with a checkered band of some kind. He had no sword, but a rifle was sitting across his saddle at the pommel.

Although there were scattered shots, the Confederate skirmishers had not yet challenged them or concentrated their fire. *The darkness must be covering their movement,* he thought, *or our boys are waiting to take them prisoner.* Cadmus delayed firing while they moved closer, taking aim on the one who posed the greatest danger to him. The one with the odd cap, and the rifle.

The two officers stopped on the road, side by side. His target was on the right. Cadmus relaxed, drew in a half breath, and fired. He saw the target's horse shy just as he pulled the trigger—too late—the ball had left the barrel. He knew the shot missed, and cursed himself for not waiting an instant longer.

His target knew he had been fired at—*Like as not, saw the muzzle flash.* The horse and rider on the left reversed direction and galloped off toward their own lines. He heard shouts. His own skirmishers were finally challenging them. The second officer, his missed target, started to back his horse, then appeared to fall backward off the mount. *Maybe I did hit 'em.*

Men ran out to capture the Yankee officer who fell, and there was a tussle. Two Yankee skirmishers moved forward from their line to help, but were shot down.

Then the officer who had fallen from his mount began firing rapidly. *Must have one a them new repeatin' rifles.*

Cadmus reloaded quickly, but could not see well enough to take a second shot. He could barely make out the scene as the officer scrambled to reach his mount. Hanging onto the saddle, he was dragged back toward his own lines. Several horsemen gave chase until the Yankee skirmishers forced them to turn around.

Later in the night, Cadmus heard more than saw the Yankees withdraw. As dawn broke, he felt refreshed. He was safe and exhilarated. He had taken lives—a God, invincible.

He stood up in the steeple to stretch his legs. It was a mistake he would regret for the rest of his days.

The shot, which penetrated the flimsy rotted wood of the lower portion of the steeple, came from somewhere well off in the open fields, toward the bridge. It hit him solidly in the right kneecap, the ball driving wood splinters into the wound. Cadmus buckled and fell backward into the bell, causing it to clang just once. He lay in shock.

Cadmus could not believe he was shot. It was a mistake—not him … no, he was under God's protection, indestructible. He tried to stand, but the pain was unbearable and he collapsed again, with a scream of agony. His hand tried to rub his knee, but felt the wetness and pulled away. He looked at his knee in disbelief. It was shattered, covered in blood, and there was a six inch piece of wood the thickness of a shovel handle protruding from it. In a daze he pulled the wood out, and lost consciousness.

When he awoke the third or fourth time, he was in a hospital. A surgeon was there. An orderly said, "Don't be worryin', son, you ain't gonna lose that leg."

Cadmus was ecstatic at hearing this. He knew well enough that in military hospitals limbs came off like pulling petals off a daisy. He lost consciousness again.

What they failed to tell him was that although he was not going to lose the leg, it would not be of much use, either. He was a cripple, and always would be.

When he was finally told, "You'd be too slow to be of any use in the army," his madness crystallized. It focused as never before, and begat a pure virulent hatred of the enemy who brought this thunder down upon him, and made him nothing once again.

Chapter 10

---

17 September 1862, evening along Antietam Creek

The note Captain Hiram Dryer wrote after their ride into Rebel lines reached all the way to General McClellan. Carried by one of Dryer's lieutenants, it went up the chain of command through Dryer's brigade commander, Lieutenant Colonel Buchanan, and division commander, Brigadier General Sykes. The note asked permission to assault the Confederate positions with all the regulars on the field, quickly, before the Confederates were reinforced.

It was approved by Buchanan and by General Sykes, who saw the opening. However, as Ian had suspected, the request was denied by Little Mac. Ian looked on in astonishment as McClellan told his generals of his decision.

McClellan seemed to be composing his words, perhaps rehearsing them for posterity, "Gentlemen, at Borodino, Napoleon was asked why he refused to send in his Imperial Guard at the critical moment. I believe he answered something like, 'If I am defeated this day, where is my army for tomorrow's fight.' General Porter has urged caution. His counsel reminded me of Napoleon, which forced me into sober reflection. I am exactly in Napoleon's position now."

He paused for effect, then said carefully, "Despite Captain Dryer's fine, brave initiative, and excellent intelligence, we have done enough for today."

"But, sir—," Sykes started to say, not wanting to believe the general would hesitate in the face of such a clear opportunity.

McClellan cut him short, "No more. Recall the regulars, secure the bridge. I'll have orders for the corps commanders shortly. Gentlemen, we'll fight again tomorrow."

He turned his horse and walked it into the dark toward his headquarters at the Pry family's house. His staff followed, some trying by moonlight to scribble notes as they rode.

Dryer's lieutenant rode away to give his captain the unbelievable news. Sykes just shook his head in exasperation. He glared at Porter. Porter bowed his head and drifted away.

An aide handed Ian a note signed by McClellan, himself. It summoned him to headquarters at once. There would be no time to reach Dryer to commiserate.

Ian feared the worst—that General McClellan was given the information that he, a foreign observer, was with Dryer on his wild ride into the Rebel lines. He knew he was dead wrong in following Dryer forward, but he had no regrets. Now if he must pay the piper, so be it.

An hour later, Ian climbed the steep hill toward the Pry house. The hill, and what looked like every inch of ground around the house was filled with wounded. Orderlies attended them as best they could. It was dark, and small fires appeared everywhere.

Ian approached the two guards standing outside the front door. They knew him by sight and snapped to the position of present arms, a sentinel's salute reserved for senior officers. He returned the salute casually, with his right hand to his cap.

He kicked the caked mud off his boots in the entrance hallway, which was rapidly filling with more seriously wounded officers and soldiers. General McClellan heard him enter and called from a room off the hallway, "Come in, Carlyle."

The room where McClellan had set up his office was small, but he was noted for his penchant not to inconvenience civilians just to cater to his needs. In fact, given what Ian had seen in the past, he was amazed that McClellan opted to use the inside of the house at all. He thought the general might have preferred to establish headquarters within the massive, dirty-white circus of tents that surrounded the back and sides of the house—grounds which were now a sea of doctors, orderlies, and wounded in blood-soaked bandages.

As Ian entered, two staff officers frantically gathered maps from a table. One scurried from the room, stumbling over a wounded soldier propped against a wall in the hallway. The man screamed in pain.

"Apologies, soldier, very sorry," the officer said as he passed.

The other staff officer left saying, "Sir, the orders will be on their way within minutes, minutes, sir."

"They'd better be," the general replied. The wounded soldier was still moaning. The general added, "We need to move this headquarters, and soon!"

"Yes, sir, I'll see to it," the staff officer shouted as he left the house. *The general is obviously not in a good frame of mind*, thought Ian.

He was not asked to sit ... *a bad sign*. The general stood, paced, making Ian wait while he intently examined a document in his hand ... *a worse sign*.

Ian was somewhat in awe of Little Mac. He was such a diminutive, natty, little man, with so much power. Ian was only of medium height, but he felt, uncomfortably, that he towered over the general.

Although Ian agreed with Lovell and thought him too timid on the battlefield, he respected McClellan's other leadership talents enough to show him deference. He stood at attention while he waited.

During previous meetings, Ian had noticed that when the general was agitated, the tiny square patch of beard directly under his lower lip, bounced about like a horsefly, crawling around his chin, trying desperately to belie his smooth, boyish face. The forced silence continued.

McClellan finally stopped pacing and looked up, the "horsefly" bobbing rapidly. His light gray eyes glared steadily into Ian's. It made Ian extremely uncomfortable, partly because this was usually his favorite ploy. With unwavering penetration, Ian's clear blue eyes had softened the heart of many a maiden in recent years. These same eyes could turn hard and ice cold in an instant, cutting through the confidence of an opponent like the downward stroke of a razor-sharp saber. This time he was on the receiving end ... and it was not to his liking.

"So, what the devil did you think you were doing out there?" the general asked. His cold stare never faltering.

"Sir, I ..."

"Never mind. You'd just make excuses or tell me a pack of tall tales. That's not why I called you here."

Now Ian was truly puzzled. He wanted to defend himself, but held his tongue. There was not much he could defend.

McClellan shook the document in his hand at Ian. "I've orders for you, Carlyle, direct from your War Office, through mine. I assume that's Horse Guards for you, right?"

He did not wait for an answer. "You're to report immediately to the British Legation in Washington, and await further instructions. Perhaps you're in as much hot water with them as you are with me."

Ian accepted the orders. *Hmmm, could be something to do with my report on breech-loading rifles ... or could just be my brother, Peter, meddling, trying to get me out of harm's way or to come home.*

Ian's mind raced forward. "Sir, I honestly don't know what this is about. I did not request it."

"Didn't think you had."

Ian was respectful. "I shall obey my orders and take my leave immediately," ... and contrite. "Please accept my apologies, sir, if I have been the cause of any inconvenience or offended you in any way."

McClellan's voice softened, "No inconvenience or offense, Carlyle. Fortunately, your audacity with Captain Dryer didn't cause your demise. Had it, I'd have a time explaining it to your government."

He paused, then said, "No. In the end, Carlyle, you've been an asset to my staff since first we met. Done your country proud as far as I'm concerned, and given me good service."

"Thank you, sir."

Because the general was being so unexpectedly cordial, Ian pressed his luck. "Sir, may I discuss with you this proposed night attack on the enemy center. We're running out of time, and ..."

McClellan was looking down at his desk after thinking he dismissed Carlyle. He jerked his head up, stared frostily into Ian's eyes, "No, you may not. You are dismissed."

Pushed that one a jig too far, Ian thought as he turned sharply toward the door. "Yes, sir. I'll depart for Washington at once."

McClellan shouted as Ian left the makeshift office. "Good luck, Ian, I mean that, and keep your head down in Washington. Damned sight more dangerous there, than here."

As he left the porch and walked back down the hill, Ian heard the general chuckling.

Chapter 11

As the train pulled into Washington's Baltimore and Ohio Railroad Station, a small, bouncy man made his way through a smoke-filled car. He wore a plain brown corduroy coat with a Victoria Cross, Britain's highest award for valor, pinned to the left breast. He was looking for someone.

Private Broderick Swann, former London pickpocket, had been called "Little Twig" by his mates long before Ian first laid eyes on him. He was a disheveled mess of a soldier then, hardly the image of a member of the elite Scots Fusilier Guards.

In the old days he had perpetually unkempt blond hair, a stick-like build, and had a rather sickly look about him. In uniform, no matter how pressed or well turned out, he looked like a ragbag. The war in the Crimea and six years as Ian's soldier servant changed and matured him in many ways. He was no longer so tousled or fragile.

The metamorphosis began shortly after the Queen, in person, awarded Swann the Victoria Cross for heroic deeds in the Crimea. He had taken up the color from a fallen Ensign, rallied Ian's company around it, and then led the

61

charge up a hill into withering Russian fire. Though wounded twice, in the left side and left upper arm, he hung on to the color and still kept going.

Since the day in London when Ian brought him before the Queen to receive his medal, Swann had gained considerable confidence. With it came pride in himself and his regiment. He now cut his hair extremely short and kept it well groomed. Although still not a big man, he had added twenty pounds of pure muscle. When he wore his uniform, it fit him trimly, and it was immaculate—indeed, diamond sharp. He walked with a purpose, which made him look taller and more formidable.

After receiving the medal, Private Swann could have been brought up to Corporal, and likely to Sergeant, several times over. He turned down promotions to remain the soldier servant, the personal valet, if you will, of Lieutenant Colonel Ian David Carlyle. His selfless devotion to his officer meant more than his own advancement.

His emergence was spectacular in one other respect. The ugly caterpillar had indeed become the butterfly. Unlike the withdrawn, introverted individual of before, the new Swann left a string of disappointed hearts in his wake across two continents, including a slight, red-haired lady he met, wooed, and left behind on the very train they were taking into Washington.

"Are you ready, sir," Swann asked his officer. He had found Ian jammed in a seat, playing cards with an obese American major.

Ian replied, "I'd better go, Swann, before this clever American puts me in debtor's prison."

"Sir, your trunks'll be brought up soon's we're stopped. We should be makin' our way, sir."

"Right you are. Good day ta you, sir," he said to the officer, "and please try not ta spend all my money too quickly."

The American laughed. "Sure thing, Colonel. It has been pleasant. Sorry to see you go."

Ian smiled, "I'm sure you are. God speed."

Gathering up his small valise, he followed his soldier servant through the swarm of passengers in the aisle. Swann made a zigzag path through the passengers standing in the aisle to get luggage off the overhead racks.

On the railway platform a pale, well-fed, roundish man, dressed in a gentlemen's black suit, held his tall top hat in one hand, by his side, and with the other held up a white card. His small-set eyes squinted through spectacles watching the crowd depart the train. He continually pressed his spectacles back up on his nose with a chubby index finger, as he waited impatiently. Thick brown side-whiskers hung down framing his bright, kindly face, but there was scarcely any hair atop. He looked to be in his mid to late forties, very British and very official.

Ian and Swann made their way off the car onto the platform. Swann took note of the man immediately, even before he saw the white card with large black letters which read: "Lieut-Col Carlyle."

Swann managed to shout above the din of the moving, jostling crowd on the platform. "Look there, sir, we've a welcoming committee."

"Didn't realize I was so popular, did you Swann?"

"No, sir. With yer permission, I'll be off to sort out the trunks."

"Wait a mite, Swann, let's see what's what."

Ian walked directly to the man. "Sir, I do believe yer lookin' for me. Ian Carlyle, at your service."

"Ah, w-wonderful. Thought I m-might have mmmissed you," the man said in a pleasant middle-class English accent, with a noticeable stutter. His eyes blinked repeatedly when he struggled with a word. "I'm B-B-Benjamin Tasker, B-British Legation. Come to take you in tow—get you ssssettled." His face broke into an engaging smile.

"A pleasure, Mr. Tasker. We must arrange about our baggage."

Tasker was fussy and nervous, with a somewhat theatrical manner. "We've put you up at the WWWillard." Then with a sweep of his hand, "Many of us s-stay there; a grand place. I have r-rooms there myself."

He addressed Swann directly. "Tell them to s-send the t-trunks, or w-whatever, along to the Willard on P-Pennsylvania, under the colonel's name. Bill the delivery to the B-British Legation. They'll know w-what to do."

"Right you are, sir," Swann disappeared through the crowd.

All very efficient, Ian thought, *an odd character, but definitely efficient. He seems anxious to please, but not in an unctuous way.*

"Colonel Carlyle, shall we m-make our way outside the ssstation. Your man will find us. I've a carriage w-waiting." He poked his spectacles up on his nose with his finger.

Leaning against a wall in a corner of the platform was a large, powerfully built, roughly dressed man, with what appeared to be no neck at all. From beneath a wide-brimmed hat he watched their movements with interest. He followed them from the station, remaining well out of sight.

The station was on the corner of New Jersey Avenue and C Street. The journey over crowded streets to the Willard Hotel gave them enough time to talk. It reminded Ian of London, with hansom cabs, carriages, and carts of all sorts starting and stopping, occasionally bumping into one another. Walkways, when there were walkways, surged in a sea of people moving somewhere with a purpose.

"What is it you do at the legation, Mr. Tasker?" Ian asked once they were on their way. Swann was up front riding with the driver.

"Oh, please, C-Colonel, w-we'll be wwworking together for d-donkey's years. You really must call me Benjamin, or B-Ben, if you like."

"And I am Ian, not Colonel, or I'll start feeling like I'm my own father." At this, Tasker gave out a rather too-high laugh, almost a giggle. *Odd, but likeable creature*, Ian mused.

He guessed from the words and his accent that Tasker had some degree of formal education; likely more self-taught.

For a reason Ian could not articulate, he knew Tasker was never in the military.

Ian asked a second time, "So what is it you do again?

The more comfortable and relaxed Tasker seemed to become, the less his eyes blinked as he spoke. "Oh, a bit of everything. Like s-sorting you out. M-My official t-t-tit ..." Tasker paused, taking a breath, blinking again ... "I am s-secretary to the British Minister, Lord Lyons. He has a few s-secretaries, a busy man. You'll meet him tomorrow. You'll be w-working directly for him, as I understand it." Tasker came down harder and slower on some words in a sentence, which Ian felt sure was to help counter the stutter.

"I'm most curious as to what I'll be doing?" Ian said, as a question.

"Can't help you there, all v-very hush-hush. Should know t-t-tomorrow, though."

The Willard was indeed a fine hotel. To Ian's delight, he was registered in a set of rooms—a sitting room, bedroom, and an ensuite combination bathing room and water closet. *A most pleasant change from a tent in the field.*

Ian thanked Tasker and bid him farewell with a glass of port at the Round Robin, a small, but comfortable bar within the Willard Hotel. A completely round bar dominated the center of the round room, ringed with tables and chairs. The room was all mahogany, brass, and stained glass.

In saying goodbye, Tasker added, "Your appointment with his l-lordship is for n-nine tomorrow morning. I'll call at your r-rooms around ssseven for breakfast."

"Splendid," Ian replied.

Ian's two large trunks were soon delivered. He and Swann unpacked and settled in. Swann was given a small, but decently appointed room several doors down the hall from Ian. He had one large valise, which contained most of his worldly possessions.

Before retiring, Ian wrote three letters. He had no news from the battle, but nonetheless he wrote a note to Hiram Dryer, and a second to Poland. He apologized to both for his urgent departure, and gave his rather unflattering opinion of

General McClellan's decision to disapprove the night attack. He knew the bitter disappointment of these fine officers, and the entire regular division.

The third letter was to Major Charles Lovell, who so admired his horse, Jass. He had run into Lovell at the Pry house headquarters as he was packing to depart. In the letter he thanked Lovell for volunteering to take care of Jass and Blackie. He had become quite fond of them both. He also suggested they needed riding, and that Lovell should treat them as his own until he could make further arrangements to collect them.

At the same time Ian was writing letters, the solidly built no-neck man from the railway station sat in the lobby. He rested in a soft chair reading a newspaper, trying, unsuccessfully, to look like he belonged there, his shabby clothes aside.

Hulking shoulders, thick arms, and massive hands did not help his effort to remain unnoticed. He removed the wide-brimmed hat, to reveal that he had no hair on his head or face. Bushy eyebrows were low set over almost black eyes, and, of course, a neck so thick it looked like his huge head rested directly on his shoulders.

Chapter 12

---

19 September 1862, British Legation, Washington

Housed in an elegant three-story, Georgian-style house on I Street in northwest Washington, the British Legation was once the home of President James Monroe and his wife. Richard Bickerton Pemell Lyons, 1st Viscount Lyons, and British Minister to the United States, headed the legation.

"You know, Tasker, I've actually met Lord Lyons," Ian stated.

"R-Really?"

"My father, the Earl of Dunkairn, was friends with the Minister's father, who was Royal Navy you know, and killed in the Crimea. I was introduced to the entire family on more than one occasion, when they visited our home at Dunkairn Hall."

"You should r-recognize each other, then."

"I doubt it. Too long ago." Ian had little memory of the British Minister he was about to meet.

Tasker volunteered, "His lllordship is a quiet, reserved man. He listens well, but s-seldom speaks. Despises Washington District, as many of us do ... too hot, too uncommonly dull, too d-dirty."

"And the Americans? How is he thought of?"

"Excellent question. You'll d-do nicely around here." Tasker paused, Ian waited.

"Avoiding the answer, Benjamin?"

Amused, Tasker replied, "Not at all. F-Frankly, I think at first it was thought he is t-too little experienced, almost an insult to America."

"But there's been a change?" Ian asked. Thinking, *Getting answers out of these diplomats is a bit like what it must be to extract teeth. Perhaps it's merely his effort to control the stutter.*

"SSSpot on, it's been rocky going, especially with S-Seward, their S-Secretary of S-State, but he's earned their r-respect."

Benjamin Tasker escorted Ian into Lord Lyons' presence. Ian saw a fine looking, well-tailored gentleman in his early forties. He was only slightly more than ten years older, but easily looked twenty. He moved slowly and deliberately, almost as though in constant pain.

Lord Lyons had graying hair, severely combed across the top—parted on the left—then both sides combed forward toward his soft, sunken eyes. Side-whiskers ran down to his jaw line, ending in a straight, tight mouth, until he smiled. His smile was both warm and charming. A high white collar and precisely knotted dove-gray cravat meticulously covered his slight double chin.

It was a huge, spacious office, covered in wood paneling with a large number of windows. Through them Ian saw hansom cabs and omnibuses passing on the bustling street below. Lord Lyons' desk was also huge, concealed under mounds of letters, dispatches, courier pouches, and other papers, all scattered in apparent disorder.

Ian was not looking forward to this meeting, but Lord Lyons made him feel comfortable immediately. "Ah, Ian, my dear fellow, not the first time we've met, what? Was quite fond of your father. Sorry to hear of his sudden passing. A cough turned lethal—bad business. Sit down, please." Ian felt Lord Lyons' sincerity.

He sat in a luxurious leather easy chair, and found himself alone with the minister. Tasker, who had come in with him, had discreetly left the room. Ian was impressed by his quick, stealthy exit—like a cat.

"Thank you, my lord."

"Your mother?"

"She became quite ill soon after father's passing. I believe she misses him a wee bit too much. Lost without him, I fear. Remains to herself at Dunkairn Hall. My brother takes care of her."

"Sorry, I hadn't heard." He waited before continuing to give a moment of deference to this sad news.

Lord Lyons continued, "Yes, your brother, Peter. As I recall a recluse. I heard he came out of his shell. Now the Earl of Dunkairn, and doing well in business."

Lord Lyons did not mention that Peter's "business" was selling weapons to foreign buyers. Ian knew his lordship was fully aware of that fact, and thought more of him for leaving it out of their conversation.

Ian replied, "I was happy to see him coming out, my lord. I look forward to seeing him and mother when I return home."

Lord Lyons turned serious. "Right then. Well, I'm certain you're curious. Let's get to it, shall we?"

"Aye, sir."

Lord Lyons walked out from behind his massive desk. As he sat in a chair opposite Ian, he whisked both tails of his black frock coat behind him with one smooth motion, using both hands at once. Thus, he did not sit on, crush, or wrinkle them under him. The gesture was as precise and graceful as the man.

Lord Lyons became entirely business. Even his facial muscles tightened. "You know what we do here?"

"No, my lord, I'm afraid this is my first excursion into the world of diplomacy."

"Allow me to clarify. Simply put, we protect British citizens and British interests, such as the rights of our seamen, the shipping trade, imports and exports, and lately, the prevention of our resident citizens from being forced into the Federal army against their will."

Ian knew none of these things. Particularly, he had not thought of the Federal army's draft practices affecting British citizens living in America.

"From time to time, we also gather bits of intelligence to send back home. Not that we consider America our enemy … anymore … quite the contrary. These days we are growing ever closer in our bonds of trade and mutual respect." He paused, and leaned forward before continuing.

"You must understand, however, that there is a large, well-financed, and politically well-connected faction in Britain that think our interests should be more aligned with the 'Gentlemen of the South.' Do you understand my meaning, Ian?"

"Of course, my lord."

"Others believe we should never support recognizing the South as long as they would be a slave-holding nation."

Lord Lyons turned emphatic and deadly serious. "For now, our government's public policy is one of total neutrality. Some might say that advantages the South, but that is the way it sets, for now. You should be perfectly clear on that point."

"Is there a movement to change that policy, my lord?"

"I can tell you, at this minute, the strength of the neutrality policy is dicey. There's yet another faction bent on our intervening in the war, to bring, or indeed force it to a close, one way or another. Complex set of issues," Lord Lyons continued, "most complex, and I dare say we're caught right in the middle."

"I see."

"Much depends on the outcome of the battle you just left. The news today sounds like Lee is in retreat, south. What's your opinion? Federal victory?"

Ian realized how important his answer might be. "My lord, I must confess I doubt there has been a decisive victory. It's not the soldiers, they do just fine. Both sides, with few exceptions, lack the discipline we're used to seeing, but man for man, they're a formidable lot. Each side gives as good as it gets."

Lord Lyons asked, "Where do you see the problem?"

"In command, without question. McClellan is a fine officer, but on the field he's too cautious. I've heard his officers say, 'Mac has the slows.' Frankly, my lord, I also don't believe this Lincoln fellow has control of his own generals. He seems ill-suited as a leader."

Lord Lyons' eyes narrowed. "I'd reserve my decision about Mr. Lincoln, Ian, at least until you meet him."

Ian was shocked—*Meet him?*

He replied, "I shall, my lord.

"You were saying. About the battle?"

"My guess is there'll be no clear victory at Sharpsburg, or any decent pursuit of the enemy, whether Lee is moving south or not."

"I suspect you're correct. Not a good sign," Lord Lyons muttered, "not a good sign at all." Then louder, "Fever to intervene is peaking back home. Have to see how the cards play out. Until further orders, strict neutrality is the path for us. Thank you for your insights. That will be part of your job around here. Keep me from getting into trouble."

Lord Lyons settled back in his chair. "More to the point, to accomplish our mission, and therefore your mission, we must cultivate friendships at all levels among the American political, military, manufacturing, trade, and even social, communities. We've been known to entertain a great deal. Do it well, if I may say so. We also regularly attend social events around the District."

Ian looked puzzled, "My lord, surely I wasn't assigned here to entertain politicians."

Lord Lyons' smile was infectious and actually made Ian blush. "Direct and to the point, that's refreshing; but you'll have to learn to curb that enthusiasm a mite. 'Pon my word, man, you're not here merely to entertain, but it will be part of your duties."

He let that sink in. "It seems you sent a report, or something, home, which found its way into the hands of the

Army Board, and then to the War Office, then the Foreign Service, and, well, here we are."

"Breech-loading repeating rifles?"

"Yes, yes, repeating rifles. That's precisely the one. Well, it appears you got their attention. Hence, you are officially assigned to this legation as a temporary military attaché."

"Can you tell me how that happened, my lord?"

"You had orders to remain with McClellan's army and observe these weapons in use. Am I right?"

"Aye, sir."

"Your brother orchestrated that. Your current assignment is a continuation of that task, but out of the legation. Continue observing, as required, but your primary task will be to acquire samples—the best of these arms. Send them to the Army Board, along with reports of everything you can learn."

"It seems to me the American military might not be too keen on this, my lord. Particularly if they are in any way aware that a foreign government—ours—might be on the verge of intervenin' in the war, or recognizin' the Confederate Government."

"An excellent observation. That's exactly why you were chosen. You've spent more time with them than any of our officers or diplomats, and they like you, Ian. I received letters mentioning that. If anyone can ease this task through, you can."

Ian thought a moment before continuing. "I shall do my best, my lord ... Reporting, your lordship?"

"Reporting, yes. You'll report to Horse Guards in writing or by telegraph ... through me. Any legation matters you'll report direct to me. Tasker, by the by, is a wonder—he's invaluable. Don't be put off by his mannerisms. He'll sort you out with the details in no time. But there is something else."

Ian waited.

"The Foreign Office thinks it best at this particular time to show the military flag. This means you'll be tagging along with me to social and State occasions, in full dress uniform, bearskin cap and all. Shouldn't be too much of a burden; plenty of lovely ladies at these things. You'll be the center of attention, I suspect. Any objections, my boy?"

"None, my lord." At least it sounded more promising than his experiences on a military staff. He did not have his full dress uniform with him. It was in his trunk in Canada, but he could have it shipped rather quickly.

Lord Lyons got to his feet and walked back behind his desk and sat down. "Good. Now go and see Benjamin. If you need me, come see me, but for the most part, you'll deal with our whimsical Mr. Tasker. If I need you, or your counsel, I shall call upon you."

Lord Lyons rose again. This time so did Ian. "By your leave, my lord."

"Of course."

Ian did a smart about face and left the office, his head spinning. He had not expected the report of his mere observations to his brother to stir up such a commotion.

He found Tasker waiting outside. His amused expression made it apparent that he knew how the meeting went, and could pretty much guess what was said.

Ian was perplexed. "You said he didn't talk much. Were you having me on?"

"Not at all. Y-Yes, first meeting, this t-time, but from now on you aren't likely to hear two c-consecutive s-sentences from him."

Ian said, "Let's talk, but not here."

"R-Right you are, Ian. The WWWillard over a glass."

Later, as Ian looked over the top of his third or perhaps fourth glass tankard of dark ale, he asked Tasker, "Why am I *really* here?" He liked these large tankards in which the Round Robin served robust ale. The handle made them somehow easier to deal with as the night, and the drinking, progressed.

"P-Precisely what his lordship explained, Ian. No m-more, no less."

"How the devil am I to accomplish this mission?"

73

Tasker showed mock surprise. "W-Why with guile and initiative, I sssuspect. You are a resourceful G-Guards officer, aren't you?"

"Hummmph," Ian responded.

"The l-legation will provide you with letters of introduction to allow you to t-travel back and forth to the army in the field, or just about anywhere you wwwant to go. I'm not p-privy to those kinds of details. My job is to get you what you need."

"His lordship said you were very ... creative ... shall we say."

Tasker smiled, pushing his spectacles up on his nose—it was like a trademark gesture, and could grow to be annoying, Ian thought. He said, "I need another drink."

"I am, I am creative," Tasker replied, "but n-not in those areas. I can get you t-transport, food, ssspirits, get you invited to the best p-parties around town, even ladies ... if that's your desire ... but not the hush-hush s-stuff. Not my department. No, no—much too d-dangerous."

"I see. I'll make a note. Waiter—another round!"

Ian and Tasker talked into the night of many things, as they sat in the Round Robin. A bond between this unlikely pair quickly developed. At some point Ian explained his rather intense opinions about the American President, especially his poor judgment, and lack of leadership.

Tasker reminded him, "It's b-best to present a face of neutrality to those you meet in Washington. Everyone here has their own interests, which c-come first. N-Never know who you're t-talking to or who might be in earshot. K-Keep your own counsel, Ian, about those feelings you have about Lincoln."

"I'll take yer advice, Benjamin. Not to worry; I won't embarrass his lordship."

Ian was more than a bit tipsy. Perhaps that is why he failed to see the dark complexioned, somewhat untidily dressed man at the next table. It was his acquaintance from Antietam, Simon Oldham.

In contrast to Ian's lack of focus, Tasker made note of the man, whose eyes darted from side to side, apparently involuntarily. He suspected from his bohemian style dress and demeanor this was merely one of the vast sea of journalists sniffing for news.

Chapter 13

1 October, 1862, Washington

According to all the reports Ian heard, the battle around Sharpsburg was a Northern victory. Indeed, it was seen as so, internationally. However, as Ian predicted, McClellan failed to follow up aggressively, and Lee was back in the South wreaking havoc.

"Th-This should put a s-stop to our g-government's meeting to decide to m-meddle in American affairs and force a negotiated p-p-peace. At least I should b-bloody hope so," Tasker said to Ian in confidence, as he pushed his spectacles up onto his nose for the ten thousandth time.

"Wasn't aware such a meeting was contemplated," Ian said.

"Not sssupposed to know." Tasker touched the side of his nose twice, indicating secret doings. "P-Palmerston was s-scheduled to meet before the end of S-September to make just such a d-decision—if there was a C-Confederate v-victory. Well, there's no d-decisive Federal victory, but there's c-certainly no win for Lee."

They were at the Round Robin, where Tasker was introducing Ian to someone useful. "Ian, this is C-Captain

Gregory P-Prescott, Ordnance Department. On s-staff at the War Office. He might prove valuable, and he's a fine bloke." The spectacles up on the nose yet again.

Prescott seemed an easygoing chap, big broad smile, unpolished in appearance, with a bulging forehead. He looked out of place in uniform, as though he was being compelled to wear it by some outside force.

According to Tasker, Prescott, although a volunteer with no military background, was a splendid ordnance officer. On this first meeting at the Round Robin, Prescott was quite drunk.

"Captain Prescott, my name is Ian Carlyle. May I stand you to a whiskey?"

Prescott, who was one of those rapid talkers, replied almost too fast for Ian to master the thick Bostonian accent, "Of course you can. Carlyle is it? Another damned Englishman, I suppose."

Ian could not let that pass. He could never let that pass. "Hardly … I'm a Scot, and we're a good distance away from being English." He was about to order three whiskeys, when he noticed Tasker had disappeared. *He has a bad habit of doing that, but not quite as irritatin' as the spectacles.*

Over the next weeks, Prescott and Ian met frequently at the Willard, either dining or drinking until late in the night. Benjamin Tasker often joined them. The three became close comrades.

Ian was also progressing in his mission at the legation. It was easy to obtain a Henry repeating rifle easier than Ian ever expected. A salesman from the New Haven Arms Company out of Connecticut, was staying at the Willard. For the modest sum of forty-two American dollars each, he purchased two fine Henry rifles, with no help from anyone.

Ian eventually approached Prescott for a favor, "Pres, I must impose on our friendship."

"Impose away. I'm at your service."

"I need reports that involve the use of repeating rifles."

Prescott looked quizzical, wrinkling his massive brow. "Official reports? Whatever for?"

Ian told him the truth, "Well, frankly, my country may be thinking of adopting one as our service weapon. Down the road, of course."

Tasker, who was at the table this night, pushed his spectacles up onto his nose before contributing to the conversation. "I would consider it a personal favor if you would help Ian out, Pres. He's having the devil of a time going through channels." The truth was, Ian had not even tried going through channels yet, but suspected it would be a tough road to travel.

With Tasker's intervention, Prescott seemed to take the issue much more seriously. Ian also noticed in passing that Tasker had not stuttered once in asking Prescott to go along. He made a mental note that there was some history between them, perhaps a debt to be paid.

"Why not," Prescott finally replied, "with my country and yours getting tighter every day. I'll do what I can. You can count on it."

"And I shall buy the drinks," Ian exclaimed. "What can I get you?"

"About time," his comrades both muttered.

The contact Ian reported to at Horse Guards in London was a Major Alfred Garrison, of the Royal Scots, an ordnance expert. Ian packaged one of the Henry rifles and a box of .44 caliber rim fire cartridges, and sent the package off with diplomatic mail. It included a brief report introducing himself, providing the basic specifications for the Henry, and reporting what little he had heard and observed, of its effectiveness, including his personal use of it. The other Henry he kept for himself, thinking he might someday give it to the officer whose Henry he had lost near Sharpsburg.

Captain Prescott was a man of his word. He examined incoming letters and reports from the field. Although he drew the line at providing actual documents, if any mention was made of repeating rifles, he made notes and passed them on to Ian when they met at the Willard. There was not much.

"Appears to me, Ian, that the army doesn't have the time, or doesn't see much promise in these rifles," Prescott said one evening, handing Ian a jumbled batch of handwritten notes.

"Thank you, Pres."

Prescott added, "There does seem more interest in the Spencer, than the Henry, especially for those knights of the battlefield, our illustrious cavalry. I'll keep after it."

"Thank you, again," Ian said.

Interest or not, every morsel of information added grist to Ian's reports to Major Garrison at Horse Guards, who seemed quite pleased with what he was receiving.

*   *   *

1 October 1862, outside Parliament, Westminster, London

They conversed in low tones, just out of hearing of the many passers-by streaming past the Parliament buildings. "The plan has been authorized. We are to assassinate President Lincoln as soon as practicable."

"I understand, but isn't there another way? Must he be killed?" Peter asked. This time he was approached by a man on the street who knew his name and mentioned his brother Ian. They all seemed to look alike; very military, and very well dressed.

"There's no other way, and we're not to question what is already decided. Will your brother cooperate?"

"I don't know. He can be stubborn."

"You'd better pray he does, or you'll be ruined and possibly hanged."

There it was. Peter had never actually said the words, but there it was—ruined—hanged. "I understand. I'll do my part, and I'm certain Ian will do his." Secretly in doubt, he prayed that Ian would do what was asked of him.

After all, Peter reasoned, it would not hurt Britain to be rid of Lincoln, and would likely be of benefit to British interests. What kept Peter going was his rationale that the people behind this were so high up, and so intricately connected to the British Government, that what they asked was merely an extension of Britain's foreign policy.

I'm merely doing my duty, he told himself, but then why did his insides tumbled over and over?

Chapter 14

Late 1862, Washington

Ian received most of his information about politics and the war from American newspapers, even though many of the events discussed were happening in Washington, itself. Lincoln had signed the Emancipation Proclamation, and the furor following it had dissipated. General McClellan, Ian's personal choice as the next President of the United States, was relieved, and General Burnside took command. The Fredricksburg campaign was fought and lost.

Accusations of who was at fault were rampant, and Ian found the entire matter most entertaining. To his delight, there was even serious talk in some circles of recalling General McClellan—yet again—to rectify the ills of the Army of the Potomac, and "save the Union." The Joint Committee on the Conduct of the War was having endless meetings, and showing little, if any, progress. Ian suspected the real cause was jealousy and possibly insubordination among senior officers—the original and continuing evil he saw in the American military system.

He blamed it on President Lincoln's meddling in strategic and even tactical military matters, rather than concentrating on overall national strategy. Ian concluded that Lincoln was an utter failure at leading his country in time of war.

Presently, General Burnside too, was relieved and General Hooker given command of the Army of the Potomac. The fighting down south abated for a time during the winter months of 1862.

*   *   *

April 1863, Washington

Spring was not yet smiling upon the busy streets of the District of Columbia. At times, the cold was still bitter.

Although tiresome, there existed a brighter side. Lord Lyons found much for Ian to do. He was shown off at every opportunity, at least once each week. His social calendar ranged from small intimate parties at the legation with a few select foreign and American dignitaries, to lavish receptions and balls at mansions in Georgetown or downtown Washington.

At Lord Lyons's continuing insistence, Ian often wore his scarlet tunic, and tall bearskin cap. He soon became known in Washington society, and found his position gave him a certain social cachet. Astonishingly, he did not mind. It was his duty, and there were compensations. He had met some rather fetching ladies.

Tasker was correct when he told Ian that he would seldom be spoken to by Lord Lyons, unless to introduce him to a dignitary. The exception was a small dinner on a chilly night in April.

"Will you be going out this evening, sir?" Swann asked.

"Yes, I'll need my dress uniform laid out. Thank you, Swann."

Swann saw to it that Ian's trunk was shipped from Canada and arrived safely. He acclimatized himself quite well to Washington, and had actually become a most excellent valet. He was also becoming quite adept at anticipating Ian's requirements on a daily basis; forever the scrounger in adding to their creature comforts and the needs of the inner man.

Ian gave him a modest clothing allowance, from which Swann acquitted himself with a brown vest and tan trousers to go with his brown corduroy coat. He added a formal business suit and the required accessories to his wardrobe—a sedate frock coat, a vest and pants, a couple of dress shirts, and a cravat. Ian insisted, no matter what he wore, that Swann place his Victoria Cross over his left breast.

Swann also became quite popular with the ladies of the Willard Hotel service staff. While Ian was out and about, Swann found much to hold his interest. Occasionally he was required to accompany Ian to a legation function, but not often. Thus he had a lot of free time in the evenings.

On this night, Ian was attending a dinner party on a yacht. Swann heard that it was a wealthy merchant's boat, docked in Georgetown. Lord Lyons needed to cultivate this particular businessman, Joshua Billings. Swann discovered he owned a fleet of sailing and steam ships, and was trading in large monetary transactions with Britain. He passed this intelligence on to Ian, as he assisted with his wardrobe for the evening.

"How do you come by all this information, Swann?" Ian asked.

"Ear to the ground, sir, ear to the ground ... always listening. Never know what might be useful."

"It is most useful, so keep at it."

"Well sir, it's my job, in'it, sir. Will you need me tonight, sir?"

Ian surmised at least some of Swann's extra activities included the ladies, "You're free, but you mind yer manners."

Swann responded with a small, knowing smile, but did not answer. He enjoyed that his officer was concerned about him, but would lend a blind eye on occasion to his little mischiefs. These two had earned each other's trust, affection, and respect, in the cauldron of battle.

Swann hailed a hansom cab outside the Willard for his officer, and Ian picked up Lord Lyons at the legation. The hansom made its way to the Georgetown dock area where the yacht was moored.

Usually on these trips to social engagements Lord Lyons was polite, but always busy with documents he would bring along or deep in his own thoughts. On the way this time, he was uncharacteristically conversational. "Ian, tonight should be interesting. I'm told, by the way, that regards our possible intervention in this American conflict, the worst of the political storms may have passed."

"Does this mean, sir, that Britain will not be intervening in—"

"Dear me," Lord Lyons interrupted, "I must remember to be more precise when I chat with you, Ian. The words 'will not' are far too absolute in the diplomacy business. I said 'may have passed.' I simply mean that at the moment, neither Britain nor France see compelling advantages in changing the status quo. Neutrality is still the watchword as far as we are concerned."

Ian remained silent, thinking whimsically, *Could you try to be a bit more vague yer lordship?*

Lord Lyons abruptly announced, "You ask me, it's Russia. We need Russia to show a wide coalition for intervention or whatever course we might decide."

"Russia won't join the enterprise?"

"Russia is and always has supported America, meaning the Federal government, not the Confederacy. Damn me, the United States was sending money and supplies to Russia when you were in the Crimea being shot at by Russian bullets."

"Didn't know that, my lord."

"You need to know these things." Lord Lyons looked at Ian with a curious smile. "You may run into Russians."

Ian said, "Right, my lord. I understand." Ian was amazed at this outburst from the usually silent and circumspect Lord Lyons. He carried on in an unusually good mood.

In his resplendent dress uniform, Ian played the role Lord Lyons gave him. Show the colors, and let them know we are armed and ready, so to speak. As the hansom approached the yacht and he heard the faint sounds of a violinist hired for the occasion, he was all the more certain this would be just another in a long line of dinners and receptions.

Two crewmen met them at the gangplank dressed for all purposes as American sailors, which Ian knew was not the case on this private yacht. Lord Lyons and Ian boarded carefully and went immediately below decks to the large main salon where the dinner guests were congregating.

Their host, Joshua Billings, was in excellent form and already tipsy. White-gloved waiters passed about, with generous portions of Champagne. Although Ian was fully prepared to be bored out of his boots, this would by no means be just another dinner.

Ian did his duty, mingling with those guests he knew, to include the tall, semi-bald, yet handsome Secretary of Treasury, Salmon Chase; the rather prodigious-nosed Secretary of State, William H. Seward, an old enemy of Britain whom Lord Lyons had converted into a more friendly associate; and the short, round, bespectacled, fully-bearded Edwin M. Stanton, Lincoln's Secretary of War.

Ian had met these prominent gentlemen previously in the social world of the United States capitol. He felt somewhat comfortable engaging them, but studiously avoided discussing international politics.

Ian's only relief to the tedious prattle was Kate Chase, the Treasury Secretary's beautiful and delightful daughter. She was a charmer of the first order, and no slacker at political intrigue to further her father's ambition to one day be president. That ambition was the worst kept secret in the District.

She was one of only two women at the dinner. Kate wore a white muslin dress adorned with flowers, which accented her graceful and willowy figure. Ian found her most refreshing, and was glad she was there to chat about one of her favorite subjects, the London social scene.

There was another bright and unexpected note in the evening—the only other woman at the dinner party. Ian noticed this wondrous, chestnut-haired beauty the moment she entered the yacht's main salon, accompanied by Kate. Obviously they were good friends.

This lovely creature was presented on Kate's arm to other guests. Ian observed Kate introduce her to a tall American officer, an army captain, then he seemed to monopolize the beautiful lady's time. *That will never do*, thought Ian.

As a diversion, Ian plucked a glass of champagne from the tray of a passing waiter, and presented it to this exquisite woman, whose glass was quite empty. In his best Scottish brogue, Ian said, "Excuse me Miss, I know we havena been formally introduced, but I couldn'a help noticin' yer glass needed chargin'. Please allow me the honor, by acceptin' this refill."

The brash interruption seemed to irritate the officer, who mumbled something, but it pleased the lady. When she spoke to thank him, he detected the delicate trace of an Irish accent.

"You are so sweet to notice among all these people. Thank you, sir."

"No Miss, it is I who should be thankin' you. Yer presence has brightened the entire room. It is indeed my pleasure." Ian bowed slightly, and moved away.

Ian later found Kate Chase when she was alone, which was not often. In a whisper, he asked, "Kate, might I ask the name of that lovely lady who accompanied you ta the dinner?"

"You most certainly may not. I'm jealous, and I simply won't have it," she said, lightly.

Ian replied in an equally light tone, "Kate, my precious, ya simply can't have us all. You already have every man in Washington crawling at yer feet, including a certain gentleman from Rhode Island. So, tell me, is it true?"

"That I'm engaged to be married to William Sprague? ... Perhaps."

Ian bowed his head slightly and looked at Kate with piercing blue eyes from under thick, brown lashes, a small smile creasing his lips. "You see, Kate, there you are. Ya do have us all."

Kate giggled, "Ian, you lie so well. You are a scoundrel. I cannot resist you, although I think I'd rather have you at my feet than all those incessant crawlers. The problem is, you'd never grovel, and I know it. I think that's what intrigues me."

"The name, Kate?"

"The name—if you insist—is Elizabeth Callaghan. Before he passed away her father was in a business similar to our host, Mr. Billings ... ships and the like. She's studying to be a nurse at the hospital made up in the Union Hotel here in Georgetown."

Ian said nothing, knowing Kate couldn't resist gossiping.

"She does, of course, have her own inheritance. I believe she sees nursing as her patriotic duty." She added rather haughtily, "Only God knows why."

"Thank you, my dear friend, a full and complete report. You'd make an excellent soldier." Ian cocked his head to the side again, waiting ...

Kate scolded, "No! Absolutely not. I won't introduce you. That's going too far. Besides, I already introduced her to that handsome captain she has been talking with, and he has so much more money and influence than you. He's our host's son, the young Justin Billings."

It was Ian's turn to laugh, "Kate, yer priceless, my dear. You'll never change, nor would I want ya to. You've been most helpful already."

"Humph."

A bell tinkled, calling them to dine. Ian was seated at the massive table in the main salon dining area across from the beautiful vision with the Irish accent, he so wanted to meet formally. Unfortunately the table was wide, and she was too far away for decent conversation without shouting.

Billings had certainly gone the limit in lavish good taste and expense. During his mingling with the guests Ian heard a rumor that Lincoln, himself, was supposed to attend. Perhaps that was why Billings had spread such a sumptuous repast.

The table was laid out with starched white linen and polished silver. So many forks and spoons at each place—it made Ian think of his mother, and smile to himself. He recalled how she had nagged him to learn the proper use of each piece in a place setting. And he fondly remembered this as the one thing his mother had insisted upon teaching him herself, without the nanny's interference.

That brief, but vivid memory of her swept over him, warm and loving, to the exclusion of those guests about him. She had been quite ill since his father died, and he wondered if she was recovering. *I must write her soon,* he thought. *I'm not the best son in the world.*

He was so wrapped in his reflections that he did not engage in dinner conversation, or notice that the American officer who had been talking to Miss Callaghan was seated near him. In fact, he hardly tasted the pheasant and cream pearl onions, or partook in the plentiful plump strawberries, so difficult to obtain these days.

When he came out of his nostalgia, he had to force himself not to stare at the lovely Irish lass across the table. Did he detect that she was glancing at him? No, she must be looking at the American captain seated close by.

Even through the cacophony of jokes and voices around the table, it seemed he could hear the light rustle of her dress as she turned to speak to one of the guests at her elbow. Guiltily, Ian wondered what lay beneath.

The gentle rhythmic movement of the yacht—small waves from the Potomac River washing against its sides, and the soft violin music wafting in from the quarter-deck—turned Ian's thoughts to his first love, his dear Jasmine. He saw her face for a moment, her silky black hair. He could reach out and gently stroke it—then it was gone—replaced by the beautiful face of the Irish lass, Elizabeth Callaghan. He jerked back his hand, which had mysteriously stretched in front of him. What was he thinking?

After the splendid meal and a few too many glasses of an exceptional Lafite Bordeaux Red 1858, Ian excused himself from the table. He found Lord Lyons already in a corner with the other gentlemen, about to light a cigar. For some reason Ian was incredibly tired, and small talk with this group would have driven him absolutely mad.

Ian quietly asked Lord Lyons for permission to retire early, claiming a headache. Dutifully he said goodbye to the host, but doubted if Billings understood a word of it, having progressed from tipsy, to modestly inebriated, to almost blind drunk.

Ian looked about for Miss Callaghan in the hope he might at least bid her farewell, but she was nowhere to be found. When Ian thought about her, it made him smile. He determined to find out more about this lovely Irish creature, who so recklessly invaded his thoughts.

Ian disembarked, noting that the crewmen were no longer at the gangplank. He began walking the considerable distance back to the Willard. He cherished such quiet times. It was a brisk evening, but walking several miles a day was the only thing keeping him fit, while he drank and ate his way around Washington.

Chapter 15

Early 1861, Georgetown area, outside Washington

It was true that to look at Elizabeth Callaghan, one was stunned by the perfection of her delicate facial features and the fire in her deep-set green eyes, her face surrounded by long, flowing chestnut hair. Even dressed in a corset and hoop skirt, the observer knew that below her small supple breasts and narrow waist was a sensual delight. She took obvious great care in her appearance, always wanting to look her best.

Elizabeth had that mysterious ability to glide, rather than walk, across a room. When seated awaiting a suitor's attentions, she personified grace and charm, her perfectly designed dress flowed about her like a meadow of wild flowers, every curve and fold planned by some accomplished artist posing her for a portrait. When she spoke, her disarmingly soft and ever so light Irish accent kept suitors spellbound.

Washington society gossip described Elizabeth as a rather colorful socialite in her twenties, somewhat shallow and self-absorbed, worried more about which dress to wear to an evening gathering than her obligations to a better society.

This was neither completely true, nor entirely false. Although charm and grace came naturally to Elizabeth, she was far more than appearances would suggest.

Her roots were firmly planted in an Irish family. They lived in a mansion in Georgetown, off M Street. Her mother, Constance Callaghan, was a famous beauty in capitol society, when she was in good health. She met Elizabeth's father, Seamus, at a summer picnic on the Potomac. She was captured by his thick Irish brogue, and he by her gentleness.

Constance seemed content to do nothing more than attend dinner parties and other prominent social events, both in and out of season. Eight years after Elizabeth was born, she gave birth to a second child, a son, Patrick Edward Callaghan—a wild boy from the time he left the cradle.

Elizabeth's father was a robust man, an immigrant from County Kerry. At sea by the age of eleven, he made his way to America by eighteen. His experiences at sea taught him many things, not the least of which was to gamble. He loved to tell his daughter, "Lizbeth," the story of how he won his first ship from a pompous German, the beginning of the Callaghan Shipping Line.

Seamus Callaghan loved the sea and his ships, but not more than his Constance. Unhappily, Constance Callaghan became chronically ill, and began gradually wasting away. She developed a hacking cough, eventually spitting blood. When Elizabeth was still quite young, her mother died of consumption.

Her father committed suicide not long after, leaving his business interests in the hands of lawyers, and the considerable family fortune in a trust for his son and daughter. He earned his money from shrewd investments in steamships and international shipping, making him one of the wealthiest men in Washington.

At any given time, half a dozen of his ships would be docked at the Georgetown wharfs, spilling out or taking in precious cargo. The business was still active, but in somewhat of a holding pattern, awaiting Seamus' only son, Patrick, to come of age and take over.

Thus, after losing both parents, and when most young ladies were worried about coming out socially, Elizabeth became de facto guardian to her unruly younger brother, even though they were only separated by eight years.

The lawyers hired several nannies, but Patrick was too high-spirited, and each was soon driven off, cowering. It became Elizabeth's duty to raise him. She tackled this daunting obligation as she did everything else in her life, with tenacious devotion and perseverance.

In addition to her responsibilities toward Patrick, or perhaps as a result of them, Elizabeth developed an incredibly sharp mind, and painstakingly educated herself to use it. Unlike the social creature her mother had been, Elizabeth felt a passionate need to contribute to the greater good.

By the time "this dreadful war"—as she called it—loomed as a menacing reality, her charge, Patrick, whom she loved more dearly than life itself, grew into a strong-willed young man. He was the very image of his father, tall, robust, and very handsome. Unfortunately, he had no desire to run his father's shipping business.

To her dismay, he told Elizabeth, "I'll not be tied down to a life in some dreary office. No, by God, I'd rather be sailing father's ships on the high seas. That's the life for a man."

He was attending Columbian College on College Hill in Washington. He studied Latin, philosophy, mathematics, and religion. This was boring enough, but it was dreadful after Fort Sumter was fired upon. He could barely sit still in classes, jiggling in his seat, tapping his scuffed toes. He wanted to *do* something.

"Lizbeth, I can't stand it. I'm going to shrivel up and die."

"Patrick, please," she pleaded. "Your time will come. Be patient and finish your studies.

The college was split, as was the nation, with half its student body for the North and half with Southern sympathies. In a burst of patriotic enthusiasm for a strong Union, the young Callaghan stole away from school, and from Elizabeth.

From his trust, Patrick was allowed an accessible account sufficient to ensure his education and comfort at school. By writing a sizable draft on this account, Patrick was able to quietly acquire funds to travel north. He packed a small valise and boarded a train headed for New York City, adventure, and glory. In a flash, he was gone for a soldier.

He arrived in New York, and found he had too many choices. Numerous regiments were recruiting, and Patrick was prime pickings. In deference to his Celtic heritage, he enlisted as a private in Company D of the overwhelmingly Irish 69th New York Volunteers. He wrote Elizabeth a long letter, asking her forgiveness.

Elizabeth was devastated. She unburdened her heart to her friend, Kate Chase, "I know I couldn't have stopped Patrick even if he'd confided in me. He is so headstrong, impetuous. I can't stand that he is going to be in danger, and here I am, safe and secure. Father would never have forgiven me for letting him go."

"Nonsense, Lizbeth, you couldn't have stopped the boy, and you know it."

Elizabeth burst into tears, but quickly recovered. "I really must do something myself, Kate. Be with him, or at least near him. I think it my patriotic duty. I can do something—anything."

"I don't understand. Whatever will you do?"

"I'm not at all sure. I have some money from the trust. I've heard they're going to need nurses for the war, and—"

"But you know nothing of such things," Kate burst out.

"There are places where they teach you. I hear there'll be some new agency certifying nurses for the army. How difficult can it be to give the simple comforts to wounded soldiers? Perhaps I can go near the fighting as a nurse, be close to Patrick."

Her friend Kate was shocked, "Surely not, Lizbeth! You can't possibly mean to pursue this wild escapade. I hear these nurses are no more than common women of the streets. They only recruit plain, ugly women, who won't upset the soldiers. You can't—"

"Perhaps you're right, but I must try … I simply must."

"Lizbeth, this is madness. They won't allow women near the seat of war. They'll keep them in hospitals, safe from the hazards. It would do you no good."

"All the same, I'm immovable on this. If not a nurse in the field, perhaps I can apply here in Georgetown, at a hospital. I will do my share."

Kate tried desperately to dissuade her, but no argument held sufficient weight.

Chapter 16

July 1861, Georgetown

Elizabeth, true to her word, found work as a nurse-in-training at a hospital established in Georgetown's Union Hotel. It did require an exception direct from Dorothea Dix, who superintended recruitment and training; because Kate was right, they wanted only plain women.

An exception, however, was not difficult, with a bit of help from some of her father's business associates; gentlemen who contributed large amounts to political campaigns and the Union cause in general. She was well on her way to being certified by the United States Sanitary Commission, and in the right place at the exact right time to find out the reality of war, and its horrible truths.

Late July, 1861, the news came with the not-so-quiet dignity of an Irish wake—shrill and raucous. A tremendous battle was being fought just outside Washington, near Centerville. The whole town erupted in a frenzy of chaos and fear. Many of the naïve believed this battle would decide the issues, and the North would prevail. Others, equally naïve, were certain the entire Confederate army was about to come crashing down 14th Street, rape all the women, and kill all the men.

Wagons loaded with the wounded poured into Washington, clogging the streets. The drivers, wild-eyed, bellowed at their horses to go faster, then yelled, "Whoa!" to slow them down before they turned over on sharp corners. Desperate to get their bleeding, moaning, often screaming cargoes to hospital, they tried to avoid running over pedestrians or crashing into Washington's street traffic full of private coaches, hansom cabs, and hackneys.

A particularly muggy, hot day was even more stifling within the stuffy rooms of the Union Hotel turned hospital. A fat, sweating orderly lumbered toward Elizabeth. He asked, breathlessly, his double chin bouncing, "Aren't you the one ... inquiring about ... the 69th New York?"

"I am that person. Have you news?"

"What a day—hot as blazes." He was sweating profusely.

"The 69th New York?" she asked, not hiding her irritation and impatience.

"There's a bunch of those Irishmen raising holy hell in Ward Two."

"Thank you," she said, rushing off down the hall. Five or six burly Irishmen, who were demanding whiskey from a harassed doctor, greeted her in the ward. "We need it to dull the God-awful pain of our wounds. Them we got in the fight fer the glorious Union."

The boyish doctor trying to tend their wounds was out of his element, frightened to death, and entirely overwhelmed. Elizabeth knew just how to handle this, and she had not learned it in nurse's training.

Placing her hands firmly on her hips, she bellowed, "Quiet, now! Get back in yer beds. There'll be no whiskey this night. What would yer blessed mothers say if they saw you acting such hooligans?"

The strong woman's voice, the clear Irish accent, her demanding to be obeyed ... there was instant silence. The doctor let his breath rush out in relief at being saved from what he thought would be a certain beating.

The Irishmen grumbled a bit, but generally calmed down. Elizabeth, in a softer voice, added, "Thank you, gentlemen, that's more like it. Now do what the kind doctor tells you."

Elizabeth moved gently among them. She wore no hoops, only petticoats to give her dress a slight form. This way she could navigate between the crowded beds unhindered. She saw a sergeant with a nasty leg wound.

While changing his linen bandages, she asked, "69th New York?"

"Yes, Miss, we're all 69th."

"Do you know a Patrick Callaghan?"

"Officer, Miss? Don't recall an officer by that name."

"No, Sergeant, he's just a private."

The sergeant apologized, "Miss, I just assumed you'd be asking for an officer. Sorry, but I don't know any Patrick Callaghan. We do have Callaghans in the regiment, but no Patrick I can think. Would ya be knowin' what company?"

She hesitated, "Company D, I believe?"

"Sorry, Miss, I'm A Company. Don't know of a Patrick Callaghan."

She looked disappointed. "Thank you Sergeant. I'll try to get back to keep the linen fresh on that wound."

"You're an angel, Miss. Patrick is a lucky man."

"He's my brother," Elizabeth replied somewhat defensively, then added, "but thank you for the kind words."

Elizabeth asked others from the 69th for word of her brother, but to no avail. One soldier, who was the only casualty thus far brought in from Company D, verified that there was, indeed, a Patrick Callaghan in his company. "I don't know him, Miss, I only just enlisted and was sent to fight without even being told how to load and fire the musket they give me."

The D Company private was coughing, and his voice was weak. He had a very small hole in his right side. The wound did not look serious to Elizabeth. "That's all right, soldier, it's a great comfort just knowin' that I've met someone in his company. I'll come back and dress your wound shortly."

Elizabeth went about her immediate duties, examining wounds and changing dressings where needed. She returned to the D Company private later, but the bed—in this case a thrown together cot—was empty. A male orderly saw her distress. "Died quietly, Miss. Just closed his eyes and was gone."

"That can't be so. He was resting quietly, but awake when I walked by just minutes ago."

"That's the way it happens, Miss Callaghan. Better that way. Peaceful like."

Elizabeth thought, *I never want to go like that ... so quietly ... I want to make a fuss, go out screaming at the top of my lungs.* They were already bringing in another wounded soldier to place on the empty cot. It seemed to never end.

For the next twenty-four hours, Elizabeth, without sleep, was surrounded by the gut-wrenching terrible toll of human flesh taken in battle. She was rapidly losing her fascination with "patriotic duty," hardening to the pain and suffering she could do little about.

This was the first time masses of wounded had been seen in Washington. They ran out of everything, cots, medicine, linen for bandages, solvents to try to keep the place clean, while trying to get rid of the blood that was everywhere and in everything. Even straw for makeshift mattresses on the floor became scarce. She gave what comfort she could.

As time passed the sounds were getting to her; screams, constant moaning, death rattle breathing, the raised voices and shouts of orderlies and surgeons, the bone saw. *The bone saw. That sound. Merciful God,* she thought, *will it not be over?* She cleaned wounds, changed linen until there was no more linen, scrubbed floors until her hands were raw, and worse, watched the surgeon's bloody work with growing horror.

The next evening Elizabeth was making her way from bed to bed, sharing a few words with each patient. She often moved among the wounded in the 69th "Irish" ward. It made her feel better, tending to Irishmen and members of Patrick's regiment.

The sergeant she first spoke with barely more than twenty-four hours ago called her over. "What can I do for you, Sergeant?"

He was shocked by her appearance. Looking ten years older, she was haggard, her hair in disarray. She had lost her apron, or used it in some fashion to comfort a soldier, and her dress and hands were covered in blood and filth.

"Miss, are you all right?" The sergeant was staring at her.

Touched by his concern, Elizabeth realized for the first time in days, what she must look like. "I'll do nicely, Sergeant. Just a bit of dirt's all. Underneath I'm fit as a fiddle. You're right though ... I'd better clean up or I'll scare the doctors away."

"God Bless ya Miss. To us yer an angel. I thought you'd want to know. They brought in a corporal from D Company. He's over there. Looks pretty dreadful, won't be with us long I'd be thinkin'." He pointed at a nearly naked man, whose entire body was charred black, blistered, and raw with the most severe burns—the first she had encountered.

"Thank you." Elizabeth moved quickly to the man, whose eyes were closed. The pungent smell of cooked flesh was overpowering. She gagged, brought her hand up quickly to cover her mouth. Regaining control, she forced herself to look at the ghastly, scorched body—what remained of a once vibrant young man.

She looked inquiringly at a nearby orderly, proud of his uniform and duties, in spite of gray hair and a leathery face; indications he was beyond the prime army age. She knew him, but not his name. He said, "This is one of the worst I've seen, Miss Callaghan. I heard he was trapped in a supply wagon that caught fire. When they pulled him out he was still ablaze."

The orderly shook his head and looked down at the bloodstained floor. "There are so many, too many."

Elizabeth was about to turn away from the soldier, in spite of her lingering questions, finding it hard to believe he could be alive. She would come back when the man awoke, she vowed, if he lived.

"Ahhhhh!" the man screamed.

Elizabeth jerked her head back toward him. His eyes were wide with pain and fear, like two red and white pools with round blue centers, peering out of the crusty blackish-red, oozing mess that had been his face.

An orderly whispered, "These are the most terrible. Burns I mean. I suspect every pore in his body, every inch of skin, is in excruciating pain."

Through the charred mass two red lips began to move, "Water ... please ... water."

Elizabeth knelt by the hospital bed. She poured a glass of water from a pitcher on a nearby table, and glanced up at the orderly for approval. He seemed to know how to treat these cases, and certainly cared about their welfare.

He shrugged, leaned down and whispered, "It doesn't matter, Miss. Piece of shell hit him full in the chest. We didn't see it at first, 'count a the charred skin. Surgeon says we can't help him much, just make him comfortable as possible."

Now she noticed the bandage on his chest, soaked in blood, no white showing. Elizabeth tried to give him a drink. He choked, spit most of it up, spattering her face and apron—water mixed with blood and pieces of cooked flesh.

"Sorry," he squeaked in a strained voice. That he should worry in his pain about splattering her made Elizabeth's heart break. His eyes pleaded. "Miss ... I ... am I going to live?"

She hardened herself, knowing the answer they trained her to give. She said, with as much conviction as she could muster, "You'll be fine, soldier, you be resting now."

"Irish, you're Irish," he whispered.

"I am that, now you rest. We'll talk later, I promise."

"Are you ... the one looking for ... for someone in D Company?"

She stuttered in wonder, "Well, y-yes, but how did ..."

"Sergeant, yonder ... we talked some. He told me. S-Said you had the old sod in yer voice. Said you're lookin' for a soldier named Gallagher? Afraid I don't know him."

"No, no, it's Callaghan, Patrick Callaghan."

The corporal stiffened, let out a small cry from the pain it caused. He was silent for nearly a full minute. Elizabeth saw the recognition in those watery red eyes. She bit her lip, but held herself from speaking. "If you don't mind my asking, Miss, what would be your interest in Patrick Callaghan?"

Elizabeth sucked in air. "My brother—do you know him?"

The soldier's eyes filled with tears, "You're Lizbeth ... Y-You must be."

"You do know him," she exclaimed. Now her eyes were pleading.

The corporal paused, and said tenderly, through his broken lips, "He was my friend. He's gone, Miss Lizbeth."

Elizabeth let out a cry of anguish, collected herself, then demanded, "Gone ... No! ... How do you know this? You could be wrong."

"Not wrong, Miss," he rasped. "He was standing next to me ... I saw it with me own eyes. A few minutes b-before I went back in that wagon for more cartridges ... and the fire boxed me in."

He added after a second or two, "I can tell you it was quick. He never saw it coming ... like he lay down and went to sleep ... that gentle." His tremulous voice cracked. It could have been his own pain, or the remembering.

There was silence. She tried desperately to conceal her grief. Inside, Elizabeth wept. The elderly orderly was tending a patient on the next cot. He saw her distress and placed his hand on her shoulder. The corporal closed his tear-filled eyes, moaning in pain from the movement.

Elizabeth could not bring herself to think of Patrick being burned like this man. She had to focus on the corporal's words, "... next to him ... before the fire ... quick, never saw it coming ... like he lay down and went to sleep ..." She was more thankful for those words than the corporal would ever know.

It took some minutes to compose herself, staring at a corner of the blood-stained wool blanket. Then Elizabeth saw the blanket move, heard a long wheezing sigh. She looked at the corporal. His eyes were open, but he saw nothing. *At least not in this world,* she thought. *His suffering is over. He is with God, as is my beloved Patrick.*

The orderly took another blanket, covered the corporal's body, gently pulling it up over his face.

Chapter 17

April 1863, downtown Washington

Elizabeth browsed the small marketplace buying fresh fruits and vegetables. The reticule she carried matched her plain black bonnet, gloves and mourning dress, trimmed with white collar and cuffs. She had dressed like this for nearly two years. Elizabeth knew she was not expected to mourn so long for her brother, but she loved him so. She could not bear going back out in the social world. It was just easier this way.

Most of her long grieving period was spent alone, except for a maid who had been with the family for many years. Seclusion from her friends and the world in general was entirely by choice. She had her work at the hospital, and that was enough. Wearing mourning clothing helped give her the plainer appearance expected of a nurse attending soldiers on a daily basis.

"Kate, my dear friend," Elizabeth shouted as Kate Chase walked toward her, "it is so wonderful to see you. It's been so long." The last time she really spoke to her was when she announced that she was going to train as a nurse. They were out of touch since. Life is like that sometimes when you are good friends. They both knew it.

Kate, being rather notorious in Washington society as the daughter of the Treasury Secretary, often acted more like her father's wife and social secretary, than his progeny. Elizabeth had seen her before, walking or shopping in the streets of Washington or Georgetown, but avoided contact, preferring to be alone with her grief and her thoughts. Now, she deliberately sought her out.

"Lizbeth," Kate cried, "is that really you? How wonderful. We must go shopping together. You must dine with us. Father would so love to see you."

"I'd be pleased," Elizabeth replied. "I think seeing old friends would be a great pleasure now."

Kate said, "What brings you to this rather out-of-the-way part of Washington, anyway?"

"Fresh vegetables."

"Well, you look a fright." Kate beamed. She was, as ever, perky and undaunted. Elizabeth took no offense. *This is exactly what I need.*

"The first thing we must do for your sanity," Kate insisted, "is get you out of those mourning clothes. Get you out—period."

This is why Elizabeth liked her so. Kate is as beautiful and graceful as she is intelligent and witty. If there was any way at all, you could count on Kate Chase to brighten things up.

"I just haven't felt, well ... right about it," Elizabeth replied.

"Just look at these flowers, aren't they beautiful?" Kate picked up an attractive arrangement from a stand they were passing.

"They are quite exquisite," was Elizabeth's smiling reply. She doggedly returned to her mourning, "I was having a difficult time getting over Patrick's death, and blaming myself for it."

"Nonsense. Enough. Well beyond your obligation."

There was a pause, then Kate said wryly, "You think Patrick would want you hiding away this long?"

"Actually, I think he'd be angry with me."

"Certainly." Kate paused, deep in thought. "I have an idea."

Elizabeth looked at her friend quizzically.

"Look, I must rush off. Let me arrange a few details. You leave this to me. I'll be in touch ... soon."

As Kate whisked off, waving goodbye, dress swaying, she called back, "Wonderful to see you. Missed you so much. Bye for now."

Elizabeth thought, *Very much like Kate. Flitting about like a butterfly. Now that I think about it, I do miss her, awfully.*

Elizabeth headed toward the corner to catch an omnibus back to Georgetown. The most vivid thought on her mind, *Oh, Patrick ... forgive me, but I believe it's time. I shall deal with my demons later.*

Elizabeth received a note from Kate the week after they met at the outdoor market. It was an invitation to accompany her to a dinner party. The party was aboard a yacht belonging to a wealthy New York merchant, and anchored at the Georgetown wharfs. The note was persuasive. It ended:

"... you really must come, dear Lizbeth, you really must. I beg you. It is time for you to allow the world the pleasure of your company again, and I miss you, terribly.

This dinner will include an exclusive assemblage. It is rumored that the President, himself, has been invited, as well as Lord Lyons from the British Legation. Of course my father will attend. Mr. Joshua Billings, owner of the yacht, is excited at the prospect of meeting a new lady of breeding, just like you, with a reputation for beauty and social position. As an aside, he has a wonderfully handsome son. You never know what the fates will dictate."

The next day there was a knock at Kate's door. A young man in a messenger's uniform handed Kate a note from Elizabeth. It read:

Dearest Kate,

You are so right. I would deem it an honor to join you at the party. It is most assuredly time for me to return to life and society. I look forward to seeing you and your father, and to meeting Mr. Joshua Billings. As for his son, my mischievous friend, we shall see.

Your Loving Companion,

Lizbeth

Chapter 18

April 1863, Georgetown wharfs, outside Washington

Everything about the rig was old. The tiny carriage Kate sent for her was old, the one horse pulling it was old, and it came equipped with a lazy-looking elderly driver, wearing a battered top hat and dusty coat. He apparently did some work for Kate's father on occasion, and drove the horse carriage in his spare time for extra income. Elizabeth noticed an attitude of rudeness and indifference about the man right off. It was obvious he did not like toting "rich folks" around.

As the carriage made its way to the slip where Mr. Joshua Billings' yacht was moored, Elizabeth thought about the vessel's name, "Precarious." For her own amusement, she had looked it up among her father's old records before coming to the party. She thought, *Hmmm ... Precarious ... Let me see ... dangerous, uncertain, unstable, unsteady ... not a name to build confidence in a seagoing craft.*

From a distance it appeared beautiful and seaworthy, large, sleek, and sturdy, in spite of its unfortunate name. Being her father's daughter, she was well acquainted with such things. But she vowed not to think of her father tonight, or Patrick. *I shall have some fun.*

The carriage stopped at the top of a small hill, about fifty yards from the yacht, which was down a cobblestone street, lined with a few warehouses, and the odd business establishment. At this time of day the street was busy with wagons and workmen. The driver sullenly dismounted and reluctantly helped Elizabeth from the coach.

He said, "I can go no further, Miss. The road is too steep and broken for this old horse." Elizabeth did not know if he meant the animal or himself, or both. "I'll wait here, Miss. See you safely aboard. I'll try to be right here when you're ready to go home, but I've been pretty sickly of late."

"Thank you, you're most kind," she said, but his words about waiting for her didn't sound too convincing. She was almost positive he would be gone as soon as she disappeared.

Actually, she did not mind the walk. It was dusk and the crisp breeze off the water was, for a change, refreshing, even if the fish smell left a bit to be desired. There was enough light on the horizon to see that the short distance to the yacht's mooring was filled with workers, intensely busy with their chores before heading home. She spotted two of the yacht's crewmen waiting at the gangplank to welcome and assist guests aboard.

Elizabeth made her way cautiously down the hill on the cobbled street. The crewmen touched their caps as she approached. One of them took her arm when she stepped gingerly up the gangplank, which rose and fell with each wave. She stepped aboard, turned and waved, smiling, at the coachman atop the hill.

Lively voices came from below decks. Elizabeth heard music, and saw a lone violinist on deck, playing what she believed was Johann Strauss, one of her very favorite composers.

A sturdily built man was approaching. She assumed this was her host, Joshua Billings. He appeared to Elizabeth to be dressed in a United States Navy uniform. She was curious about Billings, because he had been a friend of her father.

By asking around to her father's employees, she discovered that Billings had been a member of the elite New

York Yacht Club since its founding in 1844. She suspected the uniform reflected that affiliation. She did not believe Billings had actually been in the Navy. *How quaint,* she thought. Old or not, he still looked fit.

"Ah, you must be the dear Miss Callaghan. I'm Joshua Billings, your host. Knew your father —a fine man—I'd know you anywhere. You have his flashing eyes."

"You're too kind, sir, and it is a pleasure to meet you."

Billings continued without missing his rhythm, "What a lovely sight you are to the eyes, and how fortunate I am that you decided to grace my poor vessel with your presence. Good evening, and welcome aboard." Billings swayed uncertainly as he gave this tedious speech. It was not the roll of the yacht that caused his lack of balance.

"Mr. Billings, although we haven't formally met, I've always been an admirer of yours. My father spoke often of your amazing business acumen. I'm glad you invited me tonight." She reached out her delicate gloved hand.

Billings beamed at her compliment. He took her hand tenderly, and kissed it. As he did so, Kate appeared on deck with her father, Salmon Chase—balding, built much like their host, and attractive as well. Unfortunately, he was at least as drunk as Billings, and seemingly supported solely by Kate's tight grip on his arm.

Elizabeth turned to her, as Billings mumbled his apologies, drifting unsteadily, but with purpose, toward the other side of the deck.

Elizabeth said, "Kate, I'm so pleased to see you. Thank you for sending the carriage and driver."

"My pleasure, Lizbeth, we can't have you traveling around unescorted, can we father?" She turned to the Secretary of the Treasury, yanking on his arm, but he said nothing, staring distractedly off in space.

"I'm just glad you decided to come," Kate continued.

Shaking Salmon Chase's arm vigorously, she insisted, "Father, you remember Elizabeth Callaghan, the daughter of Seamus Callaghan?"

Hearing the name of Elizabeth's father, his interest perked. "Of course, of course. Wonderful to see you again. I beg your most humble pardon. Must talk to Billings. He asks my advice constantly y'know." Without awaiting a reaction, he crossed the deck to chat with Billings, who was by now leaning precariously over the starboard rail of the "Precarious." He straightened as Salmon Chase approached, but his face was colorless. The whole scene rather tickled Elizabeth.

"My dearest Lizbeth, let's go inside so I can show you off. That is a marvelous dress. What wonderful silk, and I love the flowing shades of green and tan. The colors are stunning ... so much better than black."

"Thank you, Kate, but I must confess I'm a little uncomfortable outside of mourning. For one thing, my wardrobe of late has made it so easy to choose."

Kate looked at Elizabeth for a long moment before realizing she had made a small joke ... they both laughed and everything was magically back to normal. There would be no more talk of mourning and such, just two old friends having a night out together.

Elizabeth was in awe of the ornate wood and polished brass fixtures as she entered the companionway leading below deck to the main salon dining area of the yacht.

What greeted her there was a spacious, beautifully appointed room with deeply polished wood beams, planking, walls, and wainscoting. A long wooden table dominated the center of the main salon, covered in an array of sumptuous food—pheasant, beef, ham, mutton, salads, oysters, game pastries, fruits, including strawberries, cakes, ample wine decanters, and other provender.

The guests had arrived, most standing about talking and sipping champagne. Several white-gloved servants in white cotton jackets moved about in a semi-successful attempt to keep glasses filled.

Elizabeth was somewhat amused to note that she and Kate were the only women on board. Kate's rather unsteady father returned to the salon and was talking with a distinguished looking older man. She thought this might be Lord Lyons, because a striking British officer in scarlet tunic accompanied him.

Prominent political figures in Lincoln's cabinet were scattered about the room, as well as a small number of younger, uniformed American officers. There was no sign of President Lincoln, but then she had not expected him to attend such a small, intimate dinner. His name appeared on numerous guest lists, but he was frequently unable to attend.

Kate said, "Come, my dear, as I mentioned in my note, there's someone I'm dying you should meet. He's tall, incredibly handsome, a military officer mind you, and I should think very much available game."

"Goodness Kate, you do go on so. I am not at all on a hunting expedition. How can I meet this man now that you've completely embarrassed me?"

"Waste not a moment's thought, you'll get on famously, and," under her breath, "you're long past due finding a suitable match. Come along." Elizabeth had an amusing thought. *Perhaps I should be happy Kate wants to match-make for me, considering my rapidly approaching dotage at age twenty-five.*

A very young and nervous servant offered her a glass of champagne from a tray full of them, all shaking unsteadily. The young man furtively shot his eyes around the room apparently looking for watchful supervisors.

Elizabeth took a glass carefully. "Thank you. You are both kind and efficient." Her radiant smile and gentle words of encouragement immediately put the young man at ease.

"Yer most welcome, Miss." She took a sip, nodding appreciatively to the servant. He was still staring at her, spellbound, as she glided away across the room.

She and Kate came upon a group of officers. Kate singled out the tallest, perhaps the most attractive man Elizabeth had ever seen. He was touching his expertly cut black hair, as if some of it were out of place. Elizabeth saw nothing out of place in his hair, granite features or round blue eyes, but she found it annoying that he felt the need to check.

Kate said formally, "Elizabeth Callaghan, I want you to meet my dear friend Captain Justin Billings, our host's son. Captain Billings, this is Miss Callaghan."

The two touched gloved hands and exchanged pleasantries. Kate remained just long enough to start the conversation, then floated off to chat with other guests and continue her thus far unsuccessful efforts to playfully seduce the senior Billings. She had told Elizabeth that she thought him a wonderfully appealing older man.

"Well, Miss Callaghan, your first time aboard the 'Precarious'?" Billings said, spitting out the yacht's name with arrogance and disdain, as though it were some loathsome bug on the wall. *Not an auspicious beginning,* thought Elizabeth. Her glass was empty and Billings showed a marked lack of interest in refilling it.

"Yes, it is my first time here, actually. I wouldn't have come tonight had Kate not insisted." Elizabeth noticed the appearance of indifference in Billings' face. She found it most unappealing.

I guess when God makes them as tall and attractive on the outside as this one, he must get a perverse pleasure from giving them an inner malady to compensate, such as an arrogant and obnoxious personality.

She knew it was rude, but could not resist teasing, "Are you bored, Captain Billings?"

Billings was uncomfortable, but apparently did not catch the jibe. "Just a little. I must tell you, Miss Callaghan, and with the greatest of joy, that I for one am happy you joined us this evening. The usual crowd my father invites to these affairs is just that ... boring, and frankly, not very pretty, if I may be so bold." He had slandered the word "father" with venomous contempt.

Elizabeth replied, smiling too sweetly, "You've already been so bold, but I doubt I could have stopped you. So, if I may sum up, Captain, you don't like the yacht, you're not too keen on the host, who is your father ... and you have great loathing for the guests. You're not a happy man, are you Captain? One might wonder why you came at all?"

Billings was set back by her sharp retort, not being accustomed to such wit and directness in the ladies he romanced. He was far more used to having women fawn over him.

He recovered swiftly and chuckled, too loudly, "Why, Miss Callaghan, I came here just to find you. You are a beauty, and I mean to make the most of this happy—"

He had not quite finished his sentence, when a white-gloved hand and bright scarlet sleeve appeared out of nowhere, holding a full glass of champagne. The arm moved between Billings and Elizabeth, skillfully crowding him out.

A voice with the hint of Scotland said slowly, "Excuse me Miss, I know we havena been formally introduced, but I couldn'a help noticing yer glass needed charging. Please allow me the honor of acceptin' this refill." The British officer then gracefully exchanged the full for the empty glass.

"I beg your pardon, sir," Billings said.

Before he could say more, Elizabeth spoke. "You are so sweet to notice among all these people. Thank you, sir." She gave Billings a dagger look, which he registered without a clue to its meaning.

For the first time she looked directly at the man who had brought the drink. He was the officer who had been speaking with Kate's father and Lord Lyons. She certainly detected a Scottish accent?

He carries himself with the easy air of a gentleman, but without a hint of haughtiness. She was impressed.

"No Miss, it is I who should be thankin' you. Your presence has brightened the entire room. It is indeed my pleasure." With that, the Scotsman bowed slightly, and disappeared.

Billings cleared his throat, said to Elizabeth, "Well, of all the impudent—"

"Odd, your reaction, Captain Billings," Elizabeth interrupted, "not mine at all. I thought him rather charming, and my glass was empty." The dagger look stabbed him again.

This time Billings understood the not-so-subtle rebuke, and seemed to know enough to say nothing. After a few moments of awkward silence, during which Elizabeth smiled pleasantly around the room, he said, "After dinner, my dear, you and I shall meet again, and I'm certain we'll find much to talk of through the night."

His rather blatantly inappropriate suggestion enraged Elizabeth, but she replied calmly, "Why Captain Justin Billings, you are, if nothing else, confident."

She saw that Billings took this as a great compliment. He believed, no doubt, that he was surely making headway with her. After more meaningless conversation, Billings made excuses and went off, *to acquire a champagne refill—for himself*, Elizabeth thought.

When they sat for dinner, Elizabeth found herself looking across the table at Justin Billings and, close by, the Scottish officer.

The meal was a delicious pheasant, with all the trimmings. The table talk turned from music, to philosophy, to art, and on and on. Elizabeth utterly charmed the men on her left and right, but spent most of the meal chatting with Kate. That is, when Kate was not flirting coquettishly with one or the other of the officers around her.

While all this was happening, Elizabeth's eyes continually wandered toward the two men. It seemed to her they were ignoring each other. Normally, she would have been attracted to the tall captain with the chiseled face, but his manner had thus far done nothing but irritate and on occasion, repulse her.

She tried to focus on him, but could not. Others were addressing the officer in red as "Colonel." He looked young to be a colonel, but this Scotsman, with the most pleasant accent, few words, and a glass of champagne, kept haunting her thoughts. Like a magnet, she could not refrain from stealthy glances.

What was it? Was it the smile, the flash of his eyes, or something more? He was not starkly handsome, like the taller one. She could not seem to fathom what attracted her to this particular gentleman, but attracted she was.

As the meal and table talk continued, Elizabeth began to realize it was the whole man that so appealed to her. It was his self-assurance without arrogance. She felt he was confident; a man without having to prove it in loud talk, bragging, or manly gestures. It seemed to her he personified what a gentleman ought to be, but so often was not.

Yet, with all his polite virtues hidden not too far beneath the surface, she could sense power, taut and ready, and mischief, a rogue perhaps. It brought forth in her a kind of fear—and that excited her—along with a strange and unfamiliar feeling. It was warm, moist and tingly, fascinating her, drawing her to him.

The evening wore on and she was entirely bored with the endless chatter about the war, the latest political gossip, and the never-ending competition among the men present, over almost anything. She wished there were more ladies to talk with.

Elizabeth grew tired of the prattle, and decided to leave the dinner party. She said her goodbyes to her host and Kate, who again insisted she take the coach back to her lodging. "It should be waiting," Kate said. "I told him to remain and take you home."

"Thank you so much, Kate. You are a good and dear friend." Elizabeth saw no point in mentioning the coach driver's attitude or that he was not likely to be waiting. She knew the area and could flag down a hansom cab at the top of the hill. She gathered her cloak and quietly left the yacht.

The crewmen were no longer at the gangplank, and the cobbled street seemed deserted. Elizabeth thought about going back to the party to ask for an escort, but rejected the idea as silly. *The air will do me good after that champagne, and I'm perfectly capable of taking care of myself.*

Elizabeth walked across the gangplank and onto the dock with a light, but purposeful step. She moved up the hill at a fair pace toward where she hoped there would be passing cabs. A darkened alley loomed on her left, between two warehouses. She noticed it was lit inside only by a small gaslight over a heavy metal-covered door at the far end. She kept walking.

Up ahead along the cobbled street a man appeared, partially standing in the shadows. She was not alarmed, thinking it might be the driver, after all. As she came closer, she heard a distinct scraping sound. She stopped and froze in place. She could see this was not the driver. By his movement out of the shadows she knew this was a much younger man. *This is not good*, she thought.

He was large, and wore a slouch hat. The collar of his long overcoat and the hat covered his face. He said, rather menacingly, "Evening Missy—what's your hurry?"

Elizabeth was now frightened, but refused to allow this crude person to see it. She answered him, "None of your business, sir, and I don't care to speak with you. Now, kindly allow me to pass."

With that she tried to go beyond him on the walkway. He blocked her. She spun around, started back down the hill toward the yacht, then saw the trap. There were two more men, similarly dressed, obviously his friends. They came out from the alley she had just passed, blocking her path back to the yacht. She was caught, becoming more frightened each second.

The first man said, "Now we'll have a little fun, a little scratch and tickle." He grabbed her roughly by the arm, pulled her down the hill. The man shoved her into the alley, while his two friends kept watch at its head.

"Leave me alone. Leave me be." She could smell the whiskey strong on his breath as he towered over her, saw his face and a pair of squinty eyes.

"I don't think so, Missy. Not tonight. Tonight—you're mine."

Elizabeth tried to scream. His left hand clamped vice-like over her mouth. He pushed her into the brick-walled side of the alley, began groping under her dress, tearing through the hoop skirt with his right hand, "Now let's see what we got here. Calm down, damn it, yer gonna like this."

120

Her muffled pleas went unheeded. She was terrified, squirming and kicking to get free. Both her slippers came off or were taken off, and she could feel the cool, hard surface of the cobblestones on her feet, through her silk stockings. Somehow it made her feel naked, exposed.

The metal door in the side of the alley crashed open, and a huge bearded man stumbled out, catching himself from falling. He was even larger than her assailant. He saw the man mauling the girl, and must have realized instantly what was happening. He pulled the man off Elizabeth, and threw him to the other side of the alley with the effort it might take to toss an old blanket on the ground.

Elizabeth heard a cracking sound. She saw the bearded man—now off balance—fall forward like a stone, hit from behind by one of the other men. Elizabeth's hope of getting away fell with him.

Chapter 19

April 1863, Georgetown wharfs, outside Washington

Ian left the yacht to start the long walk back to the Willard. He heard a commotion in an alley as he moved toward the top of the hill. The light from a full moon and a small gaslight gave the alley's interior an eerie, surreal look, but he could see there was trouble.

It looked like two men kicking a third man on the ground. A woman was slumped down across the alleyway. Without thinking, he demanded, "You men there. Stop what you're doing! What the hell are you about?"

Ian entered the alley and moved quickly toward the group. The men saw him, broke away from their kicking, and headed in his direction.

He heard a footstep behind him just a second too late. The blow struck the back of his head. He collapsed to his knees, then flat on his face.

*   *   *

Will Hutchison

Although Elizabeth fainted briefly, she had regained her senses. She was breathing heavily. Collapsed on the stones, she could smell the vile odor of urine.

Alarmed, she saw that the bearded man who had tried to help her was still lying on the alley floor. The man who attacked her and one of his friends kicked at him, methodically, and he grunted in pain with each strike.

She heard a shout, "You men there. Stop what you're doing! What the hell are you about?"

A form moved toward her from the head of the alley, and hope was renewed. It was a man, but she could not make out anything else in the dim light. He did look tall. The two men kicking her fallen rescuer left him and moved to intercept the intruder. To her shock, she saw the third assailant come up behind whoever was now entering the alley, and strike him with what looked like a club. The man went down on the alley floor.

Her rescuer nearby was now getting shakily to his feet. He was even larger than she had first thought. He growled loudly, and started toward the three men, arms wide, like a big bear attacking its evening meal.

The assailants stopped, two turned and ran from the alley. The giant reached out and picked the other off his feet. He pulled him close, then closed his other fist, and brought it down squarely on top of the man's head—driving him into the ground with a visible and audible shudder, like a hammer smashing the head of a nail. The man staggered to his feet and stumbled down the alley after his two friends. The giant bear gave a huge laugh and shook his fist at them.

The bear-like man turned to help the man who had been clubbed, to his feet. Elizabeth recognized him as the British officer she was so intrigued by on the yacht. Both men helped each other back to where Elizabeth was pulling herself together, and slowly rising.

Two sets of arms came down to her—strong hands gently lifting. A quiet voice said, "Are you all right Miss? Did he hurt ya?"

"No," she replied, but found she was shaking all over. "He would have ... ah ... hurt me. I think he'd have killed me, if it wasn't for the two of you."

She paused, collected herself. "You saved my life."

"Just a wee dab of luck on my part, Miss Callaghan." Ian was rubbing the back of his head, felt the pain and a large knot forming. "I left the party early. Glad I was here, but I certainly didn't do much by way of saving anyone. Merely glad my bearskin cap took most of the blow. It was this gentleman who scared them off."

The big man spoke for the first time, "Not me. I was flat on my back getting the hell kicked out of me for the most part. The bastards ... they caught me off guard." He weaved, and Elizabeth smelled whiskey.

"I believe it was the two of you, and I'm grateful," Elizabeth exclaimed, wondering how this officer knew her name. They had not been introduced, although now she regretted she had not somehow orchestrated that introduction.

"If you're certain you're not hurt," Ian offered, "let's get you sorted out, and I'll see ya home safely."

"Before this, I'd have refused assistance from someone I hadn't met formally, but I think not at this point," said Elizabeth, half-smiling. "Thank you for your kind offer. I accept."

For another moment the big man reeled from pain and possibly the whiskey, holding his side and head. But he recovered rapidly, and his rage built with each passing moment.

Ian asked, "Sir, are you all right?"

The man's anger at being bested by the thugs disappeared as quickly as it flared up. He looked at Ian. "I'll be fine ... in a year or two." They both grinned, as though it was a private joke.

"I sure let those bastards get the better of me," the big man said, shame in his voice. "Too much drink. There was a damned poker game in this warehouse and I was losing. Guess I was getting angry, cause they told me to go out to clear my head. Damned glad you came along," he said to Ian. "At least they stopped kicking me to move on you. I'm obliged to you, sir."

The large man turned to Elizabeth, who had found her slippers on the alley floor and was putting them back on her feet. "Sorry, Miss, when I'm sober I'm not so rude with my language. Forgive me. Now, what shall it be, Miss, shall we call the constables?"

She thought about it, and made her decision. "Leave it be." She looked at the big man. "I think you taught them a lesson, of sorts."

Ian looked kindly at her, then at the large man, who nodded his assent.

"Shall we go, then?" recommended Ian.

They walked out of the alley, Ian holding Elizabeth's arm in support. She did not need it, but did not pull away. She could feel the warmth of him. She could also feel a sensation spreading through her; excitement again. Elizabeth had never felt with anyone this acute heat coming in such strong waves. *Perhaps it is merely a contrast to the fear and helplessness I felt before ... perhaps.*

Ian became aware of how beautiful she really was, felt a heat rising in him, as well.

At the top of the hill the large man attempted to smooth his long wild-looking hair, and straighten his disheveled clothing. He said, "As delightful and entertaining as this has been, I really must be on my way. I'm going in the opposite direction, I fear. You will take care of the young lady?"

"Of course," Ian replied.

"Then I'll take my leave."

"Goodbye, sir," Ian said.

The man turned to Elizabeth. "Miss, you are, indeed, brave. I leave you in this gentleman's hands."

Elizabeth again thanked him, and watched as he walked back into the alley toward the metal door.

Ian and Elizabeth looked at each other. Ian said, "A bit strange, don't you think? I don't know who he is, do you?"

"I don't think he wanted us to find out. He stumbled out and found me being set upon. He was drunk and as alarmed by what was going on as I was glad to see him. Perhaps he was somewhere he shouldn't have been, gambling, and who knows what else. Perhaps the less said the better."

"You may be right."

He looked at her tenderly. "I'm Ian Carlyle, Miss, and pleased ta have been of some small assistance."

"And I, sir, am Elizabeth Callaghan."

"I know your name, Miss."

"Yes, and how do you know my name?"

"I asked at the party," said Ian, blushing slightly.

Knowing he had asked about her and seeing him blush gave her a quiet pleasure. "It's 'Lizbeth,' please, but I fear somewhere along the way we must be formally introduced. It seems silly now, I mean after—" Her voice trailed off.

As she had suspected, the cranky old driver had simply gone home. Also, there were no hansom cabs in sight. She suggested, "I live fairly close by, here in Georgetown. I could just walk."

"Not alone you won't. That's nonsense. I'll not have you wandering about unescorted any more this night. Perhaps we—"

"I'm a nurse, sir. I work a short distance from here at a hospital at the Union Hotel, and live a few blocks from there. I'm perfectly capable of walking home alone." Her voice took on a slight edge.

Ian was undeterred. "I am quite certain you're familiar with these streets, and are most capable, Miss Callaghan. Can we say this is for my own peace of mind? I'd not be able to sleep tonight if I didn't see you home."

Elizabeth thought about this. "Well, under those circumstances—I wouldn't want to interfere with your sleep, but I will have the devil to pay if we're seen together at this late hour, no matter what the circumstances."

"Let us make every effort to be discreet. Lead the way."

They began walking, slowly. Ian knew she was still upset, but held herself together well. He was taken by her strength.

127

They talked as they walked. Ian tried to be reassuring without raising her independent streak.

They had not gone far before the initial shock wore off. Elizabeth stumbled and nearly fell to the ground. Ian caught her gently, and half carried her to a nearby bench by a wall of stone, surrounding a massive estate. It was dark there in the shadow of the wall, and quiet. Ian spoke softly, helping her regain a steady breathing.

"It's all right, Miss Callaghan ... Uh, Lizbeth ... it's over. You're safe. You're a very brave lass."

Elizabeth would ordinarily have cut him short, reminded him that she could weather any situation, and did not need his patronizing comments, but not this time—no, not this time. His words were soothing, his voice comforting, mesmerizing. She folded inside them like a warm, soft blanket.

The temptation to take her gently in his arms and stroke her hair was so strong he had to forcibly suppress it, knowing it would be inappropriate, afraid of offending her. Elizabeth, for her part, was beginning to feel safe, as she worked her way out of the residual terror.

They remained seated on the bench for a time, silently. Soon they began talking of other things. Ian spoke of his family, his career in the Guards—she of her parents' deaths and her brother, Patrick, skipping out of school to become a soldier. She, for the first time to anyone, spoke of the details of his untimely death in battle. Oddly, both found themselves talking more about themselves than either were used to doing.

They talked until after midnight, becoming acquainted, liking what they learned of each other, but knowing it was time to part before they were swept up in the intimacy and intensity of the moment.

Elizabeth broke the spell. "Goodness, it must be dreadfully late. We've been here much too long."

"Aye, right you are, Lizbeth, much too long." Ian took her hand, assisting her to her feet.

When they reached her home, a large estate behind a tall wrought iron fence, Ian walked her to the door. On the porch, their eyes met for a very long moment. She made no move to go in the house.

Ian took his gloves off, then reached for her right hand with both of his, whispering, "May I," but not waiting for an answer. He slowly, delicately undid the button on her kid glove. She caught her breath. Her wrist was exposed as he tenderly, slowly, peeled off the skin-tight glove.

When he touched the bare skin of her hand with his fingertips, stroking gently, Elizabeth nearly cried out. Ian bent and kissed the top of her hand lightly. She moved toward him. He squeezed the hand harder, turned it around, kissing her palm. The fire rushed through her.

There was an intense minute of silence, as he lingered with the wetness of his kiss in the palm of her hand before saying, "You may think it inexcusable of me, but I must ask. May I call upon you, Miss Callaghan?"

She waited to answer, her independence taking control. She lightly pulled her hand away, and distressed Ian by saying, "Certainly not." There was a pause that seemed too long, "At least not until somehow, somewhere, you manage to have us formally introduced."

Ian saw her serious look, and watched it break into a beautiful smile. He let out the breath he was holding and smiled, broadly. "Of course, Miss Callaghan. Och, I'd have it no other way." He gave an exaggerated bow, sweeping his cap around and across his front.

Elizabeth gave him an impish look, abruptly turned on her heel, flung open her front door, and disappeared inside, perhaps a little too fast.

Ian stood on the porch, still bowing, still smiling, then left, still feeling the fire.

Chapter 20

April 1863, Washington

It's him, Ian thought, *what the devil is he doing here?*

It was a week later, at a reception in the East Room of the White House. The occasion was to introduce a few new diplomats and foreign dignitaries from somewhere or other. President Abraham Lincoln was attending, but that was not who Ian was looking at.

The room where it was held was not what Ian expected—a bit plain compared to where Her Majesty lived and entertained. The room shone with three huge chandeliers, brightly lit with candles that gave off a waxy odor and left a smoky film in the air. The guests, dignitaries, politicians, industrialists, military figures, and government bureaucrats, milled about sipping from wine glasses, some punctuating their conversations with a cigar.

Across the large room, Ian spied the large bear-like man who tried to help Elizabeth in the alley. He was dressed rather flamboyantly for this crowd. Though in a black suit, he wore a bright red cravat and blue brocade silk vest. He did not look at all disheveled, but had his flowing shoulder-length black hair neatly combed, and sported a thick but trim, imperial style beard. His eyes, now that Ian saw them in the light, were strong and intense.

Those eyes, his size, the hair, and his loudish dress made him an impressive figure. Ian saw nothing of the somewhat inebriated grizzly bear who stumbled unsuspecting into the late-night Georgetown alleyway. This man was all business at the reception, talking confidently and intently to various important guests.

For the first time Ian was to be personally introduced by Lord Lyons to President Lincoln. Ian stood nearby, conspicuous, he thought, in full regimental regalia, while Lord Lyons waited quietly for Lincoln to finish with other guests.

Ian was close enough to observe this American leader in action. He politely lingered near Lord Lyons, should his lordship choose to make the introduction. It was not difficult to hear Lincoln speaking. Even in a conversational tone, his high-pitched, accented voice was hard to mistake. What he heard was not what he expected—not at all.

Lincoln was approached by a senator from Maine, who introduced himself loud enough for half the room to hear. Ian watched and listened to them talk as unobtrusively as possible. He took stock of this "back country cretin" as Lincoln had been called by officers surrounding George B. McClellan.

The first thing he noticed was the change. He had seen photographic images and portraits of Lincoln when he first came to Washington. Narrow faced with a high forehead, those earlier images showed him as square-shouldered, erect, with short, dark carelessly brushed hair, and clean-shaven.

Now Ian saw a tall man, yes, but with disheveled hair, a somewhat ragged beard with no mustache, and cavernous, sunken eyes, giving him a grave-like countenance. His face was shallower, pained, and his shoulders stooped. Ian's first thought was that the weight of this man's burden must be excessive.

The senator from Maine waxed eloquent on several topics, which Ian was sure the senator believed exhibited him as an erudite man of the world and of the arts, far above this Illinois bumpkin of a president. He was condescending in tone and pompous in opinion.

Lincoln conversed with the senator articulately, and with great charm. The President smiled his warm, engaging smile, and the poor senator hardly realized that Lincoln had his measure, and was making a bloody fool of him in his homey, quiet way.

Ian found Lincoln strangely affable, with what he strongly suspected was a superior intellect and sharp mind hidden behind a witty, backwoods American sort of façade. All of this was revealing. He did not seem the crass farm boy the "McClellanites" had led him to believe. Nevertheless, Ian decided to reserve his opinion on whether Lincoln matched the low estimation he had already formed of his political and leadership skills.

Lincoln soon dismissed the senator and turned deliberately in their direction. "Lord Lyons, how very good to see you again. I'm so glad you could come tonight."

"Your Excellency, I wouldn't have missed it. It is I who must thank you for inviting me."

Lincoln was looking over Lord Lyons' shoulder. He shouted, startling everyone around him, including his lordship. "Here, Hill, over here!"

He turned back to Lord Lyons. "There is someone I would like you to meet. May I present Mr. Ward Hill Lamon, Marshal of the District of Columbia, and my old and dear friend."

Ian saw the man Lincoln referred to coming through the crowd. It was the bear from the alley, and he was being called by his middle name by the President of the United States, who was energetically summoning him to his side.

"Hill and I were law partners for a time back in Illinois," the President told the small crowd who now gathered to listen. "Then Hill was elected as prosecutor, and we were on opposite sides of the bench, where I could whip him like an ornery dog."

There was laughter, which included this Mr. Lamon. Lincoln's tone turned confidential as he leaned forward toward the listeners. "I, of course, forgave him that small period of incredibly poor judgment, and brought him with me to Washington." There was laughter and a pause.

Half turning toward Ian, Lord Lyons said, "Mr. President, there is someone I would like you to meet, as well. This is Lieutenant Colonel Ian Carlyle, Scots Fusilier Guards. On assignment as a military attaché with my legation. He was a serving officer in the Crimea ..."

President Lincoln thought a moment, then inserted, "Yes, I understand General McClellan was over there for a time, as well. Did you meet him?"

Ian was cautious. "No, Mr. President, not there. He was only in the Crimea for about a month, and arrived after Sevastopol fell. I was invalided home with a bit of bother long before that."

Lord Lyons continued, "Colonel Carlyle was, however, on General McClellan's staff last year as a representative of Her Majesty, completely neutral, mind. He observed the actions around Richmond and at Antietam Creek. Was even mentioned in dispatches by General McClellan." This was something Ian had not known before this moment.

Mr. Lincoln said to Ian, "A pleasure to meet a soldier of the Queen—a neutral in this conflict, of course." Ian thought he actually saw him wink.

Ian, in his resplendent scarlet dress uniform, and embarrassed, came to attention.

Lincoln, in his usual casual manner, put him at ease. "Please, Colonel, not so formal here. We're somewhat more casual in the former 'colonies'." There was a trickle of laughter. Ian smiled, and found that it was an unexpectedly genuine smile.

"I know of your fine regiment." Lincoln reached out and grasped Ian's hand with an amazingly strong grip, and shook it vigorously.

"It is my pleasure, Mr. President," replied Ian. Surprisingly, he meant it.

Lincoln turned to Lamon, "And this is Hill Lamon. You two should get on well. You both, I suspect, like a good scrap."

Ian thought, *Hmmm, a confidant of Lincoln with a reputation as a scrapper. That might explain his secretiveness and his rushing off so quickly after the altercation. I can see bruises around the one eye.*

Lamon said guardedly, "Actually, Mr. President, Colonel Carlyle and I have met."

"Oh, and where was that?" Lincoln inquired, truly interested.

Lamon coughed into his hand, and said, "Not long ago ... in ... ah ... in Georgetown. It was——"

Ian recognized Lamon's discomfort, and quickly injected, "Yes, sir. I was attending a dinner party." The inference that Lamon was there was a small piece of misinformation.

He saw the immediate relief on Lamon's face, and gave an ever-so-slight nod, noticed only by the two of them. President Lincoln and Lord Lyons began talking about trade agreements. Ian and Lamon excused themselves, and moved to a corner where they could talk privately.

"Thanks for that, Colonel," Lamon said quietly.

"Please, my name is Ian. I'm afraid rank doesn't count for much in yer country."

"Counts with me, but Ian it is," Lamon replied.

Ian said, "Thought it might be prudent ta leave out our little tussle in the alley."

Lamon was candid and friendly, "In my younger years, when I first met President Lincoln, I was known for being rather quick with my fists, and my mouth, and you'll be astonished to learn I drank too much."

Lamon took a small flask out of his inner coat pocket, turned his back to the guests, opened it, and took a long pull.

"Damn, sorry, I'm being rude," he exclaimed offering the flask to Ian.

"What is it?"

"Fine Virginia whiskey," announced Lamon, "the very best from my own home county."

Ian was positive he recognized a southern accent. *Even more odd,* he thought, *with the two factions at war, a southerner so obviously close to President Lincoln.*

Lamon turned an intense gaze on Ian, "I know what you're thinking ... a Virginian ... hell, I even have brothers fighting for the Confederacy. But I'm a staunch Union man, Ian, and fully loyal to President Lincoln."

Ian nodded, took a drink from the flask. He found it sweet for his taste, but certainly strong. Lamon continued his explanation, "I made my way as a young lawyer in the North. Back then, in the old days in Illinois, he was just Mr. Lincoln, 'Abe' in private. He got me out of trouble a time or two. He made it perfectly clear, though, that he did not think drinking and brawling were appropriate for a lawyer. Still jibes me about it, so my thanks to you for keeping it our tiny secret."

Ian grinned. "I can see in the short time we've known each other, sir, that you don't drink anymore, or get into fights —"

Hill laughed heartily, taking another pull on the flask. "I sure didn't need him knowing about that fight, or my gambling in that sleazy warehouse." *Ah, so that was it,* Ian thought, *Lizbeth was right.*

"Holy hell, I had a deuce of a time explaining my bruises next day." He paused, adding, "Ian, you call me Hill, just like the President does. I think he's right. We're going to get on real well."

Ian agreed, nodding, and asked, "Did you know Miss Callaghan?"

"Only her name, never introduced. I believe she won't tell a soul about that night. What do you think?"

"Yer absolutely right," Ian confirmed, "and I shall honor that silence, as well."

"Agreed. Not a word of it will pass my lips. She's here you know."

Ian was startled, "Here—tonight—who—Miss Callaghan?"

"Saw her a few minutes ago, over talking to Kate Chase. I tried to avoid her. Decent thing to do."

Ian thought out loud, "Hmmm. Interesting. Hill, I must leave you to see to Lord Lyons. Shall we have a bite to eat somewhere this coming week? Perhaps the Willard, where I have lodgings."

"Wonderful idea, shall we say, Tuesday?"

"Tuesday at noon at the Willard Hotel. Och, I'm glad we met again, Hill."

"As am I."

Chapter 21

April 1863, Washington

Ian searched the crowded reception, and finally spotted her across the room, talking to Kate Chase. He wondered how anyone could look more lovely than Miss Elizabeth. Her exquisite silver blue dress shimmered about her in the flickering candlelight.

This was his opportunity. He waited close by, and at a break in their conversation, he pounced. "Ah, Kate, how wonderful ta see you again. Is yer father here? How is he?"

Kate looked at Ian strangely. *This is just not like the Ian I know,* she thought. *He couldn't care a fig about my father.* Then she saw through him, mostly because although talking to her, he could not take his eyes off Elizabeth Callaghan standing close by. Elizabeth was smiling, shyly, and looking at him.

Was that a redness in her cheeks?

Kate shot back, tossing her head, "Ian, you beast, where have you been?"

She could not help playing with him, "Did I hear you are now engaged to some lovely lady back in England, no ... it was Scotland, the Highlands, I think?"

Ian saw her play, came back fighting. "Of course not, Kate. I'm savin' myself for someone like you. But like you, they all have so many suitors. Besides, had it actually happened, even as far away as the Hee'lands, you'd have much more detail than you appear ta possess."

Kate was pleased. She loved this kind of banter with an attractive man.

He turned toward Elizabeth, "You know, Miss, Kate here has a better intelligence apparatus than yer General Halleck, and it reaches the far corners of the world."

Elizabeth, having recovered from her pleasant shock at seeing Ian, responded, "That doesn't surprise me in the least, sir."

Ian saw that she had not told of the incident to her good friend, Kate, which supported what he and Lamon speculated. There was a pause, until Ian turned his pleading eyes on Kate in anticipation.

Kate gave a long sigh, then, in resignation, said, "Ian Carlyle, this is Elizabeth Callaghan, a dear friend of mine. Elizabeth, this is Lieutenant Colonel Ian David Carlyle of Her Majesty's Scots Fusilier Guards. He has an outrageous reputation, but I like him."

"Miss Callaghan, it is a great pleasure ta meet you, and don't listen ta Kate. I'm really quite harmless." He bowed at the waist.

The more he spoke, the more Elizabeth's pulse quickened. She said, "It is also my pleasure, uh ... do I call you colonel or Mr. Carlyle, or—?"

"You really must call me Ian."

"And I am 'Lizbeth,' to my friends. Because you are a friend to Kate, you are a friend to me." She was flushed, trembling; never knew a man to affect her so.

Ian thought he might establish the history in front of Kate, who was already suspicious. He said to Elizabeth, "You know I'm certain we were at the same dinner on Joshua Billings' yacht last week. I certainly remember you, but there was no chance for an introduction, and—."

Kate cut in, "Of course you were both there, as was I, if you'll recall—what a tiny, tiny world." Her sarcasm and mischievous grin were not lost on either Ian or Elizabeth.

Elizabeth added, "Well at least we've now formally met." Kate cocked her head to the side. These two had cleverly used her, and she knew it. *How utterly delightful of them*, she thought, smiling.

Ian's whole being cried out to be alone with Elizabeth so they might talk or touch. His excitement only heightened by the sweet sound of her voice, her nearness. Then the spell was broken ...

A rather loud voice said from behind them, over the quartet of string instruments serenading the assemblage, "Ian, my boy, aren't you going to say hello?"

Ian turned to find Sir Archibald Walsham, an old friend of his father, standing before him.

"Sir Archibald, I'm speechless. What brings you to America?" Ian asked in astonishment.

"Why, my boy, doing business with the Federal government, textiles for uniforms, various accoutrements and equipments, the general materials for war. I frequently work with Lord Lyons. Heard you'd been seconded to the legation. Jolly good, that."

Ian made introductions all around. Sir Archibald was charismatic, quite tall, and well-made, with a spruce and trim appearance. He had thick, gray curly hair bundled on his head, extending to an equally thick curly beard, which hid much of his facial expression. With his blank eyes peering through all that hair, one could never tell when he was joking or deadly serious. Sir Archibald had more the look of a store clerk than the industrial entrepreneur making deals with foreign governments. Ian recalled he had been a good friend to his father for many years.

Reading Ian's thoughts, Sir Archibald said, "Sorry to hear about your father, and I understand your mother isn't at all well."

Ian replied, "Thank you for yer concern, Sir Archibald, she's copin' with our loss. Peter is takin' good care of her."

141

Sir Archibald beamed, "Ah, yes, Peter. I already know he's doing well. Hear good things about him. Sorry, but I must be off. I know you will all excuse me."

Kate said, "Of course, Sir Archibald." Elizabeth nodded graciously.

Leaning toward Ian, the older man said softly, "We must get together, speak of bygone days in Scotland. Dinner perhaps—and soon. You remember my daughter, Hillary. She's with me; in fact she's here tonight. I'll put her to making the arrangements. Wonderful to see you again, Ian." With that he moved away, and disappeared.

Ian made an odd face. He certainly did remember Sir Archibald's daughter, Hillary. As a child, she was a pest. She professed undying love for him, but he never gave her a thought, or, indeed, a tumble.

Hillary was a schemer, a manipulator, indeed, a liar. She had got him punished at home on more than one occasion, by exposing to his father some of his wilder misadventures. He wondered if she had changed.

After a time Kate and Elizabeth drifted away, chatting with other guests. As the evening wore on, Ian could not seem to get close enough to Elizabeth to talk with any privacy. It was almost as if she was avoiding him, and it was frustrating.

Indeed, she was avoiding him. Not because she did not want to be with him, but because of her feelings when around him. She became flushed, seemed to lose her usual poise and control, to a degree that seriously disconcerted her.

Ian noticed Sir Archibald talking intently with Captain Justin Billings. He thought them an odd pair, although an acquaintance with Billings' father might be advantageous to Sir Archibald in his business dealings.

Ian was heading across the room to chat with Sir Archibald, when he heard a soft female voice say his name, "Ian, is that really you?"

He had not seen Hillary in decades. When last they met she was somewhat pimply-faced, and chubby, certainly not the raven-haired, clear-skinned beauty now standing before him. She was rather stunning in a pink and white taffeta ball gown with pinked flounces. What held his gaze were the white mounds of flesh seen above the low cut front of her dress. Her eyes were a dark coffee brown, bright and flashing from beneath long black lashes. Her teeth were small and even, made white by her perfect cherry lips.

"Hillary?" He was incredulous, almost speechless.

"Father said you were here. Said I should find you and make arrangements for a dinner at our house."

Ian stammered, "Of ... of course. Hillary, my how you've changed. Och, yer grown up and really quite delicious."

"Thank you. You appear to have filled out well yourself. I must admit I've thought of you often over the years. You know how I hate not getting what I set my cap on."

Recovering somewhat, he said, "Do I take it you were tossing your cap at me?" Ian would not have thought she even remembered him. He noticed she was now followed by a flock of young men, all looking as though they wanted to draw and quarter him for pure sport.

Hillary lit up as though she had a marvelous idea, "Ian, let's get out of here so we can talk, catch up on what we've been doing over the years. Come walk with me in the garden."

She clutched his arm with unusually strong little fingers, and literally pulled him away. There was great mumbling among her disciples as she whisked him off toward the double doors leading to the outside.

The garden was nearly deserted, and quite dark. The scent of lilacs hung low in the air. As they walked, Hillary announced, "It's settled then. Dinner at eight o'clock, next Tuesday?"

They had reached the end of a garden lane, surrounded by overhanging trees. She handed him a small card she extracted from inside the front of her dress, "I wrote down directions for you. Please say you'll come—please."

Ian seemed to recall another appointment on Tuesday, but frankly he was enchanted by this new, grown up Hillary. He replied, "Tuesday next. I'll be there."

143

She exclaimed, "Perfect!" She threw her arms around his neck and kissed him square on the lips, pushing both of them into the shadows at a back corner of the garden, well out of sight, almost as if it were planned for that exact moment and location.

Ian was so shocked by her audacity he merely allowed her to move him. The simple kiss lingered; then he felt her tongue darting inside his mouth. He responded in kind, his own tongue gliding across those small even teeth. It was easy to allow the moment to take hold of his reason. He was instantly excited. Her grinding motion below the waist said that she knew he had an erection and her breathing said it excited her, as well.

He was no longer a novice at the game of sex. He knew the intensity of their embrace in the shadows was actually bringing her to a climax. What staggered him was the speed with which she responded—from playfully cool to intensely hot, to outrageous, in less time than it took to say the words.

Her sexual appetite intrigued and excited him, but this would never do. He deliberately disengaged, holding Hillary at arm's length. She clawed at him, like a cat, until she realized he was not responding. Then there was a flash of anger.

Hillary hissed, "What's wrong? Why are you stopping?"

"We can't do this, certainly not here. Don't you understand that? For God's sake, Hillary, President Lincoln is right inside, and yer father is a family friend. Yer reputation—"

"Reputation be damned! My reputation will survive. No one can see us. Do you know how long I've waited for this moment ... to see you again?"

"Hillary, that was years ago, and we were children, playing games."

"They weren't games for me," she spat. "I never forgot." She wasn't crying—she was angry.

"Hillary, my dearest, please slow down. Let's just move more slowly, shall we? Let's get ta know each other again."

She insisted, "When I want something, I get it. I want you."

Ian thought it best to end this quickly, before it went awry. He tried to insert a bit of humor. "Well, Hillary, my pet, you'll just have ta calm yerself. I'm really not worth it."

There was a long silence. Hillary snapped back to the coquettish young lady, almost too quickly. She looked up at Ian. "You'll come on Tuesday?"

Another drastic mood change, but Ian recovered. "Aye, I'll be there."

She turned and walked quickly back into the reception, leaving Ian bewildered, confused, and, *Damn it*, exceedingly aroused.

* * *

Ian had no desire to return to the reception, and knew Lord Lyons would not mind if he left early. Walking toward the garden gate, he listened to the music playing for the guests. He saw two men near the double doors leading to where the reception was being held. Ian recognized one as President Lincoln's secretary, John Nicolay; a spindly man with a thick mustache and chin whiskers. The other was having trouble walking. He was a much shorter man in a Federal officer's uniform, supported by two crutches.

The officer was missing his right leg to the hip, but it was his face that captured Ian's gaze. It was literally destroyed. The skin was discolored red and black, and he had pronounced scars. His mouth was twisted, lips mangled, nose smashed into his face so that its outline as a nose was gone completely. One ear was missing. He tried unsuccessfully to cover it up with longish hair, sticking out from under a kepi.

Only his eyes shown bright, even in the dim light of the garden, surrounded by moonlight and flickering torches. The symbolism was unmistakable to Ian, the essence of a wounded warrior—timeless in its intensity.

Ian thought he knew what was going on, and was consumed with a burning sense of hatred and rage. This was

145

a political opportunity. There would be a parade, and this poor officer was the star performer. He was to be on exhibit, a token, a show, a dancing bear for the pleasure of the politicians, diplomats, dignitaries, and guests of this President Lincoln. Why else bring him to this reception. Ian was glad he had reserved his opinion of Lincoln, had not been taken in by his apparent personal charm.

The two men stood on a path just outside the doors to the reception, waiting, no doubt, for the grand entrance. Ian was in the shadows, unseen by Nicolay or the officer. He could not, would not let this pass. It was not in him.

About to charge out from the shadows and insert himself into a situation where he knew he had no business going, he saw a door open, spilling more light into the garden area. A tall, gangly figure stepped out and closed the door behind him. Something made Ian hesitate.

The lone figure of Abraham Lincoln moved into the light of a torch by the path and approached Nicolay and the officer. "You must be the Lieutenant Ramsey that Mr. Nicolay has spoken of so often." He reached out his hand, but as he did so, Lieutenant Ramsey came to a rigid attention on his crutches, and with some difficulty balancing, gave a smart salute to his Commander in Chief.

Where is the audience, Ian thought sarcastically, *they're missing a wonderfully staged moment. Perhaps he wants to make a regal entrance with his triumphant trophy of war.*

That was not the case. There was no audience, in fact the reception was carrying on joyfully inside, while this drama took place outside, and in private. Ian was transfixed.

The Lieutenant held his salute. The president placed his hand on the officer's arm gently, and said in a low, respectful voice, "No, no, Lieutenant. This will never do, never. It is rather for me to do."

With that, the President of the United States came to attention and returned Lieutenant Ramsey's salute. There was enough light from the torch for Ian to see clearly the tears slowly tracing down the President's gaunt face, burying themselves in his beard.

He recovered quickly. "Ah hum, uh, Lieutenant, are you getting everything you require at the hospital?"

"Yes, sir, Mr. President. I'm doing just fine." His speech was awkward, muffled, but understandable. Lincoln leaned in slightly to better hear what he was saying.

"Excellent," the President said. "What is your first name, Lieutenant?"

"Jameson, sir, after my father. He passed away a few years ago."

"They call you Jamie?"

"Yes, sir, my mother does."

"... And how long have you been in the army?"

"Two years, sir. I left our farm in Ohio two years ago next week, but I've only been a lieutenant for six months. Still not used to it. I was corporal, and they promoted me up to officer for some reason. Haven't exactly figured out why."

"I know why you were promoted, Jamie. I know exactly why, and I'm proud to know you." The lieutenant seemed to stand a bit taller. The President smiled that gentle, homey smile Ian had seen when they were introduced.

"I was a good officer, sir, led my men well, I think. Guess I won't be leading much from now on, but that's all right. It's God's will, and there's many who are worse stove in than me."

The President cleared his throat again, and looked away, briefly. "Well, Jamie, John here tells me you wanted to see me in person. You have something you'd like to say to me. Is that right?"

"Yes, sir, Mr. President. I wanted to thank you. When I was wounded, you wrote a letter to my mother. She was ailing and alone at the time, and it was a pure comfort. She talks about it to anyone who'll listen; reads your words over ten times a day."

"I'm happy I was able to help in some small way in her time of need. It was my pleasure and my honor. With God's kindness, this war'll be over soon, and there'll be no more need to write those letters. I pray for that day." The President bowed his head.

When he again looked into those bright eyes shining at him, he asked, "Your mother, I hope she is well?"

"Fit as a fiddle ... uh, sir ... sorry, sir." The lieutenant obviously thought his outburst inappropriate.

"No, no, don't be sorry, not at all. Glad to hear it." President Lincoln gave a hearty laugh. He sighed. "I must get back to my guests. I'd invite you to join me, but, frankly, I don't think many of those politicians in there deserve the honor of your presence."

He looked at Lieutenant Ramsey, but spoke to Nicolay. "John, take this young man and get him some refreshments. Bring him to my office so he can sit and relax. I'll only be a few more minutes, then I'll join you. We'll jaw some, Jamie, and you can tell me about your mother and that farm of yours in Ohio."

The shocked lieutenant could only say, "Yes, sir, I'd be happy to, sir."

The President walked slowly back toward the reception to his guests, and the politics of the day. Nicolay disappeared with the lieutenant down the path he had come from.

Ian waited a long time in the shadows, staring at the flickering torches. He was moved beyond measure. He had been so wrong, so very wrong, about this man, Lincoln. He felt somehow he owed the President an apology.

Chapter 22

April 1863, Washington

It was the following Tuesday, and Ian sat waiting in the dining room at the Willard. Lamon was late. Thirty minutes after noon, he sauntered in.

"Sorry I'm late, government nonsense. Happens a good deal in my current position."

Ian was curious. "What exactly is that, Hill?"

"I'm a little touch of everything. I'm in charge of the President's safety—in an informal way. Let's eat." He called a waiter and they both ordered a light fair and a glass of wine.

"Bring the wine at once," Lamon told the waiter. "I'm not that hungry, but I want the noon meal done with. I always feel like it's in the way," Lamon said.

"You were saying ... about yer work."

"Oh, what I do. Well, my formal title is Marshal of the District, as the President told you the other night."

"Impressive. By the way, yer Mr. Lincoln is impressive."

"I know, I know," Lamon said seriously. "If his decriers only knew the man, they'd be ashamed of themselves." Ian agreed, feeling a bit of that shame himself, but he chose not to tell Lamon about the garden.

"So tell me more about this prestigious job of yours."

Lamon put on a mockingly serious face. "Yes, highly impressive, it is. For instance, today, he was concerned over some bills his wife, Mary Todd, accumulated locally. We can't have creditors banging on the President's door, can we?"

"I should think not."

"Odd jobs, as needed. I organize some White House events, coordinate his travel. He gets me involved in some of the damnedest doings."

"Still, it sounds interesting. You seem content."

"Sometimes bored, but usually quite content. You see, I like Lincoln. He's my friend, so it's more than just patriotic duty or a job that has to get done." He paused as the waiter placed two glasses of red wine on the table. "But what about you? What keeps you from tearing your hair out?"

"You saw," Ian said. "I follow Lord Lyons about, so he can wave the flag and show off a real live Guardsman of the Queen—fierce, and in full plumage."

"Ah ha, the fierce Scottish warrior. I can see that. You were certainly fierce in the alley." Lamon laughed a hearty, rather loud laugh, then downed the wine in one or two gulps. Ian joined him.

"I also do odd bits around the legation, mostly worrying about our poor citizens bein' drafted into yer bloody army."

Lamon laughed again. "I never knew. I thought all your Irishmen were clamoring to get into the fight—any fight."

"I'm also submitting some reports on how well yer new repeating rifles do in the field. We might adopt such a weapon for our soldiers."

"Now that sounds more interesting." He shouted toward a passing waiter, "Let's have two more glasses of wine here,"

Ian said, "You could be right about the Irish ... but there are those who would prefer not, or at least don't want to be pressed into going off to another country's war."

"Now that, sir, is quite understandable. But beyond that you don't sound like a happy man."

"I'll not complain. His lordship is a fine man. I'd merely rather be doin' somethin' more active, more useful."

"Boredom is a curse."

As the wine was set down on the table, Lamon had an idea. He lifted his glass and suggested, "Let's make a pact."

"A pact?"

"Yes, a pact between the two of us. That we will do our level best to fight boredom, and make action happen when and where we can."

Ian knew he liked this big man, and after the other night they shared a bond.

"Let us start right this minute," Lamon said.

Ian raised his glass. "Och, a most excellent idea. To our pact to avoid boredom at all costs—cheers!"

They both drank to their new friendship—for the rest of the afternoon.

*   *   *

By the time Ian appeared at the door to the Walsham residence, he was quite in his cups, but managing, he thought, to at least appear sober. He fooled no one. Hillary was upset, but Walsham found it rather humorous.

Ian explained he was with Hill Lamon, and Walsham said, "Say no more. That explains it all. I don't know him, but my friends around the White House tell me he's quite a character."

Ian agreed, "Aye, indeed."

Walsham said, "I'm glad you're becoming friends with him. We all need good contacts in Washington."

Hillary sulked throughout the meal, which was brought by two servants who never spoke. During the meal Ian and Sir Archibald spoke of Scotland, England, old times, and how much Washington was like, and unlike, London.

After a delicious meal of roast beef and oysters they adjourned to Sir Archibald's magnificent library, with its shelves of classics and glowing fireplace. There was a pleasant smell of cedar and the lovely odor of leather bound books.

As the evening turned to cigars and brandy for Sir Archibald and Ian, Hillary curled demurely into a large cushioned chair, sipped port, and appeared to be intently interested in a book. She stopped sulking, and was presumably satisfied to allow the "gentlemen" to talk of subjects like politics and war. *This is somewhat against her nature*, Ian thought.

Sir Archibald stood at the fireplace in a noble pose. Ian began nonchalantly perusing the book titles as they spoke of Sir Archibald's continuing good fortune in the business world. It seemed Walsham was content that the war would go on, at least for a few more years. Thus, he would continue making exceptional profits selling war materials to the Federal government.

The evening was passing agreeably when a servant brought a message to Walsham. He read it, then looked at Ian with a pained expression. "My sincere apologies, Ian, my boy, but I've been called away. Some trouble with a shipping invoice at the docks."

"Father, must you go?" Somehow Hillary did not sound convincing, and, for that matter, Sir Archibald's reason for leaving didn't seem quite right to Ian either.

"I must, but Ian can certainly remain a bit longer."

Hillary looked innocently at Ian. He said, "Of course, Sir Archibald," and sat on a settee in front of the fire.

Walsham gathered up his overcoat and top hat. "I might be rather late. You children enjoy yourselves."

"Thank you Sir Archibald, I am most grateful for yer hospitality."

"This won't be our last dinner, Ian, and remember— should you need anything, don't hesitate to call upon me."

After he left there was a long silence. Hillary whispered something to the two servants waiting patiently by the library door. They quietly disappeared.

Ian finally broke the silence. "I really should be going soon, myself." He was still feeling the effects of the wine he had drunk all afternoon and with their evening meal, and the half empty glass of brandy he held in his hand.

Hillary came over to the settee and sat beside him. *She does have extraordinary eyes, and her scent is light and flowery. There, there, Ian, old chum, remember she is a conniving little brat underneath, and Sir Archibald was yer father's friend.* He felt himself becoming erect.

Without another word, Hillary leaned in and kissed him fully on the lips, a soft, lingering kiss. Her hand moved to his leg. Ian could feel the heat where it rested near his knee.

"Hillary, the servants ... yer father?"

"The servants be damned, and father won't be home for hours—he said so. Besides, I think he would love the idea of you and me together."

By now Ian had a full erection, as Hillary's hand moved slowly until it just barely touched his member through his trousers. *An accident? Not bloody likely.*

He pulled her face to him, and his kiss made her wild. She kicked off both slippers and moved closer, climbing onto the settee. Hillary frantically massaged his erection through his clothing, returning his kiss with her tongue teasing the inside of his mouth. His left hand rubbed her back, while his right moved playfully to her breasts.

The heated passion was building to an intensity Ian knew must be satisfied. He rose and lifted her with his left arm around her back. The settee was close to one of the enormous bookshelves and Ian pushed her up against it; books rattled, some falling to the floor.

Hillary tore at his trousers, frenetically unbuttoning them. He pushed and pulled at her dress. First he brought the dress itself up to her waist, then gathered the caged crinoline, exposing her chemise. To his wonder and delight, he realized Hillary wore no drawers. He pulled up the chemise and gazed on her lower body, naked before him, except for white silk stockings held up with bright red ribbon garters. He plunged into her with little more thought and no hesitation.

In response, she eagerly raised her legs and wrapped them around him like a snake. Her eyes were wide, mouth open.

Ian pushed her against the edge of a shelf. Books bounced aside, cascading around them. He held her up with the weight of his body, the strength of his inserted member and his left arm on her back. With his right hand he felt the silk on her stockinged right foot, massaging the sole with his fingers, all the time rubbing her back with his left hand. He began grinding his loins as well, creating a balanced tempo of movement, carrying her excitement to a new intensity.

Ian brought both arms around her small waist, and continued the tempo, increasing it slightly. He became even more aroused when he felt her feet slapping his buttocks as he thrust into her.

She squirmed wildly in cadence. By now the shelf was nearly empty of books, and she was solidly sitting on its edge. With his hands he grasped both her wrists and brought them together above her head. She threw her head back and cried out in spontaneous ecstasy, now his captive. His continuing relentless rhythmic movements allowed her time to build her passion to a peak.

Their lovemaking was frenzied and self-absorbed. Each of them moved toward their individual satisfaction. Ian did manage to maintain control long enough to bring her to one brilliant climax, followed by his own shattering orgasm. Then, after the storm's initial glorious outburst, they began, slower this time, to soar to even more amazing heights, but together.

The library door opened abruptly. One of the servants poked his head in. Hillary's immediate reaction was to shriek at him in a piercing crescendo. He withdrew in an instant.

She did not falter in her quest for further satisfaction, nor did he. They climaxed again, together this time. She screamed out loud—he screamed inside.

Hillary began to wilt—drained. Ian pulled slowly out of her, and allowed her to sink gently to the floor in front of the fire next to the now familiar bookshelf. He joined her on a thick carpet in front of the fireplace. She curled up in his arms and whispered, "That is what I've wanted since we were children."

Ian said nothing, a bit ashamed for not better controlling the situation, and for taking advantage of his father's old friend's hospitality.

After a time, Hillary began gently stroking Ian's member, then his balls. She said, breathlessly, "I want more."

Ian started to respond, erect again, but this time forced himself to stop. He sat up. "Hillary, I must go. I let things get out of hand, and I'm sorry. Now I really must go."

Hillary was in shock. Ian began straightening his clothing as he rose from the floor.

She shouted, "You bastard! You think you can have me and just leave? It's me who uses you, damn you, not the other way round. It's me—don't you understand. You're merely a prick for my amusement." Her demeanor altered so abruptly that it caught Ian off guard.

"Hillary, please." He was unable to register her venomous ferocity.

"I'll tell my father." His back was turned. She picked up a log from near the fireplace and threw it at him. It struck him violently on the shoulder. "He'll have you flogged, beaten."

Her rage was escalating, but now Ian was getting angry. "You tell yer father anything ya like, or you can tell 'im fuck all, but I'm leavin'." Ian turned and left her sitting on the floor, shoeless, legs splayed out, dress and underclothing hiked up around her naked waist. She glared at his back as he left.

If Ian had seen Hillary's eyes, he might have been frightened. *Damn you, Ian Carlyle ... I'm not through with you—you bastard.*

Chapter 23

May 1863, Washington

The second week in May, 1863, Ian received a letter from his brother, Peter. Aside from the routine hello, how are you, mother's still ill but doing fine—there seemed a powerful and disturbing ulterior motive to his missive. He was desperate for a favor, brother to brother.

Peter always worried Ian. He realized early on that Peter was shy and standoffish. Nevertheless, Ian's concerns began in earnest on a chilly evening at Eton College, when they were both struggling their way through school.

In a hazing incident, a school bully named Roger Fairbain carved his initials in Peter's chest with a fencing foil and made him do unspeakable things. Ian was forced to watch and came close to the same fate. That was the first time his leopard had appeared. It changed his life, gave him confidence, the will to orchestrate his own destiny.

It was also the first time he had to care for and protect his older brother. He nursed Peter through his dark time, but could not help him conquer the demons this incident brought forth.

Peter left Eton shortly after, in a disturbed state. He returned to Dunkairn Hall, wrapping himself in the protection of family name, titles, estate and wealth. He rapidly became a recluse, with these things as a shield against society. This went on for far too long—years. In the meantime, Ian exacted a horrific revenge on those who had attacked the brothers, leaving them wrecked, physically and mentally.

After their father died, Peter seemed to have worked his way out of his black hole. As the eldest son, he accepted the title of Earl of Dunkairn, and even assumed his father's seat in the House of Lords. When the time came, and with Ian off to the military, it was Peter who stepped up and made arrangements to take care of their ailing mother at Dunkairn. He seemed to Ian to be on the road to normalcy, at last. Ian was wrong.

Peter took up a part-time residence in London. He began drinking and socializing immodestly. Not interested in the ladies, except the occasional whore, he attacked the gambling table with a vengeance. His debt soon rose radically, and there was talk of losing the estate and disgracing the family.

Ian watched his brother's decline, and was about to step in, when rather abruptly Peter appeared to quiet down. His debts were no longer spoken of, and he assured Ian all was well. Peter even became involved in a profitable business venture in arms manufacturing and the worldwide arms trade, with several wealthy British investors. Ian relaxed, thinking his brother was at last getting hold of himself.

Then this letter arrived. In it Peter again spoke of considerable gambling debts, and some unnamed but severe indiscretion in which he was heavily involved. He wrote that his situation could cause them to forfeit their property, including Dunkairn Hall. He would lose his seat at the House of Lords, and generally disgrace the family name for all time. More importantly, Peter was convinced that in her current state of health, the disgrace would kill their mother.

Peter pleaded with Ian to help. He said he had arranged to clear the debt, and bury the indiscretion, but it came at a price; an odd one, indeed, for, according to Peter, its payment depended upon Ian.

Peter said a man, whom he described as "a friend," might approach Ian in the next few months. This friend would have a letter of introduction from Peter, in his own handwriting, which Ian would surely recognize. The man would ask Ian to become party to an endeavor to unseat the elected American leader, President Abraham Lincoln.

Peter argued that he detested this Lincoln fellow anyway, describing him simply as "not our sort." In addition, Peter believed it was the desire of the British government that Lincoln be got rid of. Thus, he justified the effort to get him out of the way.

According to Peter, Ian would only be required to provide certain general information he might glean in his travels among Washington society. He assured Ian that nothing he provided could in any way harm Britain, and would in the long view, help his country.

This letter was extremely disturbing to Ian. He could not imagine Peter being so embroiled in such misadventures. In addition, the entire idea of becoming involved in American politics was preposterous, and against what Lord Lyons told him was the current official British government view.

Lastly, after meeting Lincoln and getting to know his confidant and friend, Hill Lamon, Ian changed his opinion of this President. He was finding he liked and admired Lincoln, and what he was doing for his country.

The letter sounded so desperate. *What could possibly be so bad to cause his brother such anguish and humiliation?* On thoughtful deliberation, Ian decided to let the thing take its course. Possibly no one would approach him at all, and he could sort this out when he next saw Peter, which he hoped would be soon.

Ian was thinking about this dilemma at one of the now routine luncheons at the Round Robin Bar with Hill Lamon, Captain Gregory Prescott, and Ben Tasker. On this day they were joined by Simon Oldham, the journalist and photographer Ian met during the campaign with General McClellan. Upon arriving in Washington, Oldham had attached himself to their merry band. He stayed at the Willard, and became a regular at the Round Robin.

Although Ian's first impression on meeting him had been that Oldham was a bloody twit, he was now discovering the man had many redeeming qualities beneath the surface. In the end he was likeable enough, and a jolly addition to the "Friends of the Round Robin" as the small intimate assembly took to calling itself. Of course, with Oldham, one ignored those darting, restless eyes, flitting about the room as he talked, an affectation that seemed to come and go with his degree of anxiety.

"What do you think about brothers, Tasker?" Ian inquired.

"I don't. I have one and we have not s-spoken for f-fifteen years. Can't s-say I r-recall why we ssstopped, but there ... but there you are." He annoyingly pushed his spectacles up the bridge of his nose.

"Why do you mention it?" Simon Oldham asked.

Ian was now addressing the entire assembly. "I just received a letter from mine, and he is somehow in trouble again. So much so that I might be required to return to England."

Lamon asked, "Isn't that the Earl of something or other? How can that be trouble?"

"It is, Hill, and you can't imagine what sort of—" He was interrupted.

Sir Archibald Walsham swept into the small bar like a giant hawk searching for unsuspecting prey. He wore a broad grin and was vibrating to say something. His sharp eyes landed upon Ian, and he moved quickly to their table, knocking into a man seated in a chair in his travels. "I do beg pardon, sir. Forgive my haste."

He towered over Ian, who was startled. "Ah, my boy, I've been looking for you. Have something you'll be interested in. I happened to find it the other day. Thought you should have it." With that he showed Ian a fine-looking dark mahogany walking stick with an ivory handle.

"This was your father's stick, lad."

"I remember it," Ian said. He seemed to recall getting whacked on the bum with it a time or two, but did not think that worth mentioning.

"He loaned it to me some years ago when I had a bout with stiff leg muscles. Somehow, I never gave it back."

In spite of his memories, Ian was taken by the gesture. He accepted the stick, saying, "Thank you so much, Sir Archibald. You were a true friend to my father. I'll cherish it."

"It's a damned beauty," Lamon observed, and the others nodded assent.

"And not only beautiful," Walsham said. With that he twisted the top and pulled out a mean looking sword hidden in the stick, itself. Ian was left holding the bottom hollow shaft, and was startled by the quick movement.

Walsham slashed the air with the blade. "I dare say this sword wouldn't take a back seat in balance to your finest fencing foil. It has a beautiful feel." Walsham returned the sword to its home.

Lamon winked at Ian. "That could come in handy, of a dark night."

Ian ignored his reference to their fight in the alley, which he had never shared outside Lamon, Elizabeth and himself. "Thank you again for such a gracious gesture, Sir Archibald. It will indeed be a fond remembrance of father."

"Think nothing of it, my boy. Must be off." He turned and swept away, out the same door he had come in.

"A b-busy man," Tasker commented. "You know I h-have the impression L-Lord Lyons is not too k-keen on him, although he is one of the wealthier B-British citizens in A … A … America."

Ian replied, "My father thought a great deal of him, and I rather like him." Ian thought, *Although his daughter is an entirely different matter.*

Chapter 24

Late May 1863, Washington

"We shouldn't be meeting like this." The dark figure in the shadows of the booth spoke in a whisper, although there was no one within hearing.

"I know, sir, but I needs yer help, sir, and that's gospel," replied the stocky bald man with thick eyebrows and no neck.

The tavern was out of the way, in a seedy part of Washington. It was dim inside, and smelled of stale everything. The two men were the only customers. The barmaid sat on a stool behind the long bar, out of earshot and judging from her whistling snores, dozing.

"I can't find fuck-all about Lincoln's movements," whispered the bald man. "He ain't the most liked President, and his security ain't the best, but I've nowhere left to go. We're movin' about bloody-well blind."

"I know, I know."

The bald man's eyes squinted. "We don't have nuthin' fer the kind of action we're planning, not by half. Killing the bastard ain't gonna be that easy. We need schedules, daily routines, routes, security around him ... all that and more.

Right now we ain't got bugger all, and I don't fuckin' like it, with all respect, sir."

The other man hissed, "Take it easy, Dodger, all in due time. The wheels are in motion, and we won't act until we're ready."

The bald man, Dodger, said nothing.

"What about the shooter?" asked the man in the booth. He was sitting back purposely, so his face was always in the shadows.

Dodger smirked. "The only part of the plan that's gone well so far. I've nipped our man. Name's Buell, and he's right as rain. A bloody great marksman, but dumb as a dirt hole. A pure zealot for the southern cause."

The man in the shadows was skeptical. "Are you certain? A lot depends on him."

"Hates Lincoln, hates the bastard, blames him for a leg wound that made him a cripple—got him kicked outta the Reb army."

The shadow man was clearly upset. "Cripple? What are you on about? How can he do the shooting if he's crippled?"

"Go easy, sir, it's a limp. Won't interfere none with what he's ta do. Besides, he won't be runnin' far or fast … just what we're wanting, I says."

"Remember, I'm holding you responsible for this selection. You know what failure means. He will not tolerate even a small failure, by either of us."

Dodger said, "It'll be sorted. I know my job, sir, but it does us no good to have a shooter without the information to act. What about the Whitworth rifle?"

"Here, in Washington. Where is this Buell?"

"Also here," said Dodger, "stashed in a hotel, standing by, eager as they come."

"Good."

"So who's this bloke we're answerin' to? This prick what pulls our strings—if I may be so bold, sir?"

There was a pause. The man in the shadows leaned forward, looked menacingly at Dodger across the table.

"You know not to ask. It isn't your concern. Do your part, I'll take care of the rest. Is that understood?"

Dodger knew he had gone too far. "Course, sir, course. Forget I asked. This here Carlyle character, he's with us?"

"Not yet. Haven't approached him with the proposition, yet. I do know he has the contacts and access to get all the information we need. I plan to broach him soon. You leave that to me, as well. I won't be giving him much choice."

"What if he says no?"

"Then you'll have to take care of it."

Dodger smiled, but it came out a leer. "Ya mean take care of him." The muscles on his thick no-neck tightened. He liked that idea.

Kally was a thug, had been all his life. He was not completely stupid—clever, manipulative, maybe even crafty, but not stupid. His way of solving a problem was to smash at it until it molded itself to his needs. He tackled everything with a heavy hand and it usually worked. He rose fast in the British army, and as a sergeant major had beat his men into submission. He beat his women as well. He liked hurting people—killing them if necessary.

Dodger Kally did not understand much of politics, nor did he much care, but he wanted to survive. He was being paid well, more than he had ever dreamed even as a sergeant major, but he wanted to be around to spend it.

The other man, who drew back into the shadows again, did not like the look on Kally's face. He depended upon Kally to do things he found distasteful, but he did not like or trust him, too far. *I'll likely have to take care of this creature too, before this is over*, he thought.

He gave Kally his orders. "I want you to take this Buell out in the woods somewhere safe, with the Whitworth, and get him used to shooting it at different ranges. When the time comes we can't afford mistakes or delays. Make certain he only knows his role in this play, but knows it well. I'll leave the weapon for you at the usual place. Understand?"

"I'll fetch it tomorrow." Kally was thinking that he had to be more careful around this man. His size or brashness did not seem to scare him at all.

The man in the shadows said, "Listen, our benefactors have information that the Federal government intends to terminate many of its Enfield contracts fairly soon; as soon as they bring their own Springfield manufacturing up to where they want it. That is something our clients in England will not accept. Apparently these Enfield contracts are too lucrative to let go. The goal is to kill Abraham Lincoln, and stir up the war before that occurs. As information comes in, we'll decide on a time and exact place, hopefully somewhere here in Washington, and sooner, rather than later."

Chapter 25

---

26 June 1863, Washington

After receiving Peter's letter, Ian asked Lord Lyons if he might return to England, claiming family reasons. "I'm afraid your personal life will have to wait, Ian. Although I have no objections, I know your people in Horse Guards will not be so obliging."

Lord Lyons was correct. When Ian wrote Major Garrison with the same vague request, the Major wrote back that his mission was of utmost importance and must be completed first.

As time passed, no one approached Ian with a letter from Peter, but during the spring of 1863, Ian's personal life at least became more interesting. He was still attending various soirees, and had made progress in his relationship with Elizabeth. Lately, when he saw her at events, they were able to talk and dance together.

The longer he knew Elizabeth, the fonder he became of her. She was constantly astonishing and delighting him with her wit and imagination. At once outrageous, clever, and seductive, she was also fun.

A battle in Chancellorsville in May, followed in early June by another at Brandy Station, caused Elizabeth to work long hours at the hospital. She was now a fully certified nurse, with all the proper documentation.

Part of the reason they certified Elizabeth so easily was her extraordinary efficiency, which made her in demand. Thus, try as he might, Ian was unable to see her as often as he would have preferred.

Ian was also moving along his assigned mission at the legation. Through contacts he had made while he was with the army in the field, and with the aid of the ever-resourceful Benjamin Tasker, he managed to acquire and send off to London a prime sample of the Spencer rifle, with a box of ammunition. Now London had both the Henry and Spencer, the two repeating rifles Ian believed were most effective.

Reports he was made privy to through Prescott's friendship indicated that the Spencer rifle was being issued to select units on a small scale. Even the Henry rifle was seeing occasional private purchase use in the field.

These reports were sketchy and did not address the effectiveness of the weapons. What Ian was lacking was observation in battle. If he could but see them in action, he could call his mission a success and return to England. Then he could sort Peter out, and get on with his life—return to the regiment.

*　　*　　*

The opportunity came one Saturday night in late June at the Willard. The Friends of the Round Robin were at their usual table, including Captain Gregory Prescott's guest, a cavalry officer none of them knew.

Slightly tipsy as usual, Prescott said in a loud voice, "Gentlemen, allow me to introduce an old classmate of mine from Harvard College, Captain Wade Dutcher, current of the cavalry. He's just recovered from wounds received in the glorious service of our sacred Union, and is about to return to the seat of war. This might be his last night in Washington."

As the self-appointed spokesman of the table, Hill Lamon said, "Greetings Wade, do please join us, we'll make your last evening a joy, and we'd be delighted to hear of your daring exploits."

"You c-can sit too, Gregory, if you really must," Tasker said light-heartedly to Prescott. They were close friends, and this challenging banter between them went on incessantly.

Prescott sat with his guest and looked blearily at his friend. "I see you haven't lost your keen wit in your old age, Tasker, or that damned stutter."

"Ho ..." said Tasker, now purposely stuttering, "I c-can s-still out t-talk you, m-my ch-chubby f-friend."

"Ouch," said Ian.

"My, my, children, we must all behave. What will Captain Dutcher think of us?" Simon Oldham offered.

Dutcher ordered an ale. The entire assemblage looked at him expectantly.

He finally got the message. "And a round for the table," he shouted to the waiter.

"Here, here," chimed Lamon, "that's the spirit. We thought you'd never ask." They all mumbled concurrence.

Dutcher said, apologetically, "I'm afraid my stories would bore you to tears. I've spent most of my time on staff. That is hardly intense fighting ... and most folks call me 'Dutch'."

Ian could well relate to staff work, and could see how uncomfortable Dutcher was in being asked to speak of his field service time. In Ian's experience this was usually the sign of a soldier who has seen too much, not too little.

"Come now, fellows," Ian cut in to save him, "let us not press the good captain—let us get ta some serious drinkin'. And I'm starving."

Later, during the meal, Prescott turned to Ian. "You're always telling me you want to see repeating rifles used first hand, Ian. Still interested?"

"Of course, Pres."

"Dutch, here, is with the 6th Michigan Cavalry, currently on the staff of Brigadier General Stahel's cavalry division. Right now we believe they are somewhere near Frederick, Maryland, heading north to engage the Confederates where they find them. This division contains the 5th and 6th Michigan Cavalry Regiments, many of whom have been armed with the Spencer rifle."

Ian's interest piqued. Oldham, seated closest, was also listening intently. Tasker was absorbed with Hill Lamon, who was, as usual, pontificating in a loud and assertive voice. This time it was on the American legal system, and its superiority to the British judicial system.

Ian was forced to shout to Dutcher above Lamon's booming. "Have you seen these repeating rifles? What they can do?"

"No, I've been here convalescing for months," replied Dutcher.

"But you say these are rifles, not carbines?"

"That's my information."

Prescott added, "My sources tell me the same thing, rifles, not carbines. I have the issue documents."

"Hmmm," Ian's mind was racing, "that's most interesting'. Just where are the Confederate forces now?"

Dutcher shrugged, Prescott was blank. Ian looked at Oldham. "If anyone knows, it should be you news types, Simon."

Oldham responded, "That's easy. We don't really know a damned thing. Reports have them all over Maryland and parts of Pennsylvania. Take your pick—Hagerstown, Chambersburg, we know they were in Carlisle about ten days ago."

"Now?" Ian asked.

Oldham leaned over and all three put their heads closer together so they could talk without yelling. "Frederick, Emmitsburg, Hanover Junction, even Pittsburgh ... throw a dart. There's a host of information, but damned little of it reliable, or, I dare say, accurate. We know pretty much that the Army of Northern Virginia, under Lee, has crossed the

Potomac, and is moving north. We know that General Hooker is maneuvering to try to cut Lee off ... but that's all for certain. The rest—pure speculation."

"Did Pres say you were returning to your command?" Ian asked Dutcher, direct.

"I finally have a release from the doctors. It's no secret there's something big brewing up north, and I'll be damned if I'll be stuck here for this fracas."

Oldham added, "You're right about that. My colleagues are all abuzz. Rumors say there's to be a shake-up in command of the Army of the Potomac—Hooker's out, and whoever replaces him will be told to move quickly to find Lee, engage him, and protect Washington."

Ian turned again to Dutcher. "How might you be planning to find your regiment?" He knew it was not all that easy, especially to pin down a rapidly moving cavalry command.

"Train to Baltimore, then another north toward Harrisburg. I'll ask questions along the way, buy a horse if necessary, but I'll find them, sure enough. They can't keep me out of this one."

"A good plan, but a loose one. Suppose I could help?" asked Ian.

"What do you mean?"

"I have sources, and there's the telegraph—we might pin down a location in their path. Then you could travel there, and simply await their arrival."

"You'd do that for me?"

"With one tiny proviso, yes."

Dutcher said nothing, waiting.

"I'm comin' with you," Ian said. "You can introduce me ta those Michigan laddies. I can then perhaps see the Spencer repeating rifles in action—report somethin' useful to Horse Guards for a change, and get home."

Dutcher was smiling, "I can do that. General Stahel, I'm sure, would be happy to help."

Ian was jubilant, "Splendid! It's settled then. When shall we leave?"

"I'd say soon, because—"

"Hold on a minute," Oldham interrupted. "You can't have all the fun, Ian. I know something's happening up north, and I need to be there, as well. My employers would sack me if I wasn't there to report, whatever it might turn out to be. I should be able to sell my stuff to New York, Washington, my own *Manchester Guardian*, and even the *London Times*. Perhaps I can skunk one on old William Russell. We've been friendly adversaries for the last few years."

"Thought he returned to England after he wrote that scathing story on the first battle around Bull Run creek," Ian put in.

"He did, but he has cronies here who send him tidbits, and he writes stories under his name, using their information. Shoddy ... shoddy, and devious, don't you think? So what say you, shall I go along, chaps?"

Dutcher said, "With all respect, sir, some of my fellow officers are not too keen on journalists, especially foreign ones."

Oldham was adamant. "They'll like me, because I'm a photographer as well. Everyone is eager to have his image preserved for posterity. Moreover, my connections through the newspapers in all the small towns from here to Harrisburg will make Ian's sources pale. How about it, am I in?" Oldham's eyes were darting from one to the other, wide and eager.

Ian looked at Dutcher. The cavalryman said, "It's fine by me, but I plan to leave in the next few days."

They settled back in their chairs. Tasker was still shouting at Lamon, who was raucously laughing, "If you d-damned lawyers weren't involved, your judicial s-system in America might actually dispense justice! I for one—"

Prescott cut Tasker off, announcing loudly, "Friends ... friends, I have news. Ian, Simon, and Captain Dutcher are embarking on a grand adventure."

Tasker said, "No d-doubt to go north to join our army in its f-fight for God and your g-glorious Union."

Having had his thunder stolen, Prescott pouted, "Well, yes, but how did you know that?"

"I can listen to more than one c-conversation at a t-time, can't I?"

Prescott, not to remain outdone, said, "I propose a toast, then. Gentlemen, raise your glasses. God speed, safe journey, and a safe return."

Chapter 26

28 June 1863, Washington

Swann would not hear of his officer going without him. Their necessaries were packed in two small valises, one for each of them. Swann purchased rail tickets for four through Baltimore, all the way to Harrisburg, just in case.

Through the efforts of Benjamin Tasker, Ian received permission from the legation for he and Swann to join the Federal army in furtherance of his assigned mission. His identification documents classified him as a neutral, with travel vouchers and sufficient funds. He was also provided safe-conduct passes, which allowed him rather broad access and passage through Federal checkpoints or patrols.

Ian carried a letter to American military authorities, introducing him as a lieutenant colonel of the Scots Fusilier Guards. It officially explained his mission to observe repeating rifles in action, and requested their assistance. Tasker had also engineered this. General Halleck signed it, himself.

"I wish you were going with us, Benjamin."

"F-fear not, I'll be there in ssspirit, if n-not in p-person."

Ian meant what he said. In the past months he had grown to value and count on Tasker's friendship and counsel, to say nothing of his amazing ability to get things done. He saw Tasker as a specter at the legation. His hand could be seen in just about every aspect of the legation's mission, yet he was nearly transparent in the way he managed to manipulate and orchestrate events without seeming to be involved himself.

"I'd rather you were there. There's still time for you ta come along."

Tasker pushed his spectacles up and said, "No, I'm n-no s-soldier. I have my duties here. His lordship couldn't s-spare me you know," he smiled. "You g-go and do what you have to do, but keep your d-damned head d-down."

Oldham, true to his word, telegraphed ahead to his newspaper contacts. According to his sources, the Federal cavalry was somewhere southeast of Frederick, Maryland, moving generally north. Their train would be more or less paralleling that movement even farther northeast.

On 28 June, at the Baltimore and Ohio Railroad Station, they boarded a train for Baltimore. Benjamin Tasker and Elizabeth were there to see them off.

Ian enjoyed traveling comfortably. He wore his blue forage cap with the diced Scottish headband, a dark blue vest, and his plain blue American-style officer's sack coat, with no rank showing. Swann wore his brown civilian coat, Dutcher his captain's uniform. Oldham's civilian attire was toned down somewhat from his usual flamboyance.

Elizabeth was not pleased by Ian's going, but somewhat understood the necessity. They found themselves a private place among the luggage carts stacked high on the platform, out of sight of the passing public. Ian looked into her eyes, and saw tears welling up.

"Lizbeth, don't be worrying about me. I can take care of myself. I'll be fine. I'm a soldier, remember?"

She looked at him sternly, thinking of Patrick. "I am going to worry, and there's nothing you can do about it … except come back." The last three words were said slowly, with great emotion.

They held each other briefly, neither wanting to let go. He kissed her tenderly on the forehead, the fire of their touch consuming them. In this frozen moment, they both realized how much they had grown to mean to each other.

Ian escorted her to the boarding area. Before he stepped up and into the rail car, he said softly, "You stay right here, where I can see you."

She was quiet, unable to form the right words.

Ian removed his right glove, kissed his own fingers, touched them to her lips, then turned and boarded the train. As the cars moved along the platform, he watched Elizabeth grow smaller and smaller. *My God, but she is beautiful*, he thought. There was an unfamiliar pain inside him. Ian brought the fingers that had touched her lips to his mouth. He could still smell her scent.

Then he turned to his comrades. "Well, we're off," he proclaimed as the train jerked out of the station.

Oldham pulled a flask from inside his coat, and four small glasses from his valise, even one for Swann. He poured a fine brandy from the flask for all. "Gentlemen, a new adventure."

Swann, although a bit taken aback at being included, joined the others. "Here, here," they shouted, then drank the brandy down.

Oldham had the most luggage. He brought his large boxy Anthony camera. The photography and developing paraphernalia were secure in wooden boxes and canvas bags in the baggage car.

One box contained the camera with lenses, another the plates. Yet another was filled with well-padded bottles of collodion, silver nitrate, and an acidic solution. The fourth contained the heavy black cloth and odd items needed to create a mobile darkroom. His clothing and other necessaries were in a small valise to hand carry. The others traveled light, with only bedrolls and valises.

The train journey was generally unpleasant—a smoke-filled car, hard seats, and a rough ride—and this was in the first class accommodations. The train halted frequently for wood and water, or for one repair reason or another. After many boring hours of playing cards, they finally arrived in Baltimore, barely in time to catch a northbound train toward Harrisburg.

This was the North Central Railroad, and its cars and tracks were a disaster. Most of the traveling was being reserved for soldiers, and it took all of Ian's documents and powers of persuasion to get them seats. In the end, it was more Simon's journalistic prowess that got them through.

After leaving Baltimore, the train was held up at Relay House, a stop where Simon went off to make further inquiries by telegraph. It was a good thing, because other than his reports from sources, everyone else seemed totally confused as to where the army was located, let alone the rapidly moving Federal cavalry. This included the military authorities.

"It's Littlestown, gentlemen," Simon explained, returning from the telegraph office. "That's our best bet to intercept. It came from a good source, who is, I understand, actually with them now. They're scattered all over from Harrisburg down to Frederick, Maryland. They're said to be converging somewhere. Littlestown is more or less in their path wherever they decide to consolidate."

"Good," Dutcher said, "We can take a train almost all the way there; at least to Westminster."

"How do you know such things?" Ian asked.

"Family builds trains. I've picked up a few things. We change here to the Western Maryland Railroad. It's a single gauge track, but adequate. Should be there in a few hours."

"With luck, we'll beat the cavalry and can merely wait for them," added Ian.

Dutcher frowned. "Not quite that easy, Ian. Westminster's still a dozen miles south of Littlestown."

"Can we wait in Westminster?"

"I wouldn't," said Simon.

"I agree," injected Dutcher. "Too far south. We could miss them. I say we go to Westminster, find horses and a buggy for Simon's equipment, then move on to Littlestown."

"No buggies," said Ian, emphatically. "We'll pair down. Rent horses, saddles, and a pack animal, somewhere. Swann!"

Swann, who had been sleeping, awoke, yawned, and asked, "Where are we, sir?"

"Almost there. We're changin' trains. When we arrive at a place called Westminster we'll need horses and saddles immediately for the four of us—oh, and at least one sturdy packhorse. Would you be kind enough ta sort that out?"

"Most certainly, sir."

The others seemed satisfied—they had a plan. By now they had complete confidence in Swann's resourcefulness; in fact, they were highly impressed, all except Ian, who was used to it.

They settled back for the bumpy, smoky ride north. Only Simon appeared apprehensive.

Ian asked, "Anythin' wrong, Simon?"

"Don't know. I should be feeling good. Russell's gone home. My way is clear with the *London Times*, and they've asked for my stories now."

"So what's botherin' you?"

"Nothing specific. There are reports, uncorroborated mind, about movements: Ewell's army somewhere around Harrisburg; more at Carlisle, Pennsylvania; Confederate cavalry at York, demanding money from citizens; Baltimore in danger; and, most disturbing, Confederate patrols seen on the road between Westminster and Littlestown."

"All unconfirmed, you say?"

"Uh, yes, but—"

Ian was amused by Simon's fears. "Well I suppose we'll find out soon enough, and we should be a mite careful, what?" He closed his eyes and was quickly fast asleep. The rocking of the train helped. Simon, wide-awake, stared out the smoke-smudged window.

Chapter 27

28 June 1863, Westminster, Maryland

"Your man, Swann, is an absolute marvel," Simon commented to Ian as they left Westminster, their horses at a casual walk.

"That he is, and you've not seen him at his best. Still worried?"

"No, whatever will happen, will happen." Simon looked back at the others. "We make quite a spectacle."

Swann found four suitable horses and saddles, and a giant draft horse with a packsaddle. There was a time when Swann did not know one end of a horse from the other. In the past years, while Ian was convalescing at Dunkairn, Swann took an interest in the Carlyle horses. He learned not only horsemanship, but how to take care of them in the field, and he became a rather good rider.

Their four saddle horses were tiny in comparison to the draft horse, and with all Simon's various boxes hanging off it, this mighty beast looked formidable. It gave the entire entourage an outlandish and eccentric facade. Dutcher summed it up, "Don Quixote ... with an entourage."

Westminster was in an uproar. Rumors were rampant that a large Rebel army was marching toward the town. The major railroad depot, the obvious target, was under guard by a small detachment of cavalry and a few infantry. Their orders were to protect it at all costs.

Ian's party rode north, away from the turmoil. It was a sunny, beautiful day. A short distance from town Ian shouted to his comrades, "It seems hard to believe we might run into hostile patrols, but best we take no chances. I assume we all carry weapons. Check them."

There was no question of Ian's leadership, even Dutcher, the only uniformed American officer deferred to him. The order was carried out without comment, as they reined to a halt on the road.

Simon perpetually carried a small, deadly Colt pocket-model pistol under his coat. Just to be safe he took this opportunity to replace the five percussion caps on the cylinder with fresh ones.

Dutcher gently patted a brace of two big Remingtons in pommel holsters, one on each side of his saddle. "I checked these a few minutes before we left. They're ready for whatever comes." He also carried a heavy enlisted cavalry saber fastened to his saddle. This was a fighting saber. He preferred it, as many officers did, to the lighter model made for officers.

Swann had a Deane-Adams revolver Ian gave him, and made lovingly certain it was capped for action. Ian checked the old Colt Navy .36 he had carried in the Crimea. He hated leaving his Henry at the Willard. It was a weapon he could count on in a tight spot, but it seemed impractical to carry with him on this trip.

The small party moved into an easy trot toward Littlestown. Ian took lead. He chose this pace because it would cover a lot of ground without tiring the horses. Swann brought up the rear with the packhorse in tow.

When they came, Swann heard them first—the pounding of several horses coming up from the direction of Westminster, behind them.

"Visitors, gentlemen!" he shouted.

They all looked back, to see ten or so horsemen coming fast, pistols drawn. Ian and Dutcher both knew these were Confederates, even though they couldn't make out their uniforms—who else would assume a group of horsemen on this quiet northern road was an enemy and attack with a purpose; and who else favored pistols over sabers?

Dutcher nodded understanding to Ian, "Let's move!" Ian bellowed.

As one, Ian's party accelerated to a gallop, their faces tight, jaws clenched. In a few seconds the horses were flying through the narrow streets of Union Mills, nostrils flared, mouths beginning to froth. Ahead was a cluster of horses and dismounted men.

Damn, thought Ian, commanding, "Ride through them!"

So they did, packhorse bringing up the rear, its reins in the outstretched right arm of Swann. He struggled to control his own mount, left hand on its reins.

They're Confederates, all right, Ian thought as they passed—noting their dust-covered uniforms, an odd mix of gray and light brown. A few of the startled Confederate cavalrymen tried to mount and join the pursuit; most were merely stunned. Several with more sense quickly pulled their carbines around on their slings and fired at least one round at Ian's fast-disappearing party.

Swann was having trouble with the overburdened packhorse. He was falling behind. He heard the shots, ducked involuntarily in his saddle, then felt a jolt as the reins of the packhorse were yanked from his grip. He tucked in his head and looked back over his right shoulder. The poor packhorse was hit somewhere vital, and stumbling. The weight shift of the onerously awkward load did the rest. Swann saw the horse go down and careen over on its back.

The pursuing horsemen pulled to a sharp halt at the fallen horse, which gave Ian's party a new lead. They were soon out of sight of their pursuers.

Ian pushed the horses for another mile before he led them to a halt in a dense clump of trees, twenty or thirty yards off the road. There was a frightening silence as they, and their horses, caught their breath. Curiosity over the fallen animal or, more likely, looting through Simon Oldham's photographic equipment had saved them.

"Sorry about that, Simon," Ian said.

"I just couldn't hold 'em, sir," Swann added, "wounded badly in that volley, he was."

"Not your fault, Swann," Simon replied. "Better it than us."

They started back on the road north at an even faster trot. Soon they arrived at Littlestown. It appeared deserted. Only one old man was shuffling along the street near the town center. He was all gray—hair, beard, plain shirt and vest, baggy coat, even his shoes were covered in gray dust.

"Where is everyone?" Dutcher asked.

"Hidin'," the old man said. "In their houses, cellars, off in the woods. Some just headed out to get away, tryin' to get 'cross the Susquehanna. Rebs came through and scared the b'Jesus outta them."

"And you?" Ian asked, with some curiousity.

"Too old to worry 'bout it. I been thinkin' our own boys'll be here soon. I guess I'll be the town greeter," he said, proudly.

"Yer a brave man," Ian said. The old man's chest puffed out.

"You the advance party of our boys?" This was directed at Dutcher, the only one of the party who actually looked the part of a Union officer.

"No," Dutcher said, "but we expect them. We're waiting for them ourselves."

The old man looked disappointed, thought a moment, then suggested, "That case, I'd wait a ways outside town, up north. Rebs might be back."

"Good advice," Ian said, and led the way, waving at the old man as he rode off.

To lessen the load on the packhorse, they had packed as much personal kit as possible on their own mounts, including their bedrolls. As it turned out, it had been an excellent idea.

They camped by a stream north of town. No fire—their supper was cold beef jerky and uncooked potatoes they brought along. The raw potatoes, sliced thin, with a bit of salt, tasted fine. They slept in shifts the night through, and spent the following morning waiting in the semi-hidden campsite.

Around noon a large patrol of Federal cavalry came from the north toward the town. Dutcher hailed them. The others remained in camp. He returned almost an hour later, jumping down from his mount like an excited child.

"Easy, Dutch," soothed Ian.

"Damn, the whole world's gone crazy," he stammered.

"So, what is it?" Simon asked.

"Hell, don't know where to start … All right … First, we're exactly in the right place, but the cavalry coming isn't the same cavalry I left a few months ago."

"What the hell does that mean?" demanded Ian, becoming impatient.

"Just what I said. All shaken up. General Meade is going to command the army. General Pleasanton has been given virtually all of the cavalry, and has reformed the entire Cavalry Corps. Stahel's out—apparently on his ear. Stahel's men have been fashioned into a 3rd Cavalry Division under a brand new Brigadier General, Judson Kilpatrick, and I imagine they're not too happy about it."

Simon had a pad out and was frantically taking notes, ever the journalist.

"It gets worse." They all waited, but Dutcher had calmed down, now savoring his news. He kneeled down by the creek, filled a tin cup, and took a long pull of water.

"Pleasanton's appointed three new generals, brigade commanders for Kilpatrick's spanking new division—Elon Farnsworth, George Custer, and Wesley Merritt. Brand spankin' new"

Ian was caught off guard. "What? I know who they are, but they're junior officers."

Dutcher continued, "They were! Hell, Farnsworth and Merritt were captains, and last I heard Custer was only a first

185

lieutenant … but it seems true. They are now all brigadier generals of volunteers. He's consolidated the Michigan regiments in one brigade, the second brigade, under Custer."

There was a long silence as they soaked it in. Not much would change, except for Dutcher, who was now out of a staff job. Simon would always have news he could report, and Ian could still observe the Michigan cavalrymen with the Spencers.

Ian asked, "Who, exactly, is coming through here?"

Dutcher replied, "Well, I guess that's the only good news for me. The entire 3rd Division is converging on this very town. Should be here in a matter of hours."

Chapter 28

Throughout the afternoon and evening of Monday, 29 June, scattered elements of the newly constituted 3rd Cavalry Division arrived in Littlestown. As Federal horse soldiers began to appear in considerable numbers, the townsfolk emerged, slowly at first, not sure it was safe, then in relieved welcome. The 3rd Division began setting up camps around the small town, mostly to the north.

Ian's party moved into town and found accommodations at the Union Hotel. By late evening, refugees began streaming into Littlestown, having fled Westminster. One obviously wealthy merchant came into the hotel lobby excited and distraught. "It was awful. The two Delaware cavalry companies and a few New York infantrymen guarding the railway depot took on Stuart's whole cavalry. Damnedest thing I've ever seen."

"What happened," he was asked.

"They were outnumbered and outgunned. Poor bastards were run over almost before it began."

There were shouts, "Where's Stuart now?" "Are they coming here?"

Overwhelmed, the man answered as best he could, as they crowded him into a corner of the lobby. "Hell, I don know. All I know's when I left, Stuart was prancing around the town square like he owned the damned place, and I guess he did." The refugees also passed on the news that days ago the Rebels had captured an enormous Federal supply train, over a hundred wagons, in Rockville, Maryland.

Simon disappeared, apparently off to gather as much information as possible, and send telegrams to his various journalistic employers. Ian, Dutcher, and Swann, stayed close by the hotel.

Around midnight, Brigadier General Judson Kilpatrick and his staff came in a cloud of dust. He established his headquarters in the same Union Hotel where Ian's party was staying, using the lobby and two or three rooms on the second floor. Officers tramped up and down the stairs all night, talking in rapid, hushed voices. The air was tense with the urgency of impending conflict.

Dutcher heard that the 5th and 6th Michigan were camped north of town. Before leaving to report for duty to the 6th, Dutcher introduced Ian to General Kilpatrick. "Sir, I'd like you to meet Lieutenant Colonel Ian Carlyle, of Her Majesty's forces. Here to observe our army."

Ian came to attention, "Sir."

The first two things Ian noticed were Kilpatrick's rather sizeable beak-like nose and his bushy sideboards, which seemed to curl back up from his cheeks to form a sparse mustache. His hair was straight and stringy, pointing to a soiled white shirt, cravat, and open dark blue vest. His thigh-high boots made him look every inch a cavalry officer, even in his shirtsleeves. A double-breasted frock coat and rakish brimmed hat hung off a chair behind him. Each shoulder of the coat, and the hat, bore a crude single brigadier's star—*No frills*, thought Ian.

"Delighted," Kilpatrick said. "I don't mean to be rude, Colonel, but I'm extremely busy right now. What exactly can I do for you?"

"This should explain my purpose," Ian said, handing the general a leather pouch containing his letter of introduction and other documents regarding his mission. "You may be certain, sir, I won't be a bother."

As Kilpatrick read through them, two senior officers entered the small room he was using as an office. They looked worn, the shorter one was slapping a layer of dust from his coat with a soft slouch hat.

Kilpatrick looked up from his reading, "Good. Now we can get moving. Uh ... Colonel, these are two of my brigade commanders, Generals Farnsworth and Custer."

There were nods of recognition and handshakes. Elon Farnsworth was young. He wore a shell jacket with a velvet collar. His new-looking one-star shoulder boards were trimmed on the edges with excessively ornate gilt. George Custer looked even younger, although a thick mustache made an effort to give him maturity. He was hatless, because his hat was covered in the dust he had been brushing off. This made his curly, fair, shoulder-length hair stand out. He wore an officer's sack coat, rather tailored, with a somewhat makeshift general's star sewn on each corner of the collar of a light blue shirt pulled out over the coat collar. Ian thought he saw a red scarf, but it was hard to tell under the dust.

Kilpatrick, facing Ian, said firmly, "Allow me a word with them, Colonel, then I'll get back with you."

"Of course, sir." Ian left the room with Dutcher trailing behind.

"There you have it," Dutcher said, once the office door was closed. "Custer's my new commander. Kind of eccentric, aye?"

"Sometimes they make the best soldiers, and leaders," Ian offered.

"We'll see. You'll likely be assigned to ride with his brigade. Perhaps you and I will see each other down the road. I'm off to report to Colonel Gray of the 6th. You're on your own from here, Ian. Best of luck."

"And to you, Dutch, take care. We'll meet again." Dutcher left the hotel, while Ian waited.

Soon, the door to Kilpatrick's temporary office opened and Farnsworth came out. Kilpatrick called, "Colonel Carlyle, do come in, and close the door."

He turned his head toward Custer. "George?"

Custer took his cue. "Repeating rifles, Colonel?"

"Yes, sir. I'd like to report on their effectiveness; it'll go a long way to help our ordnance lads make decisions for our own army."

"Hmmm. I see. All of the 5th Michigan, and some companies of the 6th have been issued Spencers, but we'll be leaving first light tomorrow heading north. Can one of Her Majesty's finest handle that, Colonel, first light?" Custer asked this rather playfully.

"Och, I'll make every effort, sir," Ian replied casually, accepting the slur and moving on.

"You two work it out," Kilpatrick ordered. "Carlyle, keep your head down and stay in the rear. I think tomorrow we'll meet the Reb head-on." He handed Ian's document case to Custer.

Ian and Custer left the room. Custer cleared his throat, looked at Ian, his bright blue eyes piercing. "Report at dawn to Colonel Russell Alger. He commands the 5th. I'll have explained your mission to him by that time."

"My thanks, General Custer. I do appreciate the courtesy."

Custer nodded. "Just stay out of his way." They walked out of the hotel together. In the entrance, Ian saluted as Custer mounted and rode off.

Ian returned to his room to think about the coming day. Sleep impossible, it was past two in the morning when Ian rousted Swann to get their kit together. He wanted them ready before the dawn reporting time.

"May I ask, sir, are we observing the action, or will we be in the uh—shite—sir?"

Swann's guarded concern over his officer's past lack of caution was not lost on Ian. "Swann, lad, you know I always strive ta observe from afar, but often one just can't see that

190

well from the rear. You have my permission, though, ta remain there if I choose ta advance."

"Humph. Right as rain, sir. You already know where I'll be, sir, watching your arse, as usual."

"And thankful I am, as always. I do appreciate your concern, Swann, and I promise ta be careful."

Swann busied himself cleaning his revolver—just in case.

They reported to the camp of the 5th Michigan around four. Colonel Alger, a young, but highly competent officer with well-trimmed black hair and beard, explained to Ian, "The 5th and 6th are to remain behind in Littlestown for a few hours after the division moves north. We'll patrol all around the town to protect their rear."

Colonel George Gray, a plain man with full beard and short-cropped hair was with Alger. He was introduced as commanding the 6th Michigan. Gray said, "General Kilpatrick told us what you're interested in."

Alger added, "He showed us your papers." Alger took out the leather-bound document pouch, returning it to Ian.

Ian accepted the pouch, nodding his thanks.

Alger said, "You won't be disappointed in the performance of our Spencers. They're a wonderous thing to see."

"This is an opportunity I've long anticipated. I have one man with me, hope you don't mind."

"Not at all," Alger assured him. "Now, let me see where to put you."

"Russell," Gray injected, "may I suggest?"

"Of course, George."

"I'm sending my most experienced company on patrol south. They're to locate the Reb cavalry we suspect are around Union Mills, and report directly to Kilpatrick as soon as possible. It's Captain Thompson. His men all have Spencer rifles ... and know how to use them."

Ian offered, "I rather know that area, Colonel. Rode through it recently."

"That could be damned helpful," Gray said.

"Good idea," Alger added. "Colonel, you go with Thompson's Company A? Should be enlightening. He's a fine man."

Chapter 29

---

30 June 1863, Littlestown, Pennsylvania

Captain Henry Thompson was a trim, compact man in his early twenties; an experienced soldier. His only other officer, 2nd Lieutenant Stephen Ballard, was as green as they come, but rapidly approaching maturity the hard way. They were pleased to have Ian and Swann along, especially because they were familiar with the road and Union Mills. Ian did not mention the mad dash they had made through the small town.

After meeting Thompson and Ballard, Ian watched Kilpatrick lead his two brigades north on Hanover Road. First to set out was the 1st and 7th Michigan of Custer's Brigade, with him at its head. They were followed by Battery M, 2nd US Artillery. Finally, Farnsworth's Brigade, composed of regiments from Vermont, West Virginia, New York, and Pennsylvania, with another battery of regular artillery. The day was turning warm and bright. A slight breeze stirred dust whorls on the road.

Around nine in the morning, after patrolling the town and its immediate surroundings, Gray left Littlestown with the 6th Michigan. He followed the route of the division toward

Hanover. About the same time, Captain Thompson's A Company advanced south toward Union Mills, with Ian and Swann tagging along. They were only about seventy-five cavalrymen, but were experienced, well-mounted, rested, and each man carried a Spencer rifle.

Lieutenant Ballard, perhaps the youngest looking baby-faced officer Ian had encountered in America, spent the ride south from Littlestown extolling the virtues of the Spencer. Ian listened carefully. Swann, riding close behind, felt nervous moving in the opposite direction from the rest of the division, especially knowing Winchester had been taken, and thinking about what they had run into only two nights before.

He inquired in a low voice, "Sir, in'it a mite dodgy separating from the main troops? We're bloody lonely 'ere."

Ian either didn't hear, or was ignoring him. Swann said nothing further.

Captain Thompson sported a long heavy beard, which made him look older. He was the kind of man one liked immediately, with an affable way that made him not only good-natured, but a good officer. Ian knew leadership. He had seen the good and the bad. He noticed quickly that Thompson's men would follow him through fire. Despite his early years, he was their father image.

"How soon before we reach Union Mills, sir?" Thompson inquired of Ian. He removed his forage cap, and scratched his thick, longish dark hair. This was a gesture Ian would learn was characteristic of Thompson when thinking. When not scratching his head, the young captain unconsciously stroked his beard down to a point, even as he rode along.

"Not far. Two days ago the Confederates were staying to the roads, so yer advance party should be the first ta see danger, if they're still there."

Though they could see no visible signs of the enemy, they certainly knew they had been there. The closer A Company rode toward Union Mills the more they encountered indications that a large body of Confederate cavalry was heading north behind their 3rd Division. There were tracks in the mud of hundreds of horses, and they found occasional pieces of discarded clothing and equipment.

The company entered Union Mills and spoke to several citizens, confirming the evidence they saw. A man, apparently a town official, told them, "You be careful, hear. They're mostly to the east, movin' toward Hanover."

"Thank you, sir," Lieutenant Ballard said.

There was a commotion from behind. An enlisted courier came up at a gallop. He shouted, "Looking for Captain Thompson!"

"Here," Thompson yelled.

The rider explained, as he handed a paper to Thompson. "Orders, sir. You're to return to Littlestown at once."

"Thank you, soldier," Thompson said. The courier saluted, turned his horse, and galloped off.

Thompson muttered, "That's odd. You heard him, gentlemen, back the way we came." Thompson reversed his horse, and headed north. His men did the same without command.

Thompson leaned over to Ballard, "Good thing, actually, we need to get the information to the colonel quickly, about the Rebs in rear of 3rd Division."

As he spoke, Confederate cavalry appeared on the road to their front, blocking the way to Littlestown. Again without command, Thompson's men unslung their Spencers, still mounted. They spread out, and exchanged fire with the startled Rebels.

It was no contest between the repeating rifles and the Rebels' single shot, mostly muzzle-loading carbines. The fire Company A laid down even astonished Ian. Although the Rebels had seriously superior numbers, they soon fled to the east, across the fields and away from the sting of Company A. There were no casualties.

"Now you see why we love these rifles," Ballard exclaimed to Ian.

"I'm beginnin' ta get the idea."

It was shortly after noon when Company A arrived back in Littlestown. Thompson was ordered to report to Colonel

Alger, commanding the 5th Michigan, because Gray's 6th was already well on its way north, behind the rest of the division. Colonel Alger's horse soldiers were just coming in from their various patrols.

Ian and Thompson rode to him. "Captain Thompson reporting from a scout to the town of Union Mills. Sir, there's signs of—"

"I know, I know, Thompson, but thank you for your efforts. We've seen the signs ourselves, all over the place. One hell of a lot of Rebs—and they're moving north right up the ass of young Kilpatrick."

As if to punch the point home, the distinct sound of cannon fire came from the north. "Gentlemen, Farnsworth's Brigade must have overtaken the Rebs, probably in Hanover, itself, or on the way."

Alger looked at his adjutant. "Mount the regiment. We're moving to the sound of the guns. Thompson, you'll attach yourselves to us for now. Bring up our rear with your company. Watch yourself back there."

"Yes, sir." Thompson turned and rode back to his waiting cavalrymen.

"Mind if I ride with you, sir?" Ian asked Alger.

"Come along, but it may get hot."

"I was feeling a bit chilled anyway," Ian beamed back. He looked at the regiment forming on the road. Over six hundred Spencer rifles. Now he would find out for certain. There was only a fleeting thought running through his mind that he was getting a bit far away from merely observing, as he rode at the head of the column next to their commanding officer.

"You hear those big guns, sir," Swann asked from just behind him. He referred to the cannons they could clearly hear, now even closer. It appeared the 6th had engaged the enemy on the Littlestown-Hanover Road, not far ahead.

Ian remained deep in thought.

Swann merely shook his head in exasperation. *Here we go again ...*

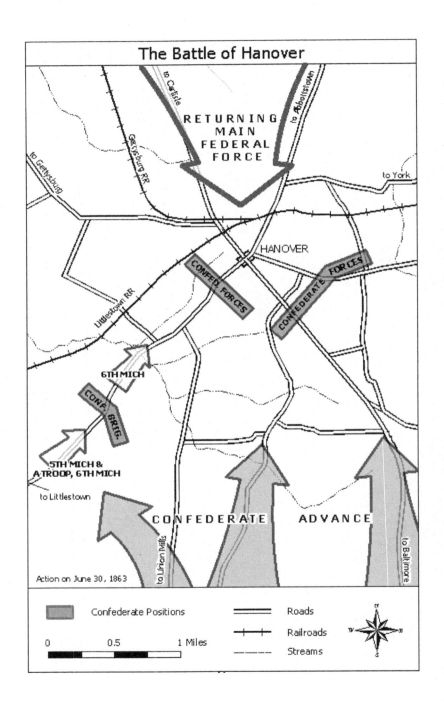

The Battle of Hanover

to Carlisle
to Abbottstown

RETURNING
MAIN
FEDERAL
FORCE

Gettysburg RR

to Gettysburg

to York

HANOVER

CONFED. FORCES

CONFEDERATE FORCES

Littlestown RR

6TH MICH

CONF. BRIG.

5TH MICH &
A TROOP, 6TH MICH

to Littlestown

CONFEDERATE   ADVANCE

to Union Mills

to Baltimore

Action on June 30, 1863

Confederate Positions   Roads

Railroads

0   0.5   1 Miles   Streams

N
W   E
S

Chapter 30

---

30 June 1863, on the road north of Littlestown and south of Hanover, Pennsylvania

"They caught us on the right flank, hard," Captain Wade Dutcher reported, breathless, sweat dripping from his chin. "We fell back, then stopped three charges from the bastards."

"Are you wounded, Dutch?" Ian asked. Dutcher's horse had what could have been a bullet hole in his chest, and was bleeding from the flank as well. Dutcher was covered in blood.

"Where's the rest of the division?" Colonel Alger demanded—impatient.

"Fighting up in Hanover, in the streets, I'd guess, sir. Too many Rebs between them and us to know for certain. Colonel Gray's trying to circle west around them with the 6th so he can join the division. He left about a half hour ago." He turned to Ian. "I'm fine, Ian, not my blood. The two men with me were both shot out of the saddle getting through. Tried to help one stay mounted. No use. It's his blood."

Alger looked puzzled. "What in hell's all that firing on the road ahead if the 6th Michigan is gone?"

"Gray left Major Weber and two companies to hold off the Rebs. He knew if they tried to disengage without covering fire, the 6th would be slaughtered."

"Smart move," Alger said. The road in front of Alger's column looked clear. "What exactly's up ahead, Captain?"

"The bunch we ran into, sir, was an entire Reb brigade, mostly Virginia boys, blocking the road between us and the town. From a couple of prisoners we found out it was Rooney Lee's old brigade, commanded by General Chambliss. Real fighters, those Virginians."

Alger was worried. He wanted to know what was right in front of him, between him and Weber's two companies. "How'd you get to us, Captain? What's up there, right there?" He nodded toward the road ahead.

"By the time the Colonel sent me back to warn you, the road behind us was full of Rebs. No idea how many. We veered right off into the woods, at a full gallop, and came around them—west of the road. Still ran into heavy patrols, but their horses weren't as fresh as ours."

It was already approaching late afternoon. "Get the regiment moving," Alger barked.

The adjutant nervously shouted orders and the column began advancing, slow and steady at first, like a giant caterpillar, then quickly picking up to a fast trot. Ian knew what Alger was thinking. He must relieve Weber, and, more important, try to place himself between the Rebel cavalry and the division.

As they advanced, these plans came to a screaming halt. Blocking the road north was a strong Confederate force. Ian estimated it was two, maybe three regiments of cavalry. More regiments were advancing toward them across the fields east of the road on their right flank.

Alger knew that if Rooney Lee's old brigade was up toward Hanover in force, then these Confederates moving at him were an entirely different brigade. This was a trap, whether planned or not.

Hell, we're cut off, he thought. *We can't get to Weber, and we'll be hard pressed to even get to the division before nightfall.*

Alger did not hesitate. "Draw sabers! At the walk … march." He rapidly brought the 5th Michigan from a walk straight to a no-nonsense galloping charge at the Rebels to the front. The Rebels' disbelieving expressions were plainly visible. They were used to a more timid Federal cavalry.

"They're falling back!" bellowed Alger. Ian saw it as well, but there was still a major threat advancing rapidly on their right flank. There were too many to break through.

Alger had to deploy, and quickly if he was to avoid disaster. "Halt! Get these men in ranks!" The charge had somewhat broken up the formation, but it was not difficult to reform, not for these veterans.

Alger needed to make some time, slow down the action. "First Squadron, as skirmishers, advance!" The First Squadron of two companies instantly advanced, spreading quickly into a skirmish line covering the road ahead, and around to the right in a half circle, to screen the regiment from the Rebels advancing on their right flank.

The skirmishers remained mounted. Their company commanders ordered, "Firing by sections, at the halt, commence fire!" Ian sat his mount next to Colonel Alger and Captain Dutcher. He was again shocked when he heard the volume of fire coming immediately from the skirmish line. The firing did not sound like a squadron of two companies. It sounded like at least a regiment.

"Now that's something," Dutcher said. Ian was caught speechless, even the stoic Swann's eyes blinked wide open.

While the skirmishers were deploying, Alger was stabilizing a strong line to their rear. "Second, Third, and Fourth Squadrons, front into line … march!" Like a machine, the three squadrons obeyed the order, chivvying their men and horses on line in a large semi-circle from the road ahead, out into the fields on their right. Sporadic fire from Rebel skirmishers was having little effect.

The Colonel shouted, "Fifth Squadron will remain with me in reserve."

Colonel Alger was going to use his edge with the repeating rifles to best advantage, fighting with his regiment dismounted. He commanded, "Prepare to fight on foot! Horses to the rear!"

The cavalrymen moved quickly. Their most experienced horseman, one man in every four, remained mounted. He held the mounts of the three horse soldiers who unslung their Spencers and formed a line about eight yards forward.

Company commanders were echoing the order, "Horses to the rear!" There was a welcome dip in the ground not far back, on the east side of the road. The horse-holders quickly moved the mounts into it, out of the line of fire.

The heavy fire from the Federal skirmish line forced the Rebels back, but not too far. They established a hasty line to reorganize for an attack, just out of range.

Colonel Alger then addressed Ian, "Colonel, would you mind finding Captain Thompson. Please ask him to move farther south and continue to protect our rear."

"Of course not, sir, whatever you need."

"... and I'd rather you remained with Thompson, Carlyle. I won't have to worry about you, and it wouldn't do any harm to have a steady hand back there. If I were them, I'd be trying our flanks first, then hit our rear."

Ian gave no argument. "As you wish, Colonel." He rode south. Swann, as ever not far behind, was relieved.

Ian found Thompson and Ballard on a small ridge. It gave them an excellent view of the fight brewing to the north and east before their eyes.

Ian said, "Captain Thompson, Colonel Alger's compliments. Would ya move yer company south on the road and continue ta cover the rear. He's worried that as thin as his line is, the Rebels will try ta come round. He's probably correct."

Captain Thompson understood, but was reluctant to change positions. He liked his view of the possibilities from right where he was. "Ballard, take the company a few hundred yards south. Stay on the road. Leave one man with me. If you're engaged, fight on foot, hold until I get there. Understood?"

Ballard smiled. "Yes, sir. We'll hold." He hesitated. They had become friends in the caldron of combat. "You be careful, Henry, you make an inviting target on this skyline."

Thompson smiled back. "Don't worry, Stephen. You too." Ballard led the company south, at a walk.

From their vantage point Ian, Thompson, and Swann, saw the mounted skirmishers soon drawn in. They came through the center of the dismounted squadrons, now ready and waiting. The skirmish squadron moved to reinforce the reserve squadron. Ian and Thompson watched the action with approval as the 5th, facing superior numbers, held off repeated assaults.

The Rebels brought up a battery of four Napoleon 12-pounders on their own left flank, and swept solid shot and shell back and forth across the entire Federal line. None of it reached the ridge where they were gathered.

The Confederates attacking the 5th must have thought it would be easy pickings, a brigade against a lone regiment. They did not know about the Spencers. Most of their cavalrymen still carried muzzle-loading carbines.

The day wore on and darkness was approaching. Each time the Rebels assaulted, they were beaten back. The field to the front of the 5th was littered with dead and wounded horses and men. Riderless horses stood with heads bowed, munching on grass—waiting—or ran about, frantically trying to flee the terror of the battle. Confederate dead and wounded, even those who had simply been unhorsed, were strewn over the fields.

Thompson casually observed, "Appears they've decided to try rolling up our flanks." He referred to several Rebel squadrons they could see heading behind the Rebel lines toward the Federal left flank.

Ian smiled. "They must be tired of butting heads with those damnable repeaters."

As he bent around in his saddle, Ian lifted his telescope to see the Rebel force riding at a fast pace, well around the Federal left, west of the road. Colonel Alger must have seen it as well, because he immediately reacted by refusing his left, curving his A Company around to meet the coming onslaught. It was too weak, and he sent a squadron of the reserve to strengthen the line. When the Rebels struck, there ensued fierce mounted fighting—saber to saber.

Ian watched this action. Swann leaned over and tugged on his sleeve. "Sir, look to yer right."

Ian swung right and saw two Rebel squadrons coming around the Federal right flank, springing from thick woods in a swift and determined mounted charge. There was no time to refuse this flank. The Rebel horsemen were on them instantly. Alger did the only thing he could. He sent the other reserve squadron to plunge into the fray, and hold the flank.

Thompson shouted, "I don't like the way this is shaping up, damn it. There go our last reserves."

Ian was closer to this desperate and bloody fight than the one on the left flank. He needed no telescope to see horses ramming into each other, men trying to stay mounted, trying to stay alive, others falling from saddles to be mangled and crushed to pulp by the hooves of their own horses. He heard the sound of swords clashing, the commands of officers and sergeants screaming at their men, and above it all, the blood-chilling yells from the thrashing Rebel cavalrymen. *God, they fight like demons.*

There was now a major assault boiling all along the line. For long minutes the battle teetered between the two sides and the outcome was by no means certain. Soon, however, the concentrated fire of the repeating rifles began shifting the odds. Slowly, the Confederate center began to withdraw. Then the unthinkable happened.

A fair distance, perhaps a mile away from Ian and Thompson, in the rear of the Federal left flank, at least four squadrons, possibly an entire regiment, of Rebel cavalry appeared out of nowhere. Apparently they could not see the fighting from their position, and were cautiously advancing in a narrow column of companies.

"Damn!" Thompson hissed at Ian. "That tears it. If those bastards hit our left from behind, they'll roll us up like a piece of bread dough."

Captain Wade Dutcher was galloping toward them. He skidded to a halt, pointing at the Rebel formation.

Ian shouted, "We see it, Dutch."

"Alger says you gotta stop 'em, Thompson." He was having trouble controlling his skittish mount.

"Hell," Thompson said, "I only make it four, maybe five hundred, and me with, what, seventy, seventy-five ... four or five to one. A walk in the damned park on a Sunday afternoon."

"He'll send reinforcements when he can."

Thompson's reply was caustic. "Why do those words 'when he can' make my stomach crawl?"

He turned to the horseman standing by. "You, get your ass down to Ballard. You see where we're going?" He pointed toward the Rebel formation, which had come to a complete halt. "The jaws of hell!"

"Yes, sir," the soldier replied. "I see it."

"You tell Ballard to follow us, at the gallop!" He twisted in his saddle. "You coming Carlyle?"

"Och, I wouldn't miss it fer all the lassies in Glasgow."

Swann was behind his officer. Under his breath he cursed, "Shite!"

Dutcher shouted, "I'm coming too."

They galloped across the fields to a place between the Rebel cavalry formation and the left flank of their Federal line. Thompson placed Dutcher where he wanted his right. Moving swiftly he put Ian, with Swann at his side, where he thought the left would fall. Ballard brought the company up on line in short order. He was a good lad. He saw immediately what had to be done, and ordered, "Company ... Prepare to fight on foot!"

The line of Spencer rifles was quickly set. "Horses to the rear—get them back and under cover as best you can, boys

... Now—steady ..." Ballard remained mounted, but drew his revolver.

They had been seen getting in position, and the Rebel cavalry formation was deploying as it rapidly advanced. Thompson had selected a good position, on a slight rise in some scrub, with a narrow farmer's field in front, fences and thick woods all around. It would make it difficult for the Rebels to deploy their superior numbers and overwhelm his small company.

He spread his men into a long skirmish line to broaden their front. With the odds he was facing, Thompson was depending upon one factor to save them—the power of sustained, accurate, and rapid fire.

"Here they come!" someone cried. There was no faltering. They were cocky. Figured this was a mere company of Yankee cavalry, who would likely skedaddle before they reached them, as they had done many times in the past. They came in a column of squadrons, two companies in each squadron; and covered the width of the field in front of the Federals. In depth, there was a fair distance between squadrons to allow the first squadron to engage and penetrate the enemy line before the second squadron hit.

The Rebels knew their business. They were precise in moving from a walk to a trot to a canter, and finally to a full gallop in the charge, bugles blaring. Unfortunately, from the canter on, they were moving up a rather steep hill to Thompson's well-chosen position.

Thompson did not need to hold his fire. The Spencer rifles were accurate at a range far beyond the length of the field to their front. He ordered volleys, one after another, in quick succession, so much faster than muzzle-loaders could have been reloaded. His fire ripped the first squadron apart, horses and men tumbled, fell, jammed up those behind, and whittled down the ferocity of the charge as each second went by.

The Confederate bugles sounded the charge, and Ian heard Thompson say, "Have them commence firing at will, Mr. Ballard." Ballard jumped off his horse in one motion, revolver in hand. He and several sergeants moved down behind the line, shouting the order.

The first Rebel squadron proved almost non-existent by the time it struck Thompson's line, and did very little damage. The second squadron was slowed, and nearly halted short of the line, about half way up the hill. The momentum was gone. The horsemen turned back, and collided with the squadron to their rear. This caused a general melee of disorganized horses, as the Rebel cavalrymen withdrew beyond the far ridge to regroup.

Thompson's company withstood three more such attacks in a similar manner. Their position on the military crest among the scrub bushes was sufficient to limit casualties, but each time, the Rebels seemed to get closer in before the attack lost momentum and they withdrew. As darkness fell, they tried a last charge.

Both Ian and Swann had recovered Spencer rifles from wounded cavalrymen, and plugged themselves in with the rest of the A Company soldiers, firing at the charging Rebels. Ian was pleased at how quickly the rifle reloaded seven cartridges in the pre-loaded tubes they carried.

This time the Rebel charge was a bit different. Its strength focused on the left of the company's line, where Dutcher had joined Ian and Swann. The first charging squadron actually reached the crest. It did not disintegrate like the ones before, possibly because the semi-darkness foiled the aim of the Federal cavalrymen.

Ian never realized how huge a horse could look until that moment, when he saw the silhouette of a horse and rider coming over the scrub bushes and down on top of him. He staggered back, as did Dutcher and Swann.

Dutcher had his sword in one hand and a pistol in the other. Swann had his Spencer reversed, and was swinging it like a long club at a Rebel closing on horseback. Ian's rifle was freshly loaded. He fired at the silhouettes, horses and men in rapid succession until his rifle was empty.

Some of the Rebels had dismounted or been unhorsed, because there were three of them coming toward him on foot. Ian tried to grab the rifle by its barrel, as Swann had done, but the exposed metal of the upper part was scalding hot.

Dutcher ran forward directly at one of them, pushed the Rebel's carbine aside, and brought his saber down, severing his neck. The blow carried the blade into the man's shoulder and chest at least six inches, but then it would not come out.

Dutcher was tugging at the blade. Another of the Rebels, a big man with long, flowing black hair and two enormous revolvers, turned and moved in behind Dutcher, only a foot away.

"Dutch!" Ian screamed—too late. The Rebel fired both pistols. The shots exploded into Dutcher's back, propelling him forward and down on his face. Ian could see the massive holes surrounded by black smoking powder stains, and knew Dutcher was dead.

Swann swung his rifle, turned club, in a wide circle, catching the Rebel who had killed Dutcher full in the back of his skull. There was a thud, and a loud snap. The man crumpled to the ground.

There was only one Rebel left. He belonged to Ian, who saw in the man a look of pure hatred. Ian had his rifle turned around again and held across his chest. His finger was on the trigger, but the rifle was empty. The Rebel swung his saber down at Ian, who lifted his rifle and barely blocked the blow. The blade narrowly missed slicing the fingers off Ian's left hand. Wood chips from where the blade connected with the stock bit into his face and eyes, causing him to flinch back.

Out of pure instinct, half blinded, Ian brought the rifle's butt up with all the strength he could manage. It landed in the Rebel's groin. The man gave a high-pitched scream and went down. Ian felt no compassion as he lifted the rifle and smashed the butt into the man's nose. There was a loud crunch. The skull unexpectedly came apart, the rifle butt sinking into what had been his face. There was no need for a second blow.

It dawned on Ian that this time he was in complete control of his actions, not as it had been in the trench in the Crimea.

This was different—a deliberate, calculated move. For good or bad, he was crystal clear about this. It was a question of simple survival. He was a soldier, and killing before someone killed him, was part of it.

Something else crossed Ian's mind, as he became aware that he had callously taken a life without remorse, and now stood among a pile of torn, bleeding bodies, listening to the groans of the wounded. At first he couldn't put his finger on it. Then the realization came to him—the leopard did not appear at this battle. Ian had not called him forth, nor had he come on his own. He smiled to himself.

"Hot work, sir," Swann said as he casually tossed aside his Spencer.

"Hot work," echoed Ian, discarding his own rifle on top of the body of the Rebel he had killed.

The Confederates had enough. They withdrew into the darkness. Later, Thompson sent a patrol, who reported back that they had left the field.

Alger was apologetic. "There just weren't enough of us. It was in doubt 'til the end, when they withdrew. I had no one to send to you. You did magnificent work, Thompson. I'm in your debt."

"Thank you, sir ... my men did the work." He was genuinely proud of them.

Ian remained with Colonel Alger after the fight while he spent a few hours reorganizing the regiment. The casualties were light, and a blanket of coal-black night hid the carnage of the battle.

The road having been cleared of Rebels, the 5th Michigan finally entered Hanover for a few hours of deserved rest. "With yer permission, Colonel, I'll spend the evenin' with Captain Thompson and his lads." Ian had grown very fond of A Company.

"Of course, Colonel, thanks for your help today."

"I assure you, sir, it was my pleasure."

Captain Thompson had already found his regiment, the 6th, and reported to Colonel Gray. With enthusiasm the members of Company A, having now fought alongside these two strange British folks, welcomed Ian and Swann to their camp. They spent the evening recounting the day's adventures around bright crackling fires.

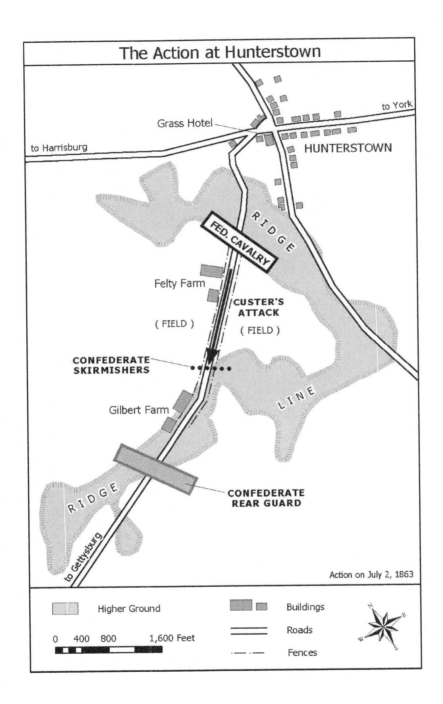

The Action at Hunterstown

to York

Grass Hotel

to Harrisburg

HUNTERSTOWN

R I D G E

FED. CAVALRY

Felty Farm

CUSTER'S
ATTACK

(FIELD)

(FIELD)

CONFEDERATE
SKIRMISHERS

L I N E

Gilbert Farm

CONFEDERATE
REAR GUARD

R I D G E

to Gettysburg

Action on July 2, 1863

Higher Ground

Buildings

0 400 800 1,600 Feet

Roads

Fences

Chapter 31

2 July 1863, Hunterstown, Pennsylvania

"What is this place?" Swann asked an 18th Pennsylvania horseman riding next to him. Swann took his feet out of the stirrups and stretched his legs, allowing them to dangle loose along the horse's sides. He had been cramped up most of the day.

"Far as I know, we're in the great Commonwealth of Pennsylvania, but can't swear to it. Not from hereabouts."

For two days Kilpatrick had been trying unsuccessfully to find Stuart's cavalry. Thus, Ian and Swann passed two uncomfortable nights in the field with no shelter, reminding them of other such nights and battles, in another time and another country. Most of the day before, they had heard the distant rolling thunder of cannon.

By late afternoon they were in a village, passing through a small town square with a two-story hotel on their left. The sign read: *J. L. Grass Hotel.* Kilpatrick's lead elements had already driven Rebel skirmishers out of the village. The rumbling of cannon fire to the south and west pointed to a major battle waging somewhere fairly close.

The 6th Michigan led the whole division. Ian rode with Colonel Gray behind the advance guard. Swann was far back in the column, passing the Pennsylvania regiment, working his way forward.

A short distance past the hotel, Gray, according to his orders from Custer, had his regiment turn left heading south on the Gettysburg-Hunterstown Road, toward the town of Gettysburg. They advanced slowly, halting at a ridge to clear a woods. A few hundred yards south on the west side of the road was a small farm with a brick two-story house and a barn.

Ian said to Colonel Gray, "That's a fine farm. Shame ta destroy it."

Gray replied, "I agree. My map says it's the Felty farm, but I don't see a family anywhere."

He called to his adjutant, "Lieutenant, let's see if we can do as little damage as possible to this farm, and the farmer's fields."

"Yes, sir."

Beyond the farm, fields of wheat and corn swayed in the brilliant afternoon sun, like ocean waves pounding an imaginary shore. At the far end of those fields, no more than a quarter-mile, another two-story farmhouse sat with yet another rise in the land beyond it. Ian, looking through his telescope, spotted Confederate horsemen in the road, and dismounted men around the second farm.

He was not the only one to see them. Their movements were visible to General Custer, Colonel Gray, and their staffs. Gray wisely strengthened his skirmish line at the Felty farm and on both sides of the road, facing the Rebels.

"Who do you suppose they are?" Ian asked Gray, pretty much knowing the answer.

"Rebs marching south to the battle—to the guns. Likely that's their rear guard, maybe only a company in sight, but can't tell what's over that ridge or in the woods on the flanks. They're getting set to hold us up and protect their main force."

"What will you do now?"

"Just like always, Colonel Carlyle, sit tight and await orders."

It was not long before General Custer, himself, rode up to Colonel Gray. His excitement showed, but his voice was calm and he was direct in his orders, "Get your men deployed. Use the farm buildings, but I want at least two companies off to the side, able to cover this road."

"Yes, sir," Gray replied.

Gray and his adjutant turned their horses and began barking orders.

Custer shouted to Gray, "Point out your leading company commander. I want him to attack those Rebels at that next farm."

Gray leaned back, said, "That's Captain Thompson, Company A, sir, over by that tree, but is that wise, sir—?"

Custer ignored him, riding over to Thompson. "Captain, as soon as you can get your men organized I want you to attack those Rebels down this road. I need time to set my artillery in the proper place, and you're going to buy me that time."

Ian followed behind Custer, heard his order. *Not a wise move,* he was thinking. He saw a sinister cloud fall over Thompson's already dark features. He took off his cap, scratching his hair vigorously. Captain Henry Thompson was around the same age as Custer, but had been an officer much longer. He was not about to go charging off with his men without some deliberate thought.

Ian knew he was going to question Custer's order, smiling at the thought, and waited for the fire to ignite. He suspected who would get burned, and felt empathy for the young captain he had grown rather fond of over the past few days.

Thompson looked at the Rebels. It was apparent now that they were no longer moving south, but were preparing positions to defend against a possible assault.

Thompson made his argument, "With respect, sir, we've no idea what strength is out there in the woods or back behind that ridge out of our sight. I'm wondering if one company will be enough, sir."

Ian saw Custer redden. He did not like being questioned, but kept his outer calm. With an edge in his voice he said, "Carry on, captain. Get your men ready—now."

Thompson saluted, "Yes, sir."

He and Ballard formed the company on the road, back from the farm. Around a slight bend and out of sight of the enemy. The nature of the road and the fencing on each side only allowed them to form in column.

The men saw what was happening. They were nervous. Their horses felt it—shied and jigged about.

Ian said, quietly, "Thompson, I'm going with you." Swann, behind Ian, started to say something to his officer, but thought better of it.

Thompson looked at Ian for several seconds. "Suit yourself, Colonel, but this jaunt won't be without cost. I think the entire affair ill-advised, but that's that."

"I'm comin'," was all Ian responded. He knew he had done enough, proved his point, observed the Spencers in action as close as one possibly could. It did not matter—his blood was up and he was going.

Other companies of the 6th dismounted and took positions on both sides of the road, as Gray ordered. Ian looked at Gray. The senior officer seemed to be purposely avoiding looking at Thompson and Company A, busying himself with the other dispositions.

Six 3-inch Ordnance Rifles, arrived on the field. They came to action front on the rise in ground, with an excellent field of fire on the Rebel positions. Ian thought, *I've no idea what Custer was on about, but his reason for this attack can't be time to get his artillery in place—they're already there.*

Things were moving rapidly, yet Thompson waited to begin his advance, stroking his long beard and looking concerned. Custer impatiently rode toward the head of Company A. His staff began to follow. He motioned them back, and rode alone in front of the cavalrymen.

Custer drew his saber, and addressed the sullen Thompson and his jittery men, "I'll lead you this time, boys. Come on!"

Damned fool ... but you can't fault him for a lack of courage. Even Ian was swept up in the enthusiasm. Thompson commanded, "Draw sabers!"

Ian drew his pistol at Thompson's command for sabers. This was a different kind of fighting. The thought of being in a cavalry charge exhilarated Ian. Swann drew his pistol as well, but with considerably less enthusiasm.

They advanced—first at a walk. As they passed the Felty farm they came to a trot. About half way to the next farm and the Rebels, Thompson brought them to a full gallop. They were still hemmed in by the fencing on both sides of the road, unable to deploy. They charged in a crowded column.

Company A smashed into the initial mounted Rebels, who were at a halt in the road a hundred yards from the second farmhouse. Thompson's horse soldiers cut through them like a runaway train, scattering the enemy soldiers from their immediate front. This precipitated a disorderly retreat by the Rebel skirmishers.

Custer's and Thompson's relatively small band of cavalrymen were soon at the farmhouse where the fences ended, and they could begin to deploy in a wider front. They clashed with more Confederate soldiers, both mounted and on foot. The Rebel rear guard around the farm collapsed, and more of the enemy ran under the relentless pressure of the charging horsemen.

There was momentum in their charge, and as well in the Rebels' retreat. The Federal horse soldiers felt it, pushing, thrilled and delighted, they pressed beyond the farm toward the ridge. That was their mistake.

A scathing fire opened from their right flank. It came from the farmhouse, its out buildings, and the surrounding fields. It hit with devastating effect. Horses and riders were cut to pieces by the withering fire. Company A was instantly leaderless. Custer, Thompson, and Lieutenant Ballard all went down at once. Rebels began reorganizing and coming at them from the front and both flanks.

Custer's horse dropped dead from a lethal wound, sending the hapless general to the ground in an undignified bundle. Captain Thompson was severely wounded in the chest, and thus unhorsed. Bent over, clutching at the wound, he wandered in a daze among the struggling animals and men. Ballard received only a slight wound, but his horse became frantic and he was unceremoniously tossed from the saddle.

To his credit, Ballard came immediately to his feet, and grabbed the reins before the horse ran off. He made a heroic, but futile attempt to remount the skittish animal.

Ian saw Ballard's distress, one foot in the stirrup and one on the ground, hopping wildly. The horse bolted and circled away. Ballard's foot jerked out of the stirrup. He looked around helplessly as his horse disappeared.

Ian maneuvered his own horse through the melee to assist Ballard. A sudden sharp pain stung the right side of his neck. A bullet had grazed him. He ignored it.

Horses were jammed up all around. To his horror, he saw a huge, riderless horse violently charging at him. The animal was trying desperately to get out in the open, wounded and screaming, with his head up, ears back, nostrils flaring. The poor creature collided with his mount, plummeting both horses hard to the ground.

Ian scrambled out from under flailing hooves. He saw at once the two horses were useless.

As he looked about, he caught site of Custer on the ground near him. One of the Michigan cavalrymen came to his aid, trying to help him. A mounted Confederate was charging toward Custer. The soldier shot the Rebel in the head.

He managed to get to the general, who quickly mounted the rear of the soldier's horse. The horse with both riders plowed up the road north through the fighting, toward the Federal lines they had just left.

The situation for Company A was perilous. Firing into them was increasing, as was hand-to-hand fighting. Ian saw a large body of Confederate cavalry coming at them over the rise up ahead. They would be on them in moments, and it would be all over.

Ian was amazed to find he still had a tight grip on his revolver. With his left hand he felt his neck—torn skin—fingers coming away bloody.

From his left he caught the specter of a mounted Confederate cavalryman bearing down on him. With no time to aim, Ian twisted toward the danger, pointed the pistol, and fired four rapid rounds at his assailant, thumbing the hammer back as quickly as he was able. One shot was effective. The man's face exploded in bright red. He fell backward off his horse, yet the animal ran into Ian, knocking him to the ground. He almost lost his revolver, but managed to hang on to it.

As Ian recovered his senses, he rose to find a horse at his elbow. He did not believe who he saw in its saddle. "Simon? Is that you? What the devil ..."

Simon Oldham, controlling his frightened horse, fumed at him, "You damned idiot, get your arse up here." Simon had acquired a saber from somewhere, and as he spoke was busy hacking at a Rebel soldier trying to pull him to the ground. He raised the blade and swung it full force down on the head of the Rebel. The blade cut through his gray kepi and continued slicing through hair, brain matter, and skull.

Ian saw this just before he heard a voice cry, "Watch yer back, Colonel!"

Ian looked behind in time to see two dismounted Rebels running at him with bloody sabers raised. One screamed, "Git that fuckin' officer!"

Swann, still mounted, brought the barrel of his pistol down hard on the head of the Rebel who shouted. The man crumpled, and was promptly trampled under the hooves of several horses milling about, including Swann's animal.

Nearly on top of Ian, the second Rebel let out a fierce war cry as he prepared to cut Ian in two. Ian brought his pistol straight forward, cocked the hammer, and fired into the man's face, dodging away from the blade, which was already coming down at him. Ian stumbled to the ground, and never saw what happened to his assailant. He was too busy scrambling out from under horses, hooves, and viciously struggling men.

Now he had lost his revolver. As he got to his feet he saw Simon Oldham again, trying to get his horse through the pressing fight to where Ian was standing.

It took some doing, but he made it through. Simon reached down. Ian grabbed Simon's arm, and swung onto the back of the saddle. Simon deftly reversed his mount, then headed toward Federal lines.

Ian felt a strangely eerie moment happening. The irony was inescapable. He remembered a ride almost exactly like this in the Crimea, on the back of a fellow officer's horse with Russian Cossacks closing in for the kill. They had made it that time. That was his friend, Lewis Nolan. A month later Nolan was killed in a futile charge much like this one, led by another damned fool officer, Lord Cardigan.

They passed the farmhouse full of Rebels firing at them from both stories. Bullets were now whizzing by from the left and rear. A smashing blow struck Ian in the back; an excruciating pain on his left side practically unseated him. He tottered on the brink of passing out completely, his arms slipping from their grip around Simon's waist.

A strong hand took his arm, stopping his fall. He was pushed back onto the horse behind Simon. It was Swann, who had ridden up close beside Simon's horse, straightening his officer on the horse's back and holding him there as the two horses made their way out of the fighting.

The horses rode side by side the quarter-mile back through the Federal line and on past the Felty farmhouse. Ian was only semi-conscious, barely holding on. Simon and Swann slowed to a walk. They brought him to a temporary hospital set up at the Grass Hotel in Hunterstown.

"Back to Washington," Ian pleaded, "Simon, Swann, fer God's sake, take me back ta Washington. Don't leave me here ... not in a field hospital ... you know, Swann—you remember." Ian did not feel much pain yet, but he passed in and out of consciousness, and knew it was bad.

Swann told Simon in a soft voice, "In the Crimea, sir. We lost most of them what we knew who went to field hospitals. Weren't never seen again."

"I understand," Simon whispered.

A tall, lanky surgeon, with spectacles, shirtsleeves bunched up on his arms, wearing a bloodstained apron, looked at Ian. He was thorough, and efficient. He had a lot of soldiers to look after.

"Your man's lucky," the surgeon reported. "The neck wound is only a graze. Should heal soon enough if kept clean. The wound in his left side is worse, but went clean through and out the front. Always preferable to its lodging inside."

"I know," said Simon, picking up the left side of his frock coat, which showed a blood-spattered rent in the cloth. Apparently without harm, the spent bullet that went through Ian tore through his own garment.

The surgeon nodded, "You're a lucky bastard, too."

"What do you think his chances are?" Simon asked.

"Bullet didn't do too much damage in its travels; fortunately it was below the rib cage and above the pelvis. Only time will tell," the surgeon said. "If he doesn't develop an infection and gets past the initial—"

Simon was impatient, "Can he travel?"

"On horseback, you damned fool? No!" the surgeon barked.

"What about a wagon, then by train?" Simon asked. "We're headed back to Washington."

The surgeon knew well why they were reluctant to leave him in a patched-together temporary field hospital in Huntertown, Pennsylvania. "With care, and moving slowly, perhaps. What I was about to say was that if he gets past the initial shock, and the real possibility of infection from whatever cloth or other nasty things were left inside as the bullet passed through, he should make it. I looked pretty good—couldn't see anything in the wound, but ..."

"Tell us what we have to do," Simon cut in.

"I can bandage him up, but infection is still the biggest danger. The wounds have to drain. I'll pack them with linen, that's all I've got. It'll hurt like the blazes, so I've given him medicine to ease the pain. If you're going to travel, you'll have to change the linen packing often for drainage, clean the wounds, and change the outside dressing. I'd say at least twice daily."

"I understand," said Simon.

"If you can handle that," he looked critically at Simon and Swann, "he should do, but I can't recommend it, no sir!"

Swann said, "I've packed wounds and changed dressings before, sir. Could do with some linen, though—maybe something to dull the pain ... ah ... sir, as what you just give him wears off."

"Of course, take what linen you need, and Laudanum for the pain."

The doctor thought about it for a long moment, then made up his mind, "I release him to your care."

"Thank you, doctor," Simon turned to Swann. The surgeon was already working on another casualty.

Swann anticipated him, "I know, I know. A wagon, sure enough. I'll be back."

Within an hour they were on their way. Swann had "found" a substantial buggy hidden in an old shed by some enterprising Hunterstown resident. There was room in it for Ian to lie on a cushioned rear seat, with Swann holding him secure and Simon navigating the bumpy roads. Miraculously, two fine-looking draft horses, also "found" by Swann, were harnessed to the rig and ready.

Chapter 32

---

2 July 1863, Frederick, Maryland

Rumors were circulating with great intensity. It was hard to know where embellishments stopped and truth began. The chatter up and down the rail line was that the Rebels had burned the railroad bridge south of Hanover Junction, and were roaming toward the southeast in small patrols.

Simon thought it too risky to ignore a chance encounter while they transported the wounded Ian. He decided to cut over to the Emmitsburg Road and travel more directly south toward Frederick, Maryland, then catch a train there. It was longer, but safer, and allowed them to pass over better roads with the buggy.

They looked a sad and worn out trio, Simon, Swann, and their often delirious charge, traveling through the long, dark night. The buggy ride was jerky and slow, with little talking, listening to the sounds of battle not far away. The road was clogged with wagons hauling supplies north, and wounded south.

They spoke to no one. They sat in the buggy stiffly, Simon holding the reins, nodding off occasionally, only to be jolted awake at the next bump. Ian was in Swann's lap, braced against his dirt-encrusted corduroy coat.

Upon arriving in Frederick, they easily found the railway station on Market Street, and brought Ian gently inside. The station was already filled with wounded from what they were told was "a huge battle at a town called Gettysburg just a few miles north." Simon and Swann looked at each other, realizing how lucky they had been to have avoided the fighting so near their route south.

"I'd better change the linen again," Swann said. Ian was in a fitful sleep. Gently, Swann removed the old bandage to examine and clean the wound. Simon marveled at Swann's tender care of his officer.

Despite Swann's kind hands, Ian awoke with a start, and moaned in agony. A film of perspiration covered his pasty pale skin; his eyes glazed. The old station master, carrying a lantern, saw him, and croaked, "You better get him seen to. He don't look so good a'tall."

Simon asked, "Where, old man?"

"Up the block there. Old Hessian Barracks. Been converted into a hospital. They call it General Hospital Number 1. They got everything this young man needs."

"What about the time?" Swann asked. "It could go worse for him if we miss the next bloody train. We ain't leavin' 'im here."

"Just up the road. You can get 'em there and back 'fore the next train to Washington. Don't leave 'til mornin', in two, three hours. Plenty a time."

Simon looked at Ian and silently decided. He turned to Swann. "Come on, we're wasting time. Let's get him looked at by a doctor before we try this next leg."

The doctor at the hospital looked pleased. "Excellent job, young man," he said to Swann. "Wish you were working for me."

He spoke to Simon. "The wounds are clean, best I can tell. The surgeon who saw to him did well; couldn't see any bits or pieces inside. Slight fever, no sign of infection, but he's been jolted around some. The neck wound is clean as a whistle. I repacked the entry and exit wounds in his side."

Simon asked, "Can we get him by train to Washington? We're taking him directly to hospital in Georgetown."

"The train will be better than that buggy. Just keep him padded as best you can, and he should be fine. Don't feed him much except broth. Best he remain on light fare."

They returned to the railway station in time to catch the B&O train to Washington. It was indeed better than the buggy, but not by much. The railway car's seats were hard. Air whistled through the open windows permeating the car with thick smoke and an acrid smell from the engine.

The car was crammed with wounded from the Gettysburg battle. The horrible sights and smells of blood, infection and vomit, were everywhere. As the train chugged along their screams at every shudder or shake made the journey a nightmare.

Ian regained consciousness from time to time, but mostly he slept, fitfully. The Laudanum the doctor gave them kept the pain to a minimum. It caused him to remain mercifully oblivious to the world and horrors around him.

In his dream state he saw Elizabeth in candlelight, sunlight, and dusk, always with a lilting laugh. He gazed into her knowing eyes, felt her soft skin and the light touch of her gloved hand. She would fade out of his vision, and he would feel a knife-like pain in his stomach without her being there.

In moments of lucidity, Ian's thoughts were intense—a sadness, that he might never see her again. The sadness also made him realize how much she meant to him.

His eyes opened, fluttered briefly, and closed. They opened again, a hazy vision, but she was there. He thought it a hallucination. Radiant, she leaned over and gently kissed him on the forehead. He felt the warmth of her lips ... *This is so real*, he thought.

He tried to rise, but a sharp pain in his left side felled him. "Lizbeth," his voice rasped out.

Tears appeared in her eyes. "You stay quiet. Lie still. You're going to be fine, but you must rest."

225

It is real, Ian sighed in relief.

She was probably right, that he should lie still, but it was impossible. There were too many questions. "Ballard," he whispered, "Ballard ... he was all alone. Tried to help him. Safe ... is he safe?"

Elizabeth's face went blank.

Swann's voice came from somewhere out of his line of sight. "We don't know, sir. He never made it back, sir. They think he was taken prisoner."

"Damn," he stopped to catch his breath, "he was a good man."

Ian tried to turn his head to see Swann, but flinched as the neck wound flared. Swann came around next to Elizabeth. "Captain Thompson was seriously wounded. The surgeon wasn't sure he'd live. I asked because I knew you'd want to know, sir."

"Custer?" Ian's voice showed just the edge of disdain.

"Not a scratch, sir, except to his dignity I suspect, if you'll pardon the liberty, sir."

"Damned fool." He was becoming more wide-awake by the moment. He looked around the room, cautiously, the neck stung like crazy.

"Where am I?"

"Union Hotel Hospital, in Georgetown," Elizabeth said.

"How?"

"Swann insisted," she said, "I think he thought I might be concerned. He was right."

"Oldham? Simon saved my life. I remember, and the wagon ride, and the train. Where is he?"

"No idea, sir," Swann replied. "He and I brought you here, then he disappeared, like a ghost. He's a strange one, sir, but he got us through without a hitch, he did."

In her best matronly Irish voice, Elizabeth ordered, "Tis time we got out of here and let you rest, Ian. Your wounds are clean and thanks to the fine efforts of Swann and that other man, there's no sign of infection."

"Must you go?"

"I won't be far away, and Swann is a permanent fixture."

"Yes, he and I, we've been through this before." He closed his eyes, remembering the painful journey from the Crimea back to Scotland, and Swann's help during his convalescence.

"Now you sleep the angel's sleep for as long as you can."

Ian closed his eyes, said softly, "What saved my life, Lizbeth, was seein' yer face ... your beautiful face ..."

South of where Ian was wounded, the great battle at Gettysburg was a victory for the Union forces. When he was well enough, the details came to Ian through Swann.

"Look, sir, I saved the old newspapers for you. Stories about how Meade won at Gettysburg. It's been the talk all over. Lee's now movin' south—withdrawing, you was to ask me. Meade's right on his arse ... beg pardon, sir."

Ian relished the news. "I don't see anything about our fights."

"Right you are, sir. The brawl at Hanover was outdone by a big cavalry fight the day after you was wounded, not far away from where we was. Custer led another charge, he did, with the whole bloody Michigan Brigade. They say he's a hero."

Ian listened intently as Swann continued, "The tussle where you was wounded was a place called Hunterstown. No more n' a skirmish compared to the fightin' in Gettysburg, itself."

Ian was happy his new friends in the cavalry fared well. Swann seemed to read his thoughts. "I hear Custer and the Michigan boys was magnificent, sir."

"Excellent," Ian said, "most excellent."

Ian was in hospital six weeks. Lamon, Tasker, and Prescott visited regularly, but not Simon Oldham. He seemed to have disappeared. Elizabeth was at his side several times a day tending his needs. She made certain the wounds drained, changed bandages, ensured the doctors examined him often, and even, to his embarrassment, washed and scrubbed him every other day, on the non-delicate parts of his body.

Evenings, when Elizabeth was off duty, she came and read to him. She was a great admirer of Robert Burns. *A*

Scotsman like Ian, she thought. She could never understand his poems written in the ancient Scottish, although she loved to listen to them spoken. Elizabeth did enjoy reading his work—written in English, but with a Scottish dialect.

What she did not know was that Ian was never fond of Burns. Of course, he never mentioned it. Listening to her soft, gentle, lilting voice gave a new, sweet life to the bard's magical song-poems.

One of her favorites, *A Red, Red Rose*[2] she read just before leaving every night:

O 'my luve's like a red, red rose, that's newly sprung in June; O 'my luve's like the melodie, that's sweetly play'd in tune.

As fair art thou, my bonnie lass, so deep in luve am I; And I will luve thee still, my dear, till a' the seas gang dry.

Till a' the seas gang dry, my dear, and the rocks melt wi' the sun; And I will luve thee still, my dear, while the sands o' life shall run.

And fare-thee-weel, my only luve, and fare-thee-weel a while; And I will come again, my luve, tho'' twere ten thousand mile.

Elizabeth would invariably change the original words "bonnie lass" to "handsome lad." Then she took his hand and kissed him on the lips, before gliding out of the room. Ian began to notice that he felt more pain at her departures than his wounds were causing; but it was an oddly pleasant ache, knowing she would come again.

---

[2] "A Red, Red Rose" or "My Love is Like a Red, Red Rose" was written as a song by Robert Burns in 1794, but often published as a poem. There are a number of slightly different versions. I picked one I believe would do justice to his original text.

On his last night in hospital, Swann, his constant companion, was strangely absent. Elizabeth arrived very business-like, prepared to give him his last washing. Usually there was a male nurse or Swann present, but this time they were completely alone.

Ian mildly protested, as he usually did, although he enjoyed such attentions from her far more than he would ever admit to himself. Elizabeth started the cleansing ritual in the usual way. She changed his dressings, examining the wounds to ensure they were clean and mending—the neck, left side rear entry wound, and left side front, where the bullet exited.

Then she began washing his hands, arms, chest, back, feet, and legs. As she did so, she bent over him to check his neck dressing. Her hair brushed his face, and he could smell the fragrance of lilacs. His immediate erection was quite apparent and he tried to pull away.

Elizabeth said, "No, my sweet Ian." Her hand moved slowly over the sheet, which covered his lower stomach and upper thighs. It rested gently on his erection, sending waves of the most intense pleasure through his every fiber and nerve ending.

Elizabeth's body touched his side as she stood next to the bed, leaning in. She breathed in his ear, *"O 'my luve's like a red, red rose, that's newly sprung in June; O 'my luve's like the melodie, that's sweetly play'd in tune."*

She kissed him on the forehead, but this time her lips slowly kissed him on the eyes, the nose, and finally full on the lips. It was at first a tender kiss ... then they were both swept into its depths with an excitement neither had known before—long and sweet. Ian felt no pain—no pain at all—only wondrous passion.

He strained to rise up to her ear, the pain nothing to him, and whispered, *"As fair art thou, my bonnie lass, so deep in luve am I; And I will luve thee still, my dear, till a' the seas gang dry."*

Chapter 33

Mid-August 1863, Washington

Ian was released from hospital, still feeling wobbly. He had mixed feelings—anxious to get back in the game, at the same time feeling regret that his evenings with Elizabeth would come to an end. He spent the remainder of his recovery in his rooms at the Willard. Lord Lyons would not hear of his returning to the legation until he was fully mended.

The Friends of the Round Robin, or at least Lamon, Tasker, and Prescott, came to his rooms, bringing a draught or two, or three, of one of his favorite single malts. Simon Oldham had seemingly vanished.

Although Washington was a beehive of activity, the legation by comparison was relatively calm. Benjamin Tasker kept Ian informed of the diplomatic doings. Nothing seemed of real importance, and Tasker made certain Ian did not feel guilty about convalescing.

Elizabeth visited occasionally, always with Swann present. She read to him, and they talked endlessly, boring Swann to a fare-thee-well.

Ian used his time to write reports to Major Garrison at Horse Guards, a copy to his brother, always with a brief note. He was convinced more than ever that repeating rifles were Britain's future in weaponry. He liked the Henry well enough, but the Spencer had proven itself the better all round choice for the military.

He wrote that although he had asked to be sent home, he wanted to remain in America longer to see more of the Henry for comparison. Of course, the underlying reason for wanting to remain was Elizabeth, pure and simple.

With regard to the strange letter Peter sent, no one had been in contact with him. He had just about decided—and hoped—that whatever the problem, it passed. In any event, he did not mention a word of it when he wrote notes to Peter, for fear it might surface again and end up in the wrong hands. Peter mentioned nothing in his replies.

Then one late August night a knock on his door changed Ian's world forever.

Elizabeth had left and Swann had returned to his rooms. Ian was reading accounts of the war in a two-day old copy of the *New York Times*. He thought the war effort was wearing thin, and Lincoln's unpopularity growing. He was thinking of that night in the White House garden, when his musings were interrupted by a soft, but insistent, knock on his door. Opening the door revealed a tired, grimy Simon Oldham.

"By God, Simon, my dear fellow. Where have you been? We thought you'd deserted us. Come in, come in." Ian was genuinely glad to see his friend.

"Around, Ian, around. I had some things to take care of."

"How mysterious. Involving a woman, I hope. I've been waiting ta thank you. You pretty much 'saved my bacon,' as the Yanks say!"

Simon brushed the thanks aside with a hand gesture. He examined Ian, standing before him, with his hand held lightly on his injured left side.

"You seem to be in good spirits. I'm glad to see it," Simon added.

He appeared fidgety, not able to hold his gaze on Ian— eyes flitting about like fireflies. By now they were close enough that Ian recognized Simon's darting eyes as not a permanent affliction, but a sign that he was nervous, disturbed, or uncomfortable about something.

He looked at Simon seriously. "Let's talk about it, old friend, what's wrong?"

Simon waited, held Ian's gaze steadily for almost a full minute. *How very odd*, Ian thought.

"Ian ... sit down. I have something to discuss with you."

"This sounds serious," Ian said, sitting in his favorite chair, and offering a cigar. Simon declined with another gesture.

"Cognac then?"

"Yes, if you don't mind."

Ian poured two snifters of cognac from a decanter next to his chair. "Warmed?"

"No, this will do nicely."

Ian handed one of the glasses to Simon, who sat in a comfortable wing-backed chair across the small room.

Simon began, "We're both soldiers, both professionals, so I will be straightforward with you, and get right to it."

Ian had a strong foreboding. Now he was the one who was uncomfortable. He remained silent, listening, but gripped the chair arm tightly with his free hand.

"I know you received a letter from your brother, Peter, Earl of Dunkairn, not too long ago."

Ian couldn't believe his ears—*Simon?* His mind raced ahead. He had to be extremely careful from here on. Simon was searching his face.

"Yes, I did," Ian replied tentatively.

Simon reached in his pocket and withdrew a sealed piece of folded parchment. He stood, walked across the room, and handed it to Ian. "This is from Peter." The seal was red wax, impressed with his family crest from a ring Ian knew their father gave to Peter. He reached for the letter opener on the table next to his chair and sliced the seal open.

The letter was written in Peter's unique hand. It introduced Simon as the "friend" he had mentioned previously. It again implored Ian to be of whatever assistance was asked, and reiterated that the family fortune, the family name, Peter's own freedom, and, most important, their mother's health depended upon his full cooperation.

Simon sat heavily in the chair opposite Ian. Ian placed his hand to his head, rubbing his fingers over his forehead, scratching his eyebrow intently. He realized his brother was deadly earnest and in great peril, or he would never have pleaded so. He remained silent for a long time. Simon waited, allowing Ian to come to terms with Peter's request.

Finally Ian asked, "Are ya even a journalist?"

"Ian, I'm hurt. Of course I'm a journalist ... and a photographer, and with a fairly good reputation in some circles, as you well know. All of that is true. Although I may not be as active a journalist in this country as I pretend."

Ian probed, "So why are ya doin' this—whatever 'this' is? You don't strike me as some zealot for the Rebel cause. Yer too pragmatic."

"It's rather simple, really. I'm a professional soldier, a leader of men, and an organizer, much like you. My rather unique skills are required in this instance. I don't care who wins this bloody war, and neither should you. It's not our war. I have clients, and they're paying me a tidy sum to dispose of this little problem they have."

Ian was becoming increasingly aggravated at having been played the fool by someone he thought was his friend. He suspected Oldham's military skills for hire meant that any planned action was more than mere political persuasion or manipulation.

Oldham also offended his sense of honor and duty as a soldier of the Queen. He reacted with venom. "Rather mercenary of you, old boy—rather pathetic as well. Tell me, is it enough ... what they're paying you ... ta buy yer honor?"

Simon frowned, "You're upset. I'll let that pass—this time."

Ian looked at him, hard, was silent for a time. "You said you'd be straightforward with me. What do 'they' gain from somehow gettin' rid of the current American President?

After all, that's what Peter is saying here, ain 't it?" He shook the parchment at Simon.

Simon sipped his brandy. "I will be as candid and direct as I can, while keeping faith with my employers."

"Well—yes. We wouldna want to offend yer 'employers'."

Simon ignored him, "Clearly, there is a major and influential political faction in Britain who wants Lincoln gone. They feel strongly that Britain's interests, indeed her national character, are kindred with the aristocracy of the South."

Ian recalled his conversations with Lord Lyons. "And that's behind all this?"

"No. Just like my mercenary bent, this all boils down to money, as does most politics. In this case, it is primarily cotton and the sale of arms for the war—to both sides, I might add."

"You have my attention, Simon, go on."

"If Lincoln prevails and the North wins this conflict, slavery is finished. Money interests in the textile industry in Britain would be seriously injured without America's inexpensive cotton—the bastard child of slave labor, and slavery, itself."

Simon waited, but Ian made no retort. He continued, "Simple economics. The price of cotton without slave labor would increase tremendously. My clients are a group of money people, investors, industrialists, and such, who merely find that prospect too great a loss … unacceptable. They believe Lincoln is the paste that holds the Union together. With Lincoln out of the picture, they believe the Union will fall apart and the Confederacy will win."

"Let me see if I have this right in my mind. Slavery, the trafficking in human misery, will be safe, and, more important ta yer clients, the price of cotton will remain low."

"There you have it, Ian."

"And the arms sales?" Ian pushed.

"Just another richly rewarding aspect of the money profits. This group is heavily invested in arms transactions, as well as textiles and other war materials. For instance, they've been selling Enfields to both sides since the beginning of the conflict. Big money, many lucrative contracts, endless paydays all round, including your brother, Peter."

Ian wondered if Lord Lyons was aware of this, then thought, *of course he is.*

Oldham went on, "We've learned that the United States government has increased its manufacturing and production of their own Springfield rifle musket to the point that they are about to cancel many of those contracts for Enfields—a huge loss to our clients—again unacceptable. If war fever on both sides could be shaken up, say by eliminating a critical leader like Lincoln and blaming the enemy, this would stir up the pot—lengthen the war—perhaps generate even more lucrative contracts, and not only in arms sales."

Ian saw it all, but did not like it. He asked the crucial question, "Just what do you mean by 'eliminating' Lincoln?"

"As you may have deduced, we are going to kill Abraham Lincoln, and soon."

"You're goin' ta kill him? That's yer grand plan?"

"Yes, the war will escalate because we'll find a way to blame the assassination on the Confederacy. With Lincoln out of the way, my employers feel they can control the slavery issue."

Simon was convinced that this was the critical moment. Either Ian would come along, albeit reluctantly, or Dodger, who was waiting a short way down the hall from Ian's room, would kill him.

Ian looked at Simon, incredulously, "You can't be serious."

Simon chose his words carefully, "Ian, be aware that these people are quite serious. They are ruthless, more powerful than you can imagine, and will stop at nothing to gain their ends. Believe me when I say that Peter's freedom from jail, your family name, and your mother's continued good health are in the balance. Even your own life."

Ian came up out of his chair, crossed the room in a flash, and knocked Simon's glass to the floor. Then he backhanded him across the face. The glass shattered, and Simon's lip split open, his nose pouring blood, as he fell back in the chair. Ian grabbed his shirtfront, tearing it as he hauled Simon up. He whispered, "I should kill ya right now, ya evil bastard."

"But ... you ... won't." Simon paused, catching his breath. "Ian—calm down. Don't be a fool."

Simon's chest wheezed a deep breath. He wiped the blood off his face with his coat sleeve. "If you kill me ... your brother, your mother, will be dead in a few days. This isn't my plan, Ian. I'm merely the messenger. It's their idea, although I will execute the part where we kill Lincoln—it is their master plan. You gain nothing by killing me. It will happen with or without you, or me, but you'll have lost everything ... everything, including your own life."

Slowly releasing his grip, Ian allowed Simon to sink back in the chair. Simon watched Ian for signs of another outburst of rage as he composed himself.

Ian's eyes glazed over. He slumped back into his own chair, saw the futility, saw the trap he was in. He resigned to control his rage, deliberately put his leopard back in its cave ... *For now.*

"Who's behind all this? Who are they? Tell me?"

"You don't need to know, Ian, and you won't—ever. More political figures than you might imagine are either directly involved or supportive. I can tell you that your Lord Lyons is one of them. The real money is a small group, but the movement grows daily. As Peter may have mentioned, you'll never be asked to do anything against Britain's interests."

Ian did not believe this for an instant, but he went along, formulating the germ of a plan of his own. He saw that he had to back off, convince Simon he was beaten.

He breathed heavily, and sighed. "All right, Simon, I blew up. Sorry. I don't like being bullied or threatened, even if I might agree with some of what ya say, or what these people of yours think."

Simon also breathed a sigh—of relief. He had him, and he knew it. "I suspected from our past conversations that you weren't that keen on this Lincoln."

"You'd be right. Lamon is my friend, and in front of him I must sound at least sympathetic, but that isn't my true feelings. I tend to agree with McClellan, that he's a baboon, and bad for this country. Perhaps McClellan should replace Lincoln."

"We've thought of that, and may be able to influence it," said Simon, feeling more relieved.

"Too many bad decisions," Ian said. "In my opinion he's merely a poor and unsophisticated leader. I've had a chance ta meet him, you know. I found him every inch the boorish clod most Americans think he is."

Ian hesitated, looking thoughtful, then convincingly continued, "In the fullness of time, his demise might be the best thing for this young country."

Simon nodded his agreement.

"Right, then. So what is it ya need from me?" Ian asked.

"You're smart enough to figure that one out. You have access we don't. For instance, you've met him. There's the social scene, as well as your friendship with Lamon and others close to the White House. We need a time and location where there will be optimal chance of success, and, of course, escape—an acceptable risk. We're not zealots. To find that delicate balance, we need information on Lincoln's daily activities, his security, and the like. That's where you come in."

"I see, but you said 'we'. Who else is involved?"

"The less you know the better. You'll meet them in the course of time. Meanwhile, you'll report directly to me."

"How much of this was planned—my assignment to the legation, my meeting you, even you saving' my life?"

"We're not that good, I'm afraid. Not all of it, but some. You give us too much credit. We certainly couldn't have planned that episode at Hunterstown, but I did go with you, at least in part, to observe you up close."

"And my brother," Ian demanded. "Just what did he do, aside from incurring gambling debts, that has caused him to be in this bind?"

"Hmm. It will do no harm to tell you that much. Peter is the elected treasurer at his club, White's in London—"

"Of course, I know that," Ian said in frustration. "Our father was also a member. What of it?"

"I'm afraid he used a rather substantial amount of club funds to gamble. My clients have covered the funds without any of it getting out, but retained evidence of Peter's criminal involvement in their misuse."

Ian said, "Good God! What possessed him? How much money are we talkin' about?"

"Don't know the exact figure, but over 70,000 pounds."

"Damned fool," Ian muttered, "but I might have guessed." He poured Simon another cognac.

Chapter 34

Ian sat in the Round Robin in the quiet afternoon hours, sipping a glass of whiskey, deep in thought about his encounter with Simon. He was still having trouble believing it. *I cannot accept that a group of prominent British politicians and citizens support this diabolical plan.* He knew the English could engage in foreign intrigue well enough, but to kill a nation's leader? *No, definitely, no.* He most assuredly did not trust that Lord Lyons was involved in any way.

Nevertheless, Simon had convinced him that this mysterious group of money-grubbing industrialists was a serious threat to Peter, his ailing mother, and, indeed, the diplomatic integrity of Britain, itself. There was no telling how deep their influence and power reached.

One thing Ian knew as a certainty. The worst course for both Britain and America was to allow the President of the United States to be assassinated, regardless of who might be blamed. Despite what he said to Oldham, he had come to think of Lincoln as the right man, in the right place, at the right time.

"Another whiskey, my man," Ian said to Collins, the chubby, over-friendly bartender.

"Certainly, sir, the same?"

"Aye, the same."

Ian carefully selected a cigar from a tooled leather case, a gift from Jasmine a long time ago. Collins leaned across the bar and struck a match to light it. Ian drew a long, satisfying smoke, and enjoyed for a moment the smooth taste of the fine Virginia tobacco Lamon had given him.

The cigar and the whiskey settled Ian. He put it to himself—*Ian, my boy, you have a dilemma —a choice between two unsatisfactory courses of action. First, if you go ta the authorities, British or American, they might stop the plot, but they would discover Peter's involvement and indiscretions. Second, if ya try to foil the plot yerself, say from within the assassination team by pretending to join them—you chance exposure and death at their hands.*

If Simon's threats are real, and I believe they are, they would destroy Peter, yer good name, and yer mother's health, just as the result would be with the first option of going to the authorities.

Ian downed the last drops of single malt, tapped his fist on the bar, and said out loud to no one, "Well, that's it, fer better or worse, the second choice it is."

Collins, startled by Ian's outburst, said, "Of course, sir, of course. You're absolutely right ... the second choice is the best one." He had no idea what that meant.

Ian chuckled, "Another, Collins. This is goin' ta be a long afternoon."

Ian decided the risk of the second alternative was worth it. He must go it alone, try to destroy the plot from within and take his chances. He fully appreciated the perils he faced.

To minimize the danger of later accusations that he was, in fact, one of the conspirators, he needed protection of some sort. He thought of going to Sir Archibald, but rejected the idea because his rather unstable daughter, Hillary, was in Washington, and he did not trust her at all.

He decided to write his old friend from the Crimea, The Honorable Robert Lindsay. His friend was awarded the Victoria Cross for bravery as a captain at the battles of Alma and Inkerman. He was not only highly decorated, but extremely well respected in British government circles.

In his letter, Ian explained the entire situation to his friend. He told Lindsay about Peter's part in the affair, why he needed to protect his brother, and why he felt he must work from within the conspirators to stop their plan from being executed. He wrote: *My dear Lindsay, no need to tell you how important it is to keep this matter confidential; and if events go terribly awry, you might at least speak for me at my trial or court martial.*

The next day, Ian sat down with Swann and laid out the entire unvarnished truth. "You have a choice, my friend. I will not ask you ta become involved in somethin' that could go as badly as this enterprise might. You could be ruined for life, even jailed."

Swann's response was predictable. "Bollocks to that, sir," he said. "I've had yer back all these years, and you'd want to have a go at this without me? Not on yer life, uh, sir. More my world you'll be goin' into than yours, and that's God's truth. Just tell me what you want done."

"Thank you, Swann. Most appreciated. I've a feeling we'll be needin' yer rather special talents before this little adventure ends." Swann knew already that if it came to it, he'd die for Ian Carlyle.

*   *   *

By early September Ian's wounds were almost healed, thanks to Swann and Elizabeth. He had deliberately not told Elizabeth about Simon's plot or of his intentions. If anything went wrong, he did not want her involved. But she suspected something was afoot. Though Ian acted nervous, no matter how much she prodded or probed, he remained stubbornly silent, mumbling something about his wounds itching and making him edgy.

It seemed to Ian he had two tactical alternatives. He could give Oldham little valuable intelligence about security and such, in the hope he would cancel the plot because of the lack of information. Or, he could give Oldham excessive, even false information if need be, building up the security aspects, hoping he would see the enterprise as too risky and terminate the project.

He chose the latter tactic, and began gathering information. It took time to accumulate, but it was there. Some came from Hill Lamon, but most of what he reported to Oldham was, although difficult to locate, public knowledge in one place or another. Of course, he would allow Oldham to believe it came from various sources close to Lincoln, and embellish it. He was actually amazed by the limited degree of Lincoln's protection.

Not long after Simon's visit to Ian's rooms, they met upstairs at Butler's Restaurant, across from the Willard Hotel. It was in the same room where Major General Fitz-John Porter was court-martialed.

He had not seen Oldham since the night he showed up at Ian's rooms. This was a test meeting, set up by Oldham, because none of the usual crowd from the Willard frequented Butler's.

Ian began, "I don't like meeting so close ta the Willard and all our friends."

Oldham was adamant, "You let me worry about that. What have you found out?"

Ian looked about, nervously, then reported, "Lincoln and his family are presently living in a two-story cottage on the grounds of the Soldier's Home. He'll reside there, according to my sources, until the first part of November, then return ta take up residence again in the White House. As you may know, the Soldier's Home is about three miles from the White House on Rock Creek Church Road. I found out his bedroom is at the southeast corner of the cottage, but I don't know which floor—I'd assume the second."

Oldham said, impatiently, "Who guards him out there? When and how does he get to the White House?"

"An infantry company from a Pennsylvania regiment—I think the 150th. They camp on the Soldier's Home grounds and patrol them extensively. They guard all access ta the grounds, and the cottage, itself. Lincoln commutes daily. He leaves no later than nine in the morning, and is usually back ta have dinner with the family by six each evening. He travels either on horseback or in an open barouche style carriage."

Oldham's interest perked, "That seems somewhat foolhardy. Who accompanies him?"

"He's well guarded. He routinely brings along the captain who commands the infantry company, and sometimes others of his own staff or the cabinet. There is also an escort of around twenty cavalrymen from the 11th New York Cavalry."

"I see," Oldham said. "Continue."

"Lincoln's daily routine varies sometimes, but there is, nonetheless, a fairly stable schedule. In the morning after he arrives at the White House, he reviews mail his secretaries have sorted out. He then meets citizens and petitioners, something they refer ta as 'office hours' 'til noon. He eats the mid-day meal at the White House around one, then it's office hours again 'til four. There are periodic cabinet meetings that cause alterations in this routine."

"Excellent work, Ian. I'm impressed."

What Oldham did not realize was that all of this information was available merely by asking the right people, and diligently examining the newspaper archives. The bit about the infantry captain accompanying him to Washington came from a past conversation with Hill Lamon. The captain's name was Derickson. According to Lamon, he was highly favored by Lincoln, who ordinarily detested any visible security.

Oldham added, "One more thing. What route does Lincoln take to and from the Soldier's Home?"

"I've no idea."

"Find out ... and find out more details about his daily routine at the White House. You're doing fine, Ian."

They left the restaurant separately, arranging to meet again in a few days. Although it was not his country, and the information he gave was more or less in the public domain, Ian still felt like a traitor. Somehow he had to convince Oldham that any attempt to assassinate Lincoln was futile and doomed to failure.

Chapter 35

Late September - early October 1863, Washington

Over the next several weeks, Ian met Oldham at Butler's regularly. He also found that acquiring even rather public information took some work. Nevertheless, with the unwitting help of Lamon, and other acquaintances he met at social functions, he was able to piece together a significant pattern of Lincoln's daily life, which he successfully fed to Oldham a bit at a time.

Oldham was gaining trust in him, as he planned, but it was not easy on Ian. He felt himself the treacherous bastard every time he gave Oldham anything.

His information was becoming progressively more critical as time passed, and he still had no clue who the other conspirators were or what they planned. He knew it was coming to a head, but did not know how he was going to handle it.

It finally began to come together in late October at their weekly meeting. Oldham was unusually cordial. "Ah, Ian, so good to see you. Tell me, where do we stand?"

Ian thought, *An strange question. He usually only asks what I've found out.*

"Does that mean ya want my opinions, as well?" he asked rather sardonically.

"Of course, of course. I value your mind for detail, and your intellect, more than you know. Again, that's why you're here. That's why we chose you."

Good—that will help me stop you. Any kinship or debt Ian felt he owed for Simon's saving his life had long disappeared. *Phase one of my plan—convince him I'm with them—check.*

"First, Simon, based on common sense and what I've been able ta glean from my acquaintances, it wouldn't be prudent ta try this at the White House. There are many guards and too many of Lincoln's armed associates about. Chances of success are extremely low, and chances of escape are almost non-existent."

"I'd already decided that, Ian, but I'm glad you focused on it just the same. Shows you're looking out for our interests. Please, carry on."

So far, so good. "The only time Lincoln is away from the White House seems ta be his walks to the telegraph office at the War Department. It's his habit to determine the current status of his military forces. He goes more often when a major engagement's brewin'."

"Yes, a possibility we've considered. When does your information tell you he does this?"

"He visits the telegraphers around 7:00 p.m. If somethin's afoot, he may repeat that visit as late as 11:00 p.m., but that's only when he's in residence at the White House. As I may have mentioned, until early November he's at the Soldier's Home. Unless something's loomin' on the military front, he's home by six and doesn't return 'til mornin'. According to my sources he currently travels to the War Department during the day. In broad daylight, Simon—and damned well-escorted."

Oldham said, "A good analysis, but it merely confirms what we already know. At least for now, I've eliminated his travels to the War Department as a possible location to strike. We may have to revise our plan if we can't get it done before his return to residence at the White House in November."

Ian was somewhat alarmed, but pleased. It was the first time Oldham confided any of their plans to him.

"As far as I can tell," Ian summed up, "there are only two other possibilities. The Soldier's Home, or along the road to or from it."

Oldham's smile broadened, "Perfect, Ian, you've paralleled my thinking precisely, but I've also eliminated the home, itself. Too many soldiers, and, the same as the White House, too bloody risky."

"So I take it you're focused on the route Lincoln uses. I think I can help with that."

Oldham leaned into the table, listening closely.

"You wanted the exact route from the White House to the Soldier's Home. Unfortunately, it varies from day to day. Not as a security precaution, but simply because Lincoln likes ta stray off the direct route to visit cabinet members or whoever he damned well chooses. It apparently drives his escort crazy."

"So what is the basic, most direct route normally followed?"

Ian responded in more detail. "If Lincoln doesn't decide to deviate, his entourage travels northeast on Vermont Avenue, takes a right turn onto Rhode Island Avenue to Seventh Street, then north on Seventh all the way to Rock Creek Church Road. They turn right on this road and travel to the Soldier's Home. This route is reversed when he comes in to the White House in the morning."

"Good, good, in fact most excellent," Oldham sounded almost jovial.

Ian disagreed, "No, not good at all."

Oldham was cautious, his bright mood broken. "What do you mean?"

Ian continued, forcefully, "Ya want my opinion ... Here it is. If yer thinkin' of making yer move on Lincoln either when he's traveling to the White House or on his return, it'd be suicide."

"Why, pray tell?" Simon was not a happy man.

"Weren't you listening at our last few meetings, Simon? His twenty-odd man cavalry escort is extremely conscientious and diligent ... and armed ta the teeth. Those staff members who might accompany him are also armed and ready. Soldiers at Fort Slemmer and Fort Totten, not that far away, are alerted to his travels and stand ready to support if any trouble arises. Even if we succeeded, I doubt we'd escape capture." Ian purposely used the word "we" to assure Oldham he, too, was now part of the plot.

Oldham did not like where this was going. It was one thing for Ian to give his opinion, quite another for him to come on strong in an area not his concern. Ian sensed this immediately. He had gone over the line.

Must be more careful.

Oldham reminded Ian of his place. "This isn't your problem. You've given us the information—we'll do the rest. Those forts are too far away to count much. Besides, we'll watch the route closely for a time, before we strike. We'll handle this, Ian."

This was not working out at all. Ian had too little control, and his information was not deterring Oldham; indeed, it appeared to embolden him. He would have to rethink his strategy.

To his astonishment, Oldham became all smiles again. "My friend, I can see you're only concerned with success, and I appreciate your efforts. In fact, the information you've already given us has been substantiated as accurate."

He paused. "What? You didn't think we would take all you reported as gospel, surely. Well, you passed the examination. Now it's time you moved up a step, and met our little band. Come with me."

Oldham took Ian by carriage to a warehouse near the Georgetown wharf, not far from where he and Lamon had the altercation with the three thugs in the alley. The faded sign above the door read: Billings Shipping—*a coincidence?* There was a room in the warehouse containing several chairs and a long table. Maps of Washington were laid out in scattered fashion. Smoke filled the room with the strong odor of cheap cigars. It swirled about the two men who were in the room when they arrived giving it an eerie texture, like a graveyard scene.

One of the men was a young red-haired somewhat creepy-looking fellow. He was tall and thin, with a generally unkempt appearance. He lovingly wiped an oiled cloth over what Ian thought by its checkered stock and telescopic sight to be a British Whitworth rifle musket. The other was bald, thick-necked, and mean-looking.

Oldham's introductions began with the mean-looking one. "Lieutenant Colonel Ian Carlyle, Scots Fusilier Guards, this is Thomas Kally, late of the Rifle Brigade. We call him 'Dodger'. He is my invaluable second in command and confidant. And this rather undernourished -looking gentleman fondling his weapon is Cadmus Buell, late of the Confederate Army; Palmetto Sharpshooters, as I recall—an expert rifleman."

Ian thought he recognized the one called Dodger from somewhere, and pegged him as a former non-commissioned officer. *In this team*, Ian thought, *Dodger is the muscle.* Buell, obviously the shooter, showed almost immediately he was not the cleverest member of the assemblage.

Buell said, "Scots Fusil—what? I ain't never heerd'a that regiment. You from Texas?" He pronounced it "Tex-ass."

Oldham dismissed him quickly, with a smirk. "Not your army, Buell. He belongs to the Queen. Never mind, it isn't important, except you need to know Carlyle, here, is an experienced, professional soldier, and an officer. Have you got that?"

Buell was contrite, and looked genuinely hurt, "Yes, suh. Sorry, suh."

Kally had not said a word, merely tried to stare Ian down with a strong gaze beneath thick eyebrows. Ian had encountered non-commissioned officers like him many times—surly, manipulative, intimidating when they could get away with it—dismissive of officers, yet fearing them.

Ian stared back, hard, until Kally dropped his eyes and shuffled his feet. *Good, first score to me, but this one could be trouble. Better be on guard. Don't give him any room.*

Oldham shook Ian's hand. "Welcome." Ian shook hands with the other two men. Kally's handshake was a test. Ian anticipated it and jammed his hand into Kally's first, giving him the advantage. He squeezed, hard ... knew it hurt. Kally's eyes blinked and Ian knew he'd won another round.

Ian felt he had to say something. "I've no love lost for this Lincoln baboon. Happy to be with you."

"So what is it, sir?" Kally asked Oldham, ignoring Ian's attempt to be friendly.

"Not sure just yet. Ian's given us the route our target takes each day to and from where he resides, but it does seem a bit crowded with armed escorts. I'm worrying it through. Ian doesn't think it's feasible. Too risky."

Oldham outlined what Ian told him so far. Ian filled in a few blanks.

When they finished, Kally suggested, "If we have this much information, why waste it. Let me do some quiet watchin' along the route, a day or so, see just how dicey it might be."

"Good," agreed Oldham. "Buell, you help Dodger, but be careful, not too public. Plant yourselves along that route at the appropriate times, morning and evening. Be there an hour before and remain an hour after; say between eight and ten in the morning, then again between four and six in the evening."

Dodger said, "Sir." Buell nodded his head. Dodger gave another scathing look at Ian. It was apparent he did not trust Ian's information, and thought him far too timid.

Oldham was ending the meeting. "Ian, see what else you can find out. Concentrate on the route." Ian also nodded his head.

"All of you, meet back here in three days at seven in the evening, sharp. Understand?" Nods all round. They left separately, each going his own way.

Ian was already planning his new strategy as he headed back to the Willard on foot. He hoped that these were the only men involved in the plot; at least in America. He had to get to Swann first, then Hill Lamon, and quickly, if his new plan was to work. He decided to forego his usual walking and take a hansom cab to the hotel.

He found Swann in his room, and told him what transpired at the meeting with the conspirators. He needed Swann's help.

"I'm going ta tell Hill that you overheard two men talkin' in a tavern. Say they were definitely anti-Union men, discussing how easy it would be to assassinate President Lincoln ... tell him that they said they'd been watching him with a hand gun on his daily rides to and from the Soldier's Home, and were convinced they could get close enough ta shoot him as he rode past."

Swann was skeptical, "You think he'll accept that, sir. It's pretty risky."

"Hill and I have talked about this very thing. He's been worried for some time about Lincoln's safety on these rides. It'll confirm his worst fears. At the least he'll bolster the security around the President while he tries ta look into the matter. That's what Kally will observe, and, not knowing of the threat situation, he'll think it's the routine security. That should substantiate my information and cause them to abort any attempt ta kill Lincoln during those rides."

"I hope yer right, sir."

"So do I, Swann. So do I."

Chapter 36

Late October 1863, Washington

Ian and Swann found Hill Lamon at the Round Robin, a few hours after Ian's meeting with Oldham. He was feeling the whiskey he had consumed, and not so quietly singing songs, playing his banjo, and regaling a small gathering of regulars with tales of his exploits in exotic, faraway places. He often did this of an evening, and his following was growing.

Lamon was actually a fine entertainer, his music spirited, setting even the most reserved to toe-tapping. Ian knew his stories were not entirely true, but they were humorous and adventuresome. The kind of story you would tell a young lad while staring into a blazing campfire. His following never tired of Lamon's tales—true or not.

Oldham was not there, as Ian suspected. In fact, Oldham rarely joined the "friends" these days.

Ian interrupted Lamon between song and story, whispering, "Hill, we need to talk—in private. It's urgent."

Lamon, irritated at the possibility of being dragged away from his admirers, asked, "What in hell is so urgent, Ian?"

"I brought Swann with me. Last night at a tavern near the river he overheard a conversation that is most disturbing. It involves President Lincoln. You be the judge."

Lamon sobered instantly, made an excuse to the gathering, and pulled Ian and Swann to a table away from the other patrons. He turned on Swann. "Tell me," he demanded rather harshly.

"Well, sir," Swann began, showing just the right amount of fear and excitement. "I was sitting at this here bar, the *Rusted Spike*, minding me business and drinking a nasty tasting ale. These two men, rough trade you ask me, were down the bar, whispering. Had a mite too much, mind." Swann was perfect.

"Their whispers were loud enough fer me to hear. I paid them no mind until I heard the name Lincoln, then 'kill the bastard.' Me ears perked up, right enough. I heard the one say he'd been watching Lincoln on his morning and evening rides. I didn't know what he was talking about, but it sure sounded evil." Ian thought, *Good lad, Swann, all that lying and cheating growing up in the London streets has worked for you this evening.*

"I know exactly what they're talking about," Lamon said, his eyes set hard as he thought about the implications. "He rides each day to and from the Soldier's Home, where he lives during the hotter months."

"Well that scares me, then, sir, cause they was sayin' as how they might just get close enough to shoot him with a pistol as he rode past. Jesus, Mr. Lamon, is that bleedin' possible?"

"More than possible," Lamon replied. "We protect him. He has a cavalry escort, but nothing could stop a determined sharpshooter or a close-in gunman from getting off at least one shot."

Ian, as always feeling like a first class bastard, clenched his fists to keep his voice from breaking, and added, "This doesn't sound good, Hill. I thought you should know."

Lamon was insistent, "Swann, could you point a finger if you saw them again?"

"No, sir, too dark. Followed them outside, but even there, too dark. They split up. I kept after the bigger bugger of the two. He caught one of them omnibuses a few blocks away, and were gone. Sorry, sir."

Lamon pondered for a moment, then said, "Good job, Swann, my thanks. I must go now and take care of some business." Just as Ian hoped, Lamon appeared to be taking the threat seriously.

The next day Lamon doubled the President's existing escort from the 11th New York Cavalry. In addition, he placed soldiers at critical locations, clearly visible along the route in the morning and late afternoon.

He took the precaution of adding a second detachment from the 11th New York riding a hundred yards behind the entourage. It was just out of sight of President Lincoln, but ready to pounce if there were shots fired or a commotion of any kind.

Lamon and Ian sat around a small wrought iron table, hardly touching the steaming, fragrant coffee before them. Lamon explained the additional security. "Ian, my friend, I feel better. I think I may have plugged the hole, or at least made a decent stab at it, thanks to you and Swann."

Ian asked, "Why not have the second detachment of cavalry merely ride along with him?"

"He'd never stand for it. Might not even tolerate the soldiers along the route. He just doesn't believe there's danger, and doesn't want the citizens to see all that protection. Wants to seem courageous to them, accessible."

"I suspect what you said is right. You can't protect him completely if the assassin is a zealot—strong and single-minded."

"No," Lamon said, "and that's what gives me the terrors, wakes me in the early hours of the morning with the sweats. I've been known to sleep at his door."

"How long can ya keep this additional protection in place?"

Lamon grunted, "At least 'til he moves back to the White House, if he doesn't notice it and pull me up short before then. Maybe next year I can talk him out of residing at the Soldier's Home, but I doubt it."

Lamon explained one last change in the security arrangements. "For the next several weeks, I'll try to personally ride with him, if I have to go out there at the crack of dawn. Even if someone gets by all the sentries and cavalry, they won't get by me." He opened his frock coat, revealing two pistols and a rather large knife stuck in a wide leather belt.

Ian pulled back, gaping at the dangerous array. "Och, I know I'd sure feel safe with you next to me." Lamon grunted.

A few days passed, and Ian met again with the conspirators, as arranged. Ian went to this meeting armed with his own revolver, a small Smith and Wesson Number 2 Army, purchased to replace the Colt he lost at Hunterstown. This revolver could easily be concealed under his coat and vest.

He also had an armed Swann well hidden outside the warehouse, within calling distance. If anything went wrong, he at least wanted a chance to come out alive.

Kally was highly agitated, almost beside himself. This made Ian nervous, until the no-neck started talking, then he sighed in relief.

Kally exclaimed, "Bloody hell, Carlyle here was right, but he didn't go far enough."

Oldham soothed, "Take it easy, Dodger."

"We watched two days, morning and afternoon, like you said. This Lincoln is pretty obvious—looks like a fuckin' scarecrow in a tall top hat."

"Get to the point," Oldham insisted. He did not like vulgarity, and he was getting nervous. Ian saw the darting eyes begin. It was the first time he had seen this disturbing habit in Oldham in a long while.

"Right. On both days there was a great huge bastard with a beard riding with him in an open barouche. This ugly bruiser didn't look like a politician to me. More like a wrestler, and he watched the sides of the road, like a bloody hawk lookin' fer its next meal."

Lamon, Ian thought.

Kally went on, "Carlyle was wrong about the size of the escort. I counted well over thirty spread out in front, along the sides, and behind the carriage—sabers drawn and at the shoulder. We could also see soldiers spaced well apart, standing guard on the roadside along parts of the route."

Oldham muttered, "Hmmm, this doesn't sound promising." His head was now jumping back and forth with his eyes. He seemed very upset by this news.

"There's more. After Lincoln's buggy passed, another cavalry detachment, of equal size, rode past with carbines at the ready. Even if we got the shot, close in with pistol or long distance with Buell's rifle, we'd have damn little chance for escape."

They talked more, but came up with nothing new. No plan proposed allowed for a shot and escape afterward.

With the possible exception of Buell, these were not zealots willing to risk capture and prison or execution, for a cause. They were mercenaries. Besides, they could not afford to risk any chance of the plot being traced back to their employers.

Oldham decided they would place their plans on hold until something else came up. In the meantime, Ian and the others would continue gathering information. They agreed to meet at the warehouse, weekly.

It was a dark night with no moon. On leaving the warehouse, and once out of the area, Swann joined him from the shadows.

"Black night, in'it, sir? How'd we do?"

"It went splendidly. Exactly as we'd hoped. All plans are on hold, and they don't know where they're going from here."

That was not exactly true, but Ian had no way of knowing otherwise.

Chapter 37

Ian had found a rare moment to lounge about, enjoying a midday glass of Cockburn's port, which he kept in a drawer in his office. Thoughts of Peter, his still ailing mother, and the lush green hills around Dunkairn, filled his mind. He often missed riding those hills with Peter at his heels, a huge black thoroughbred beneath his thighs. A rap at the office door interrupted his reverie. A messenger handed Ian a sealed note.

Ian opened it with no little curiosity. Who would send him a note by messenger to the legation? It was written in Oldham's sweeping hand, and summoned him to an emergency meeting at the "usual place." *How very odd. A bold move for the normally secretive Simon Oldham.*

It was raining, and there was a chill in the air when Ian arrived at the warehouse. His Smith and Wesson was tucked in his waistband under his vest. He was most interested in the purpose of this unusual gathering, and why Oldham had broken their secrecy protocol by delivering a message to him at the legation. At the last weekly meeting there was nothing particularly new, except that Lincoln's move back to the White House from the Soldier's Home appeared imminent.

The conspirators arrived at close intervals to find Oldham pacing impatiently, eyes flitting about. When they were all present he cleared his throat. "Gentlemen, you will each pack a small valise. Expect to be gone a week or so."

Buell asked, "Where we goin' suh?"

"Gettysburg," Oldham said, waiting for the next obvious question.

"Why?" Both Ian and Kally asked together.

Oldham smiled darkly. He simply said, "To kill Lincoln, of course."

Ian heard a ringing in his ears, felt his chest constricting. The plan, his plan, to stop Oldham and safeguard Lincoln, had instantly fallen apart. *All right, calm yourself, think, think. What had happened to cause this abrupt change of plans?* Then it came to him. He thought he knew how it had happened and where, but not who, had caused this drastic turn of events.

President Lincoln rarely left the District of Columbia, but a few weeks ago Lamon told Ian that the President was asked to speak at the consecration of the Soldiers' National Cemetery at Gettysburg. According to Lamon, Lincoln was going to accept, but for strict security reasons it was not to be made public until a day or so before it occurred. Ian chose not to tell Oldham and give him a new potential location at which they might execute an assassination plan. Unfortunately, Ian guessed, there had been a leak, a rather major one.

Social gossip can all at once be fun, frivolous, and damning. The war had not even slightly interrupted social events in Washington. This always puzzled Ian, but it was the same the world over. Perhaps it was just as well. Perhaps ordinary people back home beyond those fighting and dying, needed some sort of normal life, if for no other reason than to prove it could exist in the turmoil of war.

One of those highly anticipated social events was the marriage of Kate Chase to Governor William Sprague of

Rhode Island. The guest list read like a registry of all the elite in the capitol, including Lord Lyons, Ian, a majority of the cabinet members, senators and congressmen, Elizabeth Callaghan, Sir Archibald Walsham, his daughter, Hillary Walsham, and most important, the President and Mrs. Lincoln. No one wanted to miss this gala event.

The reception was held at the Willard Hotel. Ian, who accompanied his lordship, spent most of his time talking to Elizabeth and trying to avoid Hillary. During the course of the evening in one of the lounges, a group of men, including White House staff, was overheard in an imprudent discussion.

"Could be an important appearance," said one.

"Of course, on stage with Edward Everett, our greatest orator," added another.

A third contributed, "People like hearing him talk. Gets to their hearts. He should get out more often."

"When is it?"

"November 19th in Gettysburg, right on the battlefield."

"What better place."

The word spread throughout the reception like a slow-moving forest fire. Lincoln was going to Gettysburg to speak. Ian heard the rumor, but shrugged it off, thinking Oldham, who certainly did not circulate in this part of society, would still never hear about it.

Ian surmised that the leak could have been anyone who was a spy for Oldham, even Lord Lyons, himself; and the damage had been done. Oldham had apparently been told many details of the trip, or they would not be going to Gettysburg. Ian felt Lincoln's life was in the balance.

Oldham's darting eyes narrowed to stare directly at Ian. The other conspirators saw it, watched, and listened. "Ian, I'm surprised you weren't aware that Lincoln was going to speak at Gettysburg on the 19th. We could have used more time to prepare."

Because Ian provided false information on occasion, he had practiced responding to just such a situation. He was appropriately contrite. "I had no idea he was actually going.

All reports, and even Hill Lamon, said Lincoln had declined, that Sewell was going in his stead. I didn't feel it was important. My mistake. I should have at least mentioned it. Sorry."

Oldham remained silent for several seconds, eyes hard on Ian. Then he said, "Well—no harm. We've enough time if we move quickly."

Ian quietly let his breath out. Now, he thought might be a good time to be more aggressive—deflect Oldham's concern, and make his error seem more trivial. "A moment, Simon?"

"What is it? We're in a hurry."

"I want to bring along my soldier servant, Swann. You know him quite well. Good man and hates just about everything in America except its women."

Simon nodded. "As I recall from our adventure up north, a very resourceful chap. Could prove most useful. If you vouch for him, it's acceptable by me. Kally? Buell? What say you?"

Kally said, "We could use an extra man, if he can be trusted."

"I'll stake my life on him," Ian retorted. Kally and Buell looked at Oldham, nodding their approval.

"Done," said Oldham.

He glared menacingly at Ian. "By the by, Ian, old chap, you are staking your life on him. It will be forfeit should he prove unworthy."

Chapter 38

---

16 November 1863, Gettysburg, Pennsylvania

The train took a little less than seven hours, with a delay at Baltimore. Ian spent the time mulling over events that had put Swann and him on this train, heading into Gettysburg Station. He decided to deal with this new threat as it came at him.

They disembarked the train and Ian took a moment to look about. "I've never been to a town after a battle, except those tiny villages in the Crimea. Not quite sure what to expect." Swann said nothing, as he also took it all in.

Gettysburg was small, around twenty-five hundred citizens. Either fortunately or unfortunately there were several converging roads from various parts of Pennsylvania, all of which seemed to come together at the town square. This convergence, among other more accidental reasons, made it the focal point of the largest and bloodiest battle thus far in the American civil war. Had he not been wounded at Hunterstown, he and Swann would have witnessed this battle first hand.

As they made their way the short distance to the center of town, Ian sensed and saw that the townspeople were still reeling from the grotesque aftermath of war. Its streets and buildings showed palpable signs of the battle. Numerous holes made by bullet, solid shot, and shrapnel punctuated its buildings; but even more poignant, actual bullets and shell fragments left long-lasting scars, embedded in trees, buildings, and fences.

To Ian the most remarkable and bizarre result of the war was the storefronts of several thriving businesses that had developed, apparently for the immediate burial of the dead. *A health consideration for the entire town, no doubt.*

Ian whispered to Swann, "I'll wager those ghoulish businesses are making some folks wealthy."

Swann replied, "Yes, sir. Read a newspaper on the train. Says the dead soldiers were all below ground, and now they're diggin' 'em up. Reburying the poor sods in the new cemetery. Don't seem right, somehow, sir, after they was laid out and buried proper an all." Ian was not surprised. Although an apparent necessity, it smacked of the morbid, grisly side of man to profit from such wanton disaster.

The conspirators arrived separately during the rest of the day on 16 November 1863. Oldham, who arrived a day earlier, found modest accommodations for them at the Black Horse Tavern, two miles west of Gettysburg on the road to Fairfield, Pennsylvania. This was far enough away to give them privacy, yet close enough for convenience.

He brought with him much of the same type wet plate photography equipment he lost on the trip north to Littlestown. With photography in mind as their major pretext for being there, Oldham spent his time getting to know the town and surrounding country, making his face familiar as a journalist and photographer.

To that end he made it a point to visit the Gettysburg gallery of Charles and Isaac Tyson, located on York Street. "Charles, so good to see you again."

Oldham had met the younger Tyson, Charles, in Philadelphia just before the brothers moved to Gettysburg in 1859. Of medium height, Charles, the mainstay in the gallery, wore full facial whiskers, but with no mustache. Both were Quakers.

"Simon, Simon Oldham, I can guess what brings you to our modest little borough."

"Yes, Charles, old boy, it is my intention to get amazing photographic images of this momentous occasion, and of Lincoln, himself. It will go down in history, with my name."

Tyson smirked. "Not if I get it first." They both smiled—theirs was a gentle rivalry.

"Simon, this is Isaac, my brother." They exchanged greetings. Oldham thought, *They look much alike, same exact eyes. I think they purposely wear different beards for that very reason.* Isaac's beard whiskers were only on his chin.

"Charles, where can I rent a wagon and two sturdy horses? I have photographic equipment with me."

Charles looked blank, Isaac answered him, "Best bet would be one of the taverns, or perhaps the Wagon Hotel—they cater to teamsters and the like."

"I'll also need to purchase some chemicals from you—collodion, silver nitrate, the usual, if you have any to spare," Oldham said.

Isaac injected, "You might take a look at the upper level of the Wagon Hotel while you're at it ... for those magnificent photographic images you mentioned. It looks up Baltimore Street—the route from the square to the speechmaking site."

"You can have all the chemicals you need," added Charles, "we can stand the competition, if you can."

"Thanks to you both. I am in your debt already. I have colleagues coming into town. They'll be around to pick up the chemicals in the next few days. They'll also be scouting for locations for our cameras."

Oldham knew the word would spread among the many journalists and photographers arriving for the big event. He planned this visit, but never thought it would go quite so well.

He did not have to search much for a wagon. He rented a small canvas-covered wagon with two horses, from a Mr. Bream, the proprietor of the Black Horse; but he kept the Wagon Hotel in mind. In keeping with their pretext for being in Gettysburg, he rigged a sign on each side of the wagon canvas, reading simply, "Photographic Images."

He also set up an adequate dark area in the wagon's rear, with a large, heavy black cloth for preparing and developing the wet plates. He did not plan to use it, but it had to look functional to make the pretext believable.

*   *   *

By evening, they were all present in Oldham's room. Anxious to get started, he announced, "Good, we're all here. Lincoln should arrive late afternoon on the 18th. He has a huge entourage, and there will likely be an equal number to welcome him. He's staying the night at a local lawyer's house, a David Wills, the representative in Gettysburg for Governor Curtin."

Ian asked, "Where exactly is his house?"

"Excellent question. It's this Wills fellow who is really behind the cemetery for the soldiers, its consecration on the 19th, and the reason we're here. He wrote to ask Lincoln to speak, but took the precaution of asking Edward Everett, the famous orator, to give the main speech in case Lincoln backed out. Both Everett and Lincoln are coming. To answer your question direct, Wills' house is at the Diamond, a block from the railway station—"

"Diamond? Ain't a real diamond, is it?" Buell cut in, eyes gleaming.

Oldham lowered his head, shook it back and forth, "No, Buell, that's the name they call their town square ... the Diamond."

Kally, Swann, and Ian were grinning. Buell looked disappointed, but the rebuke was lost on him.

Oldham continued, "I believe the entourage will walk from the railway station to the Wills house. There are plans for Lincoln to speak to the anticipated crowds, and for him to tour the battlefield at some point, but all this will depend on circumstances. No one I've found has any idea of times or routes." He looked at Ian, who knew that would be his task. He nodded in acknowledgement. Ian wondered again about Oldham's sources outside those present. His information was impressive.

Kally observed the obvious, "We have a bit of work ahead."

Oldham said, "Rather ... so let's get to it, shall we? Kally, Buell, you will scout possible areas for the shot. Off hand, I'd say start with the railway station, the Diamond, and the site of the consecration. By the way, they're building a platform there for the speakers and important guests."

"Right, sir," Kally snapped. Buell bent his head sharply.

"Off you go," Oldham said, handing Kally a slip of paper with an address on it. "Use the wagon outside. Stop at this address, see either Charles or Isaac Tyson, and pick up several bottles of chemicals from them. They'll know what to give you."

Kally took the address. Oldham said, "Let the locals get used to seeing the wagon and you around town, as my assistants. I've already spread the word, so it shouldn't cause concern that we're looking for locations for our cameras."

As the two were leaving Oldham added, "We shall all meet here tomorrow."

He turned to Swann. "I'll need five saddled horses at our disposal until we leave the 19th. We'll escape on them and leave them somewhere away from here. You don't have to steal them. Here's enough money to rent. We need good, reliable horses. Have them fed, saddled and ready at dawn each morning, starting day after tomorrow, the 18th."

Swann accepted the money in a small pouch, "Right you are, sir."

"I also need sketch maps of the Diamond area at town center, and the area where the speaker's platform is being built. Can you handle that?"

"Aye, sir."

269

"Then carry on." Swann looked at Ian, who nodded slightly, then waited for his own assignment.

To Ian, Oldham said, "Yours is perhaps the most important assignment, and I think you already know it. What you may not know is that your friend Lamon arrived here a few days ago, stayed at the Eagle Hotel, and returned to Washington on the 13th. He was likely here to set up security for Lincoln. He's due back today or tomorrow. This time he'll be staying at the Harper House, which is adjacent to where Lincoln will lodge. You must get to him, and find out all you can—protection, the route to and from the dedication site, times when events will occur, that sort of thing."

Ian was even more astounded at the detail of information already known by Oldham. He knew Lamon was traveling to Gettysburg. He had deliberately not mentioned it. Lamon told him he was appointed Marshal of Ceremonies for the consecration, and not merely a companion or bodyguard to the President.

"It might be difficult ta explain my being here," Ian suggested.

"You'll think of something. Tell him Lyons sent you."

In fact, in a way, Lord Lyons had sent him. He asked Lord Lyons for the time away from the legation to go to the consecration. He thought it an excellent idea. A report could be made to London on the event.

Oldham continued more confidentially, "I waited 'til we were alone. Whatever we decide or wherever we shoot Lincoln, the plan generally has always been to leave the Confederacy-stamped Whitworth behind, traceable back to a South Carolina arsenal by the markings on the stock. Buell was to be seen escaping, wearing a Rebel uniform."

"Yes, I'm aware of that," Ian said.

"Actually, that isn't the plan. Kally is the only one, other than you—now—who will know what shall occur after Lincoln is shot."

Ian waited, thinking he knew what was coming, *the bastards*.

"We will leave the rifle, but Kally will also kill Buell as he escapes, then melt into the crowd and confusion. This will clinch the fact that the Confederates are behind the assassination—a real live dead Rebel." He sniggered at his little joke.

Nothing from Oldham or Kally shocked Ian any longer. He remained perfectly calm as he asked, "What is it ya want from me, Simon?"

"I want you to back up Kally."

"What might that mean, exactly?"

"If for some reason he fails to eliminate Buell, I want you to do it."

"Eliminate." What a quiet-sounding word for murder, thought Ian. "I'll handle it," he said, then asked in an even tone, "Do ya want Kally eliminated as well?"

This surprised and amused Oldham, "My, my, Ian, how callous you've become. No, I need Kally—for now."

"I'll take care of Buell, if the need arises," Ian said, menacingly.

Oldham seemed satisfied.

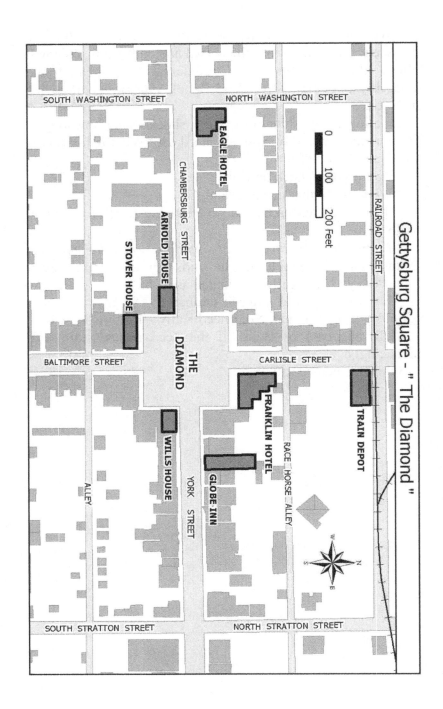

Gettysburg Square - " The Diamond "

Chapter 39

---

17 November 1863, Gettysburg, Pennsylvania

The early morning air was cold and damp. Ian watched for Swann from a window in the Franklin Hotel[3] lobby. A man drove his wagon up the near-empty Baltimore Street into the Gettysburg Diamond. The words "Photographic Images" were painted on the canvas over the back. In tow behind the wagon trotted a string of five horses.

Good, it's Swann and he's had success. How does he manage it? Ian walked out of the hotel to meet Swann and examine the mounts.

"They look fit enough," Ian observed. "Saddles?"

"Best I could do in a short time, sir—expensive, very expensive."

"Where are the saddles?"

"In the wagon, sir."

"Good, saddle one up. Leave it in front of the hotel here. I have business to do."

---

[3] The Franklin Hotel was owned by Colonel McClellan, a wealthy businessman who liked to trade and race horses. The hotel was later named the McClellan House, and is today the Gettysburg Hotel.

"Yes, sir." Swann brought a saddle from the back of the wagon, with a bridle, reins, and a blanket. He made up one of the horses and tied it off to a hitching post, while Ian returned to the lobby.

He watched Swann drive the wagon slowly out toward the west on Chambersburg Street, then turned his attention to watch the Harper House across the square. Lamon came out around nine o'clock. He walked around the corner to the tavern at the Globe Inn on York Street. Ian waited twenty minutes, and sauntered into the tavern room directly toward the nearest empty table, ignoring the patrons. Lamon was seated at a table in the far corner, eating breakfast.

"Well, what in hell are you doin' here?" Lamon exclaimed, with a broad grin.

"Ah, Hill, I was hoping I'd run into you."

"Well by God, I'm glad to see you."

"When I mentioned the consecration to Lord Lyons, he insisted. He was most keen I attend and take careful notes."

"There'll certainly be something to see, but why the notes?"

"My guess, he intends to send a flourishing report to his superiors in London. In any event, it gave me a chance to get out of Washington."

"This is a damned nightmare."

"A nightmare ... that's a bit melodramatic even for you, Hill."

"You have no idea. I'm doin' damned near everything to get the ceremonies on track, put a decent program together, and I'm worried sick about the President's safety while he's here."

"How so?" Ian asked, with that feeling stirring inside, like a first class "shite" for using his friend in such a shabby manner.

"Remember, I told you he refuses most protection. Bad enough in Washington, but here—the crowds, the dangers—it's appalling."

"Can I help, Hill? I'd be happy to do so." *God, I hate this.*

274

"I'll take you up on that, friend. Could use another opinion, you being a soldier of some experience."

Worrying over the safety of his President, Lamon was as nervous as a new bride. This made him overly talkative to Ian, whom he considered a close confidant. He explained the protective efforts thus far, the route Lincoln would take from the Wills house, and the approximate time schedule. "I have at my disposal several dozen marshals sent from the various states whose soldiers are represented in the cemetery. I'll have 'em mounted, surrounding the President, dressed in some fashion similarly, both for protection and to show the degree of security. They'll all be armed."

"That sounds helpful. In my opinion, the more visible the military and other protective measures are, the less likely anyone will try anything untoward."

Excited, Lamon exclaimed, "Yes, yes, that's why I'm havin' the cavalry and other military lead the affair in front of him. It's Lincoln, himself. That's the problem. If he thinks I'm bein' too protective, he'll try to block me at every turn."

Ian said, "What yer doin' is exactly what I'd do, but what if someone wants ta shoot at him from a distance—with a longer range weapon? Those around him won't be much help, except ta block a view or go after the culprits after they do their worst."

"I know, God, I know. I'll have sharpshooters at higher level windows or on roofs of houses to watch over things, but even that might not be enough to stop some determined bastard."

"I think you're right there. I see the predicament."

Lamon added, solemnly, "It's driving me mad. There's nothin' I can do to be certain of his complete safety—nothin'."

I can help you there, my dear friend, but I can't tell you the truth, at least not now. How did I get into this mess? Damn you, Peter!

*   *   *

Later that afternoon the assassins met in Oldham's room. They all pulled chairs up to a round oak table—Oldham, Ian, Kally, Buell, and Swann.

"Horses are in the barn outside, fed and ready," Swann said without being asked. He just wanted to get his part out of the way. "There's a saddle for each. The wagon is there also, with two good horses standing by."

Swann laid out sketch maps of the Diamond, and the site of the speaker's platform. He had also acquired a rough street map of Gettysburg.

"Good man," Oldham said. He looked around the room at the faces of the conspirators. "Ian, you're first—report."

Ian reported much of what Lamon told him, but not all. "As you suggested, Simon, he will walk with his entourage and the welcoming committee from the station ta this lawyer, Wills' house on the Diamond—probably thirty or more people. He'll be surrounded by bodyguards, military, dignitaries, and an admiring public. His arrival time depends on the punctuality of the railroad, which means it is totally unreliable. They estimate between four and six in the evening."

Ian paused to let this information settle.

"Lincoln will speak at some point ta the crowds at the Diamond, but no idea when or exactly where. It'll depend on the crowds. Also, he will tour the battlefield sometime in the early morning on the 19th, but he'll have a heavy cavalry escort with him. The time and his route are undecided, and likely won't be known until they actually depart. In my humble opinion, all of these possibilities are too risky."

Ian turned to Kally. "What do we have on the town square?"

Kally was uncomfortable responding to Ian's demanding question, but he had little choice, because Oldham was looking at him as well. "We found a possible location for the shooter on the Diamond, if that's where we decide to do it. There's a building owned by a George Arnold. Has his clothing store, and the Farmers and Mechanics Savings Institution on street level ... at the corner of Chambersburg

Street and the Diamond, itself, across from Wills' house. A good location for a shot at someone on the square, mind, but no bloody good for the entrance to the Wills house on York Street—bad angle."

Oldham inserted, "I've covered that. Rented a room on the York Street front of the Globe Inn, second floor. It's across the street, more or less, from the Wills house entrance door." He pointed to Swann's sketch of the Diamond. "I've left a few pieces of clothing and toiletries there. It'll remain empty for the next few days, but each evening one of us will go in and mess the sheets to look as though someone's staying there. That's yours, Swann."

"Sir," Swann replied, understanding his assignment.

Oldham asked Kally, "How would we get to this possible shooter's position?"

Kally was ready. "Piece of cake. Part of the second floor is storage—the rest is livin' space. There's a stairway leading up to the storage part from the back alley, with only a simple locked door securing it. We were up there today, we were ... easy in and out. Left the door locked again, as we found it. Never even disturbed the people livin' in the house."

"Good," Oldham said. "Ian, what news about the procession?"

Ian pointed at the map of the town streets. "Mid-morning, day after tomorrow, Lincoln will leave the Diamond in a grand procession toward the dedication site—about three quarters of a mile—total. He'll be preceded by a host of military units. The parade will move south on Baltimore Pike until it reaches a split, here," he pointed to a place on the map, "where it will bear right onto Emmitsburg Pike, traveling southwest ta Taneytown Road, then left and up the hill ta the dedication site. They're still working out the details of the program and seating arrangements on the platform."

Kally picked up from there. "The platform ain't complete yet. Looks like to me there ain't enough room on it for all the people they're tryin' to seat. The bad news is the speaker's platform is on a hill that's all but bald. Only trees there are too bloody small. There's only one place. The gatehouse of the old cemetery. There's an archway, bounded by two, two-story square towers, both being used as residences."

"Is there any good news at the site?" Oldham asked, dryly.

"Aye, sir, at least according to Buell here. He thinks—"

Buell interrupted, "That's right, suh ... good news. I can git a decent shot from any window on the second floor of that there gatehouse. On'y problem is gettin' up there." He gestured toward the ceiling of the room.

"We can get over that," snapped Kally, irritated by Buell's interruption. "The people who saw us accepted we was photographers lookin' for camera locations. We walked about, asked questions—no one took notice. They're expectin' ten to fifteen thousand gawkers at this little party. We should be a fly speck amongst that lot."

Oldham summarized, "Right. As I make it, there's four possibles: On the way from the railway station, during one of his excursions from the house he's staying at, during the parade to the dedication site, or at the dedication site, itself."

"Sounds about right, sir," said Kally. The others nodded in agreement.

"Let's focus on the four we just discussed. Keep at it," Oldham concluded in dismissal.

Ian and Swann had supper together, neither daring to mention the meeting or the tangled web of events in which they found themselves embroiled.

Ian decided to turn in early. He wanted time to think. Still determined to convince Oldham of the futility of his efforts, Ian was actually certain in his own mind that it was rather a suicidal venture, at best. But that would not save Lincoln. *No, I must convince Oldham.*

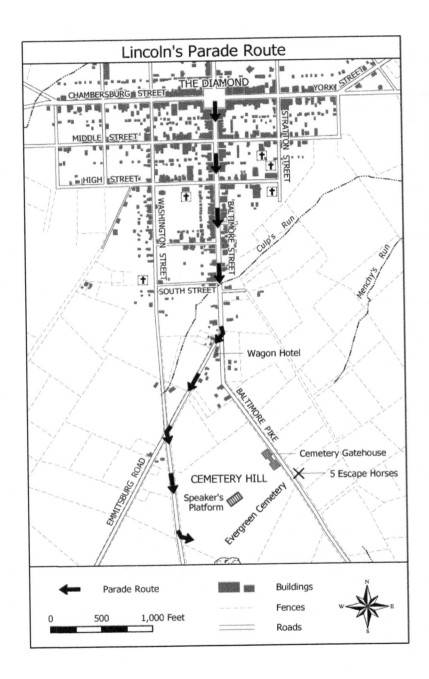

Lincoln's Parade Route

THE DIAMOND

CHAMBERSBURG STREET

YORK STREET

MIDDLE STREET

STRATTON STREET

HIGH STREET

WASHINGTON STREET

BALTIMORE STREET

Culp's Run

Menchy's Run

SOUTH STREET

Wagon Hotel

BALTIMORE PIKE

EMMITSBURG ROAD

Cemetery Gatehouse

5 Escape Horses

CEMETERY HILL

Speaker's Platform

Evergreen Cemetery

←	Parade Route	
	Buildings	
	Fences	
	Roads	

0   500   1,000 Feet

N
W — E
S

Chapter 40

18 November 1863, Gettysburg, Pennsylvania

Ian spent a sleepless night mulling over his strategy, and anticipating another meeting with Lamon the next day. They met at the Globe Inn for coffee the morning of the 18th.

Ian greeted Lamon, "My friend, I've been pondering over your security problems. Frankly, I can't think of any hole you haven't plugged; at least ta the degree humanly possible."

"Ah, thank you, Ian. I wish I had your confidence. God help me, he'll be here this afternoon." They talked more. Ian learned the details of the program and other security elements he might use to somehow dissuade Oldham.

Around noon at the Black Horse, Ian made what he hoped was his last report, and his final and conclusive arguments against any action. "The town is bursting—soldiers, dignitaries, political hopefuls, citizens from afar, and locals. Good thing you arrived early, Simon, there's not a room to be had anywhere. Even the so-called dignitaries are sharing rooms. There are no new details of his arrival or any activities on the Diamond, but tonight is expected to be a rowdy one, parties and drinking all night long. I wish to state again that I consider any effort by us to eliminate Lincoln here in Gettysburg, sheer folly."

Kally grunted in obvious disgust, and spat on the floor.

Ian ignored him, and continued his report, "Allow me ta give you my reasoning. As far as the procession to the dedication site, it's to be led by the Marine Band followed by, I believe, a squadron of the 2nd Cavalry Regiment, then Generals Couch and Stahel with their staffs, all armed. They will be followed by more cavalry and an artillery detachment."

When no one interrupted, Ian continued, "The route to and from the site will be sprinkled with armed cavalry and infantry, including sharpshooters at high-level windows and on some roofs—mostly from a local unit, Company B, of the 21st Pennsylvania Cavalry. They are also providing the guards at the Wills house—at the entrance, and presumably at Lincoln's door.

He paused again, then went on, "Surrounding Lincoln from the time he leaves the Wills house until he reaches the dedication site will be twenty or thirty marshals from different states, identified by white-colored sashes. Each is armed. Their primary duty, under the watchful gaze of Ward Hill Lamon, is ta protect Lincoln."

Ian waited. No one commented, but they were listening intently.

"Lincoln should be easy ta recognize. He'll be ridin' a large chestnut bay horse. With him will be Generals Doubleday, Gibbon, and Wright, all presumably armed, at least with swords. Of course, Lamon will be right next to him. As I recall, Lamon carries two large pistols and a sizeable knife. With this amount of layered security, it doesn't appear ta me a sound choice for us, with any reasonable chance of escape."

Kally said, irritably, "Seems to me, Carlyle, that if it were up to you, there would be no good place to do this—Washington, Gettysburg, or anywhere."

Ian bounced back quickly, "That isn't it at all. I just want this done at the right time and place, and this excursion of

Lincoln to Gettysburg doesn't fit either of those categories." He hoped this was enough to make him seem cautious, but loyal to their mission.

Ian kept going, to offset the rebuke. "The program is uncomplicated. Lamon will make introductions, there'll be a dirge, then a prayer, and music surrounding most everything. Everett is first speaker and will no doubt take the most time. Lincoln will follow, likely introduced by Lamon. Lincoln has been asked to say only a few words – but there's no telling. Betting money has it he'll talk for five – ten minutes and that's all. I believe that's about it from my end."

"You neglected the platform. Anything on seating arrangements?" Oldham inquired, somewhat harshly.

"Right, sorry. It's a large platform, as Kally said, to accommodate numerous dignitaries. No one is certain yet how many. Of course Lincoln and Everett have center stage front, as the speakers. Close by will be Lamon, as Marshal of Ceremonies, Governor Andrew Curtin and Secretary of State William H. Seward. The others on the platform will be in two or three rows next to and behind the principles I named."

There was a long silence.

"Kally, you've had time to look around. What's your opinion?" Oldham asked.

"Tryin' to get close enough for a pistol shot or explosive is not in the cards. Carlyle's right there, sure enough." Oldham was jotting down notes.

Kally continued, "I think we should forget the walk from the station. It's bad. Too many people, Too little chance for a good clean shot."

"Done. I agree on both counts," said Oldham.

Kally went on, "We could make use of the Arnold building for the shooter if we decide on any location around the Diamond, but I've found an even better spot. There's a large house on the square owned by a professor name of Stoever. Works at Pennsylvania College[4]. He's a delegate to

---

[4] Pennsylvania College was later renamed Gettysburg College.

this here United States Christian Commission. There's a store at street level, the J.L. Schick Dry Goods Store."

"Get to it, man," Oldham interjected.

"Right, sir. Seems the Christian Commission used the store and building right after the battle. It was also used as a hospital, like most places in town. When the Commission left, the top floor and attic remained as storage for bibles and tracts and such. Again, we can get in through a back entrance and stairway without being seen by the people in the store, or the Stoever family living on the first and second stories. There's windows overlooking the Diamond, and a large attic window that would do nicely."

Oldham said, "That gives us two locations on the square, but am I correct that from neither one can you see the front of the Wills house?"

Buell answered this one, "That's sure enough, suh."

Kally quickly added, "Right, but the Globe Inn allows an excellent view of the steps and front door of Wills' home. We was there today in the room you rented, to make damned sure."

"Good," Oldham said.

"If we was to do it during the procession," Kally went on, "there's another good place. At the split, where the parade turns right onto Emmitsburg Pike off Baltimore Pike, stands the Wagon Hotel. It's on a rise in the land and overlooks the procession as it comes south, then passes the hotel. There's fine vantage points from two balconies or any of the upper front windows."

Oldham said, "I'm familiar with that particular hotel, and—"

Ian interrupted, dampening Kally's enthusiasm. "Of course, Kally, that must be the reason Lamon mentioned that hotel, and told me of the many soldiers he was putting on those balconies and in those windows. My guess is it would be a battle to the death just getting Buell into position."

Kally glared at Ian, seething, "It's still the best place, it is. There's other houses, but we'd have to deal with them that lives there."

"Play nice, children," Oldham said. He was thoughtful, "And the dedication site?"

"The gatehouse is our best choice," Kally said. "The cemetery keeper, a Peter Thorn, is gone to the war. His family lives in the gatehouse—wife, three small children, and her parents. Parents are German immigrants; I don't think they speak much English. My guess they'll all be at the ceremonies and the house'll be empty. The two towers of the gatehouse are independent. The southwest tower, where the parents live, has a second floor window. The gatehouse is exactly 212 paces from the speaker's platform, facing it at a right fine angle," Kally asserted. He stared at Ian, challenging him to knock that apart.

Buell added, "They's a door at the foot a the tower, with an easy lock to bust. Then they's stairs leading up to the second floor, easy climb, even with my bum leg. Couple hundred paces—I could do that shot blindfolded."

Ian saw in his eyes the crazed look of a zealot. This man loved his work—was looking forward to the kill. He wondered what it was that made Buell such a cold killer of men.

Although Ian knew nothing of his background, his instincts about Buell were right. He was a man of unquenched obsession, and a remorseless killer by nature. Cadmus Buell saw the killing of Abraham Lincoln, the devil incarnate, as revenge, redemption, and patriotic duty, all bundled together. As he would say, this was his moment to "purely shine."

Buell continued to leer at his fellow conspirators while Kally continued his report. "We can park the wagon next to the gatehouse, ease open the door pretty as you like, then haul the camera equipment inside in plain view. We'll look like enthusiastic photographers. Simple escape afterward to Swann's waiting horses on the Baltimore Pike nearby, and we're clean away."

Ian was desperate. He knew he was losing ground. He asked, with no little disdain, "What will the numerous soldiers and marshals be doing while we fire the shot, and quietly steal off?"

Kally sputtered, showing his anger, "There'll be citizens milling around and much confusion, damn it. The sound of the shot would be distorted, because Buell would fire from inside the bloody room. We could walk away and none the wiser."

Oldham brought the brewing altercation to a halt, "Gentlemen, all possibilities have risks. It's my decision. Frankly, I've eliminated trying to do it during any excursions from the Wills house. The schedule is too vague. Would require watching for a long period to wait for him to leave the house. Too much exposure. It's down to the parade route or the dedication site. You'll all know the plan tomorrow morning at dawn. In the meantime you can relax a bit ... but before you do, I want everything ready—wagon, horses, the Whitworth, camera equipment—everything. Packed and ready to go. Understood?"

They nodded. "Get cracking," Oldham commanded.

*   *   *

After the others left, Oldham and Dodger Kally were alone, "I didn't want to tell the others, but all these plans but one, are up the spout. I've heard from our clients." Kally waited, cautious and curious.

"Theater, Dodger, my boy, on the stage of life."

Kally did not quite grasp his meaning, "Yes, sir, uh, theater."

"Don't be dense. Can't you see it? Killing Lincoln is one thing, but killing him at the very moment of his important speech, in front of thousands of American citizens, is a statement. Indeed, theater on the world stage. That's what our clients want. It will have more impact on future events than killing him anywhere else."

"I see ..." said Kally, awareness dawning.

"I want one more thing from you. I know this won't disappoint you. Afterward ... after we've eliminated Lincoln and escaped, on our way back to Washington, I want you to kill Carlyle."

"I thought you trusted him, sir."

"I think he'd as soon see Lincoln dead as not, and he knows the consequences to his family if he isn't with us, but just the same—there's something about him. Perhaps too cautious, or too much conscience, even with his family to protect. I can't bring myself to fully trust him anymore—or Swann, of course. Besides, these are also our orders from on high. Keep it clean. No one to trace it back to us, or our clients. Kill them both."

Kally could only snigger, his no-neck bulging. "My pleasure, sir, my pleasure."

At the same time as Oldham and Kally were discussing their fate, Ian and Swann were anxiously trying to come up with a plan of their own. Their deception had gone on long enough; perhaps too long. Oldham and Kally were determined to carry this to its end, for their own mercenary reasons. Cadmus Buell was pure crazy. He wanted only the kill.

Chapter 41

18 November 1863, Gettysburg, Pennsylvania - evening

Ian was now convinced no amount of logic, persuasion, or fear of getting caught would deter them. The plain fact is that the failure to convince them was Ian's burden to shoulder. It was time for brutal action. No way could Ian allow the assassination to succeed.

"Well, Swann, old son, we must decide what ta do."

"Yes, sir," he replied. "Afraid I've only one idea."

"Let's have it. I've just about run out of ideas. In any event, so far, my brilliant ideas haven't shown amazing success."

Swann said, with no apparent emotion, "Kill 'em in their beds ... sir—one at a time—quiet as the rustle of a curtain in the night breeze."

"We could," said Ian, rather shocked by Swann's modest proposal, "but I suspect that wouldn't be so easy. Buell yes, no real threat there, but Oldham and Kally are professionals, and we can't afford ta fail."

Swann thought a moment. "Then we could do it from behind at the dawn meeting, sir. You take Oldham, I'll take Kally, then we deal with Buell together."

Ian was perplexed. These could not be their only alternatives. The margin for success was too narrow, and ... it would be nothing short of murder. He recalled Simon dragging him to safety at Hunterstown—saving his life.

"I canna do that, Swann. No, I'll go ta Hill Lamon, tell him everything, and let him handle it. They can be arrested, and that will end it."

"But, sir, your brother, your mother? You'll be in for it, too, won't you?"

While Ian pondered their impasse, the germ of an idea came to Swann. He asked, as he thought out loud, "We don't know which of the two places they're gonna use, right, sir?"

"That's right, the parade route or the site. Even if we did, I don't know how we'd stop them on the spot, just the two of us. It would place President Lincoln in too much danger if we failed. I'll go to Hill. There's no other way."

"Sir, if I may, yer thinking we should stop them bastards before they put their plan in motion, have them arrested."

Ian could almost feel the wheels grinding in Swann's shrewd, street-wise brain. He'd had a childhood of surviving in a world where life was cheap, and cunning was the only way to beat the odds.

"What's on yer mind?" Ian asked, hopefully.

"Well, sir, what if we was to do something that would stop their plan whenever or wherever it might be put in play ... make it impossible to carry out?"

"I don't see how that—"

"Hear me out, sir. The Whitworth is a first class little beauty right enough, but it works like any other muzzle loading piece."

"Meaning?"

"Meaning a percussion cap on a nipple. The hammer hits the cap, puts a bit of spark through a tiny hole in the nipple and barrel, which fires the powder inside the barrel, shooting the bleedin' bullet out the spout."

Ian's eyes squinted almost shut, picturing the rifle's inner movements, but not getting Swann's meaning at all. "Where are you goin' with this?"

"Suppose we was to steal the Whitworth, plop a dab of melted lead into its nipple, kinda unseen from the outside, then screw the nipple back on—simple as pie—then it's only a great long club. The cap will spark, but no firin' … no killin'."

Ian was quiet for a long time, digesting—running the possibilities in his mind—success versus failure. He finally bellowed, "Damn me if you ain't a bloody genius, but can we do it? The rifle is either in the wagon with the camera equipment, or, more likely, in Buell's room. We'd have ta get it, do the deed, and put it back without being caught. And just how would we do it?"

"Not 'we', sir—me. Like I said a long time ago, this is my world. If I were to get caught, I'd act drunk and say I were in the wrong room—ever so sorry. Then we can still do it the hard way—tell Mr. Lamon everything and take our punishment—nothing lost."

Ian stared at Swann for a long minute. Swann was silent. At last Ian said, "You're a marvel, lad. I think yer onta somethin'. You have at it."

Swann was excited. He was at his best, his true calling. Around mid-afternoon he took a horse and rode into town. Asking around, he found a gunsmith out on the road north toward Carlisle. This gunsmith worked out of a small shop behind his house. The man was dubious at first, but after an exchange of money, he agreed to do some easy work on a weapon, sometime later in the evening.

Swann and Ian waited until well after dark. Ian remained in his room, pacing the floor, while Swann looked through the wagon in a shed behind the tavern. The canvas bag containing the camera tripod and rifle was not there. Swann never actually thought it would be. Buell coveted that weapon like a mistress—it would be close to him.

He went back to Ian's room. All their rooms were on the same floor of the tavern. They waited, allowing time for Buell to go to bed, and finally fall asleep.

Ian kept watch in the hallway. Breaching the door was easy for Swann. The lamps were out, but moonlight through the window was enough. Leaning against a chair was the white canvas tripod bag. The rifle was nowhere to be seen. *Must be in the bag already, too noisy to pull it out. Have to take the whole bag.*

He carefully lifted the bag and carried it out of the room, leaving the door unlocked for his reentry. Ian returned to his room to wait, while Swann slipped out.

In the stable, Swann looked in the bag. His normal breathing returned when he saw the sleek shape of the Whitworth nestled among the tripod legs.

He finally woke the irritable gunsmith after much loud banging on doors. In spite of his previous agreeability, he complained bitterly about the time and inconvenience. After Swann gave him even more money, the gunsmith delicately removed the nipple from the Whitworth, dropped in a dab of melted lead to seal the bottom of it, tested it, and replaced it. The work was done.

Greedy bastard, Swann thought as he rode at a gallop back to the Black Horse. The hackles on the back of his neck were dancing all the way. That sixth sense that kept him from the clutches of the law while growing up kept signaling him he was being followed. He took precautions, but saw no one behind him.

That was odd. He had checked before leaving. Oldham had retired, Kally was drinking in the tavern, and, of course, Buell was sound asleep. There was no one else who could be following him. He decided it was his overactive imagination. *Been away from this kind of life too long.*

When Swann returned to the hotel, he almost ran smack into Kally prowling the hallway, slightly drunk. He quickly hid the canvas bag behind a large standing flowerpot, and stepped into the open.

"Can't sleep either, Mr. Kally, sir?" Swann asked, rubbing his eyes. He made it a point never to call Kally by his nickname, "Dodger."

Kally gave him a hard look, then commanded, "You get some rest. I don't need no flaming sleep."

Swann returned to his room, with Kally watching. He was trapped. Unless he could get around Kally, *not bloody likely*, he had no way to return the bag, which was still hidden behind the flowers in the hallway. There was no way to alert Ian of the state of affairs.

Swann peeked into the hall from time to time. Kally was always there, pacing restlessly, or sitting in a chair at the end of the hall, sipping from a dark bottle. The night passed too quickly.

Ian was wide awake. He had seen what transpired between Swann and Kally through a crack in his door. He hoped it would resolve itself by Kally withdrawing. Finally, with dawn approaching, he knew he had to take action. He hoped Swann was watching, and would seize the opportunity.

Ian walked into the hallway and confronted the huge Englishman. "Good, Kally, I'm glad you're here. The shed where our wagon is parked—it's just below my window. Thought I heard something, someone messin' about in the shed. Thought I'd take a look."

Kally looked at him with doubt and no little show of contempt. His eyes were red. He swayed a bit, but did not seem drunk. "Jittery, are we? I don't fuckin' like you, Carlyle. I think you're a bloody coward. It's time I taught you a thing or two."

He abruptly swung his massive ham-like fist at Ian's head. Not much bother … Ian swiftly dodged the blow, bringing his right fist into Kally's stomach. The big man collapsed around it, leaned forward, and puked on the hallway carpet.

Kally was down on his knees, and Ian, with some disdain, cuffed him on the back of the head, splaying him out on the floor in his own vomit. Kally came back to his knees, then to his feet, weaving. Ian could see the hatred in his eyes, burning into him. He could smell the whiskey on his breath. He lunged at Ian again.

This time when Ian sidestepped the big man's attack, he grabbed him and continued his momentum, smashing his head against a wall. Kally went down like a felled tree, and with a loud crunch, landed on his face on the carpet.

Ian waited, thinking the sound of Kally's head bouncing off the wall should have awakened someone, but there was no sound from any of the rooms. No doors opened, no movement in the hallway.

Kally was far from unconscious. Seeing this, Ian lifted him to his knees by his hair—looking at him quizzically. Kally eventually looked back, and spitting blood, said, "You win, for now."

Ian let go of his hair, wiped the hair grease and blood off his hand, turned and headed down the hallway to the stairs leading below. He said as he walked away, "Kally, you do what you want, but I'm going ta see if anyone's pokin' around the wagon. I'd guess that's what Simon would expect, but you suit yerself."

He had him. Kally showed a flash of concern at the mention of Oldham's name, then stumbled to his feet and followed Ian down the stairs and out the back door of the tavern, holding his bleeding nose and mouth.

Swann watched, astonished at his officer's speedy dispatch of the much larger man, saw the two of them heading down the stairs. He took his cue, worried that with the commotion in the hallway, or the sunlight creeping in the window, he might be too late. He grabbed the bag from behind the flowerpot and entered Buell's room, only to find him drowsily waking up. *Shite!*

"Hey, mate!" Swann shouted at Buell, who was sleepily lifting himself in the bed. The bag was behind Swann's back. "Get yer bloody arse up, ya lazy bastard. We're waitin' on ya! Dodger and my officer 'ave been tryin' to kill each other in the hallway. Wonder that didn't wake you."

He turned his back away from Buell, placed the bag quickly where it was leaning on the chair, picked up Buell's Confederate jacket from the same chair, turned and threw it at him.

"How ... how'd you git in here?" Buell stammered.

"Ya left yer bleedin' lock undone, ya damned fool. Now get up, and be quick about it."

Buell pushed aside the jacket, said groggily, "Yeh, yeh, I'm up. Y'all er worse than my ma."

"Right. Get yer arse up!" He left the room, mission accomplished.

Ian and Kally were coming up the stairs as Swann emerged from the room. Ian was saying, "I must have been hearin' ghosts, but better ..."

Kally cut in, bending over slightly and holding his stomach, "Time to get up anyway."

Kally saw Swann in the hallway, ordered, "Get us some coffee."

Swann said, "Right!" He looked at Ian—they both smiled.

Consecration Site - Cemetery Hill

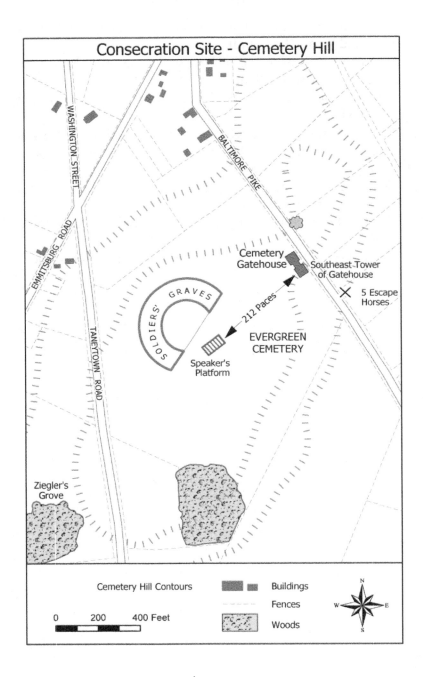

WASHINGTON STREET

BALTIMORE PIKE

EMMITSBURG ROAD

TANEYTOWN ROAD

SOLDIERS' GRAVES

Cemetery
Gatehouse

Southeast Tower
of Gatehouse

✕ 5 Escape
Horses

212 Paces

EVERGREEN
CEMETERY

Speaker's
Platform

Ziegler's
Grove

Cemetery Hill Contours

Buildings

Fences

Woods

0   200   400 Feet

N
W   E
S

Chapter 42

---

19 November 1863, Gettysburg, Pennsylvania

The conspirators met for their last time at dawn in Oldham's room at the Black Horse. Oldham said, "It'll be the dedication site—we'll kill him there. Time for discussion is over." He looked directly at Ian.

"We'll follow Dodger's initial plan, leaving in an hour or so, after breakfast. Dodger, you and Buell will take the wagon, the rest of us on horseback, with your two extra horses in tow." Dodger Kally nodded in satisfaction. Oldham must have noticed his bruised face, but said nothing.

"Buell will park the wagon next to the gatehouse. Everyone will assume we want good photographic images of the crowd, then of Everett and Lincoln, as each of them speaks. If anyone asks, that's our story. What the hell's the name of the family living there?"

"The Thorns," answered Kally.

"You'll say the Thorns allowed us use of the upstairs window in the southeast gatehouse tower."

"What if someone gets too suspicious and asks questions about photography?" Kally asked, "I'm no photographer, and Buell here, certainly ain't."

"You only need to know a little. Remember, it is an Anthony Wet Plate Camera. The wagon has the mobile dark room for preparation and developing the plates under the black cloth. Anything else anyone wants to know, they should find me to ask."

"Right," Kally said. He seemed satisfied.

"You're my assistants—only. You can tell them I insist our photography methods be kept confidential for business reasons. But don't worry; no one will be that curious."

Using Swann's sketch map of the dedication site, Oldham pointed out positions. The gatehouse was already on the map. He had scribbled between the gatehouse and the speaker's platform, "212 paces."

"Kally, you and Buell bring the camera and equipment over to the door of the tower. Park the wagon under the archway. Kally, you'll break in, quietly, looking as though you have a key, and you'll both bring the camera equipment inside."

"What if someone's home?" Ian asked.

Oldham paused, looked directly at Kally and Buell. "You'll deal with them. Kally, you know what to do."

"Yes, sir."

"Buell ... set up the Whitworth, make certain the barrel doesn't protrude out the window. Sight it in as best you can, then get comfortable. The program indicates Everett speaking before Lincoln. Unless I miss my guess, he'll be an hour or more. He's long-winded. You'll shoot after Lincoln begins speaking. Understand? This is important—*after* he begins speaking."

Cadmus Buell said, solemnly, "I got it, suh—after. I know my duty."

"When you've accomplished your mission, come down the stairs and out the door, then run like hell. You'll be wearing this white smock over your uniform jacket." He tossed the garment to Buell. "Make certain you discard it in the tower or as your running, so the people can see your Confederate uniform."

Buell bobbed his head in assent, with that crazed, mad look in his eyes. He was picturing his magnificent flight from the tower in his uniform—broad daylight, through the crowd, but impervious to them—a hero, a patriot, and once more indestructible.

"Dodger, you'll be at the door, making certain Buell isn't disturbed. You'll see to it Buell gets away after the shot is fired, then fade away yourself. Both of you make for the horses, and we're gone."

Kally nodded.

"Ian, you're to be between the gatehouse and the horses, ready to help Buell and Kally, as needed." He winked at Ian, unseen by the others.

Ian said, "Right, Simon."

"Swann, you're with the horses, all five, right about here. Can you handle them?" He pointed at a place on the map southeast along the Baltimore Pike; near, but not too near the gatehouse.

Swann replied, "Right you are, sir, piece of cake."

"Remember, we leave the Whitworth, the camera equipment, and the wagon behind. Make certain the wagon has no tell-tale signs of us in it."

Ian asked, "Where will you be, Simon?"

"Don't worry about me. You each do what you're supposed to do, and I'll be where I'm most needed. If all goes well, we'll ride at a slow pace southeast on Baltimore Pike, then head generally south toward Washington—play it as it comes from there. Questions?"

No one spoke, absorbed in their own thoughts and the part in the drama they were to perform.

Chapter 43

19 November 1863, Gettysburg, Pennsylvania

They headed their horses south on Baltimore Pike, Ian and Oldham riding side by side. Oldham said, "Look at the pomp, Ian. Flags everywhere, waving gaily in people's hands—at every damned window. Some flags are at half-mast, others not. They play funeral dirges followed by raucous marching tunes and airs. Last night they partied all over town, drinking and brawling."

"What of it, Simon?"

"Well, it seems to me these addled Yanks can't make up their mind if this is a solemn, religious occasion or a damned party."

Ian kept his silence, thinking, *A consecration, a dedication, or a celebration. I think it matters not. What matters is the spirit of thanksgiving to the soldiers who died here. Pity you can't see that, you arrogant bastard.* Frankly, Ian had his doubts that Oldham ever saw action in the Rifles. He did not match the mold Ian formed having known such men.

The November day was mild and clear. It rained earlier in the morning. After-rain freshness saturated the air. The last of the leaves were falling from the nearly naked trees and gently covered the whole magnificent scene. Ian thought, *A quite beautiful day for such a poignant consecration and such a reprehensible deed.* He was still rattling at the edge of his frayed nerves, *Suppose something goes wrong?*

They arrived at the dedication site around ten thirty. Everything went smoothly. They observed Mrs. Thorn and her three children, whom Kally had seen before, leave the northwest tower of the gatehouse and walk into Evergreen Cemetery toward the speaker's platform.

A short time later, an elderly couple left the southeast tower walking in the same direction.

Kally looked at Buell. "Luck is with us. The cupboard is bare. Let's go."

They parked the wagon just under the archway, but not blocking the road into the cemetery. Breaching the door was easy. No one looked with suspicion on the two apparent photographers lugging equipment into the southeast tower.

Buell was soon in his position in the upper floor, with the Whitworth propped up on a chest, the barrel about a foot in from the windowsill, and pointing at the speaker's platform. He decided to remove the white smock. One less thing to worry about.

Kally waited by the door downstairs. It was only a few feet from where Cadmus Buell was set up, to the head of the stairs, with Kally on watch below. A rope extended from Kally up to Buell. They had worked out various signals.

Ian stood almost directly across the pike from the gatehouse. The crowd size startled him. Civilians spread over the entire old Evergreen Cemetery, the new Soldier's National Cemetery, and beyond into the fields. They were dressed in all variety of clothing, from the very best crinolines and satins, to tattered working attire. There were not only military in formations, but numerous officers and enlisted soldiers gathered as spectators, no doubt to see the President.

Later, as they watched from their positions, the long procession entered the dedication site from Taneytown Road, moving toward the speaker's platform. The soldiers slowly deployed in formations. They were two to three ranks deep, surrounding the platform.

Buell jerked on the rope hanging down to Dodger Kally. Kally stepped out of the tower far enough to give a signal by holding his hand over his heart. Ian and Oldham, who were standing together across the pike saw it. This was the signal Lincoln was coming. It was about eleven thirty by Ian's pocket watch.

Simon looked at Ian closely. "Good luck, my friend."

Ian did not want to talk, afraid his voice would reveal his venom toward Oldham. *This is it. If our plan works, when the gun doesn't fire, Buell should come down, and they will all abort the mission, heading for the horses.*

Around noon, the dignitaries took their places on the platform, including the tall, gangly Lincoln, wearing a black suit, white gloves, with his tall hat in hand. Ian watched through his small telescope. He made note of the black mourning band around Lincoln's hat. *For his son Willie? For the soldiers who died here? For both, and perhaps for America, itself? This man has had his share of trials.*

There appeared to be a holdup, which put Ian on edge. His friend, Hill Lamon, stood up and announced the cabinet members, generals, and other important dignitaries who had sent their regrets. Oddly, Everett, the primary speaker, was not yet on the platform. *That must be the delay.*

After what seemed like a considerable wait, Everett appeared. Lamon said a few words Ian could not hear distinctly. A dirge played, followed by a prayer.

Oldham walked off, disappeared toward the horses. Ian was unable to follow his progress through the crowd because it had become so dense.

Everett stood up and began speaking. Ian did not even try to listen. His mind raced, terror rushed in like a burst dam. *What could go wrong? Is it possible Buell has an extra nipple to replace the bad one? No! Too unlikely. Surely he'll try to open the hole with a nipple pick. No! No time. Must stop thinking too much. It's out of my hands now.*

From deep inside his mind, he dredged up his leopard, closed his eyes and watched it gracefully approach. Its presence, crouched and ready, calmed him, as always. In his thoughts he patted its head—the beast let out a soft purr. *Good, stay now, stay with me friend.*

Everett was still talking. The crowd seemed to be growing. He looked at Kally, saw him staring back—he was not going to let their altercation in the hallway die there. Ian figured that if they lived through this, there would be a reckoning. He was prepared for it. He tried to see Swann with the horses off in the distance on the road, but the land undulated and the thickening crowd blocked a clear view.

Ian looked at the time again. Everett had been speaking nearly two hours. *It must end soon.* Just as he began to focus on the words, the speaker stopped talking.

There was a deafening silence from the crowd as Everett concluded his oration. Apparently they were trying to show reverence to the solemnity of the occasion.

A glee club performed next; their finish greeted by ringing applause. Ian watched as Hill stood up, shouting in a resonant timbering voice, "Ladies and Gentlemen ... the President of the United States."

There was applause and musical fanfare as Lincoln stepped forward on the platform, taking out his spectacles and placing them on his nose. Although Everett spoke for two hours, apparently without notes or written text, Lincoln appeared to have a piece of paper to read from. Ian's body tightened, like the leopard, ready to spring.

Behind the upper window of the gatehouse, Buell tried to relieve his leg cramps by shifting position. Kally poked his head inside the tower and scowled up the stairs, tugging on the rope three times. All eyes in the crowd were on the platform.

Buell recognized Lincoln, the evil one, the minute he stood up. He did not need Kally pulling on the rope to tell him. This was the man responsible for the constant, sharp pain in his leg, like being stabbed with a knife. This man

304

caused him to be discarded, tossed aside like broken china ... and this was his chance.

As the crowd noises died down, he heard a measured, somewhat high-pitched voice speaking clearly to the gathering...

> *Four score and seven years ago our fathers brought forth, on this continent, a new nation, conceived in liberty, and dedicated to the proposition that "all men are created equal"....[5]*

The cramping, the pain in his leg all disappeared, replaced by the coldness before the kill. He rubbed his hand gently over the weapon.

> *Now we are engaged in a great civil war, testing whether that nation, or any nation so conceived, and so dedicated, can long endure. We are met on a great battle field of that war. ....*

Buell cleared his mind and focused his entire being on the task at hand. All sounds and distractions disappeared. As his father taught him, he relaxed, letting out some breath, focused on the center of the chest of the devil incarnate, and squeezed the trigger. There was the sharp stinging crack of the cap, but no satisfying slam of the butt in his shoulder... no loud boom as the bullet sped home. A misfire!

> *We have come to dedicate a portion of it, as a final resting place for those who died here, that the nation might live. This we may, in all propriety do. ....*

---

[5] There is disagreement among scholars regarding the exact words spoken by Lincoln during the address, and which of the numerous existing manuscripts of the speech is most accurate. I suspect we will never know. I chose the Nicolay copy for this text because there is some evidence it may have been the copy Lincoln held in his hands on the platform.

Buell looked at the weapon in disbelief. He was frozen in time, unable to grasp what had just happened. Then he snapped out of it, and leaned forward toward the windowsill, looking down at the crowd below.

Some nearby spectators were looking up or around at the popping sound of the cap, but no one seemed to think it unusual. Buell fumbled with a second cap from a small pocket in his Confederate jacket.

But, in a larger sense, we can not dedicate—we can not consecrate—we can not hallow, this ground -

Kally started running up the stairs of the tower, determined to take the matter in his own hands, kill Buell on the spot, and finish the affair by shooting Lincoln. He did not realize men were rushing forward from the nearby crowd until they burst through the door, grabbed him roughly on the stairs, and manhandled him out the door and onto the ground.

At the window, Buell heard the commotion on the stairs and was panic-stricken. *This can't be happening*, he thought. Terror set in—he abandoned the rifle, the new cap in his hand fell to the floor—the second try with a fresh cap a thing Buell now knew would never happen. At the top of the stairs he shouted, "Kally!" No answer.

The brave men, living and dead, who struggled here, have hallowed it, far above our poor power to add or detract. The world will little note, nor long remember what we say here; while it can never forget what they did here. ....

Buell scrambled recklessly down the stairs and lurched out the door with one thought—escape!

It is rather for us, the living, we here be dedicated to the great task remaining before us -

Kally was on the ground, three men holding him there. Buell rammed into one of the men as he left the tower, almost fell himself, but regained his footing. Seeing there was no one immediately after him, he started to run, limping, through the milling crowd—hands out front, smashing aside anyone in his way.

"Outta my way, ya Yankee bastards." He oriented himself as he ran, heading generally toward Swann and the horses.

that, from these honored dead we take increased devotion to that cause for which they here, gave the last full measure of devotion -

Ian, watched in shock as the scene unfolded. He witnessed Kally dragged out the door, saw Buell rapidly limping away. A small stout man stepped agilely into view from among the spectators, intercepting Buell. With one swift blow of his right elbow to Buell's neck, stopped him cold—lifting him off his feet in mid-stride. Buell lay semiconscious on the ground, coughing and holding his throat.

that we here highly resolve these dead shall not have died in vain; that the nation, shall have a new birth of freedom, and that government of the people by the people and for the people, shall not perish from the earth.

Ian was frozen in place, stunned. The man who felled Buell had his back to Ian. The man slowly turned toward him. It was Benjamin Tasker.

Tasker walked briskly over to him. "Hello, Ian. Splendid to see you again." He no longer looked or acted like the unassuming and rather humble secretary at the legation, or the friendly drinking companion at the Round Robin. There was not a trace of stutter. His annoying spectacles not only were no longer riding on his nose, they had completely disappeared. He walked purposefully and poised ... almost nonchalant, all professional. His voice was clear, level, and in charge.

Ian was speechless. Taking several long moments to recover his composure, he asked, "What the devil's going on? Who are these men? Who are *you*?"

"My dear chap, so many questions. I'm afraid I'm a bit more than a secretary, and I'm afraid I've been watching your movements for ages, with the utmost interest. These men are mine—on loan—but mine. No time for this now. I'm after Oldham. Where is he?"

Ian was still staring at Tasker. The man's whole demeanor had altered. Even his accent had a more refined quality.

Tasker brought him out of his reverie, "To work, man, there is simply no time for this. Where is Oldham? He's the bastard I want!"

Ian snapped back to reality. "Probably gone, if he heard the cap go off without the rifle firing. If he's still around, he'll be with Swann and the horses, on the road out there." He pointed toward Baltimore Pike.

Tasker waved to a couple of men to follow. Ian went with them. They hurried down the pike to where Swann waited with the horses; four of them. One was missing.

Ian shouted to Swann, "Oldham?"

"Took a horse and rode off, sir, never said a word."

"Which way?" Tasker demanded.

"First to the wagon, rummaged in the back, then headed for town. He had some kind of a canvas bag with him, like the tripod bag."

Ian said, "I didn't see him over at the wagon."

"You were pretty busy, sir, it was just after Mr. Tasker pole-axed Mr. Buell. You was lookin' elsewhere, sir."

Swann looked at Tasker. "That was a nice piece of work Mr. Tasker."

Ian thought a moment, turned pale, exclaimed, "My God, the wagon." He ran to the wagon, followed by Tasker and his men. Swann remained holding the horses.

"Ian, what the devil's going on?" Tasker insisted.

Ian was silent—thoughts running through his head, making him nauseous. He scrambled around in the back of the wagon, found the Whitworth's custom-made gun case.

Buell had used it to protect his beauty during transport from Washington. As he feared, there was something terribly wrong.

The case had two compartments, not one! The top layer was for one weapon, but a hidden catch opened a duplicate second compartment underneath—with the outline for a second Whitworth. The compartment was now open, and empty.

Ian yelled to Tasker, "It's not over Benjamin! He has a second rifle that hasn't been rendered useless."

Before Tasker could react, Ian ran back to the horses, mounted the nearest, and rode off toward town at a full gallop.

Tasker roared, "Swann go after him—you two men go with them. Follow their orders." The men mounted and followed Swann, who was already on his way.

Chapter 44

19 November 1863, Gettysburg, Pennsylvania

Swann and his two companions rode back north on Baltimore Pike, headed toward the Wagon Hotel. They had to make their way through clusters of people. Many soldiers milled about the streets. Swann led them carefully, so as not to draw attention. They arrived at the rear of the Wagon Hotel to find Ian's horse tied to the rail, but no sign of the small paint Oldham had taken. He was about to rush in when Ian came out the hotel's back door.

"Not there," Ian said when he saw Swann and the two riders. "Didn't think he would be. One of you men remain on guard here.

Swann added, "If Oldham shows, take him or kill him."

One of Tasker's men said, "Right you are, sir," and dismounted. Swann realized the man had a distinct London cockney accent, the same as his, which lent to the mystery— *Who exactly were these men?*

Ian, Swann, and the second of Tasker's men rode north at a fast clip on Baltimore Pike, toward the Diamond. *I still have a chance to make this right. Lincoln is just now leaving the platform. It'll take him some time to get back to the Wills house. That has to be the place.*

Ian led them to the rear of the Arnold building. He had not been there before, only Kally and Buell. Swann found the door leading to the back stairs. It was open. Ian rushed past him and bolted up the stairs, pistol drawn and cocked. Swann followed, after telling Tasker's man to remain at the rear door.

The second floor was packed with boxes and clothing on wooden racks. Ian slowly walked among them toward the front windows overlooking the town square.

Oldham was not there. About to leave, Ian thought of the house itself, and how it appeared from outside. There were two attic windows above the second floor.

"Swann, look for the entrance ta the attic."

Swann's reply was almost immediate. "Found it, sir. Over here."

First up the rickety ladder, Swann disappeared through the hole in the ceiling. He did not have to go all the way up. "I can see the whole attic. It's empty, just a few crates and boxes."

They moved swiftly back down the stairs. Swann told the man guarding the rear door, "You heard me tell your mate, right? You stay by here—mind the horses. If Oldham comes, take him or kill him, and be careful. He's a tricky bastard, right enough."

Ian and Swann hurried out onto the square on foot to look around—nothing. They ran around the front of the Stoever building and Shick's store on Baltimore Pike. They could see the procession slowly progressing toward them. The tall President on his big chestnut bay was clearly visible, waving at the cheering crowd.

Moving rapidly around the building, they found the back entrance. This time Swann kicked in the door and they raced up the back stairs. The third floor was packed high with boxes of bibles and tracts. Ian pushed through to the windows, shouting for Swann to locate and search the attic.

Oldham was not on the third floor, or in the attic. There was only one place left. Of course, it had to be.

"He must be at the Globe," Ian yelled as he ran into the square. Swann caught up with him halfway across.

Swann knew exactly where the room was in the inn. He had been there evenings to mess up the linen and make it look occupied. They ran down York Street, and into the Globe's lobby.

Ian asked the short, round clerk for the room key. The clerk said haughtily, "Oh, no, sir. Sorry, but I can't do that. Mr. Oldham gave me strict instructions."

Ian started to protest, "Now look here—"

Swann was far more direct in his approach. Leaning past his officer he grabbed the clerk's ear, pulling him across the top of the counter. He said with an ominous tone, "You give my officer here the key when he asks for it, you fuckin' little tosspot, or I'll tear off this bloody ear an' feed it to you."

He let go. The clerk immediately grabbed a key from the rack behind him, handing it to Ian. The room on the second floor was near the middle, along the front of the building.

"Stand back," Ian hissed softly at Swann. He delicately unlocked the door, opened it gently, gun drawn—but the room was empty.

Ian raced over everything in his mind. *Shifty bastard. Where could he be? It must be somewhere with a clear shot at the Wills house.*

He could hear the crowds outside cheering, as Lincoln entered the square on horseback. *I'm running out of time.*

It struck him like a slap in the face. He shouted at Swann, "Stay here. If he shows, you know what to do."

"Aye, sir, you, sir?"

"I think I know where he is." Ian ran two steps at a time down to the lobby. The clerk saw him coming and cringed.

Ian snarled, "You seen Mr. Oldham today? Don't lie ta me!"

"Seen him. N-no, sir, but he could've come in the back way. Wouldn't see him at all."

"Do you have a second room rented in the name, Simon Oldham?"

"No, sir. Only the one."

Ian had to think ... think ... like Simon Oldham.

"Try the name Kally, or Buell, or Swann, or Carlyle."

"No, sir ... nope. None of those names," the distraught clerk said, shakily.

"Damn, let me see that!" Ian demanded. Moving behind the counter, he grabbed the ledger.

His finger traced quickly down the list of names—there it was—"F. Abraham, Room 9" ... *Charming, Simon,* he thought. *Father Abraham—you cagey bastard.*

Ian reached over the frightened clerk, snatched the key to Room 9 from the board, and bounded back up the stairs. This room was at the end of the hallway, the southwest corner, facing the street—the corner nearest the entrance to the Wills house.

The crowd cheered louder. He could hear them below. Ian listened at the door. Nothing. Then he heard a noise—it was a scraping sound, like a window opening.

He turned the key and pushed the door open with his shoulder—empty. He saw out the window a gathering of cheering men on the porch, blocking the view. *That's why he didn't use this room, so where the hell is he?*

Ian stood in the doorway, immobilized. Then he heard it again, the scraping sound—not from the room, but above him—the ceiling.

The attic! Right! A higher vantage point with no obstructions.

Ian found the ladder, saw the hatch to the attic ajar. He lifted it and peered in. Oldham was at the small open window, slightly stooped because there was little headspace. He had moved a large trunk over to the window. The Whitworth rested on a pillow on the trunk, pointing down toward the Wills house, but still inside the window, out of sight from the street below.

Oldham knelt behind it, finger moving around the trigger. In one movement, Ian slammed the hatch aside and climbed quickly into the attic.

Oldham was startled, but recovered swiftly. He stood up from his kneeling position and twisted around, his small Colt pistol already in his hand. He said, "I thought I heard a noise."

Ian saw that the hammer of Oldham's pistol was down. It had to be cocked to enable it to fire.

"Give it up, Simon, it's all over." Ian's Smith and Wesson revolver was aimed directly at Oldham; rock steady and already cocked. He stood bent over slightly, his head touching the low attic ceiling.

"Ian, my dear fellow, what's going on here. I'd have staked my life you were with us. What's all this?"

"I'm not with you, Simon, never was 'with you.' I'm the one that bunged up Buell's weapon—made sure it wouldn't fire."

"I should have guessed as much. Should have known—perhaps I did, but wouldn't believe. Come now, don't you remember, I saved your life—must be worth something, what?"

"I got over that, Simon, when I realized you came so cheaply. You're a bloody waste, and I'm turning you over to someone I know will take excellent care of you—remember Benjamin Tasker? I suspect he's working fer the Prime Minister or Her Majesty. Perhaps you've forgot, or choose not to recall, that would be our Queen."

"Poor noble Ian, ever the naïve gentleman. This has nothing to do with our Queen. What of our arrangement? Your brother, your name, your fragile, ailing mother?"

Ian watched Oldham's hand holding the pistol. "I remember, Simon, but it's much too late. Peter, my mother and I, will take our chances. Don't be stupid. Put the gun down and come along."

"You're making a huge mistake, old man. As for me, surrender would be completely unacceptable. You see, at great expense I've purchased what a certain Colonel

315

McClellan suggests is the fastest horse in the county. It waits behind the Franklin Hotel. One shot ... Lincoln's dead and I'm away—never to be seen again in this country."

Ian was not listening to Oldham's rambling. It was almost as though time itself had slowed. While Oldham talked his thumb began to cock his revolver ... Ian's leopard tensed.

Ian shot twice in quick succession—one bullet hit Oldham in the neck, the second full in the chest. The twin impacts slammed Simon back across the trunk, knocking the rifle to the floor, followed closely by the thud of Simon Oldham's body as he went down.

Swann poked his head through the attic opening.

Lying on his back on the floor, Simon gurgled blood and made mumbling noises. His handsome face contorted, he tried to say something. All that came out was, "Iannnn ... Damn—you."

Ian looked down at his once good companion, his life spreading leisurely beneath him in a bright red pool. He said quietly, "No, I suspect the other way round, Simon ... Damn you."

Chapter 45

---

21 November 1863, train traveling back to Washington

"Are you all right?" Tasker asked Ian, with genuine concern. They sat together a few days later on a train back to Washington. Swann sat across the aisle, listening.

During both incidents, the one at the gatehouse, and the one at the Globe Inn, the thunderous shouting of the crowd and the general commotion around Lincoln swallowed any unusual noise, even the two shots in the attic of the Globe. The entire affair had gone largely unnoticed in the fury and celebration of the moment.

Oldham's body had been surreptitiously cleared from the hotel room. Kally and Buell disappeared in the hands of Tasker's men, for "questioning." Ian strongly suspected they would not be heard from again.

"I'm trying to sleep," Ian replied.

"I asked you a question."

"Yes, Benjamin, if that's your real name. I'm fine. I've killed men before."

"Benjamin will do, and it's never easy—killing."

"I'll manage. So am I right, you work for the Prime Minister, Lord Palmerston?"

"No. I refused to become political, one side or the other."

"Who then, may I ask?" Ian knew the answer.

"Let us merely say that I have a unique and special relationship of trust and confidence with a unique and special lady. Although, at the moment, she is in deep mourning over the loss of a loved one, her steadfast concern is the welfare of the people of Britain. I'd prefer to leave it just so. I shall say no more about it, and I will expect the same discretion from you."

Ian remained silent, his eyes attempting to stare down Tasker, who stared straight back. He had answered Ian's question. Their Queen remained in mourning over the death of her beloved Prince Albert.

Finally Ian asked, "If you knew what I was doing all along, why did you let me bumble about? Why not stop me earlier? I could have done real damage, you know."

"We didn't know everything, still don't," said Tasker. "There's more to this group here in America. In fact, the real leaders remain at large. Oldham was only a small but dangerous piece in this game. We also don't know all the major players in Britain yet."

"Can't help you there, I'm afraid." Ian wondered to himself just how much Tasker knew about Peter's involvement.

"Come now, Ian. We can be honest with each other. I'm the best friend you have right now, old boy. Would it help if I told you The Honorable Robert Lindsay is a close friend of mine, has been for over twenty years? He felt it his duty to his country and to you as his friend. I've read a copy of your letter to him."

There was a long silence. *So it's out in the open.* This all seemed to smack of that old "nobility incest"—aristocracy protecting its own. He would have bet a tidy sum that whatever Benjamin Tasker's real name, there was a "Lord" or a "Sir" in front of it.

"What happens now?" he asked, afraid of the answer.

"You're a bit of an unsung hero. If it weren't for you, God knows what might have happened ... but I'm afraid 'unsung' it must remain. Lord Lyons has briefed Secretary of State Seward directly. Fortunately there was only one American involved, and he's a Rebel—no loss there as far as the American government is concerned.

I briefed your friend Lamon. A minor incident in Gettysburg as far as President Lincoln was informed, and the world will never know how close he came. Lincoln was merely told of another foiled plot, and Lamon graciously took the credit for preventing its execution. After all, it was his security measures which were largely responsible."

"And that's the end of it?" Ian asked.

"I expect it will remain that way. No one wants to cause a bother or upset the new understanding between the United States and Britain."

Silence, as Ian absorbed what he was hearing. It gave credence to his suspicions.

"What about my brother?"

"I can't really answer that. As far as we're concerned, he's clear of any serious transgressions. You'll have to sort that out with him. His name will not be mentioned in any of my reports, but we'll want to talk to him at length some time later—confidentially, of course."

Ian said, "Thank you for that, Benjamin." He paused, "Hill Lamon must think me a right bastard, using him and our friendship so shabbily."

"Not really," Tasker replied. "At first he was a might angry, but I explained to him the whole story, what you were up against, your mother, why you felt you had to do it. He's fine. Said to wish you his best and you owe him several drinks at the Round Robin."

Ian was relieved. "Can you tell me 'the whole story'?" Ian asked.

"You mean what happened behind your back? Yes, most of it, I think I owe you that much."

"Yes, I think you most certainly do." Swann, across the aisle, leaned toward them. He did not want to miss a word of this.

"Well, after receiving the letter from Robert, I set up surveillance on you and Oldham—later on Kally and Buell—and eventually Swann. By the way, Oldham never served in the Crimea, and neither did Kally. They both spent time together in the Rifles, but in England. Oldham as an officer and Kally as a sergeant major. That is until Oldham was cashiered, and Kally left with him, under unusual circumstances."

"I'd guessed it was some such."

Tasker continued, "I used my own men imported from Britain, to keep it in the family, if you will. Most are officers or senior sergeants of the Royal Marines, if you want specifics—seconded to me. It all fell in place quite nicely as we went along for the ride. It wasn't difficult to follow your activities, or grasp what you were trying to do. Your moves, and I might add, motives, were rather obvious. You are not, my friend, a master of treachery, but I never once doubted your loyalty to the Crown."

"Yes, I suppose I should thank you for that. But, as you say, I'm an amateur at all this deception and manipulation. The more reason why I should think you wouldn't want me mucking about. Especially in Washington."

"Ah, you may be certain there was never any danger to President Lincoln in Washington. Had it seemed so, we'd have most assuredly pounced."

"In Gettysburg?" Ian inquired.

"Now there it was a bit more dicey; at least until we saw what you had in mind. We watched Kally and Buell picking out the Arnold building, the Stoever building, the Wagon Hotel, even pacing off the distance from the gatehouse to the speaker's platform. By following Swann, we also knew about the room at the Globe, but we had no idea of the second room, or that he might use the attic. Good thinking that, my dear fellow."

Ian was more curious than ever. "You took an appalling chance allowing Buell to pull that trigger."

"Not really, Ian. We do actually know what we're about. We followed Swann to the gunsmith both times, and questioned the man after his second visit, in the dead of night. He was greedy, but most cooperative with a bit of pressure. We finally bought his silence with threats of turning him in to the American authorities, and even more money than your man, Swann, gave him."

Swann thought, *I was right. There was someone following me from the gunsmith.*

"We pieced it together," Tasker continued, "and saw your ingenious plan."

"Not mine ... Swann's."

"When all went well the next morning, we knew Swann had got the weapon with the doctored nipple successfully back to Buell, and none the wiser."

"We were lucky, sir," Swann said out loud. He, like Ian, found it hard to believe they had let it go so far, allowing Buell to actually pull that trigger, and Oldham and Kally to run free.

Tasker looked back and forth between Ian and Swann. "You're both incredibly resourceful and courageous."

"Don't feel very courageous, sir," Swann said.

Ian added, "Nor do I."

Tasker shook his head. "Look here. We were onto this group of disgruntled industrialists as subversives, and even knew the name Oldham, but we had no idea they were plotting an assassination over here, until Bobby Lindsay wrote me."

Tasker looked for a reaction, but saw none. "You brought that to light, Ian. This plot came to an end thanks to you and Swann, here. I must admit we were hoping the main villain might show his hand during the execution of the plan, but, alas, he did not."

So that's it! That's why they let it play out. They waited to try to catch the bigger fish. If things went bad, and President Lincoln was actually assassinated, they thought the risk worth the prize. It's a funny old world. He would have wagered a fortune that the Americans were not made privy to this little twist.

321

Tasker continued, "We bagged what we had, and called it a day. Oldham is dead, Kally and Buell whisked away, and no one will miss them. We're still, of course, after the rest, both here and in Britain, but we're a good deal closer thanks to your work; even if you were helping us unknowingly. I should mention, Ian, if your brother will help us now, he could do himself and his country some good."

Ian shook his head. "I tell you, Benjamin, or whatever your name really is, I'm not certain how I feel about all this, or even about my brother. It is a great deal to digest at one sitting."

"Think on it, Ian, we'll talk more tomorrow after you've rested."

As the train rocked its way south, Ian's thoughts about what occurred in Gettysburg were overwhelmed by a deep yearning. He was consumed with an image of Elizabeth. All he wanted was to see her, hold her. Ian fell into a troubled sleep. He saw the bullets striking Oldham, the blood splatter as he fell to the floor. It had been a very personal kill.

*   *   *

When they finally reached Washington, a carriage from the legation waited for them. Tasker wanted a drink at a nearby tavern. "I'll make my own way back to the Willard. Ian, you and Swann take the carriage. We'll talk more at the Round Robin later this afternoon."

"If you insist," Ian said.

As they pulled away from the railway station, Ian said to Swann, "Mind if we take a roundabout way to the hotel?"

"Not at all, sir," Swann said, smiling. "Going to Georgetown, sir?"

Ian smiled back. He gave the carriage driver Elizabeth's address. On his arrival, the door was opened by Elizabeth's trusted maid, a diminutive woman of about forty, carrying a few too many pounds around the middle. "Oh, Colonel Carlyle, I'm afraid Miss Elizabeth isn't here."

"Is she at the hospital, Angela?"

"I really don't know, sir. She must have left quite early today."

"Didn't you see her?"

"When I went to her room, she'd already gone. Not like her, must have been important."

"Thank you, Angela, I'll find her." The door closed and Ian returned to the carriage. He felt he must see her.

"One more stop, Swann?"

"At the hospital?"

"Yes."

Elizabeth wasn't there either, and they said she had not been in. Ian was bitterly disappointed, but thought—*She has a life to lead, by damn. Why should I expect she should be waiting around for me? After all, she was unaware I was returning.*

They went to the Willard, and headed straight for their rooms. When they reached Swann's door, the ever-loyal soldier servant asked, "Will you be needin' me before tomorrow, sir?"

"No, not at all. You get some rest for what's left of today and tonight. Wake me for breakfast early in the morning." He paused, "… and Swann … thank you. Thank you for helping me, and for being a good friend."

Swann beamed. "A pleasure, sir, a right pleasure. Any time you should need me."

It was late afternoon, and Ian hoped for a long rest before facing the new day and whatever might come out of this monumental misadventure. He opened the door to his rooms, walked in, and came face to face with a grinning Sir Archibald Walsham. Behind him, wearing what looked like a tentative smile, was his brother, Peter Carlyle.

"Peter—Sir Archibald? What—" He felt the blow to the back of his head … saw the carpet rushing toward him, then blackness.

Chapter 46

21 November 1863, Washington

He heard voices before he saw anything, coming through a dull fuzziness.

"You didn't have to hit him." *Peter*, Ian thought; the voice seemed concerned and upset.

"Shut your trap!" Walsham's forceful voice, commanding—not his normal jovial self.

"He's coming out of it." An American voice Ian did not recognize.

"Ian, wake up. Please. Are you all right?" Peter asked.

As he regained consciousness, he tried to move, but could not. He was tied tightly, wrists and ankles, to a heavy chair. He struggled, but to no use.

Ian opened his eyes to find Sir Archibald, Peter, and another man in a Union captain's uniform, standing before him. Slow recognition—the officer was Justin Billings, the twit he met at the party on the yacht. *He's the same officer who chatted with Lizbeth.* He remembered Oldham using the Billings warehouse for meetings of the conspirators.

"No, I'm not fuckin' all right, Peter. My brother and my father's friend have given me a bashing, and tied me to a chair. What, pray tell, is all right about that?"

Peter cried out angrily, "You just couldn't do what I wanted you to do, could you? Just couldn't help me as I asked. Now we're all in for it. God knows what's going to happen."

Ian grew more angry, "Let me loose a moment, and I'll show ya what's goin' ta happen, you damned fool. Don't ya see it? You think these people are on yer side, yer friends?"

"Of course they are," Peter said with conviction, "we're in this together. Our entire family fortune is wrapped up in this."

Ian merely looked at his brother. "You are indeed a fool, Peter."

Walsham was holding Ian's father's sword cane—the cane he gave Ian at the Round Robin. The blade was exposed. It was pointed casually in Peter's direction, unnoticed by Peter, himself.

"What the devil are you playing at Walsham? You were our father's friend. He trusted you."

"Sorry, old man, things change."

"What do you want?" The question was asked to both Sir Archibald and Peter.

Peter replied, "Just for you to remain silent, leave America, go back to Britain. This is all over. We are finished here. That's why I came with Sir Archibald tonight. To convince you to leave at once, and—"

"Enough of this idle family chatter," Sir Archibald cut in. "I'm afraid you're quite wrong, Peter, and I'm actually tired of listening to your whining. Ian's right. You truly are a fool. I brought you over here to America weeks ago, purely to serve as leverage with Ian here, if I needed it. Turns out I do, but not the way you think. Not to convince him of anything with your pathetic words."

"What do you mean?" Peter asked, finally registering concern.

"Shut your mouth," Walsham commanded, then turned to Ian, "Can't you guess what I want, my boy? Come now, you're a smart little tin soldier, Guards Brigade and all that."

Ian professed ignorance, "You're connected ta this thing Peter wrote me about. Is that it?"

"Don't play me for an idiot," Walsham spat sharply, slapping Ian across the face. "You know very well what this 'thing' is. In fact, I understand the plot we hatched in Gettysburg was a complete shambles. Oldham dead, the others disappeared."

Ian felt the slap, but it merely angered him more. Peter turned pale.

Walsham deliberately calmed himself. "I don't care, my boy, really. Whatever happened there is in the past." He did not sound convincing.

Ian said nothing.

"You see, Oldham worked for me, but as I said, that was in the past—this is the present—the here and now. Oldham's quite dead, which you know, because you killed him; and his accomplices, who also worked for me, are nowhere to be found. I can only assume they are being held and interrogated. A pity, but I can live with it. They don't know, of course, who they worked for. Only Oldham knew ... and you conveniently disposed of him."

Ian decided to probe deeper, because playing ignorant did not seem to be working at all. "Just how much of all this was part of yer plan?"

"From the beginning, I'm afraid. Even you coming to Washington, with Peter's help. Then there was the attack in the alley on Elizabeth Callaghan, which caused you to meet Lamon, all carefully staged by me, without either of their knowing. Clever, what?"

Ian was dumbfounded. He had been used and manipulated from the start. They'd used Lizbeth, Lamon, Lord Lyons, and even Benjamin Tasker.

"I needed you and Lamon to become close to give us access to the President's movements. You did just fine, by the way; well beyond my expectations. I merely put the two of you in a situation, and you did the rest. You know I'm a member of the London and the Edinburgh Chess Clubs. Consider myself a fair hand, if I do say so. It was much like playing chess, but with real pawns."

Again, Ian struggled ineffectually with the bonds.

"Easy, my boy, you'll hurt yourself. You really didn't think Oldham capable of putting all this together, did you? No, he was merely a thug. I was there every step, moving the pieces about the board. I know about Tasker. Although it was a bit of a surprise, it matters not a jot. In chess one needs always to be several steps ahead of one's opponent. I have had an alternative plan in place for some time, which you, my boy, will now carry out. You are my knight, and you shall vanquish the king."

"Not bloody likely," was Ian's too quick reply.

Walsham moved the point of the cane sword to Peter's neck, drawing blood. "I think you'll decide otherwise." Billings moved behind Peter.

Peter cried, "Ian, I'm so sorry, so very sorry." His voice was shaky, and Ian knew he was terrified. He remembered the night long ago at Eton when Peter's nice, safe world first shattered. The look now on Peter's face was the same.

"It's all right, Peter," Ian said softly, "stay calm."

Then with an edge Ian asked, "What is it you want, Walsham?

"Why, simply for you to keep our bargain. Well perhaps a wee bit more. I want you to kill Mr. Lincoln."

"You're a daft bugger."

Walsham hissed, "I don't think so. You think about this. If you don't do exactly as I say, several things will happen … First, I will kill Peter with this sword cane, in your rooms. You, of course, will be blamed for the murder. Your father's cane, which I gave you in front of all those people—killed in your rooms. A quarrel between brothers."

His leopard appeared in Ian's mind. He was having difficulty keeping it crouching still. The animal wanted to rip out Walsham's throat. He could visualize the skin tearing open, the blood gushing out.

Walsham let his master plan sink in, savoring the pleasure. "Second ... the Carlyle name will certainly be ruined, your estate seized, by us, of course, and your poor ailing mother left penniless on the streets—while you rot in jail or meet your maker at the end of a hangman's rope. This will surely kill her, and if it doesn't, we will, and none the wiser."

A sound came from Peter's lips, unintelligible, horrifying.

Ian remained calm this time. "What if I say no? After all, you're likely to do all that anyway."

"Ah, what lack of trust. If you agree, I will give you my word, Ian ... but if you are foolish enough to say no, I give you my word on this, as well—I will pierce Peter's Adam's apple and force this blade out the backside of his throat; then you can watch his life ooze away before your eyes. I will see you and your name ruined, and I will ensure your mother dies with the knowledge that you betrayed her, the family, and your country. You see, we have the power, influence, and wealth to do all that. So you'll have to chance it. You don't have many options."

He carried his point home by pricking the sword cane blade into Peter's throat. Peter flinched, letting out a cry of pain. Billings held him.

Ian knew what he must do. No matter how unwise Peter had been, Ian knew he must save him. He saw it as clear as he had that night at Eton. He also understood that everything, his family name, his mother ... everything depended upon him.

He must play along to get free. This playing along was becoming a dangerous habit. The beast inside him settled back, but still wary. Ian's eyes turned to animal cunning— bore first into Walsham, then Billings.

Walsham was oblivious, too wrapped up in his own ego, his magnificent plan. Billings felt the burn, cast his own eyes down.

Billings had been cocky, feeling superior to this arrogant Scotsman, knowing Walsham had him ... had him good. Now he was no longer comfortable that Walsham was in control. Ian had calmed. He was no longer struggling ... but those eyes—the wild madness in them, made Billings feel like he was about to be devoured.

Ian said to Walsham, "So what would you have me do?"

"That's the spirit. Knew you'd see it my way. It's tonight. Your invitation to a White House reception is on your desk. I took the liberty of responding that you'd be honored to attend."

"And how am I supposed to kill Lincoln? With my bare hands?"

"Your bare hands—clever, and it might be fun to watch, but no. I'll give you a tiny concealable Derringer with one shot in the barrel. You'll get in, get close enough, and shoot this fellow dead. Simple, aye?"

"You really are insane," Ian said. "Even if I did, I'd be killed or imprisoned, then hanged."

Walsham wrinkled his brow, "Yes, shame that, but it is the exquisite beauty of my ploy. The price of your folly in Gettysburg. Cost me a great deal of money, time, and trouble. Afraid I lied. I can't really forgive that. At least your brother will be alive, his fortune secure, and your mother well taken care of. Might damage your precious name a bit, but we can't have everything, can we?"

Ian struggled with his bonds, this time just for show. He knew he could not get free.

"Need your answer, my boy. You and your guest, Captain Billings, need to be leaving fairly soon. Oh, did I forget to mention Billings is going with you? He will have the percussion cap for the pistol. He'll give it to you when he feels it appropriate at the reception—that way you won't get any outrageous ideas about betraying us again, as you did in Gettysburg."

Ian knew he must be convincing. Walsham was smart, he would see through Ian if he agreed too soon. He spat, "Go to the devil, Walsham. I've had about enough of being tossed about in this scheme of yers. Sorry, Peter, but I canna do this."

Peter made another pitiful sound, pulling back. Billings grabbed him tighter, and Walsham pushed the sword point in his neck again, further this time. Peter cried out.

Walsham said, "I thought you might balk, shame on you. No trust—no brotherly loyalty? Leave your dear mom hanging, so to speak? Need a bit more persuasion, do we?"

Walsham gave the sword cane to Billings. He then turned Ian's chair toward the closed bedroom door.

Ian thought, *what now?*

Walsham walked to the door, opened it, and stepped aside with a flourish, allowing Ian to see beyond. Tears welled up in Ian's eyes.

Elizabeth was tied, wrists and ankles, to the four corners of his bed. She wore a sleeping gown, nothing else, and she struggled against the ropes. She raised her head as best she could and looked at Ian pleadingly. Elizabeth made a muffled sound, but whatever was stuffed in her mouth prevented her speaking. Standing over her at the bedside was Hillary Walsham, leering back over her shoulder at Ian. She held a long knife.

"Hello, Ian," Hillary said, "so lovely to see you again. Doesn't your Lizbeth look smashing?"

Walsham gloated. He wanted Ian to feel the shock not only of seeing Elizabeth, but of knowing that even his seduction by Hillary was part of a master plan—his plan.

"You are a silly boy," he said. "Who do you think gave Oldham the information about Lincoln's speech in Gettysburg? The information you should have provided. Hillary is not only a wonderful and loyal daughter, but she's been part of the plan from the beginning.

He let that lie for a few seconds, then added, "She's not happy with you right now, Ian. Seems you rejected her, for this unfortunate young woman … she doesn't like that, no, not at all."

Hillary said softly, "May I do it now, Daddy?"

"No, I believe Ian is going to help us—aren't you, my boy?"

Ian lowered his head, slumped in the chair, and nodded his agreement slowly. It took all his will power, all his energy—the power of the leopard—to remain still and quiet.

Chapter 47

---

21 November 1863, Washington

Before they left the rooms, Billings said, "Remember, I have a gun and I can use it. If I have to shoot you, it will be because you're a spy, carrying a pistol to assassinate the President. I'll be a damned hero. So you do as Sir Archibald told you, and nothing more."

Walsham opened the civilian frock coat Ian wore for this reception in place of his uniform. He took a packet of documents from his own pocket and placed it inside Ian's coat, then said, "Those are letters, which should prove without doubt that you have been spying for the Confederacy. Good luck, my boy, don't let us down."

"Yes," Billings hissed, "and you just keep in mind your family and that bitch, Elizabeth. They'll pay dearly if you don't follow the plan to the letter."

"I understand. I'm ready." He looked over his shoulder at Elizabeth, who stared beseechingly back at him. He mouthed the words, *I love you.*

Then he said to Peter, now tied in his place to the same heavy chair, "Don't be afraid. Everything will be fine. I promise."

Peter pleaded with his eyes, tried to talk, but could only make unintelligible noises through the gag in his mouth.

Billings pushed Ian out the door. They walked down the hall, Ian leading, and down the stairs to the floor below, then on down another flight toward the lobby.

Ian counted silently to three, one step at a time: *One, two, three.* On three he leaned back, grabbed Billings by his clothing, and threw him down the rest of the flight. Billings sailed head first, without a word, landing at the bottom, sprawled in disarray.

Ian knew Walsham would kill Peter and Elizabeth anyway. He also knew if he shot Lincoln according to plan, Billings would shoot him on the spot—and claim the hero. There was no reason not to do so. Leaving witnesses alive who could talk about their involvement in the plot just did not make sense. He had to get back to the rooms, and quickly.

Billings was groggy, but not done. He staggered up, snarled, "You bastard, I'll kill you."

Ian said simply, "I don't think I'll allow you to do that." As Billings rushed him on the landing between floors, Ian punched him square in the face, crushing his nose. He did it just right, exactly as a fierce Irishman taught him, so long ago.

The blow stopped Billings, and blood poured from his nostrils. As he sagged forward on both knees, Ian stepped behind him, placed his hands on each side of Billings' head, and gave a sharp twist. There was a crunching sound. Ian let Billings go, and the body collapsed like a child's rag doll, equally as lifeless.

Ian ran back upstairs to Swann's room. He explained quickly what was happening, and sent Swann off to fetch Tasker, hoping he was in the Round Robin by this time.

Ian went to the door of his rooms, listened, and heard a frightful gurgling sound. His gut wrenched—no time to wait. He stood back and kicked the door in to find Peter still tied to the chair. The chair had fallen over on its side. Peter's eyes stared vacantly at the wall, a neat hole in his throat. The gurgling was the blood bubbling out of the opening. Peter's hair lay soaking in his own blood. Walsham stood over him, the bloody cane sword in his hand.

Ian exploded, cried out, "Aagghhh!"—rushed at the startled Walsham, knocking the sword out of his hand. He felt himself losing control, the leopard taking over—he did not care.

He began hitting Walsham with his fists—again and again. Somewhere along the way he picked up the bloody cane sword, used it to whip at Walsham, cutting his flesh open. Walsham sank down on the carpet, pleading with him to stop. Ian did not stop. The leopard would not stop. He was slashing Walsham's face to a bloody pulp when the bedroom door burst open. Hillary rushed in, screaming.

In a crazed rage, she came at Ian slicing with the huge knife. Ian warded her off with the cane sword and his arm, but he stumbled over the body of Walsham and fell to the floor. Before he could recover, Hillary fled back into the bedroom, slamming the door behind her.

"Lizbeth!" Ian screamed. He stumbled to the bedroom and flung open the door. Hillary's back was to him, both her hands gripping the knife raised above Elizabeth, the massive blade pointed down. With a staggering realization Ian knew he could not get across the room in time to stop her from plunging the knife into Elizabeth.

It came to him in an instant that he still held the sword cane covered in Peter's and Walsham's blood. He saw the split second when Hillary reached the top of her stretch, ready to begin the inevitable downward plunge. Without thinking, he hurled the sword cane by the grip as hard as he could, blade first, screaming as he did so. It struck Hillary at the base of her skull, and came out the other side, out of her mouth—but too late.

With horror, Ian watched the knife descend and sink into Elizabeth's helpless body. Her back arched, then slumped down onto the bed again.

When Tasker and Swann arrived they saw a dead man still tied to the fallen chair. Swann recognized Ian's brother,

Peter. Walsham was also there, beaten and slashed to death, almost unrecognizable. They entered the bedroom and found Ian. He sat in a chair next to the bed, staring at some distant, non-existent peaceful place where he could someday come to terms with his pain.

The room, Elizabeth's body, and Ian were bathed in blood—Walsham's, Hillary's and Elizabeth's. After Ian pulled the knife free, even as the bright red stain spread over the sheets, he tenderly crossed Elizabeth's arms over her chest to cover the wound, itself. *She looks so serene*, he thought. He wondered why his dear Lizbeth was dead, and he still lived.

Ian felt their presence in the room. He said quietly, "I untied her wrists, pulled the rag from her mouth, but her ankles are still bound."

"I'll get them, sir," Swann said, moving swiftly to the bed.

"Thank you." He paused for a time watching Swann gently remove the ropes on Elizabeth's ankles.

Ian whispered, barely audible, "They killed Peter, then ... Lizbeth. She couldn't speak. They wouldn't let her speak. She just looked at me, her eyes asking me ta take her away from this horror. I couldn't save her. She was pleading, and I couldn't save her. I had ta close her eyes. I couldn't stand them looking at me, accusing me."

He began to sob, clutching Elizabeth's hands in his. Tasker touched his friend's shoulder.

Swann whispered close to Tasker's ear, "There's another woman. I thought I saw her move."

Tasker glanced down and nodded. Two female legs stuck out from under the bed, awkwardly. Tasker leaned down for a closer look. Ian had pushed and kicked Hillary's body under the bed like unwanted garbage, even as she was drowning in her own blood from the sword cane, which had severed her spinal cord.

Tasker stood back up slowly. He said to Swann, "Never mind her now, lad, she's exactly where she deserves to be."

Ian touched his Lizbeth's hand tenderly for the last time, as he had on their first meeting. He spoke the words softly.

"And fare-thee-weel, my only luve, and fare-thee-weel a while; And I will come again, my luve, tho''twere ten thousand mile."

Epilogue

It was a month later, late December 1863. Ian, Swann, and Benjamin Tasker leaned on the railing of a steamship headed across the ocean for home. Ian's arm was still in a sling, recovering from Hillary's knife slashes.

Tasker spoke to Ian quietly. "You really had to go, Ian. Too uncomfortable, you being in America after all that's happened. I had to go as well. I'm afraid their government doesn't think much of us right this moment; but they'll get over it."

"I know, Benjamin. It's fine. I left nothing there. I apologized to Hill Lamon, and Lizbeth will always be with me, wherever I am. It'll be good to get back to the regiment, that's my real home. Besides, I have ta make arrangements for Peter's funeral; then there's mother to see to."

In her letter, Ian's mother insisted that Peter be brought home for proper burial at Dunkairn. He couldn't deny her. With Tasker's help, he enlisted the services of Henry P. Cattell, a competent and reputable embalmer. He ordered an air tight Fisk Metallic Burial Case made of steel, and even agreed to a mix of red dye with the arsenic compound embalming fluid. This, he was assured, would retain Peter's color to some degree, for his mother's sake, should she wish to view him. Ian thought the whole affair barbaric, but he couldn't refuse their mother's request. His guilt at failing to save Peter was overwhelming.

Peter was secure in the metal case in the ship's hold. Not sure how he felt about his brother, Ian decided he would come to terms with that later.

Elizabeth's funeral proved the most difficult thing Ian ever had to do. He was thankful for the friendship of Kate Chase, and the loyal companionship of Benjamin Tasker and Swann.

Swann felt he was going home, as well. He missed Britain, and was certain that returning would help heal the physical and mental wounds his officer suffered.

Swann helped Ian clear up some of the details surrounding the embalming and transport of Peter. He even managed to round up Jass and Blackie, Ian's quarter horses, from their benefactor, Captain Lovell. They were aboard ship and bound for a new home in Britain.

Swann worried about his officer, but Lieutenant Colonel Ian David Carlyle was the strongest and best man he had ever known. He would get over this, as he had recovered from so many other trials.

Tasker said, "I'll see to it Peter is remembered with honor; least I can do for you. The record will show he gave his life in Her Majesty's service."

Ian remained quiet, lost in his thoughts and memories.

Near the end of their voyage, as the ship prepared to dock in Portsmouth, Tasker approached Ian, who was alone, gazing over the water at Britain. "You know Ian, it would be a shame to waste the amazing skills that took you through this conflagration. You've been baptized by fire in the world of intrigue like not many have, and survived. I could put those skills to good use, and Her Majesty would be most grateful. Might you consider accepting a job from us from time to time?"

"Thank you, Benjamin, kind of you ta offer."

He was a soldier, and when warranted on the battlefield, soldiers did some horrific things to their fellow man, warrior against warrior. Ian recalled the methods used by Tasker most recently. Words like cold-hearted, pitiless, merciless, without compassion came to mind.

He knew they were necessary, but he was not at all certain they were honorable ... if that word could even be used. He had been callous and brutal himself, since becoming involved in this debacle. He saw it as a brutality that went beyond the field of combat. War seemed so much cleaner than political intrigue. Ian was not certain he wanted to be that ruthless again, or lose that much control again, even born of necessity.

"And your answer?" Tasker asked.

"At this moment, Benjamin, I merely want ta go home."

THE END

Made in the USA
Monee, IL
27 April 2020